THE CLOUD ABOVE THE GREEN

This new novel by Sir Philip Gibbs covers a recent period, in England (not yet past alas!) when the menace of war with Russia has cast a shadow over many minds, though it is hardly noticeable among the mass of folk who continue to play cricket on the village greens, and go on with the daily duties and pleasures of life without panic.

His scene is set in an English village and to some extent in a guest house run by an amusing Irishman and his wife. In one of the barns they give house room to a young Austrian painter who has formerly been in a concentration camp and is still poverty-stricken. Once a Communist, he exercises a somewhat unfortunate influence over the wife of a distinguished General who lives in the neighbourhood. This lady becomes an ardent pacifist, calls a public meeting in the village and creates a scandal of the first magnitude among her friends and neighbours and in her own home life. Her son, an officer cadet at Sandhurst, provides a love story which is idyllic but unhappy.

PHILIP GIBBS has also written

EUROPEAN JOURNEY
THE PAGEANT OF THE YEARS (An autobiography)
THE WAYS OF ESCAPE
PEOPLE OF DESTINY
GEORGE VILLIERS, DUKE OF BUCKINGHAM
MEN AND WOMEN OF THE FRENCH REVOLUTION
ENGLAND SPEAKS
ORDEAL IN ENGLAND
ACROSS THE FRONTIERS
FOUNDERS OF THE EMPIRE
REALITIES OF WAR
THE SOUL OF THE WAR
THE DAY AFTER TOMORROW
THE ROMANCE OF EMPIRE
KNOWLEDGE IS POWER
TEN YEARS AFTER
FACTS AND IDEAS
KING'S FAVOURITE

Novels

THE WINGS OF ADVENTURE
THE HIDDEN CITY
THE AGE OF REASON
DARKENED ROOMS
UNCHANGING QUEST
THE MIDDLE OF THE ROAD
HEIRS APPARENT
THE STREET OF ADVENTURE
THE RECKLESS LADY
THE CUSTODY OF THE CHILD
VENETIAN LOVERS
INTELLECTUAL MANSIONS, S.W.
LITTLE NOVELS OF NOWADAYS
A MASTER OF LIFE
OLIVER'S KIND WOMEN
HELEN OF LANCASTER GATE
BACK TO LIFE
OUT OF THE RUINS
YOUNG ANARCHY
THE GOLDEN YEAR
THE ANXIOUS DAYS
THE CROSS OF PEACE
PARADISE FOR SALE
CITIES OF REFUGE
BLOOD RELATIONS
GREAT ARGUMENT
THIS NETTLE, DANGER
BROKEN PLEDGES
SONS OF THE OTHERS
THE AMAZING SUMMER
THE LONG ALERT
THE INTERPRETER
THE BATTLE WITHIN
THROUGH THE STORM
THE HOPEFUL HEART
BEHIND THE CURTAIN
BOTH YOUR HOUSES
THINE ENEMY
THE SPOILS OF TIME

THE CLOUD ABOVE THE GREEN

A Novel By

PHILIP GIBBS

THE BOOK CLUB
121 CHARING CROSS ROAD
LONDON W.C.2

Printed in Great Britain by
William Brendon and Son, Ltd.
The Mayflower Press (late of Plymouth),
at Bushey Mill Lane
Watford, Herts.

CHAPTER I

JOHN PAGET, M.D., general practitioner in the straggling village of Longmead, Sussex, forty-five miles from London, was sensitive to the human comedy and tragedy—quite a bit of tragedy now and then—of the community in which he lived and worked. In spite of the Health Act which had increased his burden he retained many of his private—and paying—patients within a radius of ten miles or so and new ones arrived from time to time. That was because there was a shifting population in the half-timbered cottages round the green or on the outskirts of the village, let furnished, or sold at fantastic prices, rising higher with every new sale. Some of these newcomers were interesting and amusing—professional men who went up to town every day or came down for week-ends, a lawyer or two, a film star, very glamorous and not unintelligent, a poet, James Stewart who slouched around the green with an Alsatian dog looking very miserable, thinking out his incomprehensible verse. Then there were the people up at Foxgloves, a guest house run by an ex-naval officer, a very humorous fellow and a very odd fish who was hail-fellow-well-met with all his customers whom he called his guests, and treated as such apart from the accounts rendered by his hard-working little wife. Now and then distinguished people put up there—a Cabinet Minister and his mink-coated wife, a retired ambassador and his mothlike lady. But Lieut.-Commander Donovan kept things going mostly no doubt by dispensing cocktails and other liquids in the lounge bar.

Dr. Paget, like all other country doctors, knew the secrets and strains of his patients' lives. He had to be a bit of a psychiatrist as well as an ordinary 'quack', as he was pleased to call himself. Probably the war, now five years gone, accounted for some of the strains and some of the breakdowns—women deserted by their husbands, husbands by their wives, illegitimate children, the anxieties and harassments due to economic conditions bearing down upon the middle and professional class and the small landed gentry; the neuroses of ex-prisoners of war, and so on. All very interesting and sometimes touched with tragedy which he felt, perhaps too acutely, being a man of compassion.

Most of such cases were familiar to him but he came across a new one which rather startled him because of its oddity.

That was when he had a call from Foxgloves. Lieut.-Commander Donovan spoke to him on the telephone with his touch of the Irish brogue.

"Is it yourself, Doctor? I hope you're feeling fine and dandy. Could you look in at Foxgloves when you're passing this way? Sure it's nothing at all, but old Henry Fairchild—one of our regulars, you know—would like you to take a look at him. He's the picture of health with the complexion of a baby's bottom, but I guess he thinks we shall be ordering his grave for him before long. No hurry, Doctor!"

"I'll be along in the afternoon," said Dr. Paget.

He drove up to Foxgloves rather later than he had intended, having had a full round taking him far afield to an Elizabethan cottage in which an old lady—Miss Molyneux-Smith—had broken her leg down the crooked staircase. He himself had taken a nasty knock from a low beam as he came downstairs.

At Foxgloves Mrs. Fairchild was waiting for him in the big lounge which had once been an ancient barn with timbers roughly shaped by the woodman's axe.

To his surprise he found his wife there having a glass of sherry with a girl in riding breeches whom he knew to be Patricia Hastings who helped to run a riding school nearby, a free-spoken, easy-mannered young woman. He noticed that Viola, his young wife, blushed slightly when he smiled at her and raised his hand. There was no need for her to blush. He didn't object to her having a glass of sherry at Foxgloves, poor darling. He was getting a little bit worried about her. His job made him leave her too much alone. She hadn't enough to do except read a novel a day and have an occasional game of Bridge with old ladies. Perhaps he had made a mistake in marrying a girl more than twenty years younger than himself—a mistake for her, an unfair act on his part. Fifty doesn't match well with twenty-seven, he thought. What a pity that they hadn't had a child!

Mrs. Fairchild gave him a bony hand to shake.

"My husband is worried about something," she said. "There's something on his mind—if he has a mind. And yet his appetite is very good and he sleeps as sound as a bell. But he's very absentminded and something is nagging at him. Last night he revoked at Bridge."

Dr. Paget laughed.

"That sounds serious! Almost a crime. I'll go and have a look at him. Where is he?"

He was in his bedroom doing a crossword in *The Times* which he dropped on the floor when the doctor entered his room.

"Hullo, Doctor! Good of you to come."

"Anything wrong?" asked Dr. Paget. "A touch of bronchitis? Tummy trouble?"

"I want a general overhaul," said Henry Fairchild. "I'm getting a bit anxious about myself."

He was an elderly, white-haired man who had been a famous oarsman in his time and still looked wiry.

Dr. Paget examined his heart, listened to his lungs, felt his stomach, took his blood-pressure.

"How old are you?" he asked.

"Sixty-eight next month. Getting senile, curse it!"

The doctor laughed.

"Well, for a man of sixty-eight you're a fine specimen. Heart as strong as a lion's, no trouble in the lungs, normal blood-pressure; nothing wrong that I can see."

"Oh!" said Henry Fairchild, in a dejected way. "Very unfortunate!"

Dr. Paget raised his eyebrows and grinned.

"Anyone would think that I had sentenced you to death. You have another twenty years ahead of you, barring accidents."

Old Fairchild went to his bedroom door and clicked the handle.

"That's the worst of it," he said. "The fact is, Doctor—

for heaven's sake don't tell my wife—I don't want to live for another twenty years. I don't want to live for another two years. That's my limit."

Dr. Paget raised his eyebrows again and looked puzzled.

"For goodness' sake, why?"

Henry Fairchild lowered his voice.

"It's like this. I'm living on Capital like most of my class. I've nearly come to the end of it. I can hang on for another two years in places like this—I prefer it to South Kensington boarding-houses or lodgings in Littlehampton. After that I'll be broke. I was hoping I might have a touch of angina. See what I mean?"

Dr. Paget gave a hearty laugh.

"My dear sir, you're the first man I've known in my professional career who was afraid of living too long! I'll have to make a note of it in my case-book."

"It's no joking matter," said the old man. "Advancing towards a precipice and blue ruin isn't amusing, you know. I blame this Labour Government—pouring money down the drain—taxing everybody up to the eyebrows, forcing all investments down, raising prices by reckless inflation."

Dr. Paget had heard all that before and, though no Labour man, had a conviction that taxation would be high whatever government were in power. Two world wars—was there another to come?—had to be paid for. But his instinct of sympathy was stirred by this old man's plight. No psychiatry could cure that trouble. Most of his professional patients were hard hit by taxation and he was not exempt himself. Everything was in a mess, including the international situation.

"We're all in the same boat, more or less," he said.

"My boat has sprung a leak," said Henry Fairchild, gloomily. "In two years I'll be sunk. Well, good-day to you, Doctor. Fortunately my wife has well-to-do relatives—whom I hate like poison. They'll look after *her*, but I couldn't bring myself to sponge on them. See. There's such a thing as pride."

An odd case, thought Dr. Paget. On his way through the lounge he had a word or two with Mrs. Fairchild, one of the old "Quality" with a back as straight as a poker in her country tweed, and a blunt way of speech. He reassured her about her husband's health. Then he glanced round the lounge. Viola had gone, he noticed. Patricia Hastings was still there talking to a young artist who had his studio and a camp-bed in a shed at the back of Foxgloves. In a corner of the room Donovan was working at some papers on a side table. He raised his head and his hand to the doctor.

"A glass of sherry, Doctor? On the house, you know!"

"No, thanks," said Dr. Paget. "Very kind of you, Donovan."

"Ah, sure it will do you no harm at all. Or a touch of Irish whiskey?"

"No, thanks. I see you're busy, anyhow."

"Football pools," said the ex-naval commander. "One must have a fairy-tale in one's life. There's a man in Bermondsey who won £20,000 the other day. What would I do with £20,000? Betty and I would have a grand time while it lasted."

"How long would it last?" asked the doctor, smiling at him.

"Ah, not long, Doctor! All my impecunious pals would come swarming round me and I couldn't refuse one of them. Even now . . ."

"I must be getting along," said Dr. Paget.

"Say a prayer for me, Doctor," said Lieut.-Commander Donovan. "I'm in need of a bit of luck."

He returned to his football pools.

CHAPTER II

THE doctor had another surprise over one of his patients whom he would have judged to be the least nervy man one might meet on a day's march. He was one of the square-jawed, steady-eyed soldiers of the old school who had been second-lieutenants in the First World War, surviving by some miracle all the massacres from the Somme to Passchendaele. This one was a Big Pot, as Bill Stokes, the hedger-and-ditcher, called him in friendly conversation with the doctor. It was Major-General Sir William Kendrick who had a flat in London and some job in the War Office—a boy clerk's job, he was pleased to call it—and came down for week-ends with Lady Kendrick to an old house beyond the village—Badgers, which had been a farm-house as far back as Queen Anne.

Dr. Paget had played golf with him now and then and had treated him for a broken ankle when he had fallen off a ladder while picking apples in his orchard. He had always been cheery and genial in his greeting when they happened to meet on the village green or in the winding lane going up to Badgers.

It was on the village green, while watching a cricket match on a Saturday afternoon, that they met again. The doctor made a note of the date in his diary. It was two months before the fighting in Korea. April 25th of that year 1950.

Met General Kendrick at cricket match. Anxiety state.

The General—a man well under sixty—was standing with his back to a pollarded willow hollowed out by age, whose gnarled roots were like the claws of some prehistoric animal clutching at the sandy earth. Dr. Paget's observant eyes glanced at him with the thought that here was a healthy, strong-nerved man who would not need quack doctors or specialists. 'Shan't make money out of him,' he thought with a smile to himself. The General had a ruddy colour on his strong, handsome, clean-cut face with its straight nose and square jaw.

Their eyes met and the General beckoned to him.

"Hullo, Doctor! Pretty good game, eh? That young fellow with the ginger hair isn't afraid of the ball."

"Tom Thrushwood," said the doctor. "Works up at Gamble's place."

The General nodded and watched the match again for a few moments with the doctor by his side. Presently he spoke again.

"Haven't been sleeping too well lately. Can you recommend some harmless dope?"

"No dope is quite harmless," answered Dr. Paget. "Better get down to the cause. Indigestion, perhaps."

"No," said the General, with a short laugh. "It's blue funk. I'm a frightened man."

Dr. Paget answered his laugh more heartily.

"You can't make me believe that! You're humbugging, General?"

"Gospel truth. I'm not joking. Blue funk, my dear fellow!"

Dr. Paget raised his eyebrows and looked grave.

"Another war? I hope to God . . ."

The General nodded.

"What astonishes me," he said, "is the lack of alarm in people's minds. Look at this cricket match on the village green. Nobody's worrying because we're living from day to day on the edge of a fiery furnace. Don't they know? Don't they read the morning papers?"

"The sporting news," said the doctor. "Princess Elizabeth's baby."

The General smiled rather grimly.

"Don't they realize that if the Russians put on their boots they can march to the coast in less than a week with nothing to stop them? Nothing whatever! Then of course this small island will be the target for guided missiles ten times worse than in the last war. There won't be any more cricket on the village green if that happens. There'll be a mad rush from London and the big cities. England will be laid in dust and ashes."

"Most unpleasant thought," said the doctor. "It doesn't bear thinking about."

The General raised both hands slightly and laughed.

"I have to think about it. It's part of my job. But England

remains unmoved, and remarkably cheerful. Is it heroism or damned stupidity? That's what I keep asking myself."

"Ignorance, partly," said the doctor.

"This government of ours, not so ignorant, is equally unmoved—and immovable—in spite of all warnings from us soldier men and others. That's what gives me restless nights."

He suddenly broke off and looked at the doctor with a good-natured smile.

"I ought not to talk like this except that every intelligent person is talking like this in the clubs, in the drawing-rooms, perhaps in the pubs. No secret really."

The doctor looked at him thoughtfully. This Major-General was only saying what had been common talk over the tea-tables and on the golf course, and now and then in the private rooms of some of his patients. He was only saying what had been in the doctor's own mind as he drove out at night to see one of his patients, scaring the rabbits by his headlights, watching the first vivid green of a late Spring, thinking his own secret thoughts in the loneliness of his journey—thinking of Viola who was getting bored, and of that poor girl who was dying of T.B. and a case of poliomyelitis in a neighbouring village. Then headlines in the morning papers yammered through his brain sometimes as he drove through the darkness. *Russian Veto in the Security Council . . . Behind the Iron Curtain . . . Threat to Berlin by Russian-trained Police . . . American Secretary Accuses Russia . . . President Truman on Aid to Western Defence . . . Winston's Warning. . . .* All very alarming, but he had shoved all this out of his mind as far as possible except for those dark, lonely thoughts creeping into his head like goblins. Most people put them out of their minds deliberately, otherwise they couldn't carry on, or make plans for the immediate future, or get on with their daily jobs, or enjoy the little pleasures of life.

But here was this Major-General in the War Office, confessing to 'blue funk', not for his own skin, of course. He was not frightened for himself but for England and civilization. Anyhow it was alarming.

"Shall I look in one day?" asked the doctor. "We must do something about that insomnia."

"Do, my dear fellow. A little harmless dope perhaps. Don't repeat what I said, of course. That's between you and me, Doctor."

"Of course!"

"How's your pretty wife? You must bring her over to dinner one evening. . . . I say, that boy knows how to flog a ball!"

The ginger-headed young man had made a hit to boundary, greeted by cheers from the spectators round the green who had brought out chairs to their garden gates or were sitting on the low walls of the gardens. It was a pleasant traditional scene, pleasing to the doctor's eyes and soul, with sunlight and shadow playing across the cricket pitch, flickering on the white flannels of the players, deepening the rose-red colour of the old bricks in the walls of Queen Anne cottages, playing below fleecy clouds, scudding over the little low hills beyond the village. No sign of menace here. No anxiety in people's eyes. Here was the peace and charm of an English village in Springtime. A cuckoo was calling in the woods. A thrush was shouting gaily in the Hookers' garden nearby.

But the doctor felt disturbed when he got into his car.

"The General," he said to himself, "knows a deuce of a lot more than most of us and he's a frightened man. Very unpleasant. I hope to God . . ."

CHAPTER III

FOXGLOVES was the cause of some scandal in the village of Longmead, which was very prone to scandalmongering, liking a little drama in life and making the most and the worst of suspicious goings-on. It was noted, for instance, by certain ladies in the village, the unofficial watch committees, that Mrs. Lucas, or dear Emily as they called her—she would be fifty-nine on her next birthday—had gone to tea twice in one week with Colonel Burton, now approaching seventy and a lonely widower, and had taken a trip to Littlehampton with him. "To say the least of it," said Mrs. Montgomery-Jones, "it's very indiscreet of dear Emily. People *will* talk, you know." It was Mrs. Montgomery-Jones who denounced Foxgloves as a den of iniquity. According to her description of this guest house half a mile beyond the village, it was given over to 'orgies'—people drinking themselves to death, and a rendezvous of disreputable company among whom, alas, were some of the younger people in Longmead. That girl Patricia Hastings, for instance, who went about in riding kit or scarlet trousers and yellow jumpers, was hardly to be called respectable even by the most charitable judgment. The most dreadful thing that happened—it divided the village by a painful controversy—was when the Vicar, otherwise a most charming man—he had been a padre in the last war—drank a glass of brown sherry to the health and prosperity of Commander Donovan and his wife Betty when they first started this place shortly after the war. He had been there since on several occasions and had been seen playing a game of darts with Patricia Hastings. Mrs. Montgomery-Jones had written to the Bishop about it but had received an unsatisfactory reply.

That was the outside view of certain critics on the character of Foxgloves. The inside view of those who stayed there or frequented it was different. Certainly there was something odd about the character of Commander Donovan.

Dr. Paget, that observant and tolerant man, who went there sometimes for professional purposes, knew that there was an element of tragedy lurking beneath the outward comedy and cheerfulness of this friendly place, once an old farmhouse dating from Stuart times, with empty barns and outhouses and a pleasant lawn beyond a vegetable garden in which Commander Donovan worked, when he felt like working.

There were financial difficulties due partly to the economic conditions of the time. On retiring from the Navy, Lieut.-Commander Donovan, full of Irish optimism (subject to bouts of moody depression), had put everything he had into buying this place at an inflated price with very little reserve for carrying on. The petrol shortage after the war, and then the cost of petrol, had cast down his hope of high profits and quick returns by the sale of drinks at his well-stocked cocktail-bar at the end of the big lounge.

"We shall attract the passing motorists," he had told Betty his wife, "as the honeyflowers lure the busy bees."

Unfortunately the passing motorists did not arrive in swarms. For two years or more, while Commander Donovan sank deeper into debt with wine merchants and tradespeople, the road was empty and silent. They had to fall back for weekly revenue on a few 'regulars' as they called them—the old moths in the bedrooms like Henry Fairchild and his wife—and a local custom of people from the village who came in for lunch or dinner to eke out their rations or for a drink and chit-chat.

Betty Donovan confided some of this to the doctor one day when he came to dress a scalded hand. She was not Irish like her husband, but a girl from Aberdeen with all the quality of a Scotswoman—hard-working, blunt of speech, utterly straight, not without humour. Also she was attractive-looking, with reddish hair, blue eyes and a freckled nose.

"How are things going?" the doctor asked, after dressing her hand which she had burnt on a hot stove.

She gave a vexed laugh.

"Not too well, Doctor! Just this side of bankruptcy, to which we're advancing slowly but surely."

She laughed again but not mirthfully.

"It might be all right—better anyhow—if Dick were a bit less feckless. I'm fair scunnered with him sometimes. That's good Scots for fed-up."

"He's a cheery customer," said Dr. Paget. "A big-hearted fellow as far as I know him."

Betty Donovan looked ironical.

"That's his trouble—and mine! Too much heart and too little head. When some of his naval laddies drive in on their way from Portsmouth he stands them free drinks all round. 'On the house,' he calls it."

"Nice for the British Navy!" said the doctor.

Betty Donovan nodded and spoke in her blunt way.

"Nice for any lousy tramp who comes this way and tells a hard luck tale and nice for Miss Patricia Hastings who entertains her friends here and runs up some pretty little bills. 'Give her time,' says my kind-hearted Irishman. 'She's a nice little slut and very decorative,' he says."

"Certainly decorative," agreed the doctor with a smile.

Betty Donovan continued her tale of woe though she saw the humour of it.

"She's carrying on with our Austrian refugee. He's another handicap."

"The artist fellow?" asked the doctor. "Yes, I've seen him about the village. Corduroy trousers, sloppy tie."

Betty nodded.

"Dick thinks he's a genius and anyhow is sorry for him. We give him houseroom in one of the barns and free meals every day while he's decorating the billiard-room walls. He knows he's on a soft thing. He'll be a slow motion painter so long as we go on feeding him."

"Well, I must say Foxgloves is full of character," said the doctor. "It puts a strain on you, of course."

"Driving me scranny!" she admitted. "Now the cook has given notice. She's the third this year. And the parlourmaid will have to go because she's fallen passionately in love with my Irish husband whose charm is irresistible of course. What a life! Thank heaven I have a sense of humour."

She thrust back her reddish hair with one hand and laughed again.

"Without that, life might be intolerable," agreed the doctor. "Well, I must go on my rounds. Good luck to Foxgloves."

He hesitated for a moment after picking up his hat.

"Does my wife come round here much?" he asked, in a casual way.

Mrs. Donovan gave him a sharp look and answered guardedly.

"Now and again. For a gin-and-orange with Patricia Hastings."

The doctor nodded.

"Good! She's getting a little bored with herself, I'm afraid. Not many young people in the village, you know. Not much fun for a young wife with a doctor husband who leaves her very much alone, poor kid."

"Yes," said Betty Donovan. "She ought to take up golf or a hobby of some sort. Well, thanks very much, Doctor. I must go and rout out Dick. He hasn't shaved yet—the lazy wretch. He was playing Bridge with some of our guests till midnight. Rooked them of three and sixpence. He's incurable!"

She came into the yard and waved her hand—her unscalded hand—to Dr. John Paget as he drove away.

He drove away thoughtfully. He would have to do somethis about his beautiful Viola. He was beginning to worry about her a little.

He looked in at Badgers a day or two after he had exchanged a few words with Major-General Kendrick on the village green. The General had said something about sleeplessness and had asked for a little 'dope'.

It was always a pleasure to see Badgers, a fine old Georgian house, standing back from a big lawn. As he drove through the white gates the doctor noticed that the lawn had not been mown lately and that the rhododendrons needed cutting back and were straggling across the path. Once there had been four gardeners here, as he remembered before the war. Now they made do with a jobbing-gardener once or twice a week. Not good enough for a big garden like this.

'Income-tax and surtax,' thought Dr. Paget. 'It's hitting everybody, even Major-Generals.'

There was a bellpull in the old-fashioned style and he gave it a tug and heard a clang in the back quarters. The door was opened by a manservant who had been the General's batman in North Africa.

"Hullo, Embry!" said the doctor. "How's the lumbago?"

"Much better, thanks to you, Doctor," answered the man.

"Good! Is the General at home?"

"In his study," said the man. "He's been looking a bit worried lately. No wonder, with all this talk about atom bombs and such like! Personally, I believe the world's coming to an end."

"Oh well," said the doctor cheerfully, "that's a nice cure for lumbago and other aches and pains."

"We shall all go out together," said the man, "or at least all the sinful ones."

"Then there won't be many left," said Dr. Paget, with a laugh. "No hope for me, Embry! But do you think I can see the General?"

The man nodded with a somewhat ghastly smile.

"Don't mention what I've said to the General. He wouldn't hold with it."

"Mum's the word, Embry."

He was shown into the study where the General was reading some official-looking documents, a few of which had fallen on the floor at the side of his desk. He looked up and held out his hand.

"Hullo, Doctor, glad to see you. Sit down and have a cigarette. I expect you're busy."

"Any more sleepless nights?" asked Dr. Paget.

General Kendrick smiled and looked embarrassed.

"I ought not to have mentioned that. Absurd of me! But you know how it is. One stays awake for a bit and then all the dark little devils of worry and pessimism come crowding in and one thinks one's had a hell of a night."

Dr. Paget nodded.

"We all have to go through that at times. There's nothing

in it. When daylight comes the little devils depart and one has to admit that one has greatly exaggerated the causes of worry. They smooth themselves out as a rule."

General Kendrick pushed the official papers away from him on the desk as though he hated the sight of them. Then he gave a rather bitter laugh.

"Not in my case exactly. They don't smooth themselves out. If one happens to be on a ship rushing at full speed on to the rocks one can't pretend that journey's end will be smooth and pleasant."

"What ship and what rocks?" asked Dr. Paget.

General Kendrick shrugged his square shoulders.

"My dear fellow," he said, "what's the good of talking about it? Winston keeps talking about it but nobody pays any attention to him—not in the House of Commons anyhow. They jeer at him. His warnings fall on deaf ears. He sees what's coming unless we call a truce to party politics and act pretty damn' quick to provide this country and Western Europe with some measure of defence. You ask what ship and what rocks. I say the ship is this little island and the rocks are those of annihilation to us all if Russia decides to risk the supreme challenge of war."

Dr. Paget shifted uneasily in his chair.

"General," he said gravely, "have you any evidence that Russia will take that risk? Perhaps I ought not to ask you."

General Kendrick glanced at him.

"No immediate evidence," he said. "I'm not giving away any secrets. Nobody knows what's happening in the skulls of those fellows in the Kremlin. You know as much as I do about that—which is nothing. I don't say they're going to risk it. In the long run that would be foolish and they're not fools. But accidents may happen. Sparks may set the world afire. Meanwhile we remain unarmed, defenceless, at the mercy of a ruthless enemy of enormous strength in man-power mobilized within striking distance of the Channel ports. They make no secret that they hate our guts. Is that a satisfactory situation for ourselves or Western Europe?"

"Very unpleasant," agreed Dr. Paget, whose observant eyes

were watching this man closely. His strong big hands, on which some golden hairs caught the light from the window beyond his desk, shook slightly as he undid a waistcoat button and then did it up again. His face had become faintly flushed and he breathed more heavily than usual. But he spoke again with a forced calm which showed that he was putting a restraint upon hidden emotion.

"Of course in the long run," he said, "American air-power and man-power, plus that of Western Europe, would make a pretty mess of Russian cities and their lines of communication. There's the atom bomb . . ."

"Which God forbid," said Dr. Paget.

General Kendrick nodded.

"Certainly," he agreed. "God forbid that we should have to use it. But God forbid also that Western Europe and this island should be laid in dust and ashes, enslaved and massacred, with mass executions and ingenious tortures while the United States were mobilizing their future strength."

"What's our best hope?" asked Dr. Paget.

"Time," said the General. "God give us time. Two years, three years. Time that our politicans will wake up from this dreadful sleep of inaction and unpreparedness. These little party politicians of ours, these little men busy with little quarrels about wages and social services and nationalization of this and that, these little squint-eyed egoists always with one eye on the next election and the winning of votes, are wasting this God-given time which might enable us to defend ourselves and the last strongholds of civilization. I've tried to wake 'em up. I write reports which they don't read. I know some of 'em —decent fellows—but blinkered. As a soldier I'm not supposed to talk politics. I'm not allowed to give away official secrets. But the Minister for War has the right to know. I've tried to see that he does know. I have an idea that he agrees with me, but his colleagues won't listen. The Foreign Secretary is quite aware of the menace, but all our so-called leaders are afraid of the Trade Unions and the rank and file of Labour. They're not free agents. Not that I'm a party man. God forbid! I'm a professional soldier. There's a general idea that professional soldiers are mostly half-wits—unless there's a war on and they become temporary heroes if they happen to win."

He gave an uneasy laugh again.

"I ought not to bore you like this!"

"It's pretty important," said Dr. Paget. "It's a question of survival for all of us. I'm one of those who want to survive—not altogether for my own sake."

He spoke half seriously with a glint of humour in his eyes, but secretly he was disturbed. It was obvious that General Kendrick took an alarming view of things and was suffering from a sense of frustration and suppressed anger and frayed nerves. He saw the possibility of enormous catastrophe, unimaginable in horror, threatening the destruction of everything, of civilized humanity, but unable to get the attention of those who might avert it by desperate and heroic action, given time for which he prayed. A psychological tragedy of Shakespearean depths, bearing down upon this man's brain, nagging at him with a kind of mental torture. An awful responsibility for any man to hold the keys of knowledge, to be aware that the end of all things might come if his advice were ignored—the end of all things in an atom war which might kill every living thing within its range of radioactive power, wiping out cities with crowded populations, destroying every vestige of man's achievement, making England itself a vast Hiroshima—but finding that no one cared a damn, no one worried, no one raised a little finger to prevent it happening. Yet here he sat in his comfortable study—a simple soldierly-looking man, heavy-jowled, unimaginative-looking, trying to talk of these things without emotion because of his tradition and the English way of understatement and casualness.

'Perhaps he's wrong,' thought Dr. Paget. 'I hope to God he's wrong. This war may never happen. It may be just a nightmare horror in this man's mind, and in the minds of other frightened people. But right or wrong, I can understand the strain on him. He might get a heart attack. He might have a stroke one day, bottling all this up, suppressing his sense of fear for the future of us all. He's up against world powers and demoniacal forces, and he can't do a damn' thing about it.

That's his trouble, and it's the trouble of all of us. We can't do a damn' thing about it, while perhaps we drift towards the fiery furnace.'

General Kendrick spoke again and seemed to excuse himself for having talked so much.

"One speaks to a doctor as a pious Papist speaks to a priest under the seal of confession. Or like city men speak to their barbers. Have you noticed how city men blab a lot to their barbers while they're having their hair cut? It's the need of self-revelation, not possible perhaps in the family circle!"

He was getting off the subject, trying to turn the conversation to a lighter mood.

Dr. Paget answered him with a smile.

"It's a doctor's privilege to listen to his patients' confidences. It's the secret of psychiatry to get in touch with the patient's psyche."

"Well," said General Kendrick, good-humouredly, "I hope I haven't given myself away too much. My psyche at the moment must be compounded of blue funk and impotent rage. When I go to the club and see fellows asleep in armchairs or playing Bridge, or looking at the tape-machine for the three-thirty winners, I feel like banging their heads together, or shouting at them like a male Cassandra. 'Damn it, you fellows, don't you know that we're at the mercy of those devils in the Kremlin? Don't you know that we couldn't put five divisions into the field?' What do you think of that, Doctor? Symptoms of a disordered mind, eh?"

"High blood-pressure," said Dr. Paget, "increased by nervous tension and emotional strains. Very understandable in your case. Let me take a test of that blood-pressure."

It was pretty high.

"Better slow down a bit," he said presently. "Play a bit more golf. Try to keep your mind off the international situation. Don't brood over the headlines in the morning papers."

The General gave a short laugh.

"Put my head in the sand and play the ostrich? I'm damned if I do."

"Look here, General," said Dr. Paget, "there's nothing I

can do to help you except give you a mild sedative. Your problems are too big for a country quack—as big as the universe, as big as the eternal battle between civilization and barbarism. You're fighting principalities and powers and I can only pray that you will wake up this country in time to save us. That's your mission in life. I can't interfere with it. It's worth dying for, high blood-pressure or low blood-pressure. I'm talking now not as a doctor but as a friend. So bless you, my dear fellow."

General Kendrick held out his hand.

"Thanks, Paget. It's kind of you to put it that way."

He turned to the papers on his desk.

"I don't want to exaggerate my own importance," he said. "I'm not the only man who's trying to get a move on. Winston, Eden, the Americans like Marshall and Acheson, a lot of straight-thinking fellows behind the scenes. But I must do what I can to shake up our own sleepwalkers. I've just been drafting out a memorandum which I propose to send to high quarters. It may get me the sack. I don't care if it does. I've set out the grim facts of our world-wide weakness. Not pleasant reading, Doctor."

"Will they read it?" asked Dr. Paget.

General Kendrick raised his hands, those square-shaped hands on which there were little golden hairs caught by the light coming through his window.

"Who knows? This time it will go straight to the Big Man. He asked for it. He's damn' well going to get it."

He rose from his swing chair and laughed and said, "Well . . ."

"Yes," said Dr. Paget, "I must be going. How's her ladyship?"

General Kendrick answered after a moment's pause.

"I'm worried about her. She's been a bit queer lately. Queer ideas. Very disturbing in a way, poor dear. Come and dine with us one evening. Bring your beautiful wife."

Dr. Paget left him and was shown out by his man Embry, who belonged to some queer sect and believed the world was coming to an end.

CHAPTER IV

THE doctor found his young wife looking rather desperate one evening.

"How have you been amusing yourself?" he asked. "Any Bridge this afternoon?"

"Oh, I loathe Bridge in the afternoons," she answered; "it's immoral when the sun shines, and very fuggy when it doesn't."

"I agree," said the doctor. "What, then?"

Viola shrugged her shoulders. She was a tall, slim young woman with big hazel-coloured eyes in which there was now an unhappy look which the doctor hated to see.

"I went for a walk on the heath with Pincher. Of course I didn't meet a soul, I had the world to myself! It's not a very amusing world if one has it to oneself."

"I know," he told her. "I leave you too much alone, my dear. But I can't help it just now. Everybody seems under the weather."

"Of course," she told him. "You have your job to do. I wish I had."

"Play a bit more golf," he suggested. "It's a grand game."

She answered with a forced little laugh.

"It's not much fun trailing round the links with one of the Ancients. Everybody in this village is so old! They've made their lives. They've done it all—quite a lot, some of them, I must admit. Now they're waiting for death, poor old dears."

"I'm a bit old myself," said Dr. Paget, taking her hand and kissing it.

"Oh lord, no!" she answered quickly. "You're on active service. I don't class you among the Ancients yet."

"Thanks a lot!" said the doctor, with a laugh. "I feel relieved about that."

"You know I wasn't getting at you," she answered. "It's

only because I want more of you and more of life perhaps. Very foolish, I know."

Dr. Paget kissed her hair as she sat down by his side on the hearthrug.

"Life is very much what one makes it," he said. "You have plenty of time to make a lot of yours, my dear."

"How?" she asked, looking up at him.

"Take up something worth while. Science. Languages. Music. Handicrafts. Be one of the active members in the Women's Institute."

Mrs. Paget laughed with a high note.

"The W.I.? Oh lord, among the old frumps!"

"Nice old frumps, and many young ones," he answered. "Jolly good at glovemaking, woodcarving, embroidery."

"Not in my line," she told him. "That's worse than Bridge with Mrs. Montgomery-Jones and her fellow scandalmongers."

Dr. Paget laughed at his young wife and bent over her and pinched her ear.

"Scandal is very necessary to social life! Sometimes it's devilish amusing, if it isn't too poisonous. Like a cocktail at Foxgloves. Not much harm in it."

His wife met his eyes for a moment and her colour deepened.

"Somebody has been blabbing about that, I suppose. Do you object to my taking a drink now and then with Patricia Hastings?"

"Not in the least!" he answered. "Pat Hastings swears too much, flirts too much, drinks too much—and doesn't pay her bills very regularly, I'm told—but she's good fun and fairly harmless."

Viola Paget answered with a laugh.

"Not a very convincing testimonial! As a matter of fact she's a good sort."

"I agree," said Dr. Paget. "She drove an ambulance in the London Blitz. I give her full marks for that."

"None for me?" asked Viola.

"Heaps for you as a V.A.D. Do you remember that night the County Hospital was hit? You didn't turn a hair. That was when I fell in love with you, with the look in your eyes, with your spirit, and the way you comforted the frightened patients. 'That kid is a pearl of great price,' I said to myself. And then I had the cheek to marry you."

"It seems a lifetime ago," said Viola.

"Seven years," he answered. "For me seven happy and busy years, thank God."

His young wife gave a long-drawn sigh.

"For me rather empty and wasted years—except for your love, my dear, and the fun we've had now and then. It's only lately I've felt—well, a bit restless and nervy and alone. I'm just the wife of Dr. John Paget—a very busy man who drives his own car so that he doesn't need a chauffeuse. All I can do to help him is to answer the telephone and put down his calls."

"Very helpful, my dear," said Dr. Paget.

Mrs. Paget went to the window and stared through the lattice panes of the old Queen Anne house which looked out to the roadway through the village.

"I might take up nursing again," she said. "Then you would have to get a lady secretary and I should be jealous of her."

Dr. Paget laughed good-humouredly.

"That's a grand idea!" he exclaimed. "And I should like you to be jealous on my account. That would be a proof of love."

She came back from the window and put her fingers through his grey hair as he stood looking at her with a smile.

"Do you need any proof, old witch-doctor?"

"Constant proof!" he told her. "Let's hear more about that nursing idea."

"It's only an idea of desperation," she answered. "I hate nursing really. I wouldn't mind going in for physiotherapy. That's more interesting. It rather appeals to me."

"Well, there now!" said her husband. "You've said a mouthful, lady! With you as a physiotherapist we should be a grand combination. You could rehabilitate all the patients I've failed to kill."

"It's nonsense really," said Mrs. Paget. "Doesn't it take three years or so? Wouldn't it mean going to London? Besides . . ."

"Besides what?"

"Is it worth while taking up anything like that?"

"Why not? Everything is worth while."

"Aren't we going to be atomized pretty soon?" asked Mrs. Paget. "The next war doesn't seem far ahead."

The doctor was deeply shocked by that frightful question. She had asked it as though enquiring about next day's weather.

"Oh, God!" he exclaimed. "Don't think about that, my darling. Don't talk about it. It's no good imagining such horrors."

"One can't help thinking about it," she answered. "The papers rub it in. Winston warns us in every speech. It makes everything seem rather futile. It makes one want to grab at the fun of life while there's still time."

"My darling," said Dr. Paget, gravely and tenderly—with what his wife called his best bedside manner—"don't let your imagination dwell on that side of things. I refuse to believe in a Third World War."

"Ostrich!" exclaimed his wife, a little fiercely.

"I prefer to be an ostrich," said the doctor. "It's better to put one's head in the sand than look out for bogeys and demons and all the devils of hell who may never appear. Our village folk aren't worrying. They ignore all this gloomy talk—very wisely."

He hid from her his disturbing talk with General Kendrick.

The telephone rang in the consulting-room where he was having his talk with his wife. She picked up the receiver and answered the crackle of a voice in it.

"Yes, I'll tell him. He'll come round as soon as possible. Yes, of course. Quite soon."

Then she put down the receiver and said: "Damn! That means you'll be late again tonight. You know you promised to dine at Foxgloves with the Kendricks. They've asked the Vicar and his sister to meet us."

"Who wants me?" asked the doctor. "If it isn't serious . . ."

"Peggy Warner has pains coming on. She expects the baby tonight."

"Oh lord!" said Dr. Paget, with a groan. "I shall have to go. I'm frightfully sorry."

He put his arms round his wife and kissed her.

"It's a darned shame about this evening. I was looking forward to it."

"The Kendricks are sending their car for us," said Mrs. Paget. "I suppose they'll bring me back again."

"Of course. Make my apologies, won't you?"

She helped him into his coat and held out her cheek for him to kiss.

"Good-bye, old witch-doctor."

"God bless you," he said. "Don't stay up too late. Don't smoke too many cigarettes. Have a good time."

She heard him starting up his car in the front yard, then the screech of gravel as he turned out of the gate into the roadway.

She went to the mantelpiece and touched one of the little brass ornaments which her mother had brought from India—a sacred cow, a little Buddha, an acrobat, shining like gold. The German girl had polished them that afternoon with the other brass things. Presently she put her forehead down on the edge of the mantelshelf and gave a little whimper.

Then she went up to her bedroom and put on one of her evening frocks, partly for the benefit of the Kendricks and more for her own. It was not often she bothered to put on pretty things in the village of Longmead where everybody was dowdy or careless about clothes. Patricia Hastings always looked smart but generally in riding kit or in the flame-red frock which made her look, she said, like the Scarlet Woman and scandalized Mrs. Montgomery-Jones when she went to church in it—as to church she went now and then because she thought the Vicar was a dear and ought to be encouraged.

Mrs. Paget decided to wear her black silk frock cut low at the shoulders. She had pretty shoulders, as she observed when she glanced at herself in a long mirror in her bedroom—this room with a low ceiling crossed by black old beams. She put a pearl necklace round her throat, a present from her husband. Her face needed no make-up but she touched it with colour after reddening her lips.

"Anybody would think I'm going to the Ritz," she said aloud.

She glanced at herself again in the mirror, switching on

another light. She seemed to be interested by her own image, gazing at it gravely.

"I still look young," she thought. "I look ridiculously young. Soon I'll be an old moth sitting down at Bridge tables on sunny afternoons. Gosh!"

Presently she heard the slowing down of a car outside the gate and the German maid, Hildegard, came to say that the Kendricks' car had come for her.

The German maid seemed struck by her appearance:

"Very beautiful!" she exclaimed. "*Wunderschön!* You are like a princess in a fairy tale."

Viola Paget laughed.

"I feel rather like it! I feel like Cinderella going to the ball, but there won't be any fairy prince."

"Perhaps that is good," said the German girl. "Fairy princes are very dangerous, especially for a *gnädige Frau*—a married lady."

She laughed merrily. There was no sinister meaning in this remark, though for a moment Mrs. Paget had glanced at her with a doubtful smile as though suspecting it.

"You'll answer the telephone, won't you? Try to get the names right."

"Some of them are such terrible names!" cried Hildegard. "Thistlethwaite . . . Entinknap . . . Hodgkiss . . . *Schrecklich!*"

"Well, don't be too lonely," said Mrs. Paget, who hated loneliness, "I shan't be late."

"Oh no, I shan't be lonely," the girl assured her. "There are always letters to write, and then I am reading Bertrand Russell's *History of Western Philosophy*. I find it very amusing. He knocks down all the philosophers—even Kant and Hegel—like a row of ninepins. He is really very witty."

"Good heavens!" exclaimed Mrs. Paget. "You make me laugh, Hildegard. Only a German girl would choose a book like that for light reading!"

"I took my degree at Munich," said the girl. "I don't want to slip back into ignorance."

"And now you're a household drudge in a doctor's house," exclaimed Mrs. Paget. "What a world!"

"I'm not unhappy," said Hildegard. "Just a little homesick, of course. But there are other German girls round about, and in any case . . ."

"In any case?" asked Mrs. Paget, touching her hair with another glance at the mirror.

"In any case it is safer perhaps in England. Just a little safer. My parents are anxious lest the Russians should advance into the Western zone. Then frightful things would happen, especially to German girls, you understand?"

Mrs. Paget looked at her thoughtfully.

"Do you think the Russians *will* advance?"

"It is very possible," said Hildegard calmly. "There is nothing to stop them."

"Oh well, we're not worrying," said Mrs. Paget, who as a matter of fact had been worrying about the atom bomb.

The German girl laughed.

"The English people do not worry about anything until it hits them between the eyes. That is a great characteristic. It is perhaps, if you'll forgive me, a little stupid as well as very much brave. Certainly the English are brave. Certainly many of them are . . ."

She checked herself and laughed again.

"I dare say you're right," said Mrs. Paget. "I don't find much intelligence in Longmead nor in my own empty head."

The girl followed Mrs. Paget down the stairs and out of the house, shutting the door of the car after she had got in.

Mrs. Paget said "Good evening" to the Kendricks' chauffeur, who had been waiting for her some time and looked sulky.

"*Gute Nacht, gnädige Frau. Amüsieren Sie sich!*"

"*Danke schön,*" answered Mrs. Paget, who knew that much German and a few other words.

General and Lady Kendrick were in the big lounge of Foxgloves with the Vicar and his sister when Mrs. Paget entered the room and made her apologies for the doctor.

"That's too bad," said Lady Kendrick, taking both her hands and holding them for a moment. "But of course we understand. The poor man can't get much peace. It's a life of self-sacrifice. But, my dear, how elegant you look tonight! You put me to shame in this old coat and skirt."

She spoke in a 'cello-like voice which was pleasant to hear.

Mrs. Paget blushed slightly and laughed.

"Perhaps I'm a bit over-dressed for Foxgloves."

She felt embarrassed for a moment as Lady Kendrick smiled at her with dark, dreamy eyes. She was not one of the 'old frumps' but had a certain grace and beauty as a middle-aged woman, tall and thin with high cheek bones and those dark deep-set eyes.

'A bit scraggy,' thought Mrs. Paget, 'but rather good looking. She must have been beautiful once.'

She remembered something her husband had said about this lady.

"A spiritual woman and rather alarming. One of those women who take up a cause with passionate fanaticism. In the old days she would have been a Suffragette and chained herself to the railings of the House of Commons."

Mrs. Paget, who did not find her alarming, released her hands to take one of the General's who was waiting to greet her, which he did with a touch of old-fashioned gallantry and a pretty compliment.

"You look charming, my dear. Portrait of a beautiful lady. How good of you to come!"

Mrs. Paget made a little curtsy in her black silk frock. It was pleasant to be admired even by a man of sixty with little pouches under his eyes.

"Good evening, Mrs. Paget," said the Vicar, who had risen from his chair at her entrance. "Uncertain weather, isn't it? Good for the roses, though."

The Rev. Gerald Langtry was a thin-featured man of middle height and an under-nourished look, though probably his dominating sister—one of the Watch Committee—as Mrs. Paget called the vigilant ladies of Longmead—fed him up all right. He had been a padre with the 8th Army in North Africa—the Desert Rats—and had been taken prisoner by Rommel's men. Now he was in this peaceful back-water of Longmead—

peaceful but for the feuds and scandals of village life in which he was one of the targets, perhaps even the chief target.

Miss Elizabeth Langtry, his sister, stretched out a bony hand while seated in a big armchair.

"Nice to see you, my dear," she said in a loud hearty carrying voice. "I understand you're not unacquainted with this hostelry."

It was a distinct suggestion that Mrs. Paget was one of its *habituées*.

'So the old cat knows that I've had a sherry here now and then,' thought that lady. 'One can't move a step without being watched.'

"It's a pleasant place, don't you think?" she answered. "I've met the Vicar here once or twice."

"Disgracing his cloth," said Miss Elizabeth Langtry, with a high-pitched laugh. "Consorting with publicans and sinners!"

"Like Jesus Christ," said Mrs. Paget.

"Exactly," remarked Lady Kendrick with her 'cello-like voice, "That's one for you, Elizabeth."

Miss Langtry accepted the retort good-humouredly.

"I must admit . . ."

"Let's go and dine," said the General.

Mrs. Paget glanced round the dining-room of Foxgloves after taking her seat at table. At the far end she saw Patricia Hastings in slacks and a yellow jumper. She was feeding with two young men who looked like naval officers out of uniform. She looked over at Mrs. Paget, grinned, and raised a little glass which doubtless contained gin-and-orange. At another table was the Austrian artist by name of Rudi Scholl in his loose corduroys and shabby sports coat and floppy red tie. A lock of brown hair fell over his forehead and he looked unshaven. He was reading a book propped up against a bottle of beer but when Mrs. Paget came into the room he half rose from his seat with a little bow in his foreign way and twice at least during the dinner she was aware of his eyes upon her—brown, animal-looking eyes, glancing at her with homage and admiration which she could not misinterpret.

'He's trying to make love to me with his eyes,' she thought.

'That's his technique with women who will stand him a drink or buy one of his paintings.'

At other tables were the regular residents of Foxgloves—the old dodderers who were waiting for death, as she had told her husband. Mr. and Mrs. Fairchild, sitting quite silent because they had exhausted all conversation after half a century of married life—an old lady with dabs of red on her cheeks and a French poodle lying at her feet—an ancient gentleman who had come in on two sticks shuffling himself over the polished floor. Rheumatoid arthritis—ninety by the look of him. Then there were two elderly sisters who seemed to be quarrelling about something with great bitterness in thin resonant voices.

"I'm sure I left it on the chest-of-drawers," said one of them.

"Are you accusing me of taking it?" asked the other.

"Things don't disappear by themselves. You know you smoked all your own cigarettes."

Commander Donovan came over to the General's table with his touch of Irish blarney and breezy naval way.

"Sure, General, it's an honour to have you here and I hope you'll find the chicken as tender as a woman's kiss."

"A seductive simile, my dear fellow," said the General with a laugh. "How about a bottle of wine? Anything good in that cellar of yours?"

"As good as gold, of which we don't get a glimpse these days. A first-class Burgundy—Nuits St. George of '39—it has a fine flavour to the palate, as rich and warm as the notes of a 'cello. I'll take the chill off it."

"Good man!" said the General. "How are things going here? Well, I hope."

"As well as may be," answered Commander Donovan, "considering that everything's against us under a Government which is dragging us all down to blue ruin."

"Hear, hear!" said Miss Elizabeth Langtry. "It's a deliberate policy. They want to liquidate the gentry and professional classes—anybody with a little capital; anybody who has put by something after a life of hard work. I'm not a vindictive woman filled with blood lust but I would willingly strangle half the Cabinet with my own hands."

The Vicar of Longmead laughed good-humouredly.

"Hush, Elizabeth! You're too violent—and mightily un-Christian. How do you think I'm going to keep peace in my own parish if you say things like that?"

"One shouldn't make peace with evil or evil-doers," said Elizabeth Langtry. "Don't you agree, General?"

"In principle," said the General, guardedly.

"I'm sure you're against appeasement with those dreadful Russians," said Elizabeth Langtry.

Glancing at the table where the Austrian artist was sitting, Mrs. Paget saw that he was listening with an ironical smile. It was cheek of him to listen to other people's conversation, she thought.

The General seemed to be amused and mildly alarmed by the blunt-spoken lady whose voice was loud and carrying. He lowered his own slightly.

"We tried that with Hitler and it didn't work. It won't work with the Men in the Kremlin."

"Thank God the Americans are getting tough with them," cried Elizabeth Langtry.

"Does God like toughness?" asked Lady Kendrick, quietly, with a dark smile at the Vicar's sister.

"It's a bit dangerous," said the General. "Berlin is like a powder magazine."

Viola Paget glanced at him. His heavy-jowled face had a grave expression.

'He thinks we're for it,' she said to herself. 'And he's one who knows. My dear old witch-doctor wouldn't like this conversation. It would make him take his head out of the sand.'

The Vicar put in a question in his mild undogmatic way.

"Can we afford to be tough? Have we any strength behind us? If the Russians attacked . . ."

The General shrugged his shoulders.

"It's to be hoped they won't. They've a hundred and seventy divisions fully mobilized. The whole of Western Europe can hardly put ten into the field. France and Italy are riddled with Communism. Where's our defence? That's what I keep asking myself."

He had lowered his voice and now looked over his shoulder as though nervous of being overheard.

Miss Elizabeth Langtry did not see any reason to lower her voice which was clear and challenging.

"But, my dear General, why don't you prod up this weak-kneed Government of ours. Why don't you wake them up and shake them up to our appalling danger? They ought to be arraigned for High Treason."

The General laughed and answered quietly:

"I'm inclined to agree. But I'm not a politician."

"What we want," said Elizabeth Langtry, "is a Charlotte Corday, who would go with a sharp knife and kill them in their baths—if they ever have baths."

The Vicar laughed but looked perturbed.

"Elizabeth!" he exclaimed, "For heaven's sake. . . . Do moderate your speech a little."

"I won't moderate my speech," she answered, firmly. "In this time of desperate danger moderation of speech is a mockery. We ought to rouse the People—our poor, dumb, deluded People—by making them realize the terror of this menace which threatens them with every kind of horror. But they're lulled to sleep. You lull them to sleep, Gerald, by your slumber-making sermons which evade the grim realities and the ghastly facts. Forgive me saying so, Gerald, but you're one of the lullers."

"I try to preach the Christian doctrine," said the Vicar, "and I have a horror of another war, having seen the last one—only five years ago."

General Kendrick gave a heavy sigh.

"We all have a horror of war, padre, soldiers most of all. But the only way to stop it is to rearm as rapidly as possible—the general rearmament of Western Europe."

"I wonder," said the Vicar, thoughtfully. "Can one fight Communism by guns and tanks?"

Lady Kendrick had sat rather silently with a dark, melancholy look as though this talk of war distressed her or made her frightened.

'She's a frightened woman,' thought Mrs. Paget, glancing at her. 'We ought all to be frightened, but somehow we don't believe it's true. Just as we don't believe in bogeys and banshees except as a thrill by Christmas firesides. It's lack of imagination, I suppose. Or else our emotions have been deadened by too much horror. We can't be bothered to be frightened any more. I'm not frightened really. I don't care tuppence.'

"My husband," said Lady Kendrick, "believes in more guns and more tanks. I believe in more faith and more charity. We ought to fight Communism with spiritual weapons. We ought to bombard Moscow with messages of good will."

The General shifted in his seat and turned to smile at his wife.

"My dear Beatrice," he said, good-humouredly, "you can't penetrate the Iron Curtain by messages of good will. They jam them out. Haven't we held out the hand of friendship many times and haven't they spat upon it?"

Lady Kendrick's dark eyes turned to her husband's florid face and she answered gravely.

"If we really were Christians, if we really believed in Christ's message . . ."

The General shook his head.

"Those cold-headed fellows in the Kremlin are utterly callous of human life and jeer at our Christian moralities. They're dedicated to world domination. They're out to stir up trouble everywhere outside their own police states, to weaken the freedom-loving peoples by dispersing their forces and wrecking their economy and creating internal disorders by strikes, sabotage and all the rest of it. They're not in a hurry. They can afford to wait until the moment has come, waiting to strike with strength against weakness, with overwhelming weight against feeble and divided resistance."

"What keeps them back now?" asked Mrs. Paget.

The General looked her in the eyes and smiled not because the subject was amusing but because she was young and pretty.

"The atom bomb," he answered. "Nothing but that."

Mrs. Paget smiled back at him but felt a little cold touch down her spine.

'I expect he's right,' she thought. 'He ought to know.

He's been to Moscow on military missions. He has met those men in the Kremlin. I'd like to ask him how many years of life he gives us. Two, three? After that most of us will be dead. That's a queer thought. This body of mine will be cold and dead. Probably I shall be blown to bits. But nobody worries except the General and a few others. There's a whist drive tonight at the village hall. They'll all be laughing. "Regardless of their doom the little victims play." I wonder who wrote that. I can't remember. I ought to be frightened but I can't say I am, except in a theoretical way. Perhaps I am frightened. Otherwise I shouldn't have spoken to John like that—my dear old witch-doctor. Perhaps it's always nagging at the back of my mind. Perhaps it nags at other people though they don't show it or talk about it.'

Her eyes strayed to the table where Rudi Scholl was eating his food—free grub for decorating the billiard-room. Pat Hastings had told her that. He was listening again with a smile on his lips.

Lady Kendrick was speaking to her husband.

"You accept this war as inevitable."

"No, no!" exclaimed the General. "I haven't said that. There may still be time."

"I refuse to accept it," said Lady Kendrick, in her 'cello-like voice. "The women of England—and France and all the other countries—should refuse to accept it. Why should our boys be driven to the slaughter-house? 'Dilly dilly come and be killed.' I'm old enough to remember the First World War with its frightful massacre of youth—three of my brothers. Is all that to happen again? Is our Mervyn sentenced to death already before he's had a chance of life? It's this dreadful acceptance of war—the Americans are the worst—which is so ghastly."

She was speaking with an intensity of emotion and had raised her voice so that her words were heard at other tables where some of the diners turned to look at her. The young naval men in civilian clothes—they looked like that—smiled at Patricia Hastings and whispered to her. The two elderly sisters stared over at the General's table and one of them raised a lorgnette.

The General spoke to his wife with good-natured patience.

"It isn't a question of acceptance. If war comes it will be forced upon us. Then we ought to be in a position to defend ourselves. *Cet animal est méchant. Quand on l'attaque il se défend.*"

Lady Kendrick had a mystical light in her eyes.

"What if we refuse to defend ourselves? Hasn't the time come to try that out? Isn't it the only way of stopping this hideous repetition of war? If the Russians come let's meet them with outstretched hands. If we don't fight them they won't fight us."

The General stared at his wife with a look of consternation.

"Beatrice!" he said, "you don't know what you're saying. Do you want this country to be enslaved and tortured? Don't you know what has happened in the satellite states? And in any case aren't you a soldier's wife and a patriotic English-woman?"

Lady Kendrick answered in a low voice.

"I want to save the youth of the world."

The Vicar had listened to Lady Kendrick with curious intensity of interest.

"Absolute non-resistance?" he asked. "I've sometimes thought that may be the only way. The early Christians didn't take up arms. . . ."

Mrs. Paget intervened in the argument and blushed as she heard her own voice, ringing in a rather shrill tone.

"No, they went into the arena and were gobbled up by lions and hugged by bears, and clawed by tigers. An unpleasant form of martyrdom!"

Her pretty white shoulders gave a little shudder.

Lady Kendrick looked into her eyes and answered in that low-toned but resonant voice.

"We ought to be ready for martyrdom if it would save the lives of the world's youth—the children who are being born into this terrible world."

"Beatrice!" cried Elizabeth Langtry. "Did you drink too much of that delicious wine? You're talking sky-bosh and high treason."

"I'm talking with desperate and passionate conviction," said Lady Kendrick.

"It's all very interesting," said the Vicar. "It gives one to think very deeply."

The General laughed uneasily.

"I'm sorry the subject was raised. Not my fault, you know. We all have different ideas. Let's get some coffee in the lounge. Mervyn may be here later on. He's coming over from Sandhurst on his motor-bike."

As they were passing into the lounge down a dim corridor the young Austrian who had been sitting next to the General's table spoke to Mrs. Paget who had met him once or twice with Patricia Hastings.

"Forgive me, Mrs. Paget," he said. "One word, if you please."

"I'm with friends," she answered, rather coldly.

"Yes, charming friends with so interesting a conversation which I could not help hearing."

He gave a little laugh as though much amused by this conversation.

"The English people are marvellous," he said, "and they talk freely even in places like this. That is so lucky for them."

"You wish to say something special to me?" asked Mrs. Paget.

"Yes, indeed. Very special. Forgive me! In that black silk frock you look exquisite. I speak as an artist. Will you allow me to paint your portrait in that frock? I ask you. I beg of you to grant me that favour."

Mrs. Paget blushed slightly and gave a nervous laugh.

"Oh no! Please excuse me."

"Please consider the idea," said Rudi Scholl, "I could make it a masterpiece. I will put all that I have into it. I will be inspired!"

He would have spoken again but she passed him with a smile. It was rather flattering of course but she did not like him as a personality. Certainly he could paint. He had done a portrait of Patricia Hastings which was very strong and vivid but made her look rather wicked. Anyhow she herself was not so beautiful as he had pretended. That was his technique again, and she found him very unattractive. He hadn't shaved for something like two days and his corduroy trousers looked as if he had slept in them. Perhaps he had. He was as poor as a church mouse according to Patricia who stood him drinks now and then.

It was ten minutes after she had rejoined her friends that a tall handsome boy came into the room and walked towards the coffee-table where they were sitting and bent down to kiss his mother. It was Mervyn who had come over from Sandhurst.

Lady Kendrick took one of his hands and raised it to her lips.

"Well, young fellow," said the General, "how's everything?"

"Not too bad," answered his son. "They've been putting us through it all right. I ache in every limb."

"Brutal!" said Lady Kendrick.

Mervyn looked at her with laughing eyes.

"Oh, I wouldn't go as far as that! Very good for one's physique.

He shook hands with the Vicar and his sister and was introduced to the doctor's wife, looking at her with a shy smile.

"Oh, don't you know Mrs. Paget?" said his mother.

"Afraid not," said Mervyn.

It was the first time they had met. He had been in London coaching for Sandhurst at Jemmy's. Then he had spent his holidays abroad before going to Sandhurst. He was looking at Mrs. Paget with a smiling surprise, a kind of startled admiration. She felt the grip of his hand. He was tall and very young and boyish, with dark hair like his mother's and her dark liquid eyes but with his father's square-cut face.

'What a frightfully good-looking boy!' thought Mrs. Paget, using the wrong adjective for good looks. 'How young and shy he is. I'm almost old enough to be his mother.'

That was a ridiculous thought. She was only seven years older than Mervyn Kendrick as afterwards she calculated. Twenty-one and twenty-eight—a big gap!

He sat in one of the deep armchairs showing a pair of crimson socks beneath his flannel trousers.

"This is a good spot!" he said, glancing round the big room with its old beams and plastered walls.

"Have a liqueur, old boy?" asked the General.

"Good idea, Father!"

"A liqueur, Mrs. Paget?"

"That would be very nice," said Viola Paget.

"Vicar?"

"No, thanks, General. I have to preach a sermon tomorrow."

The liqueur was cherry brandy and Viola Paget felt it run like liquid fire through her veins, very warming and comforting. She had been in the depths of depression before coming here—in the dark pit of self-pity because of her loneliness and sense of futility. That mood had passed from her because of a good dinner and this little drop of cherry brandy. How very absurd, she thought, that the spirit should be so affected by something happening inside one's tummy. Rather disconcerting in a way but pleasant all the same. She noticed that Mervyn, this baby boy, six foot high, looked at her now and then with that shy smile to which she gave an answering smile.

In the big room Patricia Hastings was having a good time with the two young men who seemed to be in a gay mood. They were making too much noise with their laughter to please the two old sisters who looked at them with disapproval. Presently Commander Donovan sat down with them and played some gambling game—gin-rummy perhaps. He seemed to be winning money from his own guests.

"You have the luck of the devil!" cried Patricia Hastings.

"It's my Irish blood," said the ex-naval commander. "Let's have another drink. On the house of course!"

The General was talking about the North African campaign in which he had commanded a brigade of Desert Rats. The padre had been with him. They were exchanging reminiscences.

"Those bloodhounds!" exclaimed Lady Kendrick smiling at them. "The smell of blood and death is in their nostrils. Oh, how I hate it all. War . . . War . . . War. Can't humanity ever learn sense?"

Young Mervyn smiled at his mother.

"It seems to be the natural order of things. Man is a fighting animal."

"Not civilized man," she answered. "Not man who reaches up to the spiritual ideals."

Mervyn smiled at her again.

"Lots of 'em don't!" he said. "And isn't civilization rather a myth? It seems restricted to a very small minority nowadays, judging from the news in the morning papers. Not that I know anything about it, of course. At Sandhurst——"

He was looking across the room and his attention was caught by one of those tables to be seen in country inns—with wooden mushrooms and holes in a green cloth.

"Shall we try our skill on that table?" he asked, looking at the doctor's wife. "It's rather fun."

"I should like to," said Mrs. Paget. "I've never tried it."

"Do you mind, Mother?" asked Mervyn.

"No, my dear. You two young people . . ."

She caught his hand as he passed and kissed it again.

He put sixpence into a slot, liberating a lot of little balls which rolled down into an open drawer after a great deal of whirring noise.

"Take a cue, won't you," he said. "You have to avoid knocking down the mushrooms and get the balls into the holes. It's alarmingly difficult."

He laughed at her every time she knocked down a wooden mushroom.

"Bad luck! . . . Let's have another sixpennorth!"

"I haven't got a sixpence," said Mrs. Paget.

"Oh, that's all right. It won't break me!"

Once he stopped playing and looked at her in his shy, smiling way.

"I say, it's funny we haven't met before!"

"Yes, a pity," said Mrs. Paget.

"Silly," he remarked, "belonging to the same village and all that. We must put that right, don't you think? I mean if it isn't cheek we might meet more often."

"That would be nice," said Mrs. Paget.

"There's a paucity of people of our age in Longmead," he said. "Mostly old dodderers."

Our age? She was pleased that he classed her with his own generation. But she couldn't let him be under a false illusion.

"I'm a lot older than you," she told him.

"Not to make any difference," he answered carelessly. "Are you fond of riding?"

"I used to ride. Not much though. Only on Wimbledon Common when my people lived there—after they'd come back from India."

"We might hire two hacks and take them over the heath now and then. Would that appeal to you at all?"

"Enormously!" she said.

It appealed to her very much. It would be enchanting to go riding with this charming boy. It would be a cure for loneliness. It would be a jolly escape from self-pity and boredom.

"Right! Then we'll fix it up. I get a spot of leave from Sandhurst now and then. Occasional week-ends with the family. I say, you're getting to play this game rather well. Learning the trick of it!"

They finished the game and went and joined the others who were still talking round the coffee-table. Not long afterwards Mrs. Paget was driven home in the General's car. It had been a pleasant evening. Her 'witch-doctor' had not come back but she felt less lonely as she undressed in her little bedroom with its old beams and low ceiling.

CHAPTER V

Mrs. Paget had a ring one morning from Mervyn Kendrick soon after the dinner at Foxgloves.

"It's not a bad day," he said, after one or two polite enquiries. "What about a ride this morning?"

"What about a horse?" asked the lady.

"All arranged!" he answered, "hoping you would come. Two hacks from the riding-school."

"Quiet?" asked Mrs. Paget, with a laugh.

"Most sedate. I'll come over if I may. I suppose you have a riding kit?"

"Pre-war," said Viola. "I may have grown out of it. The elderly spread, you know."

She could hear his laugh down the telephone.

"Nothing like that!"

Mrs. Paget made a dash upstairs and rummaged in one of the cupboards until she found a pair of jodhpurs and a jacket and a little peaked cap flung into a corner under some old frocks. She hadn't worn them since riding on Wimbledon Common with her father after his retirement from the I.C.S. when India, (he said), was handed over on a silver platter at the price of a Garter ribbon. She could still get into them. There was no question of the elderly spread. She had a look at herself in the pierglass and gave a laugh.

"Extraordinary!" she said aloud. "I look like a kid!"

She was tall and slim and certainly looked very young and boyish in those riding clothes. After all she was very young as age is counted nowadays—twenty-seven on her last birthday in May.

She heard the clatter of hoofs in the courtyard and was at the door before the German girl could answer it.

"Hullo, Mervyn! This is a great adventure! It's nice of you to fetch me."

He smiled at her and seemed to like the look of her.

"It's jolly good of you to come."

He had dismounted and pulled up the other horse and patted its neck.

"Quite a nice-looking beast," he said. "That Hastings girl at the riding-school says it has a placid and philosophical mind. It's ridden mostly by schoolgirls."

"Just right for me!" said Viola. "But I expect to fall off before I've gone very far."

"Not you!" answered Mervyn, with a grin. "More likely me. I'm not one of those centaurs in the cavalry."

Viola mounted while he held her horse's head.

"All right?" he asked.

"Fine! I'm feeling excited. I hope Mrs. Montgomery-Jones will be on the lookout for me. I'd like to give her a treat."

"It will be a treat for her all right," said Mervyn, getting on his own horse. "You look marvellous, if I may say so. I hope the village photographer will take a snap of us for the *Tatler*."

They rode down the village street and up the winding road which led to the heath.

"Let's have a canter," said Mervyn. "Don't laugh if I fall off."

"Let's have a gallop," cried Viola, "I'm feeling rash. I'll race you to the sand-pit."

It was not a very wild gallop. The two hacks were not to be cajoled or spurred on to excessive speed, but they cantered across the heath at a fair pace. There was a fresh breeze blowing and to Viola whose lips were half parted it tasted like the breath of life.

'It is the breath of life,' she thought, 'riding with this boy across an open heath and those blue hills in the far distance and this smell of wet earth and old bracken.'

The new bracken was beginning to show through the brown russet of the old. Silver birches alight when the sun shone through the scudding rain-clouds were touched with the little green flames of their Spring renascence. Birds were twittering and from a valley below them on the right where the heath dipped down a cuckoo was calling with untiring reiteration.

Mrs. Paget pulled up and slowed down. She was panting

and her face was glowing with colour after the whipping of the wind.

"Isn't this glorious?" she cried. "And I didn't fall off!"

"You underestimate your prowess as a horsewoman," said Mervyn, riding alongside after being behind as much as twenty yards. "I believe you belong to the hunting set. I believe you take fences like a steeplechaser. I nearly took a toss round that bend."

"It's fun, isn't it?" said Mrs. Paget. "And up here we seem to have the world to ourselves. No Mrs. Montgomery-Jones. No old fogeys with arthritis or other ailments which keep my old witch-doctor busy."

She had forgotten that she had complained to her old witch-doctor that she never met a mortal soul if she walked this way on the heath. She had bemoaned her loneliness. Now she had no wish to meet her fellow mortals. This boy by her side was good company. At least he was young with the vitality of youth. Not that he was conversationally brilliant. She hadn't had much conversation with him. He was just a shy good-looking boy to whom she might be an elder sister. She was not sure that he had any intelligence. He was probably one of a type still turned out by the public schools in spite of so many free scholarships. Now he was at Sandhurst preparing to be an officer. Probably he would just be in time for World War Three. That thought when it came into her head shocked her. One oughtn't to have thoughts like that, especially on a sunny morning with a glorious view ahead and the scent of awakening life from the earth and the bushes.

They rode on at a walking pace down sandy tracks. Mervyn rode alongside now and spoke now and then.

"Rather amusing this, don't you think?"

"Very pleasant. Nothing could be better."

"We must do it again."

"Why not?"

"Do you ever do any sketching?"

"No, do you?"

"I used to mess about with water colours. I was rather keen on it for a time. It's good fun—whatever the result."

"I'd like to have a go at it. But one can't do these things alone."

"Oh, I don't know. Let's have a shot at it one day. Those silver birches with the dark trees behind. . . ."

"I shouldn't know how to begin," said Mrs. Paget.

"Oh, one just takes a slosh at it and hopes for the best. You'd be surprised how it catches hold of one when one gets keen."

"Yes, I can imagine that. I suppose it's creating something, or expressing something inside oneself or trying to grab at beauty."

He turned his head and smiled at her.

"Exactly! You've got the idea. One forgets one's meals and the time of day."

This mention of meals suggested another thought.

"I could do with a cup of coffee and a bun. I'm feeling a bit hollow. What about it?"

"Nothing doing here," said Mrs. Paget, laughing at him. "On this blasted heath, to use the words of Shakespeare . . ."

"I know a farmhouse not enormously far from here. They do teas for hikers and that ilk. During the week-ends of course. It's not a bad spot."

"Lead me to it," said Mrs. Paget. "I, too, have a curious sense of hollowness."

It was the fresh air and the exercise which spurred them on to that place of refreshment beyond the heath where a road twisted and turned towards a neighbouring village. The farmhouse was their side of the village and it greeted them with the smell of pigs and manure heaps and rotting cabbages.

They tethered their horses and saw the word Teas written large in one of the windows.

"It looks promising," said Mervyn. "I can smell newly-baked bread. Where there's bread there may be buns."

They went into a low-ceilinged room where there were little tables covered with somewhat grubby cloths. An untidy girl appeared with a look of surprise as though customers were unusual at half-past eleven on a Tuesday morning.

"We're not really open," she said, sulkily. "Only at week-ends."

"That's all right," said Mervyn, "but we've ridden from afar and we would be most obliged to you if we could have some coffee and buns. Is that asking too much, do you think?"

He spoke with extreme courtesy as though to a duchess.

"It's asking for what you can't have," said the girl with a titter. "There's no coffee and no buns."

"Oh!" said Mervyn. "That's a blow. What about some newly-baked bread, some farmhouse butter and a pot of tea?"

"I'll ask Ma," said the girl.

Ma seemed to be better natured than her daughter and presently came in smiling and garrulous.

"Do you want a pot of tea, dearies? Well, I dare say I can manage that. Ridden a long way I expect. Dreadful weather, ain't it? Nothing but rain though it's better today for a change. And I will say you two young people look nice in your riding clothes. A sight for sore eyes, dearies. Most of our visitors come on their flat feet. 'Ikers you know—nature-lovers and all that."

"Any chance of some bread and butter?" asked Mervyn. "Newly-baked bread of course, just out of the oven, I hope."

"Well, I won't disappoint you," said this plump and good-natured woman. "But you'll get indigestion, eating bread just out of the oven. Now you can't say I 'aven't warned you! But Gord bless us, you're young enough to risk that kind of thing, and your pretty sister too. In the pink of 'ealth both of you, and nice to see, my dears."

When she had left the room Mrs. Paget laughed gaily.

"Little does she know I'm a married woman and old enough to be your mother."

"I can't deny the first part of that statement," said Mervyn, grinning at her, "but the second part is inexact to the extent of half a century."

"Oh, well, we won't go into the exact arithmetic," said Mrs. Paget lightly. "I must smoke a cigarette while we're waiting for food and drink."

From her side pocket she took out a tortoiseshell cigarette-case and flicked it open.

"Have one?"

Mervyn shook his head.

"Thanks, I don't smoke."

"Too young?"

He coloured slightly and laughed.

"Too hard up to begin a habit which is very expensive."

"Wise boy!" said Mrs. Paget, smiling into his eyes. He had hazel-brown eyes she noticed, quick to light up when he was amused. On his upper lip there were the first faint signs of a moustache. He blushed very easily, especially when she looked at him for more than half a second.

'I used to be as shy as that,' she thought. 'I'd rather like to be as shy as that now. It means that I've become old and brazen. I'd like to shed seven years and be Mervyn's age. Or perhaps I wouldn't, now I come to think of it. Youth feels everything too intensely, including disappointment and self-criticism and unkindness. I should say that Mervyn is sensitive underneath his pose of being self-assured and a man of the world—one of the officer caste. That little embryo moustache—how sweet it is!'

The good-natured woman brought in an enormous pot of tea, a fresh loaf still warm to the touch, and farmhouse butter deeply yellow.

"There you are, my dearies. Don't spare the butter. No bread and scrape in this house."

Mervyn carved the loaf and handed a thick slice to Mrs. Paget.

"Nature abhors a vacuum," he said.

Mrs. Paget gave a squeal of laughter.

"If I eat that I shall bust."

"Lord, no! What could be better than bread out of the oven?"

Viola Paget had not had such a good appetite for some time and she watched under her eyelashes the disappearance of half a loaf on the opposite side of the table.

"This is great fun!" she said. "I feel as though I were a pioneer woman in outposts of Empire, or one of those Wild West women one sees on the movies—Annie get your gun while I saddle up the mare, kid."

"Forty-five miles from London," said Mervyn, with a grin. "Too close to so-called civilization."

"So-called?" she asked. "Have you a deep meaning behind that?"

"Oh lord, no!" he answered. "But civilization at the moment is not very reassuring. I mean it seems to have lost its moral values and that sort of thing. Anyhow, the civilized world is shrinking a bit, isn't it?—and not quite sure whether it can defend its last strongholds."

"Do many of you think like that at Sandhurst?" asked Mrs. Paget, smiling at him.

He blushed hotly for a moment and then laughed.

"You're pulling my leg, of course!"

"Not at all. I'm interested. Do you think Russia is going to attack us? Say no, for goodness' sake!"

"Not yet," he answered, "according to one of the great guns who came down to lecture us the other day. He ought to know. Chief of Intelligence, or something of the sort."

"Your father isn't very happy about it," said Mrs. Paget.

Mervyn laughed again.

"Oh, the governor! He has the wind up properly."

"Well, he ought to know, too," said Mrs. Paget. "He made my blood run cold the other night. The Russians have a hundred and seventy-five divisions against our two and a half or something!"

Mervyn nodded.

"Not too good, of course. Our weakness is appalling on a short-time view. But those fellows in Russia know that in the long run—when the United States got going and Western Europe pooled its potential forces—to say nothing of the atom bomb . . ."

He checked himself abruptly and looked nervously at Mrs. Paget.

"I say, let's get off this. It's the sort of stuff we jaw about at Sandhurst. Have another hunk of bread, won't you?"

"I won't," said Mrs. Paget, firmly. "Otherwise I shan't be able to ride back. And we ought to be going."

"Oh, not yet! Aren't we having a good time? Are you getting bored?"

"I'm having a wonderful time," said Mrs. Paget.

In her own mind she thought: 'I would like to have Mervyn for my brother. We could have a lot of fun together. I would go riding and sketching with him. It would be nice to have him in the house.'

"Does this possibility of war cast a shadow over your young mind?" she asked, smiling at him again.

"It doesn't keep me awake," he told her. "In any case I'm going to be a soldier. I shall have to take what's coming. We shall all have to take it. There's not much we can do about it, is there?"

"Why are you going to be a professional soldier?" asked Mrs. Paget. "Isn't it rather non-intellectual? I mean aren't most soldiers rather limited in imagination and individuality? Pardon the insult!"

He seemed slightly disconcerted by this challenging question but answered it politely.

"I haven't found it very cramping yet, but then I don't pretend to be an intellectual. Still I must confess——"

He paused for a moment with a little furrow on his forehead and then finished his sentence.

"It's the family tradition. I took the line of least resistance. My father and his father and his father's father have all been soldiers as far back as the Napoleonic wars. It never occurred to me to be anything else. Besides, it's not a bad life—better than being a bank clerk or a tout for vacuum cleaners."

"There are lots of other openings for bright young men," said Mrs. Paget.

She was really talking to draw him out, to find out what was happening in this young man's mind—if anything. She wanted to break through his shy reserve behind which he curtained himself. For a moment he drew aside the curtain of his family life.

"In a way I've fallen between two stools," he said. "I mean as regards my father and mother."

He glanced at Mrs. Paget as though wondering how far he could trust her discretion.

"Perhaps I ought not to tell tales out of school. But the situation is getting difficult, to say the least of it."

"I won't blab," said Mrs. Paget.

Mervyn Kendrick gave a nervous laugh.

"It's a question of ideology—that frightful word which seems all the fashion now. Would you believe it?—it seems incredible—my mother has gone pacifist! She doesn't believe in our defending ourselves if Russia attacks. She's all for greeting them as friends and brothers and taming the bear by buns and cakes, even if at first it means martyrdom and the bear's hug. She quotes the non-resistance of the early Christians."

"I know," said Viola Paget. "I heard her say so when we had dinner at Foxgloves. I couldn't believe my ears. A General's wife . . ."

"An Admiral's daughter," said Mervyn, smiling. "Pretty incredible, isn't it? My father thinks she needs psycho-analysis."

"What do you think?" asked Mrs. Paget.

"I'm devoted to my mother," he answered. "She and I have always been pals. To be quite honest she has spoilt me ever since I can remember. I was in grave danger of being a mother's darling. Perhaps that's one of the reasons why I went to Sandhurst—to escape too much mother love, if you know what I mean."

"I think I know," said Mrs. Paget. "It might be rather weakening."

"Yes," said Mervyn, thoughtfully. "A fellow has to stand on his own feet. Sandhurst teaches one that. But all the same—the domestic situation is becoming strained."

"In what way?" asked Mrs. Paget. This boy was revealing himself. He wanted sympathy and understanding of a difficult problem.

"It's an anxiety complex," he said. "My father is convinced that World War III is round the corner and will come with Western Europe utterly unprepared. My mother has the same terror in her mind and takes up the extreme pacifist position. Needless to say it's pretty upsetting to my honoured father. I may say it's pretty upsetting to me, seeing that I'm an officer cadet at Sandhurst!"

He laughed nervously as his shy eyes stared into those of Mrs. Paget.

"Shall I tell you what I think?" asked Mrs. Paget.

"Do! I'd be awfully glad."

"In my belief," said Viola Paget, "your mother is obsessed by her love for you. She would go to the scaffold or the firing squad gladly enough if your life could be saved. All her pacifism springs from that. All her ideals are centred in her mother-love. When she talks about the youth of England she means your youth, when she talks about our boys she means my boy, who once fed at my breast and for whom I would give up my life. That's how I read the riddle of your mother, Mervyn."

The young man on the opposite side of the check tablecloth looked startled and distressed.

"Good lord, no!" he exclaimed. "I can't believe that. My mother is wonderfully spiritual. She's a saint really. . . . I wish I hadn't spoken about it. I'm sorry."

"I'm glad you spoke about it," said Mrs. Paget. "We're going to be friends, aren't we?"

"I should be glad to think so," he answered.

"Well then, friendship means that we can talk to each other about most things without a veil over our eyes. Friendship means that we can trust each other, Mervyn. I'm not one of the tell-tale tits."

"Of course not!" he said hurriedly. "The first time I saw you the other night at Foxgloves——"

He gave her a quick friendly look. She had won his confidence, though he was still shy in a pleasant boyish way.

"I say!" she exclaimed presently. "We must be jogging back. I don't want to be late when my dear quack returns from his rounds."

They rode back slowly. The morning sun had broken through the clouds and was warm on them. The little low hills were blue in the distance and the sunlight gleamed on the white stems of the silver birches and on puddles of rainwater alongside the sandy tracks.

"This is heavenly!" cried Viola. "I feel rejuvenated."

"No need of rejuvenation!" he said laughing back at her.

As they rode through the village Mrs. Montgomery-Jones observed them out of her lattice window and reported to Miss Careless who had dropped in to see her.

"The doctor's wife is riding with that Kendrick boy—and looks about the same age. How silly of the dear doctor to marry a chit of a girl like that."

"She's very charming," answered Miss Careless. "Always so bright."

"A little bit too bright," said Mrs. Montgomery-Jones. "I don't like these bright young things. They have no manners and very few morals. I was only reading in the papers yesterday . . ."

Dr. Paget greeted his wife as she dismounted in the little courtyard. He had just put his car into the garage.

"Now this is splendid!" he exclaimed. "Just the thing for you, my darling. And you look as pretty as a picture."

"It's been such a treat," she told him, holding up her cheek for him to kiss.

Dr. Paget turned to Mervyn.

"Very good of you to take my wife out," he said. "I hope it won't be the last time."

"It was quite amusing," said Mervyn. "We ought to make a habit of it."

Mrs. Paget laughed.

"Oh well, now and again!"

"What about Thursday morning?" asked Mervyn.

Viola looked at her husband with laughing eyes.

"What do you think, John? You won't want me on Thursday morning?"

"My busiest day?" he said. "It will make me happy to think you're riding over the countryside. I wish I could be with you."

"That's fine!" said Mervyn. "Very kind of you, sir. I mean—if you can spare Mrs. Paget."

He blushed slightly, afraid that he might have said the

wrong thing. But he had said the right thing to this good-natured doctor.

"Delighted if you two enjoy yourselves. I like seeing young people happy. Some of them don't seem to get much fun out of life nowadays in spite of all the nobs and gadgets of this modern age."

"Now then," cried Mrs. Paget, "no philosophy on the door-step, Mr. Quack!"

She waved her hand to Mervyn as he rode off with the two horses.

"Nice boy," said the doctor.

"Charming," said Mrs. Paget. "As shy as a young colt."

Dr. Paget looked his wife up and down and laughed.

"You look like Rosamund in the Forest of Arden," he said. "And you look such a kid that I feel guilty of having married you. No fool like an old fool!"

"I'm glad you married me," she said. "I feel very safe with you, my venerable one."

He took her hand and raised it to his lips.

"I'm glad you're glad I married you. That relieves my uneasy conscience. I've been worrying about you lately. You seemed to have a grudge against life, or as though life had a grudge against you."

"Just a little boredom," said Viola. "I feel better today."

"You've caught the sunshine in your eyes," said the doctor. "It's taken the cobwebs away. How about a bite of food for a starving man?"

"Twenty bites if that German girl has cooked a meal," said Viola. "But I won't bite much with you. Mervyn and I had elevenses in a farmhouse and my tummy is swollen with newly-baked bread."

"Good heavens!" exclaimed Dr. Paget. "What things these children do!"

A gong sounded in the hall. It was Hildegard, the German girl, announcing the results of her labours in the kitchen. The chief result was a cottage pie, nicely browned. Between her attentions to the oven she had read half a chapter of Bertrand Russell's *History of Western Philosophy*.

CHAPTER VI

THE Rev. Gerald Langtry, vicar of Longmead, took tea one afternoon with Lady Kendrick as a self-invited guest. There was nothing unusual about that. She was generous in her donations to any special fund of his, such as repairs to the wagon-vaulting roof of his thirteenth-century church ravaged by the deathwatch beetle, the annual outing for his choir, a pension to a bedridden verger, help to a young widow with four children, the hiring of the village hall for a boxing club he ran to keep the boys—lads of fifteen to eighteen—out of mischief on dark nights. Once a month at least he took tea with her, not because he was after her money, though it came in very handy, but partly anyhow because he liked her and found her restful. It was restful to be in her drawing-room with her as an escape from Elizabeth. He was very fond of Elizabeth but found her exhausting at times—too volcanic, too denunciatory, too passionately extreme in her views—in short too violent and high-spirited.

It was restful to be with a lady who had a quiet and melodious voice and a quiet and melodious spirit, as it seemed to him. Perhaps he enjoyed her company and went away with a sense of spiritual refreshment because, when he came to think of it, she was a good listener. He was bound to confess to himself that as a rule he did most of the talking. Perhaps that was a reaction from Elizabeth who snapped his nose off if she didn't agree with him and certainly did most of the talking at home.

That afternoon when he decided to take tea with her again he was shown into the drawing-room by a girl who was a part-time servant—Mary Newton who lived in one of the Council cottages.

"Her ladyship won't be long," she said. "I'll tell her you're here."

"Thanks, Mary. I'll make myself at home. You weren't at the choir practice last night."

The girl shrugged her thin shoulders.

"Had to put the babies to bed. Ma is down with bronchitis again. Somethink chronic. Them brats. . . ."

"Hard luck!" said the Vicar. "I hope you'll be at the choir practice next week. But your mother comes first—and the brats."

"Oh, them brats. . . ."

She left him alone in this big Georgian room with its high ceiling and french windows looking out to the lawn. He knew everything in it—the chintz-covered chairs, the grand piano in the corner, the little walnut table with its scalloped top, the writing-desk of the French Empire period, the long purple curtains to the windows, the portrait of Lady Kendrick—then Beatrice Longville—by Lazlo, the portrait of the General as a young captain in World War I by Orpen—a striking bit of work of a typical young officer of the Somme battles with his steel helmet and gas-bag and, curiously enough, a kind of shell-shock look in his eyes. Perhaps Orpen had given him that look to interpret his own horror of the Somme battles with their daily routine of massacre.

"Oh, Vicar, I'm sorry to have kept you waiting," said Lady Kendrick, coming into the room so quietly that he was unaware of her presence.

"Not at all!" he answered. "I was having a look at Orpen's portrait of your husband. A masterpiece. Was it like him at the time?"

Lady Kendrick looked up at her husband's picture.

"That's how I remember him. That's how I met him first in 1917 after the Battles of the Somme. He was in hospital for quite a time. I helped to nurse him."

"There's something odd about the eyes," said the Vicar. "A queer look in them."

"Not queer," said Lady Kendrick. "It was the look of many young officers and men who had been over the top too many times and crawled over the bodies, or the bits of bodies, of the dead in No Man's Land. I remember the look."

The girl came in with the tea things and put them on the little walnut table.

"Thanks, Mary," said Lady Kendrick. "I expect you want to go home now."

"Yes, my lady, them brats. . . ."

"Give my love to your mother. I'll come and see her one day this week."

"Very good, my lady."

"Nice girl," said the Vicar, "but overburdened with 'them brats'. Four of them and quite a handful."

"These village women are heroic," said Lady Kendrick. "Mrs. Newton's husband was killed on D-day. Even before his death she was hard pressed but never complained. Now she has only a small pension and has to eke it out by taking odd jobs. But I'm telling you what you know, Vicar. I forgot for a moment. You know the inside story of every cottage in Longmead."

The Vicar nodded.

"On the whole they're a good crowd, very helpful to one another in time of trouble. Of course a lot of gossip and scandal goes on. That's human nature. I try to be tolerant and keep out of village feuds, not always with conspicuous success. In fact I may say I'm the Aunt Sally for all to have a shy at."

He laughed good-naturedly and stretched out a hand to take a liver sausage sandwich. He knew those liver sausage sandwiches.

"What did Jesus Christ say?" asked Lady Kendrick, pouring out the tea. "Beware when all men speak well of you."

"Exactly," said the Vicar, "and even further than that. 'Happy are you when men hate you and revile you for My sake'."

"That's a lesson in moral courage," said Lady Kendrick. "Some of us—most of us—don't seem to learn the lesson. Most of us are moral cowards."

"I suppose so," agreed the Vicar, looking around for a little table on which to put his cup and saucer.

"Over there," said Lady Kendrick. "Pull it closer to you. It's very difficult to go against public opinion and stand for ideals which most people regard as senseless or treasonable, or still worse, perhaps, bad form."

The Vicar took another liver sausage sandwich. He liked them.

"Fortunately," he said, "most of us are not called upon for supreme moral courage of that kind. We don't quarrel with public opinion on most matters—politics apart, of course—because we agree with it. No need nowadays to refuse a little incense to the Roman gods, knowing that by doing so we die. I doubt if I should have had such courage as an Early Christian."

Lady Kendrick was silent for a little while and did not answer his quiet laugh. She was looking down at her plate and seemed to have forgotten his presence at her tea-table, absorbed in some secret thought. He was watching her face as she sat there very quiet and still. 'She has the face of St. Teresa,' he thought, 'or one of the mystical women who were possessed, or thought themselves possessed, by the spirit of God. She's going through some spiritual conflict,' he thought.

She raised her eyes to him and asked a question which startled him.

"Aren't you putting incense or paying tribute to the pagan gods. Aren't we all?"

"Oh, I hope not!" exclaimed the Vicar. "In what way do you mean?"

"Paying tribute to Moloch," she said, looking into his eyes. "Or to Baal who was appeased by human sacrifice on his altars—the sacrifice of children and young boys."

The Rev. Gerald Langtry made a laughing protest.

"My dear Lady Kendrick, are you accusing me of being a worshipper of Baal and Beelzebub?"

"Yes, I am," she answered with a look of smiling challenge. "Unconsciously of course, and in the belief that you're a faithful Christian."

"God bless my soul!" exclaimed the Vicar, perturbed but good-humoured. "That's worse than anything I've heard about myself in Longmead. I am encompassed by scandal. I have to walk delicately like Agag, but not even Mrs. Montgomery-Jones has accused me of being a worshipper of Baal, Beelzebub and Moloch."

Lady Kendrick smiled at the mention of Mrs. Montgomery-Jones and held out a plate as a peace offering.

"Have a bun, Vicar. Don't look so shocked. I'm only telling you the simple truth. And it's not a personal attack. You're only acting and thinking like most other clergymen, from the Archbishop of Canterbury downwards, and most of the professing Christians who go to church once a week and say 'Thy kingdom come on earth as it is in heaven'."

The Vicar raised his hands with a gesture of protest.

"This is rather a heavy indictment," he said. "I don't pretend to be a saint, but I hope I'm not a hypocrite."

Lady Kendrick reached out across the tea-table and patted his hand.

"Not consciously," she told him. "You're a bit of a saint, Vicar. I don't deny that, knowing all your kindness and tolerance and charity, but don't you see that we're all betraying Christ at the present time and giving the homage of our souls to the old devil-gods who were worshipped by human sacrifice on altars reeking with the blood of youth. Don't you admit that?"

"No, I don't!" said the Vicar, with a laugh that was not quite sincere. "I think that's a terrible accusation entirely devoid of truth."

"It's in all the headlines of the morning papers," said Lady Kendrick. "It's in all the leading articles, day by day. It's in the mouths of the political leaders in this country and the United States. It's accepted as inevitable and right by the mass of public opinion."

She spoke with a kind of quiet passion.

"What is?" asked the Vicar. "I don't quite follow you, my dear lady."

Lady Kendrick explained the mystery of her words.

"Aren't we all being asked to make ready for the Third World War which means the massacre of millions with rivers of blood? My husband pretends that he doesn't think it's inevitable—but he does. So does every American, as far as I can see by their newspapers and their talks over the wireless. My husband is alarmed because of our unpreparedness, as he calls it. He wants us to start intensive rearmament—masses of guns, masses of tanks, masses of bombing planes in the sky. In reserve the Americans keep the atom bomb. That is to say in reserve they keep the means of blotting out vast populations of innocent and deluded people who will be blasted and burnt to death. On the other side there will be atom bombs, too. They talk about bacteriological warfare and the Russians are warned that two can play at that game. I am told that in our laboratories we are experimenting with that new form of warfare in case it's used against us—to infect crowded populations with disease germs. That's what we're coming to, Vicar! That's the beautiful prospect ahead! And that's what we are all ready to accept—atom bombs and all, while every Sunday in the churches we hear the words 'Thy Kingdom come on earth as it is in Heaven!' Isn't it an absolute betrayal of Christ? Isn't it a very terrible hypocrisy?"

The Vicar of Longmead was silent. Suddenly he spread out his hands with their long delicate fingers.

"What are we to do?" he asked. "I see the horror of it all. But we must defend ourselves. If this thing comes we must defend freedom and the civilized soul of man—all the values of life for which we have struggled through the centuries. It's the eternal fight between good and evil. Evil must be defeated!"

"Not by the same Evil," said Lady Kendrick. "Not answering murder by murder, massacre by massacre, rivers of blood by rivers of blood, atom bombs by atom bombs."

"How then?" asked the Vicar. "How then?"

"By spiritual weapons," Lady Kendrick answered gently, after a long pause. "First of all by a refusal to believe in the inevitability of a Third World War. If we believe it must happen we shall make it happen. By preparing for it we shall make it inevitable. The guns will go off. The atom bombs will be dropped."

"Only if Russia attacks first," said the Vicar.

Lady Kendrick gave a queer little laugh.

"Is there any real evidence that Russia means to attack? Might it not be a monstrous bogey conjured up by fear on both sides?"

"No," said the Vicar. "It's written in their books by Lenin

and Stalin. It's in their use of the Veto. It's proclaimed by their behaviour in Berlin, and in the vast strength they keep mobilized in Europe. It's proved by their Iron Curtain behind which they are arming with intensity. Then there's their daily abuse of us and their spate of disgusting lies."

Lady Kendrick did not challenge those facts but seemed to put them on one side.

"Haven't we any answer to all that except the atom bomb? Is the Christian ideal so feeble that we have no counter-propaganda to all these falsehoods?"

The Vicar raised his hands with a gesture of despair.

"It can't get through the Iron Curtain. They jam it out."

Lady Kendrick disagreed with him.

"They can't jam out the vibrations of the spirit. If instead of threatening force against force, our statesmen and politicians and the whole of our people were to proclaim their faith in brotherhood, with passionate love for humanity, with a complete renunciation of force, those behind the Iron Curtain would somehow know. Don't you think that?"

The Vicar shook his head.

"I don't. Buttons would be touched in the Kremlin. Their armies would march—a triumphal march without a shot fired. There would be mass executions, many tortures and the debauching of youth by false and filthy teaching. There are things worse than death."

Lady Kendrick had that mystical look in her eyes again when she answered:

"Some of us would have to die. Some of us would have to be martyred."

"Very unpleasant!" said the Vicar, with a little shudder. "What about our surrender of pride, our age-old tradition of valour?"

Lady Kendrick answered after a short silence and seemed to be looking far away through the wall of this Georgian house.

"The death of civilization with only a few rags of men wandering about the ruins, is a heavy price to pay for national pride and physical heroism. I believe in saving human life rather than destroying it. I believe in converting the Communist by a better creed than his own."

Both of them were silent for quite a time—a few seconds or a minute or two. Then Lady Kendrick gave a low-toned laugh—perhaps at the Vicar's look of anger and distress.

"Have another bun, Vicar. I've been talking too much. Forgive me!"

The Rev. Gerald Langtry refused another bun. His mind was deeply perturbed. This woman, this mystical lady, who had made him think of St. Teresa, had been saying things very challenging to his faith and conscience, very undermining to his traditional allegiance and loyalties. He remembered now that they had been challenged before by questions which he had left unanswered. At Alamein he had seen the tragedy of war and the death of heroic youth. Under the stars in North Africa he had talked with officers who had found no logic in the Christian faith because of its irreconcilability with the killing game. Afterwards, in Italy, he had talked with young pilots who had dropped tons of bombs over Berlin and other German cities, knowing that they were killing great numbers of civilians, wiping out residential districts, concentrating on railway stations round which swarms of refugees were encamped. One of them had challenged him half jestingly.

"Do you think Jesus Christ would approve of our raids over populous cities, Padre? Shouldn't we be more honest if we gave up calling ourselves Christians?"

He remembered such an argument with a young officer in the R.A.F.

"We're fighting the powers of Evil," he had said. "All means are justified until victory is won. All the weapons we can get and use are instruments of our fight for righteousness and the freedom of the soul."

"Tearing women and children limb from limb?" the young flying officer had asked.

"They did it to us," he had answered. "It's the inevitable tragedy. The innocent suffer for the guilty. The wrath of God . . ."

"All very difficult!" had been the answer, with a laugh and a shrug of the shoulders. "To my mind war is black murder. It's inconsistent with Christianity. But then I don't pretend to be a Christian."

The Vicar remembered that conversation now. He rose and held out his hand to Lady Kendrick.

"All very interesting," he said, "and rather disturbing."

She smiled at him and held his hand.

"It was meant to be disturbing," she told him. "One day perhaps I shall call on you for an act of moral courage."

"That's alarming!" he told her. "I believe I'm a moral coward. I'm terrified of Mrs. Montgomery-Jones and my sister Elizabeth and quite a number of good women in this village."

They parted with a laugh.

He did not see her go to the piano in the corner of the room on which stood a framed photograph of her son Mervyn. She took it off the piano and raised it to her lips. Perhaps that good-looking boy was at the heart of her emotional denunication of war and preparation for war. Perhaps he symbolized in her mind and heart all the young manhood of the world, who might be sacrificed on the altars of Moloch. The doctor's wife had made a guess at that and told the boy himself.

CHAPTER VII

RUDI SCHOLL had made quite a good studio in one of Richard Donovan's barns with the help of Donovan himself—mightily good-natured in his Irish way. He had laid down a good flooring of deal boards which he had then stained to a rich brown tone. He had swept the dust and cobwebs from the old beams above and white-washed the plastered walls between the tall oak uprights. At one end he had made a model's throne and behind a screen was his camp-bed and an old-fashioned wash-stand with jug and basin which he had bought for a few shillings in a junk shop in the market town of Mirfield. Stacked against the walls were his unsold pictures—landscapes and portraits—which he had painted since his coming to Foxgloves eight months ago, as a paying guest for half that time until his pockets could no longer rattle two sixpences together.

"Ah, say nothing about it," exclaimed Donovan at that time. "You'll soon be earning good money, if I know anything about art. Meanwhile, laddy, you can decorate the billiard-room to keep your hand in and make it the talk of the neighbourhood. I'll introduce you to some of our guests who will be proud to have their faces made immortal by your brush."

There was always a touch of the blarney in Donovan's speech which came from a kind heart and the wish to please, but in this case he spoke with a fair sincerity touched by enthusiasm. This Austrian refugee, poor devil, had a touch of genius, he thought—not that he knew much about it. He just knew what he liked and he liked Rudi's landscape showing Foxgloves with the little low hills behind it and fleecy clouds above. And he liked Rudi's portrait of himself—Donovan—a dashing bit of painting knocked off in three sittings but lifelike and pleasing to the sitter.

"A bit too young, don't you think?" he asked, pleased but doubtful.

"That is how I see you," answered the painter.

Betty's verdict was less favourable.

"It makes you look like the boy who stood on the burning deck whence all but he had fled. You're not half as noble as that!"

"That's me at my best," said her husband. "That's me when I commanded a destroyer and risked my life for England, though I'm a true-born Irishman. You're jealous of my manly beauty. You'll feel better about it when he has painted you and made you look like Grace Darling or Mary, Queen of Scots."

"I shan't risk it," said Betty, "and I've no time to give him any sittings and we've no money to pay for his pictures. Those things in the billiard-room make me feel sick."

"I like 'em!" said Donovan. "A bit modernistic perhaps, but colourful and bright."

"I might like them better if he paid his weekly bills," said Betty, the practical one.

"Ah, he'll pay us back one day and in any case he can work off our debt to him by free grub and house room."

"Our debt to him?" asked Betty, astounded by this point of view.

"The portrait and the decorations," said Donovan. "An artist doesn't work for nothing, old girl. Even an artist must live."

"I don't see why," said Betty, unconsciously parodying a famous French epigram.

It was unfortunate that one or two of the artist's portraits did not meet the approval of certain inhabitants of the guest house. Mrs. Fairchild had agreed to his painting her husband and was prepared to pay him twenty-five pounds if she approved of the result, but not otherwise. Her verdict was otherwise.

"If my Henry were like that," she said, "I wouldn't live with him another day. He looks as if he had been buried and dug up again."

"But I may look precisely like that," said Henry Fairchild, with great good nature and an old man's asthmatical laugh.

"And by the lord Harry he does!" said Donovan in the privacy of the old barn where he tried to console the painter's pride.

"The English," said Rudi, "are incapable of appreciating Art. As you are an Irishman I venture to say that. Please do not repeat it to any of your English friends."

"Mum's the word, my boy!" said Donovan, with a laugh. "But it's doubtless true as a generality."

Rudi's eyes were blazing with the fire of wounded pride and rage.

"How am I to earn a living in this detestable country which is inhabited by pig-headed people—by people without souls and people as stupid as the dumb beasts upon whose carcases they gorge?"

Commander Donovan laughed at him heartily and then uttered a mild reproof.

"Keep your hair on, my lad. I don't allow any abuse of the English—the most civilized race on earth—barring the Irish and the Scots. Betty is one of them, thank God. As for gorging on the carcases of beasts, the weekly meat ration amounts to one and twopence!"

"I'm sorry!" said Rudi, seeing a flash of steel in the Commander's eyes. "I apologize to the English people for whom of course I have a high respect. Pardon me, my dear friend."

Donovan laughed again.

"I can quite understand that you feel pretty mad with old mother Fairchild. Better luck next time."

There was no better luck next time. At least as far as remuneration went. It was the portrait of Patricia Hastings.

Patricia had given him eight sittings sustained by an occasional gin-and-orange which she stood to herself and the artist.

"This," said Rudi Scholl, standing back from it, "is my supreme masterpiece. It jumps out of the canvas. It is alive. It speaks. Regard the pose. How natural and living! See the subtle way in which I have caught the expression of your mouth and the lurking smile in your eyes. It reveals your soul, my dear lady."

Patricia Hastings gave a squeal of laughter as she looked at her own image on his canvas.

"If it reveals my soul you had better put it on the fire pretty quick. My soul is in no fit state to be revealed. It's inhabited—crowded—by little gibbering devils."

"Do you think your father will buy that?" asked Rudi.

Patricia Hastings gave him no hope of that.

"My father? Why he's stony broke like all other English gentlemen of ancient lineage."

"Perhaps a rich aunt?" suggested Rudi.

Patricia Hastings laughed at him again.

"I have only one aunt and she lives in a bed-sitting-room in West Kensington with hardly enough to keep herself alive."

Rudi Scholl shrugged his shoulders and spoke bitterly.

"There is no place for the artist in English life. The English people do not understand art and they despise it. It is better in Russia. It is better under Communism. In Russia the artist has an honoured place as a servant of the State. I would rather be in Moscow."

"Dangerous talk!" said Patricia Hastings. "We are in a stronghold of ancient tradition. God bless Winston Churchill and the local branch of Conservative ladies."

Rudi burst out laughing and altered his tone.

"I am a little mad and a little sad. Forgive me! It is because of so much disappointment—so much frustration. I need to earn a little money. I need to pay you back for many little drinks. I need enough to buy oil colours and canvases and frames. I need enough to buy twenty cigarettes a day as a dope and an anodyne."

"Have one!" said Patricia, holding out a yellow packet.

"Thanks, dear lady. You have the soul of compassion."

Patricia Hastings gave him a searching look.

"Have you finished those you stole last night?" she asked.

Rudi Scholl looked at her with raised eyebrows.

"Stole?"

"Pinched," said Patricia. "One of those old sisters left a full packet on the dining-table. I saw you put them in your pocket. When the old dear came down to find them you pretended to search for them. I was rather amused."

She laughed and did not seem shocked by this petty larceny.

Rudi Scholl smiled back at her.

"She ought not to smoke so much," he said. "It's bad for her health at her age. For me it is a necessity."

"Rudi," said Patricia presently, "I doubt whether you have a conscience and I dislike your habit of self-pity, but you amuse me and I think I'm a little bit in love with you, strange as it may seem."

"Not so very strange," he answered. "You and I are young. You and I are lonely in this village of ancient people with conventional ideas. We talk to each other without camouflage like two souls wrecked on a desert island. We have pity for each other. That is sometimes the beginning of love."

"Why do you pity me, refugee?" asked Patricia.

He looked at her in a penetrating way as though he could see into her mind and read its secrets.

"You are a social outcast," he said, "as I am. You do not fit in with this environment of elderly stupidity and moral righteousness. You have no one to love and you want a lover."

Patricia Hastings answered him after a moment's silence.

"My lover was killed in the war. Since then life has seemed futile and empty. But I keep on laughing and drinking little glasses of gin-and-orange."

Rudi Scholl nodded.

"I am like you. I too knew love. There was a girl in Austria. She was a Jewess. She died in a concentration camp. I was in another for four years because the Nazis did not like my political opinions. I happened to be a Communist. I was betrayed by one of my comrades. I starved and I was beaten."

"Poor you!" said Patricia. "Are you still a Communist?"

Rudi Scholl hesitated and then raised his hands in a doubtful way.

"Theoretically, perhaps. It is of course the inevitable pattern of life forced upon nations by economic necessity and world conditions—too many people for too little food. Democratic Socialism as it is called in England—your present system —is half way along the road to Communism. That is bound to come."

"With concentration camps and the Police State?" asked Patricia.

Rudi Scholl shrugged his shoulders.

"Those things are regrettable," he said. "Man is a cruel animal before he becomes civilized. Few are civilized."

Patricia Hastings uncoiled her legs and rose from her seat on the floor.

"I'm going to stand you a gin-and-orange," she said. "Instead of which I ought to tell the village policeman."

Rudi Scholl gave a careless laugh.

"You have enough intelligence to discuss these things. If you told the village policeman it would be an affirmation of your faith in a Police State. Tell me how I can sell one of my paintings, gracious lady."

It was through Patricia Hastings that he obtained a commission to paint a portrait of Mervyn Kendrick in his uniform as a Sandhurst cadet.

Patricia had spoken to Mrs. Paget stressing the dire poverty of a refugee artist.

"I don't much care for his portrait of you," said Mrs. Paget doubtfully. "It makes you look more wicked than you are."

"I like it," said Patricia. "It reveals my sinful soul. Besides it's a question of doing a good turn to a fellow human down on his luck."

"Oh well, I'll mention it to Lady Kendrick," said Mrs. Paget, softening to this appeal. Lady Kendrick was enchanted with the idea.

"I'd love to have a portrait of Mervyn," she said. "As he is now, still boyish and lovely."

Mervyn took some persuading. It was Mrs. Paget who persuaded him.

CHAPTER VIII

MAJOR-GENERAL SIR WILLIAM KENDRICK had a flat in Eaton Square. Not many years previously that would have been an impossibility. A flat in Eaton Square? He remembered the time when every one of its big houses had been inhabited by a class which had now been wiped out by taxation—his own class. As a boy he had lived here with his father and mother and a big family of boys and girls, his brothers and sisters. They had had a Nanny in their childhood, one of those devoted women to whom a statue ought to be raised in London. They were always looking after other people's children, teaching them manners and morals, severe sometimes, but mostly petting them and concealing their crimes from their parents. Their own Nanny had been followed by a French governess whom they detested, making her life a misery, poor little thin-lipped creature. There was a succession of butlers, very portly and dignified but not all as noble as they looked. One had taken to drink and had assaulted one of the chamber-maids—a delightful scandal in the nursery. Another was a terrible gambler on horses and came to a bad end. In addition to a stout old woman cook there were two chamber-maids who brought up cans of hot water for the hip baths—there was not a bathroom down the whole length of Eaton Square—and sometimes played hide-and-seek with the children with squeals of suppressed laughter; and two parlour-maids changing from time to time who had their evenings out once a week and were reported by the butler now and then for coming back late at night, or worse still, embracing their lovers furtively down the area steps under cover of darkness. Now all that way of life had gone—the Nannies, the French governesses, the butlers, the maid-servants in caps and aprons. Now the tall houses in Eaton Square were divided into flats and General Kendrick had one of them.

Every morning except for week-ends at Longmead in Sussex, he walked to the War Office through Eaton Square, past Hobart Place, along Buckingham Palace Road past the Palace itself, with a glance at the flagstaff to see if the King had come back from Windsor or Sandringham, and so by way of St. James's Park.

He enjoyed this walk. It was his only chance of getting a little fresh air and exercise in London. He liked to see the fine show of geraniums in front of the Palace and the tide of motor-cars sweeping along the Mall. They had done something to the roadway—made it a kind of reddish-purple—very red under sunlight. He didn't quite approve of that. Too much like blood, he thought.

Sometimes his thoughts—anxious in this time of menace—were interrupted by meeting a friend.

"Hullo, General! You're looking in the pink. How are things at the W.O.? What do you think of the international situation?"

He didn't think too well of the international situation. Vyshinsky was putting fresh spokes into the United Nations or had walked out of it with the Russian delegation. A new fellow—Malik—was making trouble. The terrorists were killing more planters in Malaya and the Coldstream Guards were in the jungle. China had gone Communist. Things didn't look good for the French in Indo-China. . . . The General kept his mouth shut about his own anxieties, the utter frustration of his work in the War Office unless the friend who met him was one of his own pals. Occasionally he met one of his Desert Rats now in civvy street—a grand fellow like Sergeant-Major Ramsden with whom he shook hands heartily, or young officers who had served under him in North Africa and were now at office desks—as he was!—or running garages or country pubs, or doing pretty well at the Bar.

"Hullo, General! How grand to see you again! Is there going to be another war? It doesn't look too good, does it?"

Grand to see him again? He was pleased to hear words like that from fellows who had served under him. So they didn't bear any grudge against him for his pretty strict discipline, and for the way he had commanded them in action? He had tried to make his discipline as easy as possible, as human and friendly as possible. Many times he had agonized at having to give them orders which meant heavy losses against Rommel's Afrika Corps with better tanks than theirs. More than once he had wept tears of blood in his heart—that's how they felt—because of the horrible casualties. Had they ever guessed that he suffered like that—wept tears of blood in his heart?—though he had had to keep a stiff upper lip? Probably they had thought him as hard as steel, as ruthless as a bloody-minded murderer, though really he was not tough enough to be a good general—far too sensitive to the casualty lists. That was his secret weakness which he had tried to hide from them. Perhaps he hadn't hidden it altogether. Anyhow, some of these fellows seemed glad to see him again.

One morning he did not walk as usual to the War Office but took a taxi to a small house in Barton Street, Westminster. It was an unusually early hour. He had been invited to breakfast by Stephen Hartley.

He wondered why he had been asked to breakfast by this left-wing politician whose speeches in the House of Commons were always provocative, aggressive and infuriating to his political opponents. He had only met him once or twice—the first time in Moscow during one of those abortive conferences. He had struck him then as a perky cocksure glib-tongued little man, not without a sense of humour and not unattractive in private conversation, though in public at Election time he stood for further nationalization and more government controls. That was abhorrent to the Conservative instincts of General Kendrick who said that he was 'no politician' but saw in all this a stealthy advance towards something like Totalitarianism. Anyhow, he was one of the most powerful leaders of public opinion on the Labour side and very dangerous.

'What the devil does he want to see me about?' he thought, as he stood on the doorstep of the small house in Barton Street, Westminster.

The door was opened by a young girl of twelve or so with a little up-turned nose and smiling eyes.

"Are you General Kendrick?" she asked, looking him up and down.

"That's right."

"Pa's expecting you," she said. "Come in, won't you?"

She added a comment as she led him into the hall.

"We don't often get Generals in this house. Pa's a pacifist, or used to be."

"I'm a peace-lover myself," said General Kendrick, good-humouredly.

"Oh, I can't believe that!" said the little girl incredulously, as though all soldiers, and especially generals, must be lusting for blood.

"Good morning, General," said a man's voice. "Good of you to come."

It was Stephen Hartley who came into the hall of this eighteenth-century house and shook hands with his visitor.

"Come into the breakfast-room," he added. "I've adopted Lloyd George's idea of having talks over the breakfast cups. It saves time. Later on I shall be swamped in official papers, a debate in the House, and all manner of other things. I didn't get to bed until two this morning and was up again at six. Nobody can say we fellows don't work for our living."

"I wonder you keep alive," said the General. "Is it all worth while?"

Stephen Hartley gave him a sharp humorous glance.

"Keeping alive or the results of our toil?"

General Kendrick hedged slightly. That question about worth while had slipped out incautiously.

"I mean health is important," he said. "You have heavy responsibilities."

Stephen Hartley gave a laughing groan.

"Yes, they're beyond a joke. The whole world is in a mess apart from our particular problems at home."

He led the way into a small room to the left of the hall. It was panelled in the old style with a mahogany table in the centre laid for breakfast. The General noticed that it was laid for three.

"I'm expecting another guest," said Stephen Hartley. "That's why I asked you to come. He'll expect me to have a lot of facts at my finger-tips and I shall have to hand him over to you."

"What kind of facts?" asked the General.

"The strength of the armed forces in Western Europe."

"There's no strength," said the General, bluntly. "There's nothing but weakness."

Stephen Hartley gave him that sharp humorous look again.

"I know. I've read your report. It was passed on to me by the little man. Pretty gloomy, General."

"The plain and painful truth," said the General. "What is the Government going to do about it?"

Stephen Hartley smiled and shrugged his shoulders.

"At the moment nothing, I expect."

General Kendrick raised his eyebrows. He did not like the levity of this reply. If that was the attitude of a responsible leader this visit was futile.

"You know the strength of our potential enemies?" he asked. "I gave that in some detail."

Stephen Hartley nodded.

"Formidable," he said. "Nightmarish!"

He was silent for a few moments standing in front of the fireplace and jingling some coins in his trousers pockets. Then he looked at the General and spoke with apparent sincerity.

"You're not a politician, General. Of course what you're asking for, as a military expert, is an intensive rearmament. I agree with you, though I must confess I shirked the idea until I read your report. I've always been a bit of a pacifist—at one time a complete pacifist—one of those damned conchies, as doubtless you thought of them. It's written in *Who's Who* that I went to prison for that reason."

"Yes," said the General, rather grimly.

Stephen Hartley had a twinkle in his eyes for a second but then spoke seriously again.

"This question of rearmament! Not an easy thing to face the country with. The last war with all its hardships and sacrifices is only five years past. Are we to ask for more hardship and more sacrifice?"

"You must," said General Kendrick. "In my opinion it's the only way to prevent another war—by deterring an aggressor."

Stephen Hartley looked sceptical.

"Possibly. But it means curtailing the social services to which we've pledged ourselves up to the eyebrows. It means convincing the rank and file of the nation, including the housewives who have been pretty hard pressed, poor ladies. It means switching over from peace production to war production. It means—I should say—higher taxation and less goods in the shops. It means a lot of other unpleasant things, painful to everybody after six years of war—only five years ago. Particularly difficult for our party which is hopelessly divided on the subject, as well I know. Passionate differences and hot words!"

He laughed as though remembering some of those passionate differences.

"The menace is more important than party politics," said General Kendrick. "Do those matter at all when the life of our nation and all civilization is in the gravest peril?"

He had come determined to say something like that. On his way in the taxi he had thought out a sentence like that. If he were to be shot for it he would say just that to this party politician.

Stephen Hartley answered, good-humouredly, too good-humouredly for such a serious and portentous subject.

"I see your point, General. But this country happens to be run by the two-party system and whichever party is in power has to carry public opinion with it and not out-pace it on measures dependent upon the whole nation. Not even Winston could do that, as well he knows. Up and down the country, in the clubs and the pubs, especially in the little homes in back streets and country villages, there's a deep reluctance to envisage another war—the most horrible thought of all. We can't spring a plan of intensive rearmament upon the nation at the present time. The Conservatives wouldn't do it. It would be too great a shock to public opinion. Everybody would say, 'This means War!' Unless something dramatic happens, which heaven forbid . . ."

He broke off suddenly at the sound of a taxi slowing up outside his front door.

"That's my other guest," he said. "It's that American fellow, Leggett, over from Washington. One of the high pressure group. Dollar aid and all that. Well, we can't do without it but I'm damned if I'm going to be dictated to by Uncle Sam or anyone else. I refuse to crawl even in front of the Almighty Dollar!"

Leggett? Yes, General Kendrick had met him once or twice. One of the big lads over there. The General glanced at Stephen Hartley. It was obvious that he was rather nervous at the approach of this guest. He thrust his fingers through his shock of curly hair and then looked at his wrist-watch and jingled the coins in his pocket again.

The door of the breakfast-room was opened by a middle-aged woman who announced the guest.

"Mr. William Leggett, sir."

"Come in!" said Stephen Hartley. "Glad to see you, Mr. Leggett. It's good of you to come."

"It's good of you to invite me, Hartley," said the American. "I appreciate the favour of coming to your breakfast-table."

He was a tall, powerful-looking man, clean-shaven and silver-haired, with a noticeable American accent, and rather formal and courteous manners.

"This is Major-General Kendrick," said Stephen Hartley. "You may have met him at one of the international conferences when he was one of our military advisers."

"Yes, indeed!" said the American. "Moscow. Paris. Lake Success. I'm happy to meet you again, General."

The middle-aged woman who had announced him brought in breakfast—dried haddock, fried bacon, coffee, toast.

"Thanks, Mrs. Plunkett," said Stephen Hartley.

"Sit down, gentlemen. General, you here. Leggett on my right. I'm sure you're ready for breakfast on this wintry day of so-called Spring. Leggett, I apologize for the English climate. It's a disgrace."

Mr. Leggett smiled, showing very white and excellent teeth too perfect to be natural.

"No apology needed, Hartley! It's traditional. It has something to do with the heroic quality of the English people. If they can stand this—as they do without a murmur—they can stand anything, as also they do and have done."

"It's nice of you to put it that way," said Stephen Hartley, with his twinkling smile. "Haddock, Leggett, or fried bacon?"

"I hate eating your English rations," said Mr. Leggett. "One and two pennyworth of meat a week, isn't it?"

Stephen Hartley gave a little secret smile.

"Oh, well, some of us get a bit extra."

'I bet this fellow gets as much meat as he wants,' thought the General. 'Still he seems to work pretty hard—whatever the results to our national well-being. I suppose he ought to get enough grub.'

After a little preliminary and polite conversation Mr. William Leggett came to serious topics following a question by Stephen Hartley who enquired what Washington thought of the general situation.

Mr. Leggett gave a short harsh laugh.

"Washington thinks it's going from bad to worse, and I don't think Washington—meaning the State Department—is very far wrong. We take a poor view of what is happening over here in Western Europe."

"In what way?" asked Stephen Hartley.

"I am over here to speak frankly," said Mr. Leggett. "I'm over here to report back to the President as to how far Marshall Aid and the Atlantic Pact and the organization for European recovery, are contributing to the defence of the West. Will you pardon me if I say that we're deeply disappointed and view the situation with increasing anxiety?"

"It's not too good," said Stephen Hartley, serving himself another piece of fried haddock.

Mr. Leggett gave a ghastly smile which played on his lips but did not light up his eyes.

"The English," he said, "are masters of understatement! You say it's not too good. We Americans—those of us who know—say it's one hell of a mess. We're convinced that World War III is round the corner. It's just a question of timing. It's only a question of when. Our guess is 1952."

"That's a guess," said Stephen Hartley. "I very much

doubt it. I haven't seen any evidence that Russia is preparing for the grand assault."

Mr. Leggett stared at him incredulously.

"No evidence, sir? Perhaps it doesn't reach your Foreign Office. Perhaps the politicians in this country haven't time to read the morning papers."

Stephen Hartley answered with a touch of irritation.

"We're pretty well informed, Leggett. There are no flies on our Foreign Secretary."

"I apologize," said Mr. Leggett, with that ghastly smile which seemed a mechanical action of his facial muscles.

He abandoned his breakfast and leaned forward with his elbows on the table and his chin resting on his folded hands.

"The evidence is overwhelming, my dear sir. The Russians are keeping their factories going at full blast. What are they making? Not pots and pans for their slave labour. Not agricultural machines. They're turning out guns and tanks and bombing aeroplanes. They're producing submarines like sardines. They're raising a police army fully equipped with all modern weapons in the Eastern zone of Germany. They're stirring up trouble in Asia, trying to get us involved out there. They're pouring arms and ammunition into Northern Korea. They pull the strings in Communist China. They're organizing fifth columns in France and Italy. They're at the back of strikes and sabotage in many countries, including the United States. They have sabotaged the United Nations by their use of the Veto, and now by walking out of it."

"We all know that," said Stephen Hartley, impatiently, "but we're not panicking about it."

He glanced over at General Kendrick with that humorous twinkle in his eyes but the General saw no humour in the conversation. This American from Washington was only repeating what had been in the General's own mind for months past, giving him sleepless nights now and then. But that was new about the Russian arming of the North Koreans.

Mr. Leggett spread out his hands and gave a rather harsh and croaking laugh.

"Yes, sir! That's the English way. You're not panicking

about it, but if I may say so you're not doing anything about it either. You're leaving yourself wide open in case of a Russian attack. The Chiefs of Staff who are supposed to be organizing Western defence go on talking and planning but nothing is agreed. Nothing is done. There's no defence between the Oder and the Channel ports. How many divisions can you put in the field? How many divisions are available for the defence of the West to hold a line until our American units come to support you?"

Stephen Hartley glanced at General Kendrick.

"That's your department, General."

General Kendrick answered in a matter-of-fact way.

"The whole of Western Europe could put twelve divisions into the field within the next six months—badly equipped and ill-trained."

"Exactly," said Mr. Leggett, grimly. "And how many divisions have the Russians already on the line and in reserve?"

General Kendrick gave the figures. He had written them in his report. Under cross examination by this American he gave the approximate number of Russian tanks, an estimate of their strength in bombers and fighters, the disposition of their infantry divisions, the probable strength of their active reserves.

William Leggett listened intently and made a few notes on the back of an envelope.

"All that tallies with our information," he said. He clicked on his convulsive smile and turned to Hartley.

How can you people sleep in your beds?" he asked.

"Some of us don't!" said General Kendrick.

"Now, gentlemen," said William Leggett, unclicking the smile, "I'm not here to criticize or make trouble. I well know all your economic difficulties. I know that you have to carry your war-weary people along with you in any campaign for rearmament."

"Exactly!" said Stephen Hartley, as though that answered the argument.

"And I know that under your present government it's not easy to cut down on social services or abandon some of the promises you've made to your working folk—housing and all that, the redistribution of wealth and so forth, the fruits of democratic socialism to which I have not yet been converted. With American aid, if I may say so, you have pulled through the post-war years with at least the illusion of progress and prosperity."

"More than an illusion," said Stephen Hartley, sharply. "We've delivered the goods."

"With the help of American aid," repeated William Leggett, "which we have been glad to give, though it has cost us billions of dollars which ultimately come out of the pockets of American tax-payers. We've been glad to give it in the common defence of Western civilization—our interest as much as yours. But the common defence of civilization has an open gap, a yawning vacuum through which the enemy may pass almost without a fight. Not a darned thing is being done about that, except a lot of talk while time burns. Time burns, gentlemen, while civilization itself is at stake—nothing less than that—the survival of humanity itself may be. The Third World War with its atom bombs. . . ."

"Yes," said Stephen Hartley with a touch of impatience in his tone, "We all know that. The point is what do you want us to do? What's the latest idea in Washington from our American paymasters?"

He spoke testily. General Kendrick could see that his temper was rising.

William Leggett, this emissary from Washington, answered with grave courtesy.

"We do not claim any power of coercion. We have nothing but the greatest friendliness to the British people and Commonwealth. Maybe we are a bit too impatient because of our growing anxiety. But we do hope—we do venture to suggest—that the imminence of this appalling menace should be more fully acknowledged over here and that action should take the place of conferences and conversations."

"What action?" asked Stephen Hartley.

Mr. Leggett outlined the ideas of the American State Department. Immediate rearmament with American aid. An increase in the strength of European armies. The rearming of Western Germany. . . .

"Never!" said Stephen Hartley.

"Without a German army there can be no filling of the gap," said Mr. Leggett.

"The French won't agree," said Hartley, stubbornly. "We shan't agree."

"Within an international army for Western defence," said Mr. Leggett. "Mr. Acheson leans very heavily to that view. It's a realistic view. The pages of the past must be turned over for a new conception of European unity to which Germany is essential."

"Far too dangerous," answered Hartley, with an obstinate look. "Madness."

He gave an irritable laugh.

"Besides the German people don't *want* to be rearmed. They will utterly refuse to be rearmed. I don't blame 'em. They walk among ruins. When Russia was smashing them we cheered heartily. Now we want them to help us smash the Russians who would over-run them in a few hours and liquidate them all after merry tortures."

William Leggett seemed to disagree with that statement.

"According to our reports Herr Adenauer——"

"That old fox!" exclaimed Hartley, impatiently.

After further conversation mainly between his two guests dealing with more facts and figures, he looked at his wrist-watch.

"I must be going. Good lord, yes! I shall be late for my next appointment. I'm glad to have had this talk, Leggett. Tell your State Department that the British people decline to be panic-stricken."

William Leggett gave one of his ghastly grins.

"And decline to put up any defence for themselves or civilization! Forgive my putting it bluntly like that."

"We're not going to be rushed," said Hartley.

He shook hands with both his guests and made a dash for the hall. Presently they heard the click of a car door in the street. Stephen Hartley's Daimler, complete with chauffeur and private detective, had been waiting for him. William Leggett and the General departed in a more leisurely way and stood outside the little house in Barton Street exchanging a few more words.

"Not much hope in that quarter!" said the gentleman from Washington rather grimly.

"A party politician," answered the General. "I believe he agrees secretly with everything you said but he's afraid of losing votes in the next election and probably there's a split in the Cabinet. He and his colleagues are afraid of facing the realities."

William Leggett gave one more exhibition of his mechanical smile.

"We know all about that in the United States, where party politics poison the wells of truth. What's your own opinion about it all, General? Are you as easy in your mind as Stephen Hartley appears to be?"

General Kendrick shook his head and smiled.

"I'm not!" he answered. "I shudder when I think of the frightful possibilities. I've done my best to warn my lords and masters. I shall probably get the sack for being an insufferable fellow. I wish to heaven——"

"Yes, sir!"

William Leggett hailed a passing cab.

"Can I give you a lift anywhere, General?"

"No, thanks. I'm walking to the War Office. I like to stretch my legs a bit. Besides it's no use getting there too early. I should only see the charwomen. They're nice souls with whom I chat sometimes—very sensible ladies with considerable knowledge of domestic economy, but like myself, they have no influence with the little gentleman in Downing Street and his secretaries of State."

Mr. Leggett laughed loudly.

"Say, that's a good story. I must tell it in Washington. British Major-General consults War Office charwomen on domestic affairs. Arrives too early for military colleagues. The defence of the West is held up by delays in handing round the marmalade on British breakfast-tables."

General Kendrick coloured up slightly. That ironical version of his remark went a bit too far.

Leggett held out his hand.

"Come and lunch with me one day," he said. "It would be a great favour and pleasure. I'm off to Paris tomorrow and then to Berlin and I shall be back at the Savoy in ten days. Could you make a date, General?"

General Kendrick made a date.

Leggett jumped into the waiting taxi and directed the driver to the Foreign Office. He could have walked there in five minutes.

CHAPTER IX

THE portrait of a Sandhurst cadet by Rudi Scholl was a success, though it put a strain on the patience and good-nature of young Mervyn Kendrick who had to give up sixteen good hours, spread over eight days, during his leave from Sandhurst, when he might have been riding on the heath with Mrs. Paget or enjoying himself otherwise.

During these sittings he was not unamused by Rudi's conversation. In order to keep his victim alert and interested instead of his face becoming an expressionless mask, the painter kept up a constant flow of questions, dialogues, and monologues, some of which were disconcerting and embarrassing to a shy young man.

"Have you had many love affairs with pretty girls?" he asked one afternoon.

Mervyn blushed rather deeply and laughed uneasily.

"I don't go in for that kind of thing," he answered.

Rudi advanced upon him closely and stared into his eyes at six inches distance, not to discover the secrets of his soul but to get the exact colour of Mervyn's irises. Then he returned to his easel.

"It isn't a question of going in for it," he said. "It happens after a certain age. At least it happens to Austrians, Italians, French, Czechs, Germans and very likely Eskimos and Red Indians after the age of fifteen. But the English are different. They have no passion. That is perhaps due to the climate and a diet of cold mutton and Brussels sprouts. That is why they do not assassinate their politicians from time to time or storm the gates of Buckingham Palace."

"Why should they?" asked Mervyn, grinning at him. "What good would that do?"

"Partly to reveal to themselves that they are human and have the fire of life in their guts. But then the English are not really human. But let us return to the subject of love. At fifteen and a half I had my first love affair in Vienna. It was with a little flower seller in the Kârntnerstrasse. I used to take her to the Prater where we danced and drank beer and went on the roundabouts and kissed each other in the darkness behind the booths. She was a charming little creature—a Jewess. Later in history she was put into the gas-ovens by orders of Himmler and his S.S."

"How frightful!" said Mervyn, deeply shocked.

Rudi Scholl nodded and came closer to examine Mervyn's left ear.

"I had lost sight of her for some years. My next passion was for a little milliner. She used to come tripping along with her bandboxes. I met her first in the Ring when it was raining and asked her to stand under my umbrella while she waited for a bus. Of course she knew that this was a preliminary to lovemaking. The umbrella was no good. Two of its ribs were broken and rain dripped through several holes. It was just a symbol of shelter from the wind and the rain. We laughed when the rain-drops fell on our noses. Next evening she came to the cinema with me and I had to let her pay as I had no money, being an art student. She paid nearly always but she loved me very much. She died of tuberculosis in a *klinik*."

"How tragic!" said Mervyn. "I'm sorry."

Rudi nodded again and took a swift pace forward to examine his sitter's mouth.

"Then there was Gita," he said. "I can't for the moment remember her other name. She was an art student like myself. She lived with her parents in the Goethe Haus—one of those big blocks of workmen's dwellings built on the outer Ring by the Social Democrats. You remember?"

"No," said Mervyn, who had never heard of the Goethe Haus.

"They were the buildings bombarded by Prince Starhemberg in the time of Dollfuss. The artillery plugged holes into them. The rooms of Gita's parents which had been nicely furnished were made into a shambles as I saw when it had happened. She was hiding in the cellar during the bombardment. One of her brothers was shot on the roof. Another was taken off and hanged as one of the ringleaders."

"What was it all about?" asked Mervyn.

Rudi Scholl's narrative of that episode in history lasted twenty minutes or more. He had been one of the Social Democrats against whom, it seemed, that Mussolini had a grudge. Mussolini, he said, was paying pocket money to Prince Starhemberg at the time he was supporting the Dollfuss régime. The routing out of the Social Democrats was the price of his support. Later he ratted and went over to the side of Hitler."

"All very confusing," said Mervyn.

"History," answered the portrait painter, "is always very confusing. It is never clear-cut. The friends of today are the enemies of tomorrow. The enemies of yesterday are the friends of today. It is of course all nonsense. So it goes on. Having defeated Germany and made one vast ruin of its beautiful cities with the help of the Russians—who were very efficient in destruction—the United Nations—the so-called United Nations, who are extremely disunited as you know, now are wooing the West Germans to come over to their side and join them in another beautiful war, this time against the Russians. As you say, it is all very confusing."

He laughed lightly and then squeezed out some more paint on to his palette.

"What happened to Gita?" asked Mervyn, who was interested and astounded by Rudi Scholl's sequence of love affairs.

"Gita? Oh, she starved to death in the Russian zone of Germany. To tell the truth I have almost forgotten her though she was exquisite as a young girl. She had the face of Leonardo da Vinci's women, who all had tuberculosis. My fellow prisoners in the concentration camp died of it very much."

"Did you have a bad time in the concentration camp?" asked Mervyn. This fellow's history, he thought, was staggering. It seemed inconceivable that he should have had such a life behind him and now be living in this barn studio in the peace of Longmead village in Sussex. No wonder some of his ideas were queer and a bit alarming.

Rudi Scholl smiled over his palette.

"A bad time? That depends upon what you call a bad time. I was in Dachau."

Mervyn had heard of Dachau.

"It must have been frightful," he said, looking at this shabby portrait painter with two days' growth of beard on his face and sloppy corduroys stained with paint, and a dirty shirt with frayed cuffs. 'Poor devil!' thought Mervyn, who had never known poverty or the fierce struggle for survival.

"It was not lovely," said Rudi Scholl. "I was starved and beaten. You observe that I have lost several of my teeth." He opened his mouth and pulled back his lip. "They were knocked out by S.S. men who did not like ironical remarks I made about the quality of the soup."

"Why did they put you into Dachau?" asked Mervyn.

Rudi Scholl shrugged his thin shoulders and laughed.

"I left Vienna and went to Munich to study Art. My dossier was not altogether satisfactory. I had been a Social Democrat in Austria. In Munich I belonged to a secret organization which was politically opposed to the Hitler régime—that is putting it a little mildly perhaps—I was betrayed by a comrade who was under threat of torture."

"Dirty dog!" said Mervyn.

Rudi Scholl smiled at him.

"Oh no! It is very unpleasant to be tortured. Most of us would betray our mothers or wives or sweethearts or best of friends under threat or pain of torture."

"I hope I shouldn't," said Mervyn, with his English tradition of honour and courage.

Rudi Scholl gave him a quick glance.

"You are a young English gentleman," he said, stepping back from his canvas and staring at it with half-shut eyes. "You are an officer cadet in Sandhurst."

"What has that got to do with it?" asked Mervyn.

Rudi Scholl smiled at this boy, so young, so fresh, so innocent.

"You have been taught the English tradition of honour," he said. "You have been sheltered from the ugly things of life. The English people have been spared all that. England is a nursery for innocent babes—old babies and young babies petted by Fate, living in a fairy tale. They take their baths once a day like good little boys. They wash behind the ears. They have clean clothes. They have clean souls. They go to church on Sunday and thank God that they are not as other men. It is all very beautiful!"

"We had our share of bombing in the last war," said Mervyn. "We didn't do badly on D-Day and at Caen. I don't see what you're driving at."

Rudi Scholl was silent for a little while, he was busy with this boy's mouth. Some famous artist once remarked that a portrait is the likeness of somebody with something wrong about the mouth. . . . Then he spoke again.

"It is true that you were bombed. It is true that your soldiers are very brave and very well fed even in the front lines. But the English people have never been occupied by an enemy. Here in England there have been no concentration camps, no Secret Police, no purges, no torture-chambers, nor gas-ovens. None of you, or very few, have been forced to abandon your traditional moralities and become human beasts. I have seen men—and women—become human beasts, though once educated and civilized, as it seemed. I have seen them steal food from their friends under the compulsion of hunger which makes men—and women—mad. There was cannibalism in some of the concentration camps."

"How frightful!" said Mervyn.

"Not pleasant," said Rudi Scholl with a laugh. "You see such things have not happened to young English gentlemen. Not yet! It is outside your experience—so far. It is thanks, no doubt, to a surrounding channel of dirty water and the protection of the British Navy, not quite so impregnable as formerly. The Russians, by the way, are building submarines in their dockyards as thick as sardines in a tin."

Mervyn laughed light-heartedly.

"Are you trying to scare me?"

"An English gentleman does not get scared," answered Rudi Scholl with his peculiar enigmatical smile. "At the present time there are some reasons why the English gentlemen ought to get scared. Nothing stands in the way of a hundred and seventy-five Russian divisions."

"Oh lord!" said Mervyn impatiently. "Don't let's get on to that. We hear all about that at Sandhurst."

"I'm surprised," answered Rudi, with smiling irony. "But it does not make you scared, I am sure."

"We don't believe in getting scared," said Mervyn.

"No!" answered Rudi Scholl. "That is so admirable in the English character. It is also perhaps a little dangerous. But let us avoid unpleasant subjects. Let us talk again about love in which you are so inexperienced and innocent. Love, my dear young gentleman, is the awareness of life. It is the fire and warmth and colour of life. It is, I think, the only beautiful thing left untaxed and uncontrolled. Tell me, have you not had one little love affair?"

Mervyn Kendrick blushed again and laughed.

"If I had, I shouldn't talk about it."

"I forgot," said Rudi. "Pardon me, I forgot your English tradition of—is it not?—Good Form."

Lady Kendrick came in now and then to see the portrait and sit in the studio while it was being painted.

"It's coming along splendidly," she exclaimed, after her third visit. "That's my Mervyn with his laughing eyes. May the laughter never go out of them."

"I wouldn't sit again like this for a thousand pounds," said Mervyn. "I'm only doing it to please you, Mother."

"It does please me," she told him.

"It's worse than drilling on the barrack square," said her son impatiently. "Anyhow I must be off. I have an engagement. If you'll excuse me, Scholl."

He was going round to tea with Mrs. Paget at half-past four. It was now twenty minutes past when he made a dash for the studio door.

"See you at supper, Mother."

Lady Kendrick stood back from her son's portrait and studied it.

"I think you've got him," she said. "There he is between boyhood and manhood—the loveliest period of life."

"I am so glad, Lady Kendrick," said Rudi Scholl. "I have tried to keep it very fresh. I wanted to satisfy you beyond all others."

"How very good of you!" exclaimed Lady Kendrick.

"If you'll allow me to say so," continued Rudi, in his soft voice with its foreign accent and occasional word misplaced or mispronounced, "I have a very great reverence for you and for your noble ideals of peace."

Lady Kendrick smiled and looked surprised.

"How do you know about those?" she asked.

"I overheard your conversation one night," he told her. "At Foxgloves during dinner. I was very deeply impressioned."

Lady Kendrick coloured slightly and gave a low-toned laugh.

"Did I talk so loudly? That was very ill-mannered in a dining-room."

"Not loudly," said Rudi, "but I was at the next table and I heard every word. Do you forgive me for being a listener? Your words stirred me very profoundly, dear lady."

"Yes?"

She looked at him doubtfully as though not quite sure of his sincerity.

"Here, I thought," he continued, "is a noble English lady who has the courage to express opinions contrary to those held by her social environment and traditions—opposed, indeed, to the mind and mood of the English people who are deluded into the belief that another war is inevitable. They believe that their duty will be to die with heroism in great numbers until the last survivors crouch among the ruins of atom-bombed cities, and their boys—boys like your son whom I am now painting in the beauty of adolescence—lie mangled on the last battlefields."

Lady Kendrick looked at the portrait of Mervyn on the artist's easel and her eyes became moist.

"I pray that won't happen," she said in a low voice.

"No!" said Rudi Scholl. "There is no need for it to happen if there are other women like yourself—spiritual ladies who will refuse to let it happen."

"Are you a pacifist?" asked Lady Kendrick.

"In my very bones," he told her.

"It needs a lot of courage," she said. "Courage unto death perhaps."

"I'm a Tolstoyan," he told her, "and a disciple of Gandhi. I believe in non-violence and non-resistance. You see, I have known the results of war—its senseless destruction, its massacre of civilians—women and children—its legacy of ruin, starvation, misery and death. I ask myself must all that happen again? Is the Second World War to be followed by a Third World War—a Third World War to be followed by a Fourth World War, if there are human beings enough to fight it?"

Lady Kendrick's eyes softened to this young man who spoke so earnestly, and in spite of his foreign accent, so eloquently.

"I ask myself those questions, too. Must men always go on with this madness? Will they never learn the futility of war? Now that America and perhaps Russia have the atom bomb will they not shrink back in horror of mutual destruction? But I'm afraid of Russia. How can one hope to penetrate the Russian mind behind the Iron Curtain?"

Rudi Scholl shrugged his shoulders and gave a light laugh.

"It is a Comedy of Errors," he said. "Russia and the United States are like two giants, not very intelligent giants, making ugly faces at each other, uttering nasty noises at each other like two silly schoolboys saying: 'You hit me first.' 'No I didn't.' 'Yes you did.' 'You're a dirty dog.' 'No I'm not.' 'Yes you are!' It's all very dangerous, of course, when two giants indulge in that exchange of insults while each one is afraid of the other."

"Very dangerous," agreed Lady Kendrick, listening intently to this young man, shabby, with two days' growth of hair on his face, standing in front of his easel in this converted barn before the portrait of her son.

"The United States is the more dangerous of the two," said Rudi, "because it is less intelligent than the other giant."

"In what way?" asked Lady Kendrick.

"Because of fear and panic," said Rudi Scholl. "The

Americans are very liable to mass excitement and mass emotion. At the present time they have gone mad about Communism. They see Communists in the shadow of every skyscraper. They suspect Communism in the factories and workshops, at office desks, in the very State Department. They have established a secret police to investigate un-American activities, as they call it. They have made up their minds that Russia, that big sprawling giant, is going to grapple with them in a war to the death. So they keep their factories and their furnaces at full blast making guns and tanks, while their scientists get busy with big and better atom bombs. They are possessed with a great fear which is the father of cruelty and ruthlessness."

Lady Kendrick did not accept this view entirely. She could not put the whole blame on to one side.

"Russia is doing the same," she answered. "We can't deny that. They refuse all friendly co-operation. They seem very aggressive and unreasonable."

Rudi Scholl laughed again, as though amused by this reminder.

"They adopt the attitude of offensive defensive. It is in a way forced upon them. They too are afraid. Russia is quaking with fear because of American machine power and war potential. But Russia is more intelligent. Russia plays the game of chess on the political chess-board with more subtlety and more skill. The gentlemen in the Kremlin are masters of propaganda and what you call bluff. They hide their fear of another war under a mask of ferocity or stubborn adherence to the letter of treaties dictated by the Allies. Russia desires Peace above all, Peace at any price, though she is not averse to egging on other combatants and stirring up trouble to weaken her potential enemies. That is in a way reasonable. It is in a way understandable. From her point of view it is an intelligent preparation for defence and survival. I speak, you see, in a very detached way. It is possible for the mind to be detached in the remoteness of an English country village."

He smiled disarmingly at Lady Kendrick. "Forgive me for boring you," he said. "I talk too much. I think too much. I feel too much."

Lady Kendrick looked at him thoughtfully and sympathetically. Here in this barn studio, she thought—as afterwards she told her husband—was a young man who seemed to know a great deal and to have thought out a great deal. Out of his sufferings, perhaps, he had attained more wisdom than could be expected of young Englishmen who were not mid-Europeans or linguists in touch with the problems and thoughts of men and women who had been in the storm centres of war and its aftermath. He was a young man, she told her husband, of delicate sensibility and emotion and a very great charm of personality—the artist type, the thinker, the ex-inhabitant of a concentration camp where he had been beaten and starved, but not with any loss of spirit. Out of that experience he had preserved his sense of humour—a miracle really—and out of its wretchedness and pain he had worked out his own philosophy of life and his own convictions, including hatred of war and a spiritual striving for peace and human brotherhood.

"You are not boring me," she told him. "On the contrary, I am deeply moved by what you tell me."

She spoke emotionally for a moment, after looking again at her son's portrait.

"Boys like that will be sacrificed in heaps if another war comes. It mustn't come! But what can one do—a woman like myself—to work for peace? I feel so lonely in my ideas of non-resistance. In this village—everywhere in England—there is a kind of heroic fatalism. If it comes it comes they say, even if we are all destroyed. My husband thinks I've gone mad—though he's very nice about it!"

She laughed, but it was a sad kind of laugh.

"There are many people working for peace," said Rudi. "Some of them are friends of mine—refugees like myself. There is the Peace Pledge, for instance. Your name would add weight to it, Lady Kendrick."

"Aren't they rather a queer lot?" she asked doubtfully. "Aren't many of them Communists?"

"Does it matter?" asked Rudi Scholl. "At least they are working for a better understanding with Russia. If you like I would have their papers sent to you. There are many distinguished names among them—artists, actors, poets——"

"I should like to see the papers," said Lady Kendrick. "If my name is any good——"

"The wife of Major-General Sir William Kendrick!" said Rudi, smiling at her. "A very distinguished name."

"That makes it difficult," she said. "I don't want to let him down, poor man. But I must have the courage to stand by my own convictions."

"Exactly," said Rudi. "A woman's soul is her own. We must all claim the liberty of our own thoughts and faith, don't you think?"

Lady Kendrick held out her hand.

"I must be going. Thank you a thousand times. You are a very remarkable young man, Mr. Scholl. It has been a privilege to listen to you."

"Oh no!" he answered modestly. "I am just a poverty-stricken refugee branded in my soul by memories of prison life and other horrors."

"We must have some more talks," said Lady Kendrick. "We must work together for Peace."

"That would be a great honour," said Rudi Scholl, raising her hand to his lips in the Austrian way.

When she had gone from his studio, he noticed that she had left her handbag behind lying by the side of the kitchen chair on which she had been sitting. He picked it up and pressed back the little silver catch which opened it. He glanced inside smiling to himself and fingered some papers. They were mostly letters, but tucked in one of the pockets was a wad of notes. He pulled them out and counted them. Sixteen pounds ten in ten-shilling notes. He fingered them for a few moments with that smile on his lips.

Then he laughed and put them back into the handbag and snapped the silver catch to shut it again.

"Better not!" he said aloud.

CHAPTER X

DR. PAGET was busy in the early summer of that year mainly because of the weather, which was very favourable to the elusive microbe of the common cold developing into bronchitis, a light form of influenza, and tummy troubles. He liked being busy because of his keen professional interest and sense of service to his fellow humans.

He was fully aware that a country quack, as he called himself, could work no magic, and in spite of modern science was very ignorant of the workings of the human body in such maladies as rheumatism, neuritis, and even the aforesaid common cold. All he could do was to put his patients into the most favourable conditions for their own vitality to get a chance, ease them a bit by simple sedatives and drugs, get their temperature down if they were feverish and practice a little faith healing, generally camouflaged by the name of psychiatry. He was a great believer in that knowing from experience that the personality of a doctor—what was called the bedside manner—was often more efficacious than any of his drugs. Many times he had noticed that a patient would feel remarkably better almost as soon as he had entered the room. That was because he approached them cheerfully and gave out something of himself—the best in himself perhaps. It seemed to cheer them up and banish the gloomy pessimism of their own thoughts or frights.

One man—it was James Stewart the poet—amused him by a frank avowal of this.

"I feel an awful fraud in calling for you, Doctor. You no sooner come in the room than I feel a hundred per cent better. I believe you're a magician."

"My wife calls me a witch-doctor," said Dr. Paget. "I'm afraid she's right. But what's been the matter with you, my dear fellow?"

James Stewart was in bed in one of those old cottages whose

timbers were cut when red-haired Bess was Queen, and whose low beams, especially on the winding stairs, were hostile to the head of a tallish man like Dr. Paget.

Stewart looked remarkably like a poet should look, with a thin high forehead, deep sunken eyes and a light brown beard and moustache.

"I've been beset by demons, goblins, ghouls and foul fiends," he said, in a deep and tragic voice, though a smile had crept into his eyes at the sight of the doctor.

"Unpleasant bed companions," said Dr. Paget. "Whence do they come and what do they do to you?"

James Stewart gave a 'hollow laugh' as the tragedians say.

"They come crowding round my pillow at night. They follow my footsteps by day. They grin and gabble at me in lonely places. They prevent me doing any work and gibber round my typewriter. I haven't written a line for a month and my publishers are waiting for my next volume of poems which ought to be out in June."

"Translating ghouls, furies and fiends into terms of modern psychology," said Dr. Paget, grinning at him, "I should diagnose your case as one of anxiety state and neurosis. Are you in debt by any chance?"

James Stewart grinned.

"Only to the pub where I take a few drinks now and then."

"Disappointment in love?" asked Dr. Paget, jestingly.

James Stewart sat up higher in bed and laughed again.

"Go to hell, Doctor. There's not a wench in this village, barring your own wife, with whom one could fall in love."

"Fall in love with her," suggested the doctor amiably. "It might do you a bit of good and wouldn't do her any harm."

James Stewart's eyes twinkled. He was getting better already.

"Agreeable idea!" he said. "But the fact is that the world situation is not favourable to the trade of poets. It lies heavily on one's head. It darkens one's soul. It bludgeons all beauty. How can we fellows write when there's a World War round the corner? How can we sing when we hear the thudding hoofs of the Four Horsemen? How can we express any faith in humanity when the world is in a state of chaos, reeking with cruelty, torture and the smell of blood?"

Dr. Paget did not seem dismayed by this black picture.

"My dear fellow," he said, "it's up to you poets to change all that. Doesn't the idea precede the deed? Aren't you the lads who provide the ideas and convey them to other minds by the magic of your words and the melody of your songs?"

"Shut up!" said James Stewart, with his hollow laugh again. "You know damn' well you've never read any of my immortal works."

"Wrong!" said the doctor. "I've read your last volume of poems. I couldn't understand a single line. It's all too difficult for me. You and T. S. Eliot and Stephen Spender—why don't you hand the key of your cryptograms to the mass mind?"

"We don't write for the mass mind," said Stewart. "Why the hell should we? The mass mind is ignorant, stupid and illiterate. It's the mind of the lowest common denominator to which so-called civilization is being reduced, without scholarship, without perception of moral values, without a sense of beauty, but like the first sprawling protoplasm sucking around for food. The mass mind wallows in football pools, wants to know who won the three-thirty, and goes mushy over American crooners. The mass mind of today is dragging us down to a population of morons."

Dr. Paget laughed good-naturedly.

"Bunk, my dear fellow! You've got it all wrong. What you modern poets are lacking is love for your fellow man. You're all hyper-critical and supercilious and cold in your hearts and intellectually cruel. That's why the world is in such a bad state. Bill Shakespeare loved his fellow men—even the old rogue Falstaff, Nym and Bardolf and Pistol and fat old Dame Quickly, and in a way old Shylock himself, at least with sympathy and understanding. You modern poets don't love anything except a jig-saw puzzle of images and words dragged out from the Unconscious."

"Damn it, Doctor," said James Stewart, "I thought you had come to cure me. If you go on like that you'll kill me."

"Not at all," said Dr. Paget, who was enjoying himself.

"You'll find yourself much better after my intellectual purge. Let's feel your pulse. How's the old heart? I don't believe you've got one."

"James Stewart," said the doctor presently, "there ain't nothing the matter with you except the dark bogeys of your imagination."

"I agree," said the poet. "But how am I going to exorcise those demons who are fighting a battle for my immortal soul and winning all along the line?"

"Cast out fear," said Dr. Paget, "then they'll flee from you. We're all suffering from blue funk. Myself as well as you."

"I don't believe it," said James Stewart, rather cheerfully. It seemed to please him that this doctor, so serene and jovial, should be suffering from his own demons.

"I don't let it get me down," said Dr. Paget. "The worst that can happen is death, and death is nothing if one believes in a future life as I do."

"I wish I did!" said James Stewart. "Sometimes I do. But there are worse things than death; other people's agonies, the debauchery of the mind, enslavement to ruthless tyranny. That's what crowds my bedroom with abominable spooks. I quake with terror at the thought of what the world is coming to."

"It has all happened before,' said Dr. Paget. "The Black Death, the plagues, wars and revolutions. Somehow we have survived by courage and will-power and the indestructible spirit of man. I believe we shall pull out of all this darkness. It's only a passing phase."

"Don't you believe it!" said Stewart, with deep melancholy. "The atom bomb makes a mockery of your words."

"I'm going to prescribe for you," said Dr. Paget.

"Go ahead. Some of your filthy drugs?"

"Not this time. Take three plays of Shakespeare—*Henry IV*, *Much Ado About Nothing*, *As You Like It*. Take one volume of the *Pickwick Papers*. Mix it now and then with occasional doses of Charles Lamb. Add Gray's *Elegy* and ten chapters of the *Pilgrim's Progress*. Good morning, Mr. James Stewart."

James Stewart, poet, flung a pillow at him. Dr. Paget heard

his laughter as he left the room. He had done him a bit of good, it seemed.

It was his last visit on his morning round and he went home for a bite of lunch. Viola would not be there, he knew. She was having lunch with Patricia Hastings, or rather the Hastings girl was having lunch with her in the market town of Mirfield, before going to 'the pictures' to see Noel Coward's *Blithe Spirit*. He was happier in his mind about Viola. She had been much more cheerful lately and the bored look had gone out of her eyes. That was mainly due, he knew, to her companionship with Mervyn Kendrick for whom she had taken a great fancy. She made no secret of that and why should she? The boy was charming in his shy adolescent way. Intelligent too, according to Viola. "We talk about almost everything," she told him. "He's keen on art and poetry and painting, unlike the usual Sandhurst type. Also he has a sense of humour and it's easy to make him laugh."

Dr. Paget had no twinge of jealousy. It was quite all right, this friendship between Viola and young Mervyn—the best thing that could have happened, he thought. He only chaffed her for being ridiculous when she insisted that she was almost old enough to be the boy's mother.

"Elder sister, yes!" he said, "but I've never known a mother only seven years older than her son."

Well, that had lifted a cause of worry from his mind and he was glad to hear her singing about the house or whistling in a boyish way when she polished her own riding-boots when she knew that Mervyn was coming over for another gallop on the heath.

The doctor's door was opened to him by the German girl, Hildegard. She cooked the meals and joined them at table, amusing him by her broken English and views on life.

"Anything good to eat?" he asked.

"Sorry," she answered. "Shepherd's pie again. That is to say the remainings of yesterday's meat disguised under mashed potatoes. As a cook I am not given much chance in England."

"Good enough for me," he told her.

"Naturally you find it good enough," she answered. "You

are of course a saint and an ascetic. If I gave you an old shoe cooked with onions, you would say 'That is good'."

Dr. Paget grinned at her as he hung up his hat on the hall-stand.

"Don't you believe it, and don't you call me a saint, young woman. None of your German romanticism."

He went into the dining-room where presently he was joined by Hildegard with the shepherd's pie, nicely browned and appetizing, he thought. But he noticed presently that Hildegard was not eating it and looked less cheerful than usual.

"Lost your appetite?" he asked. "Sickening for something? Put out your tongue."

She laughed and shook her head.

"It's not wrong with my tongue," she said. "It's wrong with my heart."

"Fallen in love?"

Hildegard shrugged her shoulders.

"How should I fall in love?" she asked. "It would be very nice to fall in love, but in this village there are no nice young men and I do not meet anybody."

"Bad luck," said the doctor, getting on with his meal. "I must try to do something about that. Is a Poet any use to you?"

Hildegard's eyes brightened.

"A young poet?" she asked. "A good poet?"

"Youngish," answered the doctor. "A bearded young man, though I wouldn't say he's a good poet. But then I don't understand the stuff he writes. It's a fellow called James Stewart. He's very sorry for himself. You might be a comfort to him. You could talk philosophy together."

Hildegard was making big eyes behind her glasses.

"James Stewart! Oh, but he is wonderful! He is a great genius. I have read his poems. I see him sometimes on the Green."

Dr. Paget looked at her with an incredulous smile.

"Do you mean to say you understand the stuff he writes?"

"Oh no!" cried Hildegard. "It is impossible to understand it. That is what makes it so wonderful. His poems are full of mystery. They go down very deep. They are extremely metaphysical."

Dr. Paget laughed and passed his plate for more shepherd's pie.

"That's a new definition of poetical genius," he said. "Poems which nobody can understand. Well, we won't argue that point. Anything to follow this excellent pie?"

"A baked apple," said Hildegard. "Always a baked apple with a rice pudding."

She went to fetch it and he noticed again that she was not eating her lunch and looked a bit miserable.

"Down in the dumps?" he asked.

"There are too many dumps," she told him. "Life is becoming intolerable. The world is one big damn' dump."

Dr. Paget raised his eyebrows. Hildegard had been a remarkably cheerful young woman for some time.

"Bad news from Germany?" he asked.

Hildegard shrugged her shoulders again.

"There is always bad news from Germany. My parents still live in the ruins. Germany is one great ruin. But now the Americans and the English wish to make more ruin—and more death and more cripples and more blinded. When the Russians were smashing their way to Berlin the English and Americans cried Bravo! Now they wish Germany to rearm and protect them from the Russians. But our German young men are all pacifists. They will not be rearmed except in the Eastern zone where they join a police army in order to get their daily bread. Many, of course, are Communists. Others pretend to be Communists. One day they will walk into the Western zone. There will be much bloodshed."

"A grim outlook," agreed the doctor. "Is that why you don't eat your lunch?"

"There is something else," said Hildegard. "It is no good in England for a German girl. I go back to Germany. It is better to live there in the ruins."

Dr. Paget looked at her with his kindly and penetrating glance.

"I thought you were happy here, my dear girl. Haven't we been kind to you?"

He noticed that her lip trembled and that she was on the verge of tears.

"For a time I was happy here," she said. "You have been very kind to me. Mrs. Paget has been very sweet and lovely to me. I thank you both a thousand times."

"Well then?" said the doctor.

"But others have not been kind," said Hildegard. "I thought I would make good friends in England. I thought the English were so generous and forgiving. The English, I thought, do not embrace hatred easily. But in this village I make no friends and they hate me because I am German."

"No, no! I can't believe that."

"It is true," said Hildegard. "The baker will not deliver the bread because I am a German girl. The woman behind the counter at the stores keeps me waiting and serves me last because I am a German. Mrs. Montgomery-Jones has told her maid that she is ashamed of you because you harbour a German girl in your house. She says it is disgraceful for a doctor to give house-room to an enemy alien. That is what they call me—an enemy alien. I go back to Germany as soon as possible."

Dr. Paget was not often angry, but he was angry now.

"That blasted old woman!" he exclaimed. "Always stirring up trouble; always spreading scandal. I'll go and wring her neck."

"Please!" cried Hildegard. "I ought not to have told you. I beg of you not to wring her neck."

This earnest appeal disarmed the doctor's wrath and he laughed in spite of his anger.

"Well, perhaps I won't wring her neck. But I'm very cross with her. As for the others—that baker and the woman in the shop—I think it's monstrous and almost incredible. I thought we were a good-natured people. I believe we are, in spite of a few disgraceful exceptions. Have you spoken to my wife about this?"

Hildegard shook her head and suddenly began to weep, coming across the room and putting her head down on the doctor's shoulder.

"I do not talk much now with Mrs. Paget. She goes out

riding with her young gentleman. I am perhaps jealous of her because she has a young gentleman and I have none. It is perhaps a Freudian complex. I am aware of the wickedness in my own subconsciousness. In the University I did a course of Freud. It was terribly revealing."

Dr. Paget pushed her away gently and wiped his shoulder with her handkerchief.

"My dear girl," he said, "if you must cry, don't do it on my jacket. But for heaven's sake pull yourself together and forget all about Freud, who was a nasty old man with a dirty mind."

"Oh no!" cried Hildegard. "He was the revealer of the Unconscious."

"Very likely," said Dr. Paget. "But I wish he hadn't done it. The Unconscious is best left unrevealed."

"I am sorry," said Hildegard. "Permit me to wipe your shoulder. I disgrace myself. I have not behaved good."

"Now look here," said Dr. Paget, "get back to your books of philosophy, my dear child. Meanwhile, I'll think of how you can get some more companionship. I've no doubt you're a bit lonely. My wife said you were not afraid of loneliness."

"That was true," said Hildegard. "But lately I find that Aristotle is not enough. Plato is not enough. Spinoza is not enough. Even your Bertrand Russell is not enough. I desire the adventure of life. I desire the warmth of human love. I wish to be in touch with the Universal Consciousness. I feel within myself the vital urge."

"Highly dangerous!" said the doctor. "The vital urge is the very devil sometimes." He burst out laughing. "My dear child, all this is very amusing as well as a little tragic. Heaven knows what would happen to my reputation if Mrs. Montgomery-Jones were to see you weeping on my shoulder. Don't do it again, please."

"I am sorry," said Hildegard, in a very contrite voice.

"Have a sucker," said Dr. Paget.

He went to a shelf in the dining-room and took down a glass bottle half filled with bull's-eyes. He kept them for his child patients. Hildegard was not without a sense of humour, and laughed as he held out the bottle to her.

"You treat me as a child!" she said. "You offer me a sweet as a cure for all these damn' dumps!"

"You *are* a child," he told her. "We're all children when our emotions get out of control. Now if you'll be good I'll bring a beautiful young man to the house. You can fall in love with him. It's quite likely that he'll fall in love with you, though I won't guarantee that."

"May I ask his name?" asked Hildegard timidly.

"It's the poet I mentioned before. He has a straggly beard, but you might get him to cut it off. Or you might shear his locks like Delilah did to Samson. I'll lend you a pair of scissors."

"That is like a fairy-tale," said Hildegard, clasping her hands. "I should be very happy to know Mr. James Stewart. He is certainly a great poet."

"He has a benevolent aunt," said the doctor. "Now I must go."

"*Mein Gott!* I have forgotten to give you your cup of coffee," cried Hildegard. "Wait one little minute, please."

She made a rush for the kitchen.

Dr. Paget lit a cigarette and smiled as he put it between his lips. He spoke a few words aloud.

"A queer business, this life of ours! All very difficult even for a witch-doctor!"

He heard Hildegard singing to herself in the kitchen. It was 'Haiden Röslein' by Schubert.

He had pulled her out of the dumps. But it was damnable that people had been unkind to her. And how absurd of this child to be jealous of Viola because she went out now and then with young Mervyn Kendrick!

CHAPTER XI

It was Patricia Hastings, after dining at Foxgloves, who suggested what she called a spot of table-turning.

The 'regulars'—that is to say the residents—had gone off to bed by ten o'clock. It was now half-past ten. Commander Donovan had devoted some time to studying the form of a number of horses in forthcoming races, but after this intellectual toil seemed in need of drink and a little amusement.

"Anybody for a game of Bridge? Will you join us, Betty?"

Betty was not in a mood for Bridge.

"I'm calling it a day," she answered. "It began at six-thirty—when you lay abed for another two hours, you lazy spalpeen! Good night, all. Don't stay up too late, Patricia, it's time you went home!"

"Oh, not yet!" exclaimed Patricia. "I shudder at the thought of my lonely room over the stables."

Rudi Scholl also revolted against early bed-time.

"In Vienna," he said, "life got going at midnight."

"This isn't Vienna," said Betty Donovan. "For me, life has to get going at the crack of dawn. Well, don't get up to mischief, you three desperadoes."

"Good night, beloved," said Commander Donovan. "I shall join you shortly. Without you we can't make a foursome, worse luck."

He kissed his hand to her and she laughed at his humbug and left the room.

"Who wants a little drink?" he asked.

"Little me," said Patricia. "But I can't afford to pay for it."

"That's all right," said the good-natured Donovan. "How about you, Rudi?"

"I accept with a thousand thanks," said that impecunious artist.

It was then that Patricia made her suggestion.

"What about a spot of table-turning?"

"I don't approve of it," said Donovan. "The Devil goeth about like a roaring lion seeking whom he may devour. We don't want to invite him into Foxgloves."

"Oh, it's all nonsense," said Patricia. "But very amusing when the table begins to move."

"It is purely physical," said Rudi. "One creates an electrical vibration by touching hands. As we all know, we are made up of atoms and electrons. We liberate some of this electrical power."

"Shut up," said Commander Donovan. "You don't know a damn' thing about it. Personally I believe people push the table, maybe unconsciously."

"Then it can't be the Devil!" said Patricia. "Let's have a try. Sometimes it's quite exciting. Once I saw a table walk upstairs with half a dozen people clinging to it."

Commander Donovan laughed at this fantastic story.

"Ah, sure now and you're telling tarradiddles. Well, let's have a go. No monkey tricks, mind you!"

"We ought to arrange a code if we want to ask questions," said Patricia. "If the table goes to the left that means 'yes'. If it goes to the right that means 'no'."

"Yes, but how am I going to ask who will win the three-thirty tomorrow?" asked Donovan.

"Name a horse and ask if it's going to win," suggested Patricia.

She acted as mistress of the ceremonies and dragged up a light tea-table into the centre of the room. Then she switched off the lights except one table lamp.

"For the love of Mike!" exclaimed Donovan. "I'm beginning to get goose-flesh already. And I can't see the way to my glass of whiskey."

In the big lounge room it was very dim and the one lamp flung shadows on the colour-washed walls between the old timbers. Rudi knocked over his glass and startled his companions.

"For goodness' sake!" cried Patricia, giving a splutter of laughter.

Donovan also gave a guffaw.

"I thought it was the Devil himself. Did you waste your whiskey, Rudi?"

"A little drop," said the Austrian. "*Nur ein Bischen.*"

"Well, don't speak German," said Donovan. "It might have a malign influence. It's a hellish language, anyhow."

"Make a circle," said Patricia. "Touch the tips of your fingers. Don't exert any pressure."

"I'll ask the first question," said Donovan. "Will Yellow Boots win the three-thirty tomorrow?"

For several minutes they waited in silence. Nothing happened. The table did not budge by a tremor.

"This is a farce!" said Donovan with a laugh. "I don't find it amusing."

"They don't like frivolous questions," said Patricia. "Ask something serious."

"Who are 'They'?" asked Donovan. "I thought you said it was all nonsense. I don't like that word 'They'. Very sinister. Very frightening to a timid little fellow like me!"

Patricia spluttered with laughter again, seeing this big bulk of a man in the shadow world. Presently she spoke in a whisper.

"Be quiet. It's beginning to get active."

Certainly something was happening to the table. Slowly and quietly it tilted in the direction of the Commander.

"You're pushing, Rudi!" he said. "Don't be a damn' fool."

"I'm not pushing," said Rudi indignantly. "I swear I'm not."

The table tilted down again very quietly and then began to move sideways.

"Patricia, you're shoving it," said Donovan with a suppressed laugh. "You're up to your monkey tricks."

"I'm not pushing it," she whispered. "Word of honour! Rudi, ask something serious."

The light from the little table-lamp a few yards away glimmered on the artist's face, always rather pale, and deepened the shadows in the sockets of his eyes, and revealed the faint mocking smile on his lips.

"Is the Labour Government going to remain in power this year?" he asked.

The table had tilted again. It was now moving slowly but decisively across the polished floor. It was bearing steadily left and the three partners in occultism walked with it until it banged against a sofa.

"That means 'yes'," said Rudi.

"Damn!" said Patricia, who was a true blue Conservative with leanings towards anarchy.

"That's torn it!" said Commander Donovan. "That means blue ruin to Foxgloves."

He burst out laughing and accused Rudi of cheating.

"You know you pushed it, you little monkey face! We all know you're a Left-winger and fellow traveller."

"How could I push it?" asked Rudi indignantly. "I just had the tips of my fingers on the table as lightly as five feathers."

"Well, ask it another question," said Donovan, beginning to get interested. "Anyhow, it moves, as a famous astronomer once said. Patricia, your turn."

Patricia gave a little squeal of suppressed mirth.

"Now then, lady," said Donovan. "No ribaldry! No cheating!"

Patricia asked her question.

"Will a dark, rich and beautiful young man come to marry me within twelve months?"

"I am dark and beautiful," said Rudi Scholl. "But I am not yet rich."

The table moved very rapidly in the direction of 'no'.

"No luck," said Patricia, in a low and tragic voice.

"You asked the impossible," said Donovan. "There are no rich young men nowadays. They're all stony-broke like me."

"I wish to ask a very important question," said Rudi with that faint mocking smile.

"Go ahead!" said Donovan.

"Will there be another war?"

"I don't like that question," said Donovan. "It's too damn' serious for this tomfoolery."

"Oh, let him ask it," said Patricia.

"Will there be another war?" repeated Rudi.

The table quivered, its legs scraped the polished boards.

It began to move. The three table-turners followed it. It moved steadily and rapidly towards the left. The answer was 'yes'.

"Oh dear, oh dear!" cried Patricia. "We're all going to be atomized."

"Our pavement artist was pushing it," said Donovan. "He has no conscience. He's a Mid-European."

"Do you think I *want* another war?" asked Rudi, glowering through the gloom which encircled them with an outer darkness.

"Ask it *when* there'll be another war," suggested Patricia. "This year? I'd like to know how long I have to live."

"My child," said Donovan, "I don't think we ought to dabble in this Black Art. It's asking for trouble. I'm getting scared. This damn' table is too lively. I believe it's possessed by an evil spirit."

The table made a half circle on the polished floor and then came to a halt.

"Let's chuck it," said Donovan, uneasily.

"Just that last question," protested Patricia. "Ask it, Rudi."

"Will the war happen this year?"

The table was on the move again. It slid towards the left. The answer was 'yes'.

"Oh lord!" cried Patricia. "And next year I hoped to spend a fortnight in Paris with a girl I know."

Donovan laughed, but a little nervously.

"Damn' nonsense!" he said. "Turn the lights up, Patricia. I've had enough of this. It's bad for the nerves. Sure, we'll be seeing spooks in a minute. I always thought this rat-infested house was haunted."

He took his hands off the table and stood rigid staring towards a door at the other end of the room away from the light of the one little lamp.

"For the love of Mike!" he said in a low voice, which was almost a whisper.

"What's the matter?" asked Patricia, who could see even in the gloom that Donovan had gone pale and was staring fixedly at the door on the other side of the big room. She turned her head and gave a scream.

"*Um Gottes Willen!*" said Rudi Scholl, clutching the back of a chair and looking towards the door.

In the doorway there stood a white ghostly figure. It moved towards them and then stopped and spoke.

"Oh, I'm so sorry. I didn't know that anybody was here. I came down to find my bottle of aspirin. It must have slipped down the cushion of one of the chairs."

It was Miss Henrietta Jenkins, one of the two sisters who had rooms upstairs.

Donovan gave a loud laugh and striding towards the wall switched on the centre lights, dazzling to them after this session in the darkness. Miss Henrietta Jenkins was in her night-gown reaching to her feet with a white shawl round her shoulders.

"Excuse my *déshabille*," she said. "I really didn't know anybody was here at this late hour."

They found her bottle of aspirin down the side of one of the chairs and when she had departed with it, they could not restrain their mirth. Patricia fell into one of the big armchairs with a scream of laughter. Commander Donovan laughed until he nearly choked and became red in the face. Rudi retained his smile with a glitter in his eyes.

"I nearly died of fright," said Patricia presently.

"I was a bit scared myself," admitted Donovan. "I thought the family ghost had arrived. The old woman looked like nothing on earth standing there in her night-shift. We shall need another drink after that."

They had another drink.

"That table told us there's going to be another war," said Patricia presently.

"Of course there's going to be another war," answered Rudi. "How can it be avoided with the United States just asking for it?"

"This year!" said Patricia. "Frightful thought!"

"Ah, that's all blague," said Donovan.

"But what makes the table move?" asked Patricia. "It jumped about like an unbroken colt."

"It's reflex action from our taut muscles," said Donovan.

"Bosh!" answered Patricia. "We were only touching it with our finger-tips."

"That or the Devil," said Donovan, who seemed to be of two minds about this queer activity of a light-weight table. "Anyhow, I don't think we ought to dabble with such things. You never can tell. 'There are stranger things twixt heaven and earth, Horatio'——" He poured himself out two fingers of whiskey. "Help yourselves, children," he said generously.

Rudi looked at his wrist-watch.

"One minute to eleven," he said. "What about the news summary?"

"Oh, to blazes with the news," answered Donovan.

But Rudi switched on the knob of the wireless in the corner of the big lounge.

A few bars of dance music filled the room and then faded out, and were followed by the voice of a B.B.C. announcer.

"This is the late night news summary. As announced in previous news bulletins North Korean troops with tanks and mechanized artillery have crossed the 38th parallel and have invaded South Korea which is guaranteed by the United Nations. In Washington a very grave view is taken of the situation. A spokesman of the State Department talking to the Press says that it's a case of flagrant aggression which must be resisted by force if necessary. There is no doubt in American opinion that the hand of Russia is clearly visible behind this menace to all liberty-loving peoples. An American commentator thinks it obvious that Russia is ready to risk a Third World War which was not expected in the American State Department until 1952. In the House of Commons——"

"The table was right," said Patricia Hastings in a faint voice.

"Jesus, Mary and Joseph," said Commander Donovan.

Rudi Scholl laughed bitterly.

"The same old stuff," he said. "More death, more concentration camps, more ruins. The beautiful atom bomb! Russia, of course, has overwhelming strength. In a week her armies will be at the Channel ports. This little island will be a lovely target. Presently into this village they will drop their parachute troops. It is the fault of the United States who have challenged Communism instead of understanding it as the new pattern of life."

"Shut up!" said Commander Donovan fiercely. "What the devil are you talking about? Go to bed and thank God for the British Navy."

"Yes," said Patricia. "Bed-time for little me. Perhaps it's not so bad as we think it is. Korea is a long way off, thank heaven. By the way, where *is* Korea?"

It had been a remarkable evening at Foxgloves.

CHAPTER XII

SOME time later Mervyn Kendrick was home on leave again from Sandhurst just for the week-end which happened to be fine for a change. He was on his motor-bike and as he rode up the drive of Badgers he saw his father's car drawing up at the front door.

General Kendrick got out carrying his despatch-case.

"Hullo, young fellow!" he called out as he saw his son dismounting.

"Hullo, Dad. I wonder they've let you escape from the W.O. Haven't seen you for weeks."

General Kendrick smiled at his son.

"I just had to get a breath of fresh air and a game of golf. Will you join me this afternoon?"

"Sorry," said Mervyn. "I've fixed up something else. I shall be out to tea."

"Must you?" asked his father, with a look of disappointment. "I don't see enough of you nowadays, my dear boy."

They went into the hall together.

"Is her ladyship in?" asked the General, speaking to the girl who came in for a few hours a day.

"No, sir. She's at a meeting in the village hall. The Women's Institute."

"Oh well," said the General, looking disappointed again. "Any chance of a cup of coffee? One for you, Mervyn?"

"Not a bad idea," said Mervyn.

"Come into my study. I've half an hour or so before I get on to the golf course."

They went into the study and Mervyn dropped into one of the deep leather chairs with his legs stretched out while his father put his despatch-case on the desk, unlocked it, and pulled out a wad of papers.

"I'll have to deal with these tonight," he said. "How were things at Sandhurst, old boy?"

"Not too bad! Too many lectures. A lot of new geography to learn. Seoul. Taegu. Pusan. The Americans are having a sticky time, aren't they? Do you think they'll be pushed off the peninsular?"

General Kendrick raised his hands slightly as he stood with his back to the fireplace, though in summer-time there was no fire.

"I hope not! It's touch and go. MacArthur is taking tremendous risks. Of course he's fighting delaying actions with inadequate forces, playing for time until he can build up manpower and get supplies. They'll soon pour in, but it takes a month from the American coast. The American morale is magnificent. I take off my hat to their leaders, and to the fighting quality of inexperienced troops. The South Koreans are fighting well, too. That's a comfort."

Mervyn nodded and then asked a question, in a casual way, as though not much interested really.

"Do you think Russia is behind all this? Everybody says so, of course."

"Everybody is right," said the General. "Thank heaven the United Nations has shown some spirit at last. It changes the whole aspect of things. Those gentlemen in the Kremlin see now that aggression is going to be met by resistance—everywhere. That'll make 'em think a bit."

Mervyn smiled at his father, as though amused by his point of view

"Shan't we have to do a bit of thinking ourselves?" he asked. "I'm all for stopping aggression everywhere, but aren't we bluffing a bit? I mean have we any real strength to challenge Communism on all fronts? Wouldn't it be a bit awkward if we became involved in a war with China? Isn't that the Russian game? Not that I know anything about it, of course, but the fellows yap a lot at Sandhurst."

"War with China?" asked the General incredulously. "Good heavens, no!"

"That's all right then," said Mervyn, as though satisfied with his father's answer. He looked at his wrist-watch. He had promised to go for a ride with Mrs. Paget—Viola, as he now called her—at half-past three.

General Kendrick looked at him with smiling eyes.

"I don't want to spill any secrets," he said, "but the sleepers have awakened at last, old boy. This Korean affair has given them a shock. They realize the urgent necessity of rearmament. Given a bit of time—and I'm convinced now that Russia is not going to risk a war just yet—we shall get out of this appalling weakness into which we drifted. That's keeping me busy. I'll have to work late tonight on those papers. But thank God those fellows are facing realities at last. The Opposition is playing up loyally as they always do in a time of crisis. I feel happier in my bones. Korea has been a blessing in disguise. If MacArthur pulls it off——"

"I think I must be going," said Mervyn. "I'll have to change." He rose from his chair and smiled at his father. "I'm glad you're feeling more cheerful," he said. "I find it all rather boring myself. I can't work up any enthusiasm for the South Koreans and I have an idea that by the time we've liberated them, if we do, there won't be much of South Korea left. Still, I don't know anything about it, of course. It all seems to me a bit of a mess. By the way, there's a paragraph in the evening paper which may interest you. It's about Mother. I cut it out."

"About your mother?" asked the General. "What's she been up to?"

Mervyn took out his pocket-book and pulled out a newspaper cutting and laughed as he handed it to his father.

"Nailing her flag to the mast!" he said. "In very queer company—I got ragged about it at Sandhurst. One of the fellows read it in a Left-Wing rag. But I must be going, Father. So long! See you at supper."

He left the room and made a dash upstairs to change into riding kit.

General Kendrick took the bit of paper and put on his glasses to read it.

Lady Kendrick, the wife of Major-General Sir William Kendrick, is among those who have signed the Peace Pledge, which has aroused so much hostility in the reactionary press. Her name, interesting and distinguished because of her husband's position as a military adviser to the Government, is added to a long list of prominent people who believe that preparedness for peace is more important than preparedness for war and who condemn the war-mongering of right wing politicians and newspaper peers who kow-tow invariably to the dictates of our American paymasters and raise no protest against the truculent and dangerous foreign policy of the United States, which unless checked, will lead inevitably to the Third World War. That the wife of Major-General Sir William Kendrick should feel compelled to sign the Peace Pledge is another significant item of evidence that the women of England are in revolt against a blind acceptance of a so-called 'inevitable war' which would destroy the last vestiges of civilization.

General Kendrick read these words with a frown deepening on his forehead. Then he placed the newspaper cutting on his desk and took off his glasses.

"Well I'll be damned!" he said aloud.

As he spoke the door opened and his wife came in, overhearing his words.

"I hope not, my dear!" she said with a quiet laugh. "What sin lies so heavily on your conscience?"

She went over to him and held out her cheek for him to kiss. But perhaps for the first time in their married life he did not accept this invitation.

"Beatrice," he said angrily, "I don't want to lose my temper, but I must say I'm deeply annoyed with you."

"So it's my sin then," she answered lightly. "I don't feel the prick of conscience. What crime have I committed?"

"Read that!" he said.

He picked up the newspaper cutting and his hand trembled slightly as he held it out to her.

Lady Kendrick read the paragraph attentively.

"I'm sorry it drags in your name," she said. "There was no need for that. Still, there are no bones broken."

"You ought to have thought of it," he told her. "It makes me look ridiculous. They're bound to see it at the War Office."

"You'll never look ridiculous, my dear," said Lady Kendrick, sitting down in one of his leather chairs and taking off her hat which she dropped on to the floor. You'll always look a typical soldier-man *sans peur et sans reproche*, ready to die like an officer and a gentleman at any moment and in any war."

"Beatrice," said her husband sternly, ignoring her smile and irony, "you ought to have asked my permission before signing that fraudulent Peace Pledge."

"But you wouldn't have given me permission!" she answered.

"No," he said, "I would rather you had cut off your hand."

"That would have been very messy," she told him with a laugh. Then she altered her tone. "You don't mean that, my dear. I'm sorry you're fussed about it. But I had to do it to be honest with myself as a tiny proof of moral courage and conviction."

"God bless my soul!" exclaimed the General. "Don't you see that it's a surrender of moral courage to sign a document like this Peace Pledge, which is drawn up by traitors and cowards and fellow travellers and crypto-Communists? They want you to crawl to Russia. They're all Quislings who would open the gates to the enemy."

"Isn't that rather a sweeping charge?" asked Lady Kendrick. "I should say most of the people who sign are lovers of peace and lovers of their country, who don't want to be duped into another unnecessary war. Not moral cowards, but brave souls who wish to make a public affirmation of their faith in reason rather than violence and in Christian idealism as the antidote to intolerance and hatred and war-fever."

General Kendrick breathed heavily for a moment and seemed to swallow his wrath.

"I want to speak calmly about this," he said. "For Mervyn's sake I don't want to have an almighty row with you, Beatrice."

Lady Kendrick answered him quietly.

"It's for Mervyn's sake that I signed the Peace Pledge. For Mervyn and all the other boys who will be the gun-fodder in the next war."

"Rubbish!" said General Kendrick. "Don't you see that

your pacifist ideals would condemn Mervyn and all his contemporaries to death by so weakening this country that they would be shot up in no time, mown down like sheep?"

"Wouldn't that happen anyhow if war happens?" asked Lady Kendrick. "Isn't it happening now in Korea to those young American boys sent up to the front without any previous training? They're told that they're defending civilization and fighting against flagrant aggression. These are fine words to comfort their mothers when the names of their dead boys are sent back. What is all this bloodthirsty nonsense in Korea, my dear?"

General Kendrick breathed heavily again.

"Bloodthirsty nonsense?" he asked incredulously.

"That's how it seems to me," said Lady Kendrick. "The American bombers are destroying all the industrial plants, all the bridges, all signs of civilized progress out there in the pretext of liberating the South Koreans. When they're liberated, North Korea and South Korea will lie in dust and ashes. What a beautiful liberation! How happy they will be! And meanwhile the American boys are crippled, blinded and tortured when taken prisoner. Lots of our boys are being sent out there soon. What's it all for? What will be the end of it? Isn't it asking for the Third World War? Mervyn thinks we shall come up against China if General MacArthur goes beyond the 38th parallel."

"Has Mervyn been talking to you?" asked the General. "I hope you haven't been proselytizing him to your pacifist creed, Beatrice. I hope to God you won't do that."

He spoke in an anxious, nerve-strained way.

Lady Kendrick shook her head and smiled.

"He just laughs at me, poor dear. Sandhurst has got hold of him—first Sandhurst and your family tradition. A whole lineage of fighting soldiers—Generals as far back as his great-grandfather."

General Kendrick looked somewhat relieved.

"If Mervyn took up these silly ideas I should break my heart."

"If Mervyn gets killed in a Third World War, we shall both

break our hearts," said Lady Kendrick. "That's why I want to work for Peace."

They were both silent for a little while. Then the General spoke again, more calmly.

"Beatrice, you're a reasonable woman. You're no fool, my dear. I want to appeal to your reason."

"I'm not very reasonable on this subject," she told him. "It's my religion now, or part of it. People aren't reasonable about their faith. They believe. If necessary they die for their belief."

"Now, look here," said the General, "Russia is behind all this—the evidence is overwhelming. The North Koreans are just puppets of the Kremlin, trained, armed and equipped by the Russians. In defending the South Koreans we're showing Russia that her policy of aggression is going to be stopped. We're not going to tolerate it. The vast majority of the United Nations are with us, ready to put in their own contributions of men or material. The whole Commonwealth is with us. Do you think they're all wrong? Do you and your little crowd of pacifists put yourselves up as superior in wisdom and idealism to all those leaders of the free nations, to all world opinion this side of the Iron Curtain."

That question left Lady Kendrick without an answer for some time. It was rather formidable. She spread out her hands, her long thin hands.

"The small groups of early Christians might have been asked that. I think they were asked. Do you put yourselves up as wiser and nobler than the whole of the Roman Empire? Is your God, ignominiously hung on a cross, more powerful than all the Roman gods or the world-wide justice of the Caesars? The early Christians were very weak at first and in a very small minority."

The General seemed to thrust this argument away with a sweep of his hand.

"We're not talking about early Christians. We're talking about the Russian menace. It's so alarming that even this Government realizes the urgent necessity of rearmament, and I must say they're showing courage and energy. Other European nations are responding to the call. Before very long—these things can't be done in a day—there will be a United Nations army. We shall have to rearm Germany——"

"The end of all that is war," said Lady Kendrick.

"No!" he answered. "That's the way to stop war—the only way. Russia will see that we can match her in manpower and more than match her in material."

"The guns will go off," said Lady Kendrick, despairingly. "The bombs will fall, civilization will perish. That is what you're arranging, my dear, with those papers you've brought home. Don't delude yourself. Nothing can stop another war but spiritual forces and the will to peace. Russia couldn't hold out against a world-wide peace campaign—passionate and sincere, overwhelming in its mass emotion. Now they jabber at us and we jabber back. They make ugly faces at us and we put out our tongues. They accuse us of war-mongering and we accuse them. That's why I signed the Peace Pledge."

General Kendrick looked angry again.

"You should not have signed it," he said. "It was disloyal to me. It may drag my name into the mud. Have you read the names of those who have signed?"

"Not all!" said his wife. "There are thousands of them."

"They reek of Communism," said the General. "All the dirty dogs, all the long-haired neurasthenics who call themselves intellectuals, clergymen duped in the belief that Russia's Communism is a return to Christianity, in spite of its torture-chambers and concentration camps and slave labour in Siberia. Beatrice, my dear, you and I have been in harness together for many years now. I have trusted in your loyalty with never a shadow of doubt. We're the father and mother of Mervyn. Don't let us fall apart because of different ideas and very wrong ideas."

"Mine or yours?" asked Lady Kendrick, with a smile.

"Chuck all that nonsense, Beatrice," he answered. "You're a soldier's wife."

"I can't chuck it," she told him. "I should betray my own soul if I did."

He had spoken gently in his last plea, but now he turned to her harshly.

"I can only think you've gone mad. I can only think you're deranged."

"I feel remarkably sane," she assured him. "But then all mad people do. I admit that!"

He did not return her smile. He looked at his wrist-watch and spoke angrily.

"You've spoilt my game of golf. One can't play with one's nerves on edge."

"I'm sorry!" said Lady Kendrick. She came over to kiss him but he thrust her on one side almost roughly and strode out of the room.

A few minutes later she heard his car starting up.

"A soldier's wife!" said Lady Kendrick aloud. "The Christian wife of a Roman centurion. He must have thought her mad. . . ."

CHAPTER XIII

MRS. PAGET was grateful to her old witch-doctor, as she called him, for encouraging her friendship with Mervyn Kendrick. He was very understanding and good-natured about it, even when just now and again she had left him alone for an evening when she went up to town to do a show and once a concert at the Albert Hall with that boy. He had some cousins in Kensington and took her to tea with them one afternoon, somewhat apologetically, because he was afraid they might bore her.

She wasn't bored. On the contrary, it was charming, she thought, to come in touch again with a family of young people of Mervyn's age and onward who were free and easy in their ways, very prone to laughter and full of zest for life and their own adventures therein. The father—Mr. Geoffrey Brand—was a K.C. devoted to music in his spare time, of which he didn't have much. He was a humorous man who talked to his sons and daughters on the level and stood their chaff and occasional ridicule with unfailing good humour. His wife was a buxom lady who had brought up four children in a comfortable and careless way, while writing thrillers under the name of Michael Daring.

They had been very useful pot-boilers in the early days when her husband was waiting for briefs. She had written her twenty-first thriller—'Mother's tripe,' as her son Dunstan called it when Mrs. Paget first met the family with Mervyn.

Dunstan, the eldest son, outraged his family by growing a beard at the age of twenty-five. It was not a very successful beard and the others found it a cause of frequent laughter and abusive comments. 'Dunstan's face fungus' it was described by Pearl, the eldest daughter, or 'Dunstan's flea trap' as it was called by Anne, aged sixteen.

There was another boy named Lance, short, perhaps, for Lancelot, up at Oxford, from which he made frequent dashes to town with an insatiable appetite for the latest shows.

"It's like taking you into the monkey-house at the Zoo," said Mervyn. "It's jolly decent of you to come. I have to keep in touch with them now and then."

"Tell me about them," said Mrs. Paget, before her first visit. She was in a taxi-cab with Mervyn on their way from Waterloo to Edwardes Square, Kensington. She would try to pay the fare, but Mervyn always seemed hurt if she offered to pay. It made him feel as if he hadn't grown up. He had complained of that once or twice.

"You treat me as though I were still a kid!" he told her, to which she answered, "You *are* a kid," thereby hurting his feelings profoundly, poor boy.

He answered her question about his cousins at some length.

"Dunstan is one of the high-brows. He wallows in T. S. Eliot. He listens with rapture to music which is positively ear-splitting. I suspect him of being a Communist, but Pearl says he adopts that pose to annoy the rest of the family."

"What about Pearl?" asked Mrs. Paget.

"Oh, Pearl is a queer sort of creature. She studies art; makes friends with the most poisonous types of poverty-stricken art students who tell dirty stories, feed on sardines on toast and sit about on cushions in overcrowded flats somewhere in Maida Vale."

"Tell me about Anne," asked Mrs. Paget.

"Oh, Anne is developing into one of those hefty women—all muscle and physical activity—ski-ing at winter sports in Switzerland, ice hockey and all that. Of course she's just a schoolgirl. When she laughs you can hear her on the other side of Edwardes Square. She's always scrapping with Lance—pulling his hair, thumping him on the back, getting rowdy with him."

"And Lance?" asked Mrs. Paget, looking out of the window of the taxi with a smile in her eyes. The sunlight was glinting in the shop windows. Crowds of young women were on the pavement of Kensington High Street. Ahead of them a line of cars had halted at the traffic lights. This was better than the quietude of Longmead, she thought. Good old London, throbbing with life, noisy with the sounds of life, crowded with human types more amusing than the old ladies in a Sussex village.

"Oh, Lance is just a young cub," said Mervyn with a laugh. "He ought to be a music-hall comedian. I must say he's rather humorous at times in a clownish sort of way."

"They sound delightful," said Mrs. Paget. "But how is it you have relations like that, Mervyn? They don't seem quite of the same flesh and blood as Major-General Sir William Kendrick."

Mervyn grinned at her.

"Oh, Uncle Geoffrey is mother's cousin. I only call him uncle by courtesy. There's an Irish great-grandfather in the background. That accounts for it. I hope they won't bore you to death. It's rather cheek taking you there."

She was glad to be taken there. In an untidy drawing-room in one of the old eighteenth-century houses in Edwardes Square, Mrs. Brand received her in a pleasant way after kissing Mervyn.

"It's good of you to take an interest in this soldier boy," she said with a smile. "Sandhurst and all that! Discipline and duty. He thinks we're a disorderly and loose-living bunch. So we are, thank God! If there's anything I hate it's discipline and duty. I've always been a rebel against punctuality. What's time for except to do the things one wants to do without the tyranny of the clock?"

Pearl, the eldest daughter, who was in the drawing-room, laughed as she shook hands with Mrs. Paget.

"Mother is putting up a self-defence. She's always late at meal times because she's poisoning a malignant husband or inventing an alibi for one of her criminals." She looked at Mrs. Paget with friendly and approving eyes. "Gosh, I'd like to do a charcoal drawing of your head."

There was a sound of scuffling in the hall.

"Blast you!" shouted a man's voice. "If you pull my beard again I'll strangle you."

"It's not a beard. It's a bug-house," cried a girl's voice after a squeal of laughter.

The drawing-room door was bumped open and the owners of the voices stampeded into the room. A bearded young man seized a cushion from one of the chairs and flung it at the head of a pretty girl who was chasing him. It missed and knocked off a vase from the mantelpiece which smashed to bits in the fireplace.

"There goes a bit of my priceless porcelain," said Mrs. Brand, who did not seem in the least annoyed but laughed good-naturedly. "You two bandits," she cried. "For heaven's sake come and behave yourselves. Here's your cousin from Sandhurst where they get ticked off if they behave like rowdies. And here is a beautiful lady who lives in the country and is not used to barbarians. Dunstan, shake hands with Mrs. Paget and try to behave like the son of a K.C."

Dunstan gave a limp hand to Mrs. Paget.

"Have you read *Waste Lands*?" he asked. "If so, that's descriptive of my desolate soul in a filthy world."

"As bad as that?" she asked.

"Worse," he told her gloomily, but with a mocking smile on his bearded lips. In this straggling beard he looked a man of forty but he was only a few years older than Mervyn to whom he turned with a grin. "Hullo, Mervyn! Still practicing the goose-step and other exercises to fit you for the atomic war?"

Mervyn flushed slightly but answered good-humouredly. "If it comes you'll all be in it."

"True!" said Dunstan. "We shall all lie rotting under the ruins. What about tea, Mother?"

"Come and help get it," said Pearl. "Mrs. Meggs doesn't come on Saturday as well you know."

"May I help?" asked Mrs. Paget.

Pearl looked at her doubtfully.

"In that frock? The kitchen is in a frightful state. We haven't washed up after lunch."

"That's all right," said Mrs. Paget.

"Well, come along then. It's only a question of boiling the kettle and flinging some cups and saucers on the tray. I bought some cakes and tarts on the way home. Quite a spread!"

"Let me come!" said Mervyn, rising politely.

"Too many cooks spoil the broth," said Pearl. "Sit down, little boy."

Mrs. Paget followed her into the kitchen. Certainly it was in a disorderly state. There was a pile of dirty plates and dishes on the table. In the sink were unwashed saucepans.

"Mrs. Meggs copes with all this on a Monday morning," explained Pearl. "She's worth her weight in gold, poor old strumpet."

Pearl was a tall dark slim young woman wearing slacks and a crimson jumper. She had brown eyes with long lashes and she had used too much lipstick which made her mouth look hard, but otherwise she was pretty with a lot of character in her face.

She put the kettle on an Aga stove.

"Would you like to collect some of those tea things?" she asked, pointing to a dresser. "There's the tray. I'll put some buns into the oven."

Having done these small tasks she sat on the edge of the kitchen table, swinging a leg and smiling at Mrs. Paget.

"You're a doctor's wife, aren't you?" she asked.

"Yes," said Mrs. Paget.

"Mervyn has told me about you. Your husband is as old as Methuselah, isn't he?"

Mrs. Paget laughed and shook her head.

"Under sixty. The prime of life."

"Oh lord!" said Pearl. "I call that venerable."

"He's very active," said Mrs. Paget. "Always working to help other people."

"Oh, I don't believe in that much," said Pearl. "Other people ought to look after themselves. This life is a jungle really. The survival of the fittest. The weak ought to go under instead of being pampered and cossetted. We keep alive the degenerates and the morons instead of letting them fade out. It's producing a race of half-wits. It's the era of the lowest common denominator."

"That's too pessimistic," said Mrs. Paget, laughing at her.

Pearl smiled back.

"Very likely! Pessimism is the fashion nowadays. I suppose it's the threat of war and the uncertainty of the future. My crowd—all very poisonous—wallow in dark forebodings which they rather enjoy." She glanced again at Mrs. Paget. "Mervyn seems to be very sweet on you," she said. "I'm not surprised."

Mrs. Paget smiled but coloured up slightly at this very personal remark.

"Only in a boyish way. We go riding together sometimes—but not very often. They keep him pretty close at Sandhurst except for a bit of leave now and then."

"He's always talking about you," said Pearl. "To him you're the divine lady, Juliet to his Romeo, the exquisite and unattainable beauty. Well, perhaps not unattainable. Are you in love with him by any chance?"

Mrs. Paget flushed vividly and laughed. This girl was really going too far. She was outrageous. But it was best to take it as a joke.

"Don't you believe in friendship?" she asked. "Do you think it's impossible to have a decent comradeship between a young man and a woman not so young?"

"No, I don't!" said Pearl. "Not in my experience. But then I must admit I move in a rotten set. Or at least they pretend to be rotten, but I expect it's mostly verbal. I'm not quite sure. Anyhow, what do you mean by saying a woman not so young?"

"I'm old enough to be his mother," said Mrs. Paget, "or at least his elder sister. I'm twenty-eight."

Pearl raised her eyebrows.

"Gosh! You look like twenty-two at the most. I look old and haggard compared to you. Why doesn't that kettle boil? It's bewitched."

The kettle boiled almost as she spoke.

She poured the water into the tea-pot.

"I'd like to do a head of you," she said again. "In charcoal with a touch of colour."

"One day perhaps," answered Mrs. Paget, in a noncommittal way.

"Dunstan's looking for someone to love," said Pearl, taking up the tray. "He's had one or two experiments but they weren't any good. Girls don't understand his particular form of humour.

He's ultra-highbrow of course, but underneath his imposture he's really very warm-hearted and quite a dear."

"Why do you tell me that?" asked Mrs. Paget with a laugh. "Is he likely to fall in love with me?"

"Almost inevitably," said Pearl. "You're very attractive, you know."

"I'm a married woman," said Mrs. Paget.

Pearl raised her dark eyebrows.

"Does that make any difference nowadays?"

"Quite a lot in my village," answered Mrs. Paget.

"Gosh! I couldn't bear to live in a village," said Pearl Brand, opening the oven door.

"Damn!" she cried. "These buns are burnt. I've been talking too much."

They weren't burnt beyond eating. Mervyn rather liked them burnt.

Mrs. Paget enjoyed herself with this extraordinary family. They were young and it was good to be among young people again. They laughed heartily at secret jokes of their own—family jokes. They talked with alarming candour about things hardly mentioned in Longmead. They seemed to know a lot about art and music and modern poetry. They argued and quarrelled. They ridiculed their mother's literary activities. They chaffed Mervyn and seemed to think it frightfully funny that he should be at Sandhurst as an officer cadet.

But that night at the Albert Hall they sat as quiet as mice, listening to a Symphony Concert of Beethoven and Brahms, and Mrs. Paget, glancing at their faces, saw how they were in a kind of enchantment. Mervyn sat next to her and was a little restless now and then, getting a whispered rebuke from Pearl.

'This family,' thought Mrs. Paget, 'is different from most of the people in Longmead except perhaps Rudi Scholl, who is an artist. Music seems to be their passion and means more to them than anything else. Perhaps it's their religion. They don't seem to have much otherwise. I wonder if they're such anarchists as they pretend to be? That girl Pearl looks one straight in the eyes and asks the most embarrassing questions. How they would shock Mrs. Montgomery-Jones!' She smiled at that thought and Mervyn, who must have been looking at her, touched her hand and whispered a question.

"What's amusing you?"

"I'll tell you afterwards," she answered.

"Hush!" whispered Pearl, angrily.

During the interval, after terrific applause lasting three minutes, they all started talking.

"Magnificent!" said Pearl. "I was drowned in its glory. When I hear Beethoven I become a mystic and a disembodied spirit."

"It's a pity you don't hear him a bit more often," said Dunstan. "There might be more peace in the family."

"Oh, you prefer those frightful cacophanies of modern composers," said Pearl. "They represent the hideous chaos in your schizophrenic soul."

Dunstan knocked her with his elbow.

"Silence, woman! Don't intrude into the secret chambers of my troubled soul. That is far beyond your limited intelligence and degraded character."

Mr. Geoffrey Brand, sitting on the other side of Mrs Paget, turned and smiled at her.

"These young people," he said, "talk the most ridiculous nonsense. It's a sort of game they have. They never seem to get tired of it."

"It keeps them merry," said Mrs. Paget. "I envy them. I live mostly among old fogeys. If it weren't for Mervyn——"

Mr. Brand gave her a quizzing look.

"Don't lead him up the garden path," he said in a low voice. "He's very young!"

"What's that?" asked Mervyn, leaning forward.

Mr. Brand answered quite untruthfully.

"I was saying that I like some of your water-colour sketches. Pearl thinks well of them, too."

"Oh, thanks," said Mervyn, in his modest way. "They're only amateur efforts."

Dunstan changed places with his father during the next interval and spoke to Mrs. Paget.

"A very dreadful world, isn't it?"

Mrs. Paget smiled at him.

"What aspect of it?" she asked.

"Almost every aspect. This Korean business makes me sick. The Americans are bombing the South Koreans in the sacred name of liberation."

"I thought they were bombing the North Koreans," said Mrs. Paget.

Dunstan shrugged his shoulders.

"The Americans bomb everything impartially. When South Korea is liberated there won't be much left except refugees and ruins. When our turn comes to be liberated, Westminster Abbey and Canterbury Cathedral will have been wiped off the earth with other shrines of civilization."

"I don't let it give me sleepless nights," said Mrs. Paget. "Do you?"

He answered her smile and spoke with more sincerity.

"No, I don't let it go as far as that. But it does nag now and then. I mean the frightful state of the world. The fact is—only don't tell my family—I rather enjoy being morbid occasionally. It's a kind of antidote to false optimism which is the curse of the English people. Secretly, I'm rather a humorist. I see the joke of life, but I have to hide that very carefully. Hence this beard. It's a mask of my real self and my Irish upper lip. I had an Irish great-grandfather. He lurks in all of us. He was a great wit in Dublin according to family tradition; drank himself to death and died laughing."

"What a nice death!" exclaimed Mrs. Paget.

Dunstan looked at her with an approving smile.

"I see you're an intelligent lady," he remarked. "It's not often beauty is combined with the higher sensibilities."

"In my case they're not," said Mrs. Paget. "I can't claim either of these merits."

"Pardon me," said Dunstan, "I beg to differ. I trust to my own observation, which is very critical and realistic. I should like to know you better. If I might have that pleasure it would do me good in my present state of melancholy."

"But it might do me harm!" said Mrs. Paget. "I might be infected by your melancholy microbe."

"Shall we talk sensibly?" suggested Dunstan.

"A good idea," said Mrs. Paget.

"Well, look here, it would be very pleasant if you would come and see us now and again. Most of Pearl's friends are really rather poisonous, all shamming intellectuality and wickedness. One gets tired of that kind of thing. I should say you were straight-thinking and straight-speaking. You have the country in your eyes—you know—nature and all that; fresh air and sunshine. I'm in a filthy solicitor's office working by artificial light."

"Hard luck," said Mrs. Paget. "But you would get very bored in a country village."

"I'm not sure," he answered. "I have leanings towards a shepherd's life. Sheep don't give much trouble, I understand, and I could write in the school of T. S. Eliot. But of course I should need a companion like yourself. I must have someone to love and someone kind enough to love me. Complete loneliness is hellish, don't you think?"

"We have one poet in Longmead," said Mrs. Paget, "but he has no one to love him, I believe."

"Good heavens, a real poet and no one to love him! How very sad. What's his name? He's probably an impostor."

"James Setwart. I can't say I know him."

Dunstan turned to look at her in a startled way.

"James Stewart! Why, he's a great brain. Have you read his *Anthropoidal Minstrelsy*?"

"No," admitted Mrs. Paget, "I can't say I have."

"Very wonderful stuff, though rather difficult. It's a cry of despair from a man who sees civilization sick unto death."

"Beyond me, I'm afraid," said Mrs. Paget, who was modest about her own intelligence.

"You ought to get to know him," said Dunstan. "You ought to cherish him, poor ballad-maker! Will you lunch with me at the Sprig of Wild Parsley one day? It's a haunt of the lesser highbrows—a dreadful crowd but amusing to watch."

"It would be rather fun," agreed Mrs. Paget. "Perhaps Mervyn will bring me there one day."

Dunstan spoke in a murmur.

"Just a soldier boy. No intelligence, of course. His father is Major-General Kendrick preparing for the next orgy of human slaughter. You know! Major-Generals! Oh dear, oh dear!"

"We need them in time of trouble," said Mrs. Paget. "And General Kendrick is a darling."

"God bless my soul!" exclaimed Dunstan. "I've never heard Uncle William called a darling before! I've only seen him twice, but he filled me with terror. Thank goodness I escaped from being under his command in North Africa. He's one of those noble fellows who expect their men to go to face machine-gun fire, flame-throwers and monstrous tanks with an heroic smile of self-sacrifice and self-satisfaction."

"He has the gentle eyes of a deer," said Mrs. Paget. "And he's trying to save England and civilization."

"He won't do it," said Dunstan with sepulchral gloom. "Our particular pattern of civilization is doomed."

"Oh well," said Mrs. Paget very cheerfully, "I'm not worrying about it. What's the good?"

Dunstan looked at her and gave a quiet laugh.

"I only worry about it as an intellectual exercise. One doesn't really believe it in one's bones and bowels. One's imagination refuses to believe in such a possibility."

"Hush!" said Pearl. "You two jabberers!"

The second part of the symphony concert was about to begin.

On the way home in the train that night, Mrs. Paget became aware that something had upset Mervyn. He was very quiet and answered only in monosyllables to her comments on the concert and the Brand family. Presently in the railway carriage where they sat in opposite corners with three very young sailors and a sleepy soldier, she smiled at him and asked a question in a low voice.

"Anything the matter, Mervyn? I hope I haven't annoyed you somehow."

"I haven't a right to be annoyed," he answered. "All the same——"

"So you are annoyed, then! What do you mean by all the same?"

"You turned your back on me," he said. "You were more amused by that poisonous cousin of mine, who flirted with you from the word go. Of course, if you like him——"

Mrs. Paget tried to reassure him.

"I had to be polite to him when he wanted to talk. He's a queer type, isn't he? Much too highbrow for me."

"I heard him asking you to lunch," said Mervyn. "Damn' cheek I call it, after meeting you for the first time."

"I don't think he meant it as cheek," Mrs. Paget answered laughingly. "Underneath his pose of Byronic melancholy, he has a sense of humour, don't you think?"

"No, I can't say I do. Only a poisonous sense of humour. I'm sorry I took you to see those frightful cousins of mine. They're all mad."

"Oh, I'm glad you took me," said Mrs. Paget. "Of course, they're all very modern and intellectual, but that kind of thing is new to me. Longmead is such a backwater, isn't it?"

"I prefer the backwaters to the London slums," said Mervyn, as though his cousins in Edwardes Square lived in a slum tenement.

He lapsed into silence, partly because the three young sailors began to talk and laugh noisily at some joke between them which they found irresistibly funny. The soldier to the right of Mrs. Paget fell asleep and leaned against her heavily—so heavily that after a few minutes she appealed laughingly to the three sailor boys.

"This soldier is squashing me! Do you think you could shift him a bit?"

"You bet, Missy!" said one of them with flaming red hair. "Hi, Tommy boy, you can't make a pillow of a pretty lady, you know. Come off it!"

He lugged him roughly away from Mrs. Paget's shoulder. The soldier opened his eyes and said, "What the hell!" angrily, but then with a side glance at Mrs. Paget became more polite.

"Sorry, dearie. Very tired, you know. Drank too much beer."

"Quite all right," said Mrs. Paget. "Only you're a bit heavy."

"Soldiers ain't like sailors," said one of the lads. "We like our drop of beer, but we always behave like gentlemen when ladies are about. Don't we, Dick?"

"That's right!" said Dick. "Like perfect gentlemen with the old school tie." He winked at Mrs. Paget with a roguish eye.

'I'm enjoying this,' thought Mrs. Paget. 'This is an amusing little episode of life—the real thing. Those sailor boys are very sweet and they seem to be having a good time in the British Navy. I suppose they're only in it for a short time.'

She was sorry about Mervyn. He was certainly hipped. She ought not to have turned her back on him to talk nonsense with his cousin, who had certainly amused her a good deal as something quite new in her experience. Mervyn was very sensitive as she had known before. Now he was jealous. It was absurd of him to be jealous. But she supposed that was natural. Even small boys and puppies are jealous. It seemed to be an instinct of human nature. But she couldn't accuse herself of being jealous of anybody. She wasn't jealous when her witch-doctor was rather attracted by one of his women patients, though she chaffed him about it. Mervyn was very, very young. She felt a hundred years older sometimes. But she was very fond of him. She wouldn't hurt him for the world. He was the most charming boy she had ever known, kind and thoughtful and chivalrous in a rather old-fashioned way which perhaps he had learnt from his father. And in spite of his shyness he was highly intelligent and sometimes startled her by things he said, showing that he thought a good deal. His queer cousins were more superficial really, although they seemed to think they were highbrows. Mervyn had deeper chords and was utterly sincere and straight. His cousin Dunstan had talked a lot of hot air, and his gloomy pose had very little truth in it, as he had admitted. An intellectual exercise, or a deliberate exaggeration of the anxieties which everybody felt about the state of the world.

They had to get a bus from the station to Longmead and conversation was impossible because the bus was crowded and Mervyn had to stand, while she sat a few seats away. Most of these people had been to the pictures in Mirfield. Two or three of the men touched their caps to her and one gave up his place and called her Ma'am.

Mervyn showed her home.

"I won't ask you in," she said. "It's pretty late. A thousand thanks, Mervyn. I've had a grand time. I enjoyed the concert vastly. When do we go for our next ride together?"

"Are you sure I don't bore you?" he asked, in his diffident way.

"I love being with you," she told him.

It was foolish of her really to kiss him. It was a sudden impulse because he had been peeved. As they stood on the steps, she leaned forward to him and kissed him and felt his lips press against hers. She could see even in the darkness that he was blushing, and his voice was husky when he spoke.

"That's awfully kind of you, Viola! Good night."

"Good night, my dear."

She let herself in with her latch-key.

"Hullo, young woman!" said Dr. Paget, coming into the hall to greet her. "Had a good time?"

"Splendid," she told him. "A wonderful concert. Beethoven's Ninth Symphony. Have you had a lonely evening, old dear?"

"I read a bit, turned on the wireless, slept a bit and felt very sorry for myself—a deserted husband."

She laughed at him.

"Now you know how I feel when you leave me so often. Those hideous solitary evenings!"

"I know," he said. "That's why I'm so glad you've made friends with that boy. Come and have a cup of cocoa. I've just made it for you. I knew you'd be in by this bus. I packed Hildegard off to bed."

"Kind and thoughtful witch-doctor!" said Mrs. Paget.

CHAPTER XIV

RUDI SCHOLL received a cheque for fifty pounds from Lady Kendrick for the portrait of her son. That was very helpful in time of need and enabled him to pay off a debt for canvases and oil colours, to lay in a stock of cigarettes, to buy some underclothing at a cheap Jewish store in Mirfield, to stand Patricia Hastings a few drinks in return for her frequent treating and to go up to London now and then on his own private affairs. This temporary affluence was very warming to the soul of an artist who had been embittered by poverty. He lost some of his inferiority complex and became a little arrogant and dogmatic in his conversation at Foxgloves, like a man who comes into a fortune after years of ill-paid drudgery and financial anxiety.

Patricia Hastings gave him a warning jolt.

"Anybody would think you were President of the Royal Academy," she told him. "Fifty pounds won't last you more than a few weeks, my brown-eyed boy."

"It's only the beginning," he told her. "Lady Kendrick has promised to get me commissions from her exalted friends."

Patricia laughed ironically.

"Oh, so that's why you're nuzzling up to her so much. I saw you tripping off to tea with her yesterday with those roses you had pinched out of Betty's garden. Like an American boy on his way to his best girl! Say it with flowers! You're an artful little monkey, Rudi! I can't think why I tolerate you."

Rudi Scholl answered seriously, ignoring these jibes.

"Lady Kendrick has been good enough to give me her friendship. She finds me sympathetic to her ideas about war and peace. I admire her courage in breaking with the traditional opinions of her social caste. It is very rare among English women."

"Now, look here, refugee," said Patricia. "Don't you go

converting that woman to your pestilential Communism, or I shall put the police on to you."

Rudi Scholl smiled and shrugged his shoulders.

"Abuse is a bad form of argument, dear lady! I may be a little insincere at times for the sake of social courtesy and the need of survival, but I am very much in earnest as a pacifist. I have seen the folly and misery of war. I have suffered its cruelties. I detest this nationalism which is preparing another orgy of slaughter and destruction. Those false heroics dupe the young and simple minds. We must resist this declaration of religious warfare which is dividing the world into two conflicting camps, this sinister suspicion that everyone who does not conform to certain doctrines such as the American way of life must be a heretic and traitor. This new intolerance is reaching the heights of absurdity in the United States and warping the historical tradition of England for free speech and free thought."

Patricia Hastings jeered at him.

"You're not in a public hall. Don't go talking nonsense and hot air to *me*! We have a right to defend ourselves against dirty dogs who are the paid agents of Russian propaganda, forming little cells in the trade unions, converting half-wits and semi-demi-intellectuals and sentimental clergymen who have an idea that Communism is getting back to early Christianity, while the torture-chambers and the concentration camps are crowded in Russia and its satellite countries. Lady Kendrick is one of those daft women who are taken in by all that, and I expect you're getting her under your malign influence, my little Austrian devil. I dare you to take your boot off. I bet there's a cloven hoof inside."

Rudi Scholl laughed loudly.

"If I didn't love you, my pretty Miss, with a burning passion, I should strangle you. If I weren't born with a sense of humour, I should be very angry with you. As it is, Lady Kendrick, who is a most spiritual and lovely lady, is working with me in the cause of Peace upon which your own life depends. I'm trying to save you from being atomized. You show no gratitude!"

"You and Lady Kendrick!" scoffed Patricia. "What good do you think you can do between you? A daft lady and a penniless painter!"

"We can link up with other minds," said Rudi. "That creates a spiritual force. That is how minority groups grasp power."

Patricia Hastings looked at him searchingly with a mocking smile.

"I believe that's what you're after really. Power! You would like to be a pocket dictator after being kept down and knocked about. It would be your revenge on society."

Rudi Scholl flushed slightly, as though she had found a weak place in the armour of his self-conceit.

"Perhaps I'm entitled to a little revenge for all I have suffered—for the concentration camp, for Nazi bullying, for English snobbishness, for desperate and damnable poverty."

"Stand me a drink," said Patricia. "It's nice to see you pay for something now and then!"

It was true that he was seeing a good deal of Lady Kendrick. As an Austrian refugee it pleased him to be received by an English lady of her rank and quality, to sit in her big drawing-room as an escape from his wooden hut where he slept and painted, and to be handed tea and buttered toast in surroundings of elegance. Perhaps it was egoism which made him like talking to a lady—the wife of Major-General Sir William Kendrick—who listened to him with sympathy and attention. To Patricia he talked flippantly and with cynicism, but that was not the right note for Lady Kendrick. To her he adopted a tone of earnest fervour and a tragic awareness of impending doom which could only be frustrated by spiritual weapons.

"Human brotherhood," he told her, "is more important than political differences. The younger generation of life should not be sacrificed because of conflicting ideologies. Surely, dear Lady Kendrick, it is a mistake to believe in an inevitable war with Russia because they dislike American and British politicians."

"I agree," said Lady Kendrick. "But how are we going to convince Russia that we have no war-like intentions? How are we going to counteract their ceaseless propaganda? That's the question put to me by my husband and it's not easy to find an answer, I admit."

Rudi Scholl laughed as he raised his hands.

"It will be more difficult now that the Western nations are planning intensive rearmament."

Lady Kendrick sighed, and he heard the whisper of her sigh across the tea-table.

"An armaments race always leads to war," she said. "We've seen that before in history."

Once she spoke to Rudi with a kind of despair.

"I feel so lonely, Mr. Scholl. Alone and powerless. What can I do on behalf of world peace sitting here in a country house? I've no more influence than a village woman and yet, unlike those dear women in this village, I see the world rushing to destruction. If only all the women in the world would unite against war there would be no more war. But even the Women's Institute in Longmead thinks it a patriotic duty to sacrifice their sons if another war happens. How can one rouse them to a world-wide campaign for peace?"

"My dear Lady Kendrick," said Rudi Scholl, "every great movement begins in a small way by a small body of believers. By signing the Peace Pledge you have already enlisted in a noble crusade. Why not go on to the village green and proclaim your faith? Why not hire the village hall and summon a public meeting to hear your words?"

Lady Kendrick was startled and remained silent for a moment.

"I've already thought of that," she said presently. "But I'm not sure that I have the moral courage."

"You have the courage of Queen Elizabeth," said Rudi Scholl.

Lady Kendrick smiled and shook her head.

"I've already incurred my husband's wrath by signing the Peace Pledge. I don't know what would happen to him if I called a meeting in Longmead—or what would happen to me!"

Rudi gave a laughing groan.

"How often fine ideas have been frustrated by family opposition!" he said.

Lady Kendrick sighed unhappily.

"I have to think of my husband's name," she answered.

"Must you?" asked Rudi. "Isn't that a limitation of your own freedom?"

Lady Kendrick raised her thin delicate hands.

"Perhaps I'm a moral coward," she said. "As the mother of Mervyn——" She added a few words after a moment's hesitation. "If I thought I might do any good I would willingly sacrifice myself and all social conventions—even family ties. Would you support me on the platform if I were to call a meeting?"

It was Rudi's turn to be startled and to hesitate.

"I'm only a refugee," he said, "an alien. My presence would be resented. It would do you harm, dear lady."

Lady Kendrick smiled at him after a quick searching glance.

"Perhaps you are also lacking in moral courage, Mr. Scholl!"

"Yes," he said humbly. "I am certainly a coward. But for your sake, Lady Kendrick, I would dare very much."

He raised her hand to his lips again when he left her. He had lacked moral courage in not asking her whether she had obtained a commission for him from one of her friends. That fifty pounds was dwindling very rapidly.

He went up to London several times to keep in touch with friends whom he had abandoned since coming down to Longmead. Most of them were in jobs of one kind and another which resulted in a weekly pay packet. They were mostly foreigners—Austrians, Poles, Czechs, French and Italians, whom he had known in Vienna and Paris as an art student or later as a refugee. One of them had been in the same concentration camp into which he had been flung by the Nazis after the German occupation of Austria. This was Peter Oldenburg, his best friend in many ways. He had a cynical and subtle mind and a certain intellectual arrogance which Rudi Scholl admired and envied. He had been desperately poor upon first coming to

England, taking a job as a waiter in a Soho restaurant and afterwards as night watchman in a block of offices, but he had always maintained a kind of disdain for what he considered to be the stupidities of life and his fellow men. Half a Russian and half a Jew, born and brought up in Vienna, he had the quality of these two strains, Slav obstinacy and Jewish sensibility to art and music. He was now earning a fair living in a firm of commercial artists as a designer of advertisements, posters and 'jackets' for the cheaper kind of thrillers. He had two big rooms over a greengrocer's shop in the Fulham Road where he lived with his Italian wife, Maria, who had once served in a milliner's shop in Milan and now was a model in a school of art. To Rudi Scholl they seemed very prosperous and it was to their rooms he went on his first visit to town after his rustication in Longmead. He had chosen a Saturday afternoon knowing that Peter Oldenburg would be back from his office of commercial art. He went up a flight of narrow stairs at the side of the greengrocer's shop and pushed a bell outside a door on the first landing. It was opened by Peter Oldenburg himself, whose dark deep-set eyes and haggard-looking face smiled at the sight of his former friend and fellow-prisoner in Dachau.

"*Gott in Himmel!*" he exclaimed, speaking in German. "I thought you must be dead. It's more than six months since I was foolish enough to lend you five pounds, which you haven't paid back."

"I haven't come to pay it back," said Rudi, thumping him on the shoulder affectionately. "But I won't ask for any more just yet. I sold one of my pictures the other day. Fifty pounds, my dear fellow! The English aristocracy invite me to their table. I hope to get many commissions."

"I expect you're lying," answered Oldenburg. "But come in and tell us more lies. You always amused me by your incorrigible romanticism."

"How's Maria?" asked Rudi.

"Getting fat," answered Oldenburg. "Soon she will be like one of Rubens's women—all curves. Probably she'll lose her job at the school of art as I've warned her. Haven't I, my beautiful fat one?"

Maria stood in the doorway of the sitting-room and laughed good-naturedly, as she gave her hands to Rudi and kissed him on both cheeks. He noticed that her breath smelt of brandy, and he knew that she drank more than was good for her at times.

"Peter is an ogre," she said, "as well you know, Rudi. I can't think why I'm faithful to him."

"If you're faithful to me, which I gravely doubt," said Oldenburg, "it's because I keep on feeding you while you get fatter and fatter."

She was certainly a little plump and rounded, but as Rudi thought, in a most agreeable way. She was still beautiful, he thought, like one of Rubens's luxuriant women.

The sitting-room into which they went was big and barely furnished. At one end was an enormous armoire which was probably Flemish of the seventeenth century. In the centre of the room was a big oak table on which Oldenburg had been drawing one of his designs. Against one wall was a mid-Victorian sofa and on each side of the fireplace a chair covered with dirty chintz.

On the walls were some oil paintings picked up in the King's Road, Chelsea—second-class old masters or copies of old masters discovered in junk shops with broken-legged chairs, stringless banjos, tattered books and frightful vases.

"Tell me that fairy tale about the English aristocracy," said Oldenburg. "It makes me laugh. Maria, make some tea and see that the kettle boils. I'm expecting two fellow-travellers."

"Yes," said Maria darkly, "with a Scotland Yard man pretending to buy tomatoes downstairs and making notes about those who come in and go out. Do you think you're not being watched, my innocent one? Since the Fuchs case——"

"That's all nonsense," said Oldenburg carelessly. "England is still foolish enough to believe in free speech and free political opinions openly expressed."

"Are you still one of the fanatics?" asked Rudi. "Plotting like an old spider?"

"Not fanatical," answered Oldenburg, "but intellectually convinced that Communism is the only true faith. Besides, I like being on the winning side." He grinned at Rudi and pushed over a packet of cigarettes. "I expect you've ratted," he said. "I expect you've gone over to the other side in spite of all the eloquence I wasted on you in Dachau when you were a dear little Social Democrat, but with a secret admiration of bourgeois ideals."

Rudi laughed as he lit a cigarette.

"I'm an artist—I mean a real artist, not having sold my soul to commercial art. As an artist I am sympathetic to all aspects of life. I don't tie a label round my neck. I don't put on blinkers to limit my vision."

"You're a dirty little rat," said his friend, Peter Oldenburg. "You used to curry favour with the guards in Dachau to get an occasional cigarette from them or escape a beating. I know you, Rudi Scholl. You have no fixed principles and no austerity of conscience. I expect you're wallowing in the flesh-pots of your bourgeois friends or cadging from some long-toothed female of the pluto-aristocracy."

Rudi Scholl refused to take umbrage and was only amused by this abuse.

"My dear Peter," he said, "you always had a tongue like a poisonous snake. As a matter of fact, I'm living a chaste and ascetic life, and doing my bit to promote world peace and the dictatorship of the proletariat."

Peter Oldenburg grinned at him.

"You little liar!" he said. "When England goes Communist after the next war, which is coming closer every day, I'll put your name on the black list as a renegade. A bullet in the back of the head for you, my little one!"

Rudi laughed at this grim threat.

"Believe me or not," he said, "but I'm doing some pretty good work for the Cause. I'm in touch with a very important lady. I've already persuaded her to sign the Peace Pledge. It created a sensation because of her husband's rank and reputation."

"Who's that?" asked Peter Oldenburg carelessly. "Some ridiculous society female? They're no good to us."

"The wife of Major-General Sir William Kendrick," said Rudi. "Hasn't that some little importance?"

Peter Oldenburg looked at him thoughtfully.

"That's interesting," he admitted. "For propaganda purposes it might be a little useful."

"There you are!" said Rudi, looking pleased with himself. "There was a paragraph in *The Red Star* about it."

Peter Oldenburg shrugged his shoulders.

"It's only child's play to please the propaganda department," he said. "The things that matter are world forces on the move. China, Korea. The Americans will get bogged down in Korea. It's jam for the Kremlin."

Rudi nodded but then gave a groan.

"I'm not an advocate of World War III. No atom bombs for me, my friend."

"It's bound to come," said Oldenburg. "American and British rearmament is a direct challenge. If the West rearms after all its jawbation——"

"What about this Peace Campaign?" asked Rudi. "Is there anything in it? Sometimes I think Russia may mean it."

Peter Oldenburg laughed loudly.

"Of course Russia means it—as a propaganda weapon for her own people and as a lure to all those in the West who are terrified of another war. It's already having an effect upon left-wing politicians and frightened ladies and the little hairy highbrows. It's weakening resistance—the will to resist—in Western Europe. The Americans who have gone tough are already crying 'Appeasement!' to their English allies. It's a great game!"

There was the sound of an electric bell ringing and Oldenburg spoke to Rudi in a warning voice.

"Fellow travellers arriving! Two beautiful idealists. Don't drop any heavy bricks. They need a bit of nursing."

Maria opened the door to them. Their voices were audible in the passage. Presently Maria brought them into the sitting-room.

"Tea will be ready in two minutes," she said.

Oldenburg shook hands with a young man with a pale face and oiled hair, wearing a black jacket and striped trousers well-pressed.

"Glad to see you, my dear fellow."

He introduced him to Rudi.

"This is my friend Professor Austin Hood. I expect you know his name as a scientist. Atomic energy holds no secrets for him. Professor, this is Rudi Scholl, who calls himself an artist and paints bad pictures which nobody will buy. A fellow-prisoner of mine in Dachau."

"A forgotten episode, I hope," said Professor Hood, gripping Rudi's hand. His own was cold and clammy.

Oldenburg greeted the other visitor who wore a shabby sports jacket and corduroy trousers. He had a shock of reddish hair and there were little freckles on his nose. His eyes were a deep china-blue—startlingly blue—and he had a dreamy far-off look as though his thoughts were beyond his immediate environment.

"Good of you to come, my dear Thorpe," said Oldenburg. "It's an honour to have a poet in my slum tenement."

"Delighted to come," said the red-haired young man, in a melancholy voice which did not express delight.

Oldenburg introduced him.

"Rudi, this is Alastair Thorpe, the poet. You should bow your head three times in the presence of genius. Thorpe, my dear fellow, this is a pleasant scoundrel named Rudi Scholl."

A faint smile crept into the blue eyes of Alastair Thorpe.

"François Villon was a pleasant scoundrel," he said. "I adore him."

Maria came in with the tea things and put them down on the table before shaking hands with the visitors. She spoke a few words of Italian to the poet who seemed to understand them.

"What's inside that dish?" asked Oldenburg, lifting up the lid. "Good heavens! Crumpets! Now, Maria, let me implore you not to eat any of them. They're excessively fattening."

"I'm going to eat three," said Maria, resolutely.

Oldenburg continued to chaff his wife, perhaps in order to put his guests at ease. The poet sat silent with an occasional smile to show that he was still in the room mentally as well as physically.

Presently Professor Hood asked a serious question.

"Do you see by the evening papers that Pontecorvo has gone to Russia?"

Peter Oldenburg nodded and laughed.

"Good man. Did you know him?"

"Slightly," said the professor of physics. "I can't think there was anything against him."

"Nothing whatever," agreed Oldenburg. "Not that I ever met him. But I know friends of his. Perhaps that was why he had to hop it."

"He was an idealist as well as a scientist," said the professor. "To the scientific mind it's abhorrent to keep scientific discoveries secret from the rest of the world, especially of such vast importance as those of atomic energy. It's surely unfair and dangerous to world peace if the secret of the atom bomb is held exclusively by American imperialism. In my opinion, if all nations share the knowledge, the atom bomb would never be used."

"I utterly agree," said Peter Oldenburg. "It will cancel itself out."

"I'm afraid I don't agree," said Alastair Thorpe, who had been so silent that when he spoke it was somewhat startling.

"No?" asked Oldenburg genially, putting his head a little on one side as though to hear better.

"The scientists should never have invented such a frightful weapon," said Thorpe. "I blame the scientists for their betrayal of humanity. I speak as a poet."

"He speaks as a poet," said Oldenburg to Professor Wood. He turned his head slightly and gave an almost imperceptible wink at Rudi Scholl.

Professor Hood took up the challenge.

"We are bound to go forward in knowledge. We can't stay thus far and no farther."

There was considerable discussion on this point until the poet lapsed into silence again. It was Maria who intervened with a kind of laughing vulgarity.

"It gives me the jim-jams to listen to you men. I don't want my beautiful body to be blown to bits in the sacred name of science. I want to go on being alive. I find life amusing. You men talk and talk and the end of it will be war and then you won't talk any more, because you'll be dead."

"Shut up, Maria!" said Oldenburg. "You've no more sense in your head than a tame cat."

The poet broke silence again.

"It's because I want to preserve human life and the beauty of life that I lean towards Communism. If we resist the ideals of Communism, if we challenge them with guns and tanks and atom bombs, there will be few survivors, as Mrs. Oldenburg has said. The only way to avoid this final catastrophe is for the whole world to become Communist with one state and one Government and one class and one brotherhood of man."

"How right you are!" exclaimed Peter Oldenburg. "My dear fellow, that goes to the very heart of the matter."

Maria spluttered over a buttered crumpet and spoke a word in Italian.

"*Schisezza!*"

Rudi Scholl understood that word. It meant 'filthy muck'. Certainly she had been drinking.

"Maria," said Peter Oldenburg angrily, "behave yourself, and don't eat another crumpet."

"I groan when I read the morning papers," said Professor Hood. "They put up a blank refusal to the Russian offer of a new conference to arrange a reasonable peace, starting with the total suppression of atomic weapons and general disarmament. They ridicule the Russian organized Peace campaign. How can we ever bring peace to suffering humanity if we refuse all discussion and all compromise? Thank God for the Dean of Canterbury."

"The bravest man in England," said Oldenburg. "He defies the opinion of his caste and cloth. He speaks for humanity everywhere. He is trying to save the world and civilization."

For half an hour or more they talked on this subject until their conversation was interrupted by a painful incident.

Maria was stretching out her hand for another buttered crumpet—she had already eaten four—but Peter Oldenburg seized the dish and put it away from her. It was a mistake on his part. It made Maria very angry. She took her greasy plate and flung it to the floor, breaking it into several pieces.

"You do not let me eat when I am hungry!" she cried furiously. "That is the Russian way in their concentration camps and the Siberian mines. You go on talking damn' lies to these innocent English gentlemen who think that Communism means the brotherhood of man. Shall I tell you what it means? It means the tyranny of a few devils over the rest of mankind. It means slave labour and execution of all who disagree. It means concentration camps and torture and the cruelty of Devils. It means starvation and misery——"

Peter Oldenburg's face had flushed with rage. He strode round the table and put his hand over his wife's mouth and spoke to her fiercely in German.

"You damned witch," he said. "You fat slut! Be silent and go to your room or I'll strangle you."

There was a struggle on one side of the table. Maria forced his hand from her mouth and laughed loudly, though her eyes were blazing.

"If you won't let me eat crumpets, I'll spit out the truth," she shouted. "And you know it's the truth, you lying old rat. Spy of Soviet Russia! Traitor to England which allows free speech and liberty!"

Oldenburg raised his hand and smacked her cheek sharply, hurting her so that she burst into tears and flung herself out of the room.

Peter Oldenburg gave an uneasy laugh.

"I'm sorry, gentlemen! This is very annoying. My wife has been drinking. She is also a little mad. I apologize."

The two guests looked extremely uncomfortable. Professor Hood had turned pale.

"I thought your wife was one of us," he said. "She may betray us. I understood this was a place where I could speak freely, with perfect confidence."

"My dear fellow," answered Oldenburg, laughing heartily with forced gaiety. "You needn't be in the least uneasy. My wife was only angry because I wouldn't let her eat crumpets. She's a perfectly good Communist at heart."

"She said things which no Communist would dare to say," answered Professor Hood.

"I think perhaps I'll go and do a little thinking," said Alastair Thorpe. "I've written three lines of a new poem——"

Rudi Scholl was enjoying himself. He had envied his friend Peter. He had envied him these furnished rooms, his regular salary, his comfortable way of life. Peter had always been contemptuous of him with a bitter satirical tongue. Now he had the laugh of him. Maria had shouted out unpardonable things. She had spilt the beans, as Patricia Hastings would say. It was all very comical indeed. Not even Peter could cover up this humiliation, this disgrace. Not all his false laughter could hide his discomfiture.

"Sorry, old man!" he said, when he left after the two guests had gone. "Most unfortunate!"

"You know you enjoyed it!" said Peter glaring at him. Then he laughed without shamming. "Maria scared those two fellows! Well, I don't mind. They're both unimportant and as stupid as cold mutton. But I'll have to kick Maria out of these rooms. She's a female devil. She's quite capable of denouncing me to the police."

"I like her," said Rudi. "I like her type of luscious beauty, and I like her spirit. If you kick her out I'll make love to her."

Peter Oldenburg grinned at him and slapped his face, not so hard as he had slapped Maria's.

"Get out!" he said, "or I'll kick you downstairs."

CHAPTER XV

DR. PAGET who, in his simple way, was a psychiatrist or soul doctor as well as a general practitioner, was as good as his word in providing Hildegard, the German girl, with intellectual companionship and James Stewart, his pessimistic poet, with similar comfort and consolation. He was amused and delighted at the success of his introduction. It was obvious when the poet came to tea one afternoon that he was much impressed and attracted by the intelligence of this German refugee. It was equally obvious that Hildegard regarded James Stewart with a reverence and admiration due to genius. Doubtless that was why Mr. James Stewart thought her very intelligent. Poets, artists, novelists and other creators, need constant adulation as an antidote to their own inferiority complex and self-criticism and periodical despair. To Dr. Paget himself, James Stewart's poems were incomprehensible, but this German girl, reading them in what to her was a foreign language, seemed to understand them or to get something out of them, some spiritual message, some tragic interpretation of life, some philosophy in tune with her own experience and pursuit of truth. At least she said so across the tea-table where she served tea in the absence of Viola, who was up in town that day.

"I shed tears over your poem on the Scarecrow," she told him.

"Good heavens!" exclaimed James Stewart. "Have you read it? Did you understand it? How very extraordinary!"

"It was not hard to understand," said Hildegard. "It was, of course, an allegory on civilization—the rags and tatters of its former beauty. The Scarecrow personifies the degradation and despair of man himself who has lost his hopes and—how do you call it—shudders, or is it shivers?—in the cold blasts of a cruel world. Is it not so?"

James Stewart stared at her incredulously.

"Marvellous!" he said. "Certainly it might mean that. I should be glad to think it means something like that."

Dr. Paget chaffed him a little.

"You seem darned uncertain about the meaning of your own poem."

"One is uncertain," said James Stewart. "One expresses a mood. One pursues an idea which often eludes one. A poem may have many interpretations according to the mind of those who read or listen to it. No two minds interpret Hamlet in the same way. One of David's psalms has one revelation for one soul and one for another, according to what the other soul brings to it out of its own agony or its own despair."

He looked over at Hildegard with a smile.

"Do you agree?"

"*Bestimmt!*" she said. "That is getting deep in psychology which I once studied in Bonn."

Dr. Paget's eyes twinkled.

"This of course is out of my depth. I'm a simple and ignorant fellow who likes his poetry easy to understand. I can get as far as Tennyson. . . ."

Hildegard and James Stewart looked at each other and smiled, as though Tennyson belonged to the nursery-rhyme class.

"The great poets," said Hildegard, "are never easy to understand, because there are many layers of thought in what they write, very deep and very high. One has to dig down and to reach up."

"Exactly!" said James Stewart, regarding her with surprised admiration.

It was a pity that the doctor who had brought these two together with benevolent intention could not follow on their further intercourse which happened without his presence, though Mrs. Montgomery-Jones, that Argus-eyed observer of village life, became aware that these two queer creatures, as she called them, were in the habit of meeting. She feared the worst.

"You know what poets are," she said to her friend, Mrs. Maydew, "and that German girl ought never to have been allowed to come to England. She's probably a spy and, anyhow, Germans have no morals."

The next meeting took place on the heath above the village half a mile beyond Foxgloves. Hildegard had an afternoon 'off' and as it was sunny and warm for once in a somewhat disappointing summer, decided to take advantage of it by a walk with Nature. Being German she took a book with her for light reading in her solitude. It was the *Critique of Pure Reason*, by Immanuel Kant, in a German edition. As it happened, she did not read more than two pages of this philosophical work after finding a seat on the log of a tree from which she could observe a distant view of the Sussex Downs and a near view of the old tiled roofs of Longmead in the valley below. The bracken was high and green about her, a rabbit came to have a look at her and scuttled away to a sandbank. A thrush gave song in a nearby bush. From the village there floated up the voices of children, the barking of a dog, the bell-like notes of a hammer and anvil in the blacksmith's forge. Presently Hildegard heard a rustle in the undergrowth and a man's cough. It was James Stewart who strode towards her. He was wearing corduroy trousers and a short brown jacket. He was hatless and his beard had a reddish tinge in the afternoon sunshine. Not seeing the girl on the log and believing himself to be alone in the wilderness, he uttered a loud and terrible groan and cried out:

"O God! O God!"

Then he saw the German girl and stopped with a startled and embarrassed look.

"I beg your pardon!" he said.

"Don't mention it," said Hildegard, jumping up.

James Stewart held out a long thin hand and laughed uneasily.

"I get into the habit of talking to myself," he told her. "That's because I'm so damnably alone."

"It is the same with me," said Hildegard. "I catch myself talking German. That is very dangerous in an English village where Germans are not well received."

"I'm sorry to hear it," said Stewart. "Haven't we got beyond that kind of stupidity? I detest intolerance and hatred."

"They think I'm responsible for Dachau and Belsen," said

Hildegard with a smile. "I cannot blame them much. There is much to forgive in Hitler's Germany. The German people have much to atone."

James Stewart did not disagree with this and stood looking at the view over the Sussex Downs, blue in the far distance.

"One is staggered by the renaissance of cruelty in man," he said. "That's the most damnable thing of all. Shall we sit down on this log?"

"That would be charming," said Hildegard. "The view is very good. *Wunderschön.*"

James Stewart sat down next to her and prodded the sandy soil with his stick.

"It all looks peaceful," he said. "But in a few months or a few years, this countryside may be blasted by atom bombs or made unlivable even to the rabbits by radio-activity."

"That is a terrible thought!" said Hildegard. "*Schrecklich.* Is that why you called out to God?"

James Stewart turned his head sideways and smiled.

"I'm sorry about that."

"Is there any use crying out to God?" asked Hildegard. "If there is a God He doesn't seem to care."

"Most of this misery is man-made," said Stewart. "We can't blame it on to God—if, as you say, there is a God."

He looked across to the Downs again and presently spoke again.

"In this beauty and peace," he said, "one wishes to believe—one is forced to believe—in a First Cause and a great Artist and a spirit of goodness. It's the infernal stupidity of man which gets one down. As we sit here men are killing one another in Korea. Presently, perhaps, the Chinese will take a hand in it, prodded on by Russia. Then something may happen in Berlin. Before we know where we are we may be in the Third World War. Aren't we all preparing for it?"

Hildegard sighed loudly.

"If only people would read Immanuel Kant, who believed in reason, and your great Bertrand Russell who believes in tolerance and kindliness."

James Stewart smiled at her.

"Tolerance and kindess are limited to very few. You say people are unkind to you in that village down there. If that's so, how can we hope to get peace anywhere? If we can't kill hatred in our own hearts for our next door neighbours . . ."

Hildegard made a correction to her statement that she had been treated unkindly.

"Dr. Paget is an angel," she said, "and Mrs. Paget has been very sweet to me."

James Stewart rewarded this remark with a laugh.

"One angel per English village may save this country from the wrath of the Lord."

They were both silent for a little while, sitting upon the old log with the sun upon them. Hildegard did not interrupt the silence of a poet, thinking that some divine afflatus may have touched his soul or that he was drinking in the beauty of nature which later might find expression in magical words. But presently he asked a question of no mystical significance.

"How's Germany?"

Hildegard thought out her answer for a second or two.

"Germany," she said, "is escaping from its lunatic asylum, though there are still many lunatics."

"As in most countries," said James Stewart.

"The Germans," said Hildegard, "have discovered the best cure for madness and melancholy."

"I'd like to know that!" said Stewart.

"It is work. They work from morning till night as though that were the whole purpose of life. Some of it is like the labours of Sisyphus—you remember? They stand in the midst of their ruins clearing the rubble and sorting out the stones and bricks, but it makes not much difference to the ruins, you understand. Others turn their eyes from the ruins and pretend they do not exist and build little houses and little shops in front of them, leaving the ruins still standing in the background. Everybody works as though driven by demons. The young people study until late at night, as though they were searching for the elixir of life. You understand?"

"They may find it," said Stewart.

"Much of this work is useless," said Hildegard.

Stewart raised his eyebrows.

"Why?"

"It is useless because the result is ridiculous. The miners dig out coal which is taken for reparations. The steel workers work like devils but Germany is not allowed to have enough steel to rebuild the ruins. In any case why rebuild the ruins?"

"It seems to me a reasonable idea," said Stewart.

"They will be knocked down again," said Hildegard. "If England and America go to war with Russia, Germany would be the front line and immediately overwhelmed. The Americans and British would fall back to the Rhine as their main line of defence, leaving Germany to be annihilated. That is why there is a great illusion in the English and American mind. It makes me laugh!"

"An illusion?" asked Stewart, who looked interested.

"The statesmen take it for granted that Germany wishes to be rearmed. France objects to that. But the German people will refuse to be rearmed. It is only Dr. Adenauer who agrees to raise a German army for the defence of the West. Dr. Adenauer and his Christian Democrats will be swept on one side in the next elections."

Stewart turned to look at this German girl with surprise and amusement.

"You seem to know all about it," he said. "How do you obtain your information?"

"It is no secret," said Hildegard. "It is in all the papers that reach me from Germany. But it is not in the English papers. They do not seem to know. It is because they do not wish to know. The English people only believe what they wish to believe. It gives them great strength in many ways, but it is perhaps a little dangerous."

They continued to talk about Germany for a time. Hildegard was astonished to hear that this poet had been an artillery officer in the recent war and had been in the Army of Occupation for a few months.

"It is impossible!" she exclaimed.

"What's impossible?" asked Stewart.

"It is impossible that a poet should stand behind a gun and kill his fellow men. It is a terrible idea."

She looked distressed and even aghast, that this man by her side, this great poet as she believed him to be, so difficult to understand and therefore so profound and mystical, should have been one of the killers. Perhaps he had killed her own brother, who had fallen in the neighbourhood of Caen.

"Were you at Caen in Normandy?" she asked, in a low voice.

Stewart nodded.

"Yes, my battery was there for a time."

"Then you may have killed my brother, Franz!" she told him in a tragic tone.

"Not intentionally," said Stewart. "War is very impersonal. The Germans happened to have killed a young brother of mine, but I don't suppose they had a grudge against him, individually, I mean."

He saw that Hildegard was weeping a little and wiping away her tears furtively.

"That's the absurdity of war," he said. "Men kill each other in masses without any hatred in their hearts for the individuals in the opposite crowd. They're fighting for ideas imposed upon them by politicians and propagandists and maniacs like Hitler, who roll over other people's frontiers and challenge their liberties and way of life. It's all happening again. The maniacs are making faces at one another. Eleven madmen in the Kremlin will probably send millions of men to death. They're suffering from persecution mania. They're frightened men really, and fear is the mother of cruelty. They think their religion has to be defended—the new gospel of State socialism with Karl Marx as its God and Lenin as its prophet. Our side is equally afraid because they believe that Russia is going to destroy their faith and their liberties and their way of life. But meanwhile the men who will be the gun fodder have no quarrel with one another. If they meet they rather like one another. When I was in Germany I liked quite a few Germans. I fell in love with a German girl. But she died of T.B. like so many others."

This revelation of his secret history spoken in a casual way startled Hildegard so much that she stared at him incredulously.

"You fell in love with a German girl?"

Stewart nodded.

"She was very attractive. I loved her very much."

"She was very much honoured by your love," said Hildegard in a reverent voice. Suddenly she rose from the log on which they were sitting. "Let us walk a little way," she suggested. "Let us forget all this sadness and the fear that is in all our minds. The sun is warm upon us. The birds are singing. The sky is blue for once. May we not feel a little happy because of these moments of peace and beauty? All through history it has been like this—a few moments of peace, a little sunshine."

James Stewart stood up and gave a quiet laugh.

"You are very German!" he said.

She turned and looked at him reproachfully.

"Are you mocking me?"

"Not at all," he assured her. "But English girls are not so emotional."

"English girls are cold," she answered. "They hide themselves. Or perhaps there is nothing to hide."

"Let's walk as far as Foxgloves," said James Stewart. "I'll stand you a cup of tea. We might go on talking about the misery of life. I find it very stimulating. The ladies of Longmead, whom I shun like the plague, avoid talking about the misery of life. Their outlook on life is limited to the rise in the cost of living, or the latest little scandal which makes them envious of other women's naughtiness."

He slouched across the heath with his long stride and the German girl kept pace with him.

"Perhaps we had better not go to Foxgloves," she said presently.

"Why not?"

Hildegard hesitated and blushed slightly.

"People talk. I am only Dr. Paget's domestic help and, as you say, I am very German."

"Let 'em talk!" said James Stewart. "Let's give 'em

if she drew him out, he told her about a practical joke at Sandhurst, a lecture by a military expert, a field exercise which had taken the stuffing out of some of the fellows. If he happened to come on Hildegard's afternoon 'off', they went into the kitchen together to boil the kettle and make toast, and he seemed to enjoy this domesticity. He was not a great laugher, perhaps because of his shyness, but she made him grin by some of her stories of village life which she had heard from her witch-doctor.

At first he had always enquired very politely after the doctor, but now she noticed that these enquiries stopped and he looked a little uncomfortable when she spoke about him.

What alarmed her one afternoon, was when he had to go and hesitated for a moment before doing so and held her hand very tightly and said, "What about a kiss?"

It was that look in his eyes, that yearning look, which made her uneasy.

"Better not!" she said lightly. "We mustn't make a habit of it."

She had only kissed him that night when they had come back late from town and he had been sulky because she had talked so much to his cousin.

"It's not a habit yet!" he told her. "I don't see anything wrong with it. Do you?"

"Oh, nothing wrong," she assured him, "but perhaps a little—well, foolish."

"Just once again!" he asked pleadingly.

"Well, if you feel like it. A butterfly kiss!"

She wanted just to touch the boy's cheek, but he gripped her arms and kissed her lips with a touch of passion. It would have been a long kiss if she had not drawn her head back and laughed at him.

"Hi, that's not a butterfly kiss, young man! Don't forget I'm a married woman."

"I don't forget it," he said in a low voice.

"Now then, Mervyn," she said, teasingly, "be your age, kid. And remember mine!"

"Oh, that's all nonsense," he answered half angrily.

"Well, good-bye, Mervyn," she said. "See you soon, I hope. But no more kisses! What would Mrs. Montgomery-Jones say if she heard of such a thing? I tremble to think."

"Oh, curse that old witch!" said Mervyn.

"I'm glad the word begins with a 'w'," said Viola demurely.

She brought a smile back to his eyes. He had a sense of humour under his shyness.

When he had gone she spoke aloud to herself.

"He's just a boy. There's nothing in it."

But she could not quite dismiss it like that. She would have to be careful. It would be rather difficult, rather embarrassing, rather tragic even, if Mervyn became too emotional about her. She would hate to hurt him. On the other hand, she would hate to lose this sweet friendship with him. He had made all the difference to her life in Longmead where there were so few young people—hardly any young men. It had been jolly to ride with him and go sketching with him, and to have him in her room so often. It had all been very innocent—just like brother and sister. They had played gin-rummy together like two kids. He liked to hear her play the piano, sitting in a deep chair with his long legs stretched out. Now and then they had serious talks—but not too serious—about the meaning of things, books they had read, even the international situation. She had shocked him sometimes by defending the Labour Government and what it had done for the working classes, just to shake him out of his Sandhurst pattern of thought. But he really wasn't so conventional-minded as she had first thought. Sometimes she was startled by his remarks about world affairs, and even about the mystery and purpose of life. He was thinking for himself, groping his way to some philosophy of his own, though probably he was influenced by books he had been reading, like Aldous Huxley, and the critical essays of Bertrand Russell—dangerous books for a Sandhurst cadet and the son of Major-General Sir William Kendrick. She had been flattered by his opinion of her own intelligence, by talking to her now and then on such serious things and confiding in her about his conflict at home with a father who took a traditional view about everything and a mother who shocked his father profoundly by her pacifist ideals. So there he was, a rather bewildered young man but very charming as a companion, adolescent and innocent. It would be absurd to send him away because he wanted a kiss. That would be ridiculous. No, she wouldn't do that, but certainly she would have to be a little careful, perhaps a little cold now and then, poor boy.

That evening she spoke to her witch-doctor about it, her dear old John to whom she was perfectly loyal and in whose wisdom she had faith in spite of all her teasing.

"I say, John, old man, I want to consult you about a delicate affair which worries me a bit."

Dr. Paget was enjoying a pipe and browsing over that day's *Times*. The world news was not exhilarating. It seldom was these days. It looked as though the Americans might be pushed out of their bridgehead at Pusan. The North Koreans seemed to be putting up a terrific fight with good equipment, mostly Russian, and good generalship, probably Russian also.

He put down his paper and smiled at Viola.

"Got into a jam of some kind?" he asked. "Running into debt? Not murder, I hope!"

"It's about Mervyn," she said. "He's getting too fond of me."

Dr. Paget looked amused and his eyes twinkled.

"I'm not surprised. You're a dangerous young woman. I'm too fond of you myself."

"Joking apart," she said, "I'm getting a little alarmed about it. He's so sweet and innocent. I'd hate him to get hurt. I mean, I wouldn't like him to lose his head about me."

"Well, of course he will," said Dr. Paget, with his good-natured laugh. "I saw it was inevitable from the beginning. He fell in love with you at first sight. So did I, in my senile way."

Mrs. Paget knocked *The Times* off his knees and gave him a bang with her fist, as she sat close to him on the hearthrug.

"Do be serious," she pleaded. "I'm asking your advice. Supposing Mervyn falls in love with me seriously. What am I going to do about it?"

"Treat him tenderly," said Dr. Paget.

Mrs. Paget looked up at him and gave a little vexed laugh.

"You don't seem to be alarmed. You don't seem to be jealous."

Dr. Paget picked up *The Times* and put it on his knees again.

"My dear child," he said, "I'm not going to get jealous of a Sandhurst cadet. He's just a schoolboy. Presently he will join some regiment and be sent off to Malaya or North Africa. I don't smell danger to my domestic bliss."

Viola Paget raised her fore-finger.

"Don't you be too cocksure," she said. "You know a lot about human nature, don't you?"

"Almost everything," said Dr. Paget.

"Well then, you ought to know that young men of Mervyn's age are apt to be romantic and passionate."

"Certainly," said Dr. Paget. "That's one of the symptoms of adolescence. Young fellows of Mervyn's age see some fluffy-haired girl in a tobacconist's shop and with a sudden rush of emotion—young blood at boiling-point—believe her to be the ideal woman who has come to them in dreams. Sometimes it leads to a disastrous *mésalliance*, but more often the young gentleman pulls himself together, or is rescued by his anxious parents, or has to go elsewhere. Then he meets another girl of more perfect beauty and higher intelligence. Youth is fickle and experimental."

"You're talking nonsense," said Viola Paget impatiently. "You're slurring over the question of sex and passion. What about Romeo and Juliet? They risked everything for love. They died for it. And they were both kids, weren't they?"

"Agreed," said Dr. Paget. "I don't underrate the terrific urge of the mating instinct. I've seen too much of it in this village—lots of illegitimate babies, but this boy Mervyn has been taught self-control from childhood and has been brought up in a moral code which guards him from casual love affairs. I know his type. I know his taboos. I'm easy in my mind."

Mrs. Paget gave a quiet laugh again.

"You're a little too easy in your mind, old witch-doctor. Supposing I were to tell you that he wants me to kiss him and that I have kissed him—twice? Wouldn't that frighten you? Wouldn't that make you madly jealous?"

Dr. Paget took this question calmly.

"Jealous? Not me! I don't see why you shouldn't kiss him now and then. It's a harmless and natural form of salutation, very comforting to the giver and the recipient."

"John!" cried Viola Paget. "I believe you wouldn't care if I fell in love with Mervyn and did a bunk from you. Wouldn't that be very natural also?"

The doctor looked at her with smiling eyes and then spoke tenderly and seriously.

"My dear child, I shouldn't blame you harshly if one day you wanted to do a bunk from me. A man of my age has no right to marry a girl twenty years younger than himself. It would be more my fault than yours. But I don't think it's going to come to that with your Mervyn Kendrick. It's just calf love on his side. I meant what I said when I said treat him tenderly. Let him come here as often as he likes. If he wants a kiss now and then, I don't object any more than if you kissed a schoolboy home for the holidays, or a younger brother wanting a little mothering. I have a very great confidence in your sense of humour and your integrity of mind. You're dead honest, my dear. Otherwise you wouldn't have told me about this. I'm not scared—yet!"

Mrs. Paget who was sitting on the hearthrug—it was a habit of hers to sit on the floor with her legs tucked up—put her head on her husband's knees.

"Dear old witch-doctor," she said. "You're either very wise or very foolish, I'm not sure which. But I know you're very kind. I believe you're the kindest man on earth—or at least in Longmead village!"

"It's good of you to think so," said Dr. Paget. "I'm a selfish old guy, really. I enjoy being kind, as you call it. It's a kind of vanity. It's a kind of self-indulgence. I want to be loved. That's a weakness."

"I love you quite a lot," said his wife. "But I might be unfaithful to you at any moment. Don't say I haven't warned you."

Dr. Paget leaned forward and pulled her ear and kissed her on the top of her head.

"You can't scare me," he told her. "I'm not easily scared."

CHAPTER XVII

LADY KENDRICK was greatly taken with Rudi Scholl and perhaps a little under the influence of that young man. He was always sympathetic to her ideas on the subject of peace. He even went a little further than she did in believing that Russia was not intent upon challenging the Western World and had cause for suspicion and fear because of the menace of the United States who undoubtedly, he said, was preparing for a Third World War. So it was not unnaturally argued that Russia should make counter-preparations, keep a large army in being, and strengthen her outer line of defence in Germany and the satellite countries. Besides, at that very moment, Russia was organizing a great Peace Campaign for the abolition of atomic warfare and general disarmament.

She argued with him almost against her own conviction and certainly against her secret hopes.

"My husband says it is simply a propaganda campaign for throwing dust in the eyes of peace lovers like myself. I must say I find it difficult to believe in their sincerity. Didn't Mr. Molotov and Mr. Malik keep on saying 'No' to any proposal for a peace with Austria and any decision of the United Nations?"

Rudi Scholl shrugged his shoulders and laughed.

"I don't agree with their methods or manners," he said, "but when they walked out of UNO it was because the new Republic of China had no representative on the Council, although Britain has acknowledged her new form of government. It's surely most illogical that a Chinese Nationalist, one of Chiang-Kai-Shek's men, should pretend to represent the new China! All he represents is the island of Formosa, crowded with corrupt generals and reactionaries. Of course, Great Britain has yielded to the pressure of the United States who are as fanatical against Communism as the Russians are against Capitalism—a religious war again! Meanwhile, the American bombers are flying from their bases in the Arctic regions, impatient to fling atom bombs on to Russian cities. It's the Americans who are the greatest menace in the world today, because they get into panics and react to mass opinion and get 'mad' as they say, over some trivial incident."

"All that sounds like blasphemy to my husband," said Lady Kendrick, smiling at this persuasive young man. "You won't make me believe that the Russian leaders are innocent lambs!"

Rudi Scholl hastened to reassure her on this point.

"By no means innocent lambs, but genuine in their desire for peace, very terrified, I'm certain, of another war. If we could dispel their idea that we are preparing for war under American pressure, if public opinion in this country would gather weight and profess a passionate belief in liberating their foreign policy from that of the United States . . ."

So they talked and gradually Lady Kendrick began to be persuaded that this young man had very beautiful ideals and very deep sincerity, and an uncanny perception of truth regarding the international situation.

There was, she thought, the very soul of truth in his eyes. Like herself, he had a hatred and horror of war. Had he not suffered? Was he not a refugee from terror? She pitied him because of his poverty and admired him because of his genius, or, at least, talent as an artist. Because of this pity and her increasing liking for him—he was always so charming and polite—she took quite a lot of trouble to get him a few commissions and did succeed in persuading one of her London friends, Lady Harley, to have a portrait of her daughter done by him. But that would take some time, and meanwhile she knew that he was desperately poor and probably even undernourished. One afternoon, when they had been having tea together, and she had fed him up with buns and bread and butter, she spoke to him after some hesitation and embarrassment on this subject of his poverty.

"Forgive me," she said, "but I feel so sorry for you. Would you allow me to make you a little loan until Phyllis Harley's portrait is done? If twenty pounds would be of use to you——"

"You are too kind, Lady Kendrick!" exclaimed Rudi Scholl. "I really hesitate to accept such a generous offer."

"There's another little matter," said Lady Kendrick. "I almost feel ashamed to mention it in case you should be offended."

She gave a nervous laugh.

"Nothing that you did could possibly offend me, dear Lady Kendrick," answered Rudi.

"Forgive me," she said. "You look so shabby always. Now my son Mervyn has grown out of some of his clothes since he went to Sandhurst. I am sure he would be delighted if I gave you one or two of his suits. Do excuse me making such a suggestion. I feel sure they would fit you, as you are not so tall as he is now."

"How good you are!" said Rudi Scholl. "You are like a mother to me."

A few days later he tried on one of Mervyn's suits in his studio, where a neat brown paper parcel had been delivered by Lady Kendrick's man Embry. It fitted him perfectly. It was accompanied by several newly-washed shirts and collars and a dozen ties.

"*Gott in Himmel!*" he said to himself, after gazing at his own image in a cracked mirror which he put at different angles so that he could see various views of these new clothes. "I look like an English aristocrat. I feel like one." He was self-conscious when he went into dinner at Foxgloves that evening. Patricia Hastings raised her eyebrows and gave a squeal of laughter at the sight of him.

"Good lord!" she said in a low voice, as he sat opposite at her table. "Our little Rudi looks as if he had been to Moss Bros."

"How do you think I look?" he asked.

"Ridiculous!" she told him brutally. "You look like the model of a murderer in Madame Tussaud's—Rudi Scholl the poisoner. Many women fell for the charm of his dark eyes. He poisoned them in their baths."

"You're extremely cruel!" he exclaimed. "One day I'll poison you, or strangle you. Or I might get married to you in these clothes. You and I would make a fine-looking couple."

She spluttered over a spoonful of soup.

"Have you come into a fortune?" she asked.

"Almost," he told her. "It's just round the corner. Let's have a bottle of wine with a label on it tonight."

Patricia Hastings stared at him with amused surprise.

"Did you raid a till this afternoon?" she asked. "I hope you didn't leave any finger-prints."

Rudi Scholl beckoned to Commander Donovan, who was moving about the room.

"What's the matter with you, laddy?" asked the Commander. "You look as though you were disguised as a gentleman."

"What about a bottle of Nuits St. Georges?" asked Rudi Scholl. "I propose to pay for it, of course."

Commander Donovan suppressed a laugh.

"Holy Mother of God!" he said. "Our little refugee proposes to pay for something!"

Rudi pulled out a pocket book and extracted a pound note. It was one of those loaned to him by Lady Kendrick.

"Seeing is believing," he said. "Is that not an English proverb?"

"I've heard it said," answered the Commander, "but all is not gold that glitters. That's another English proverb, my little Mid-European."

He lifted the pound note to the light of a standard lamp in this big barn room.

"I'm not an expert," he said, "but I'll take a chance."

Presently he brought the bottle of Nuits St. Georges and placed it on the table with a laugh. Then he bent over Rudi Scholl and whispered a question.

"Did you have luck with the football pools, laddy?"

"Nothing like that!" said Rudi. "It's a bit on account of future work."

Commander Donovan looked disappointed. The football pools were his fairy-tale.

It was when Lady Kendrick called a meeting in the village

hall of Longmead, to discuss the Problem of Peace, as her talk was entitled, that a considerable amount of fat went into the fire with many little flames and splutterings. The Vicar, Mr. Langtry, was the first to get his fingers burnt. He had been asked by Lady Kendrick to take the chair and after an act of faith and courage had accepted. Very great courage.

"I shall get it in the neck from my sister Elizabeth," he told Lady Kendrick, with a nervous laugh.

He got it in the neck from that militant lady.

With cowardice which somewhat undermined his courage, he had kept the proposed meeting secret from her until it was announced by posters—the lettering was done by Mrs. Waggett in the village—stuck up outside the Post Office, the village stores, the church and the Congregational chapel.

THE PROBLEM OF PEACE

Address by LADY KENDRICK

To be followed by a Debate

Chairman: THE REV. GERALD LANGTRY

In the Village Hall, Wednesday next, 8.15 p.m.

Miss Elizabeth Langtry was startled by this placard which caught her eyes on her way home to tea. She was in a state of suppressed anger when her brother appeared at the tea-table, knowing that the storm was about to burst. He had put on an air of bravado and came in whistling 'Little Brown Jug'.

"Tea ready?" he asked, with forced cheerfulness—an unnecessary question because the tea things were already on the table.

"Gerald," said his sister, glowering at him, "why didn't you tell me about this preposterous Peace meeting?"

"Didn't I?" he asked, insincerely.

"No, you didn't. You kept it from me deliberately because you were ashamed to tell me."

"Ashamed?" asked the Vicar, taking a piece of toast and buttering it very carefully. "Why should I be ashamed?"

"Ashamed of being as weak as water under the influence of that ridiculous woman."

"What ridiculous woman?" asked the Vicar, as though ignorant of the particular woman to whom she referred.

"You know perfectly well," said Elizabeth Langtry. "She's a most dangerous creature who ought to be locked up for treasonable propaganda."

The Vicar put a little honey on his buttered toast.

"If you're referring to Lady Kendrick," he said, "I can't agree that she's dangerous and I've not come across any treasonable propaganda. It's surely not treasonable to work on behalf of Peace."

"Fudge!" said Elizabeth Langtry. "Those who pretend to be working for peace are all Communists and fellow-travellers. What we want is to prepare for war, to be strong in defence, to rearm with the greatest possible speed. You say you haven't come across her treasonable propaganda? Let me tell you that for the past week she has been going round the cottages and the Council houses talking to the women—even the young girls—and urging them to band together to prevent another war. If that isn't treasonable I don't know what is. She's disgracing her husband's name. She's stirring up trouble and strife in many little homes, separating wives from husbands and daughters from fathers. Do you think the ex-service men approve of their womenfolk being seduced from their loyalty to King and country? Why, damn it, the woman ought to be denounced to the police. I've a good mind to ring up Scotland Yard. And now you're going to take the chair for her. No wonder you look ashamed."

The Vicar brushed some crumbs off his waistcoat and sipped his tea. Then he gave a good-natured laugh.

"Elizabeth, I don't look ashamed and I don't feel ashamed. I happen to be a Christian, though a bad one I admit, and I happen to be a priest of the Church of England, which professes to believe in Jesus Christ who said Blessed are the peace-makers. As for Lady Kendrick, I think she's perfectly right to arouse the women to the menace which is creeping upon us all. If all the women of the world were to set their minds and hearts against another war, utterly refusing to accept it, there would be no war."

"Fiddlesticks!" exclaimed Miss Langtry, with a flushed face. "The woman has bewitched you. I believe you've fallen in love with her. Mrs. Montgomery-Jones has had that idea for a long time."

"Mrs. Montgomery-Jones ought to be strangled," said the Vicar, in a most un-Christian way. "She's a danger to society."

"Not so dangerous as your lady friend," answered Miss Langtry. "You wilt when she turns her dark eyes upon you. You're like a piece of putty in her long thin hands. Beware of her, Gerald. She's luring you into sin and leading you into temptation."

The Vicar pushed his plate away and very nearly knocked over his tea-cup.

"You forget yourself, Elizabeth!" he said sternly. "How dare you say such things?"

"It's my duty to say them," said Elizabeth Langtry. "Thank God I have never shirked my duty, however unpleasant it may be."

General Kendrick saw the poster about the Peace meeting in the village hall and read it outside the Post Office after watching another cricket match on the Green. He had missed two or three week-ends in the country, having been kept in town by his work at the War Office in connection with the Government's plan for rearmament, and consultations on that subject with some of the Big Pots, as he called them. Things were not going too well. There was a lot of planning but very little achievement. The switch over of industry to arms production was not even begun. No orders had been given for tanks or guns or other weapons. There was a horrible drag. He suspected political resistance in high quarters—perhaps within the Cabinet itself—to the whole policy of rearmament which would, of course, cut into the Labour programme for the export drive and social services. This country was not alone in hesitation and delay. The American offer of aid in rearming Western Europe—enormously generous—was accepted in principle, but still subject to endless discussion by the Council of

Ministers and European statesmen. France was resisting the rearming of Western Germany, though without German man-power, re-trained and re-equipped, there could be no real strength of defence against Russian aggression. The Germans themselves, were, it seemed, extremely reluctant to be rearmed. General Kendrick had heard that from his American friend, William Legget, who had lately been in Germany and had come back with gloomy, if not pessimistic, impressions.

"Those Germans," he said, "have gone pacifist. 'No more soldiering' seems to be their slogan for the moment. They've had a bellyfull of war and are still licking their wounds and indulging in an orgy of self-pity amidst their ruins. They don't see why they should help to defend us against the Russians who were our allies when they were being smashed, and they're convinced that they would be overwhelmed and massacred if Russia attacked in strength. Old man Adenauer who is keen to come in with us may be thrown out on his ear by his political opponents."

These thoughts were in the mind of General Kendrick when he strolled over to the Post Office to buy a book of stamps. At home there was a pile of private letters waiting to be answered —bills to be paid and so forth. Then he had missed his weekly letter to Mervyn, which he regarded as a pleasant duty. Young Mervyn was often in his thoughts and always in his heart. He was proud of him. He had a good poise, that boy, though Beatrice had done her best to spoil him by too much mother-love and adoration. Poor Beatrice! . . .

His attention was caught by the poster and he stared at it for a few seconds. Peace Meeting . . . Address by Lady Kendrick. . . .

"Good heavens!" said General Kendrick aloud.

Dr. Paget was coming out of the Post Office and greeted him.

"Hullo, General! How are you feeling?"

General Kendrick gave an uneasy laugh.

"Not too good! I've just seen this."

He pointed his stick at the poster. Dr. Paget glanced at him with amusement.

"Yes. I admire your lady's courage and idealism. I hope you're coming to support her."

"I'll be damned if I do!" answered the General. "What would the War Office say?"

"They needn't know," said Dr. Paget, jestingly. "I don't suppose they read the *Sussex Gazette*. Besides, I don't suppose any of your colleagues are yearning for a Third World War."

"They're not," answered the General. "Nor am I. My whole purpose in life at the moment is to prevent a Third World War. Not by weakness but by strength. Beatrice doesn't understand that. It's devilish awkward, Doctor. It puts me in an awful hole."

"Don't let it spoil your domestic bliss," said Dr. Paget. "After all, your wife has a perfect right to her own opinions. We stand for free speech, don't we?—even in the home—and anyhow we can't avoid it. Our women folk will have their say!"

He spoke lightly, seeing that the General was distressed and upset.

"It affects my name and position," said General Kendrick.

He strode off rather abruptly in the direction of the lane which led to Badgers, and Dr. Paget watched his sturdy straight-backed figure and his military step.

'There goes an unhappy man!' he thought. 'A fine type, but too rigid in his mind. Her ladyship is in for a wigging.'

It was not until the evening that the General broached the subject of the public meeting. He came from his study into the drawing-room where his wife was reading in the window-seat which looked on to the rose garden, now in glorious bloom. She had a passion for roses and went round every day snipping off the dead heads. A bowl filled with dark red roses stood on one of the little tables, scenting the big room. Although eight o'clock by summer time, it was still light and the lawn was bright in sunshine away from the long shadows flung by a row of blue cypresses.

"It's a wonderful evening," said Lady Kendrick, looking up from her book as she heard the General come in. "It makes one think that one might have a little summer."

The General did not pursue the subject of the weather. He gave a nervous cough before speaking to her.

"I say, Beatrice, I see you're going to address a public meeting on the problem of Peace in the village hall. Don't you think you might have consulted me about it before you put out those posters?"

She glanced at him and smiled.

"You've been up in town such a lot. Are we going to have a row, darling?"

"Not a row," he answered. "I hope I shall keep my temper, but I must say I'm annoyed—to put it mildly."

"Why?" asked Lady Kendrick. "It's going to be a very harmless meeting. It's to discuss the problem of Peace, to get the ideas of the village folk. Why does that annoy you, my dear?"

He was silent for a few seconds, but she noticed that his face was flushed slightly—an infallible sign of suppressed emotion, being a fair man who flushed very easily when put out about anything.

"It sounds harmless," he said, after that silence, "but your ideas are not harmless, Beatrice. They're darned dangerous. If they're put about they'll weaken the morale of this country. Your extreme pacifism is frightening and in my opinion deplorable. It's bad enough when you talk about it over the dining-table or in private company, but it's another thing when you call a public meeting to express such ideas."

"One must have the courage of one's convictions," said Lady Kendrick. "But haven't we argued this out before? Let's walk into the rose garden. Aren't those ramblers marvellous? I've never seen them quite so luxuriant. I suppose it's all the rain we've had."

She rose and held out her hand as though to lead him out, but he ignored the invitation.

"Beatrice, I must have this out with you. I want you to cancel that meeting. You can plead ill-health."

She looked at him with a kind of quiet defiance.

"I can't do that, my dear. I've hired the hall and advertised the meeting in the *Sussex Gazette*. Many of the village women tell me they're coming. I can't let them down. I can't show the white feather." She came close to him with smiling eyes and put her hands on his square shoulders. "Darling," she said, "do be generous. It's not going to do you any harm. I expect the audience will be mostly women, the simple souls from the Council houses, and the old cottages."

"It will get into the papers," the General said. "It will put my name into the mud. It will get as far as Sandhurst and cover Mervyn with ridicule. Think of Mervyn if you don't think of me."

He made a mistake in bringing in Mervyn's name. Her hands dropped from his shoulders and she put them to her breast.

"Don't you understand?" she said in a low voice—her 'cello voice as people called it. "Don't you see that I'm trying to save Mervyn and the lives of all the boys like him? Can't you see what's going to happen at the end of your rearmament plans? Hasn't it always happened before? The War to end War! Another generation of youth wiped out with our dear Mervyn among them. Do you think rearmament is going to bring Peace? Has it ever brought Peace? This time the War to end War will be the War to end civilization. Only the rags and tatters of men and women will crawl out of the ruins. You know that. You've told me so. In your own heart you believe it. Do you deny that?"

"I don't deny it," he said less harshly than he had spoken before.

He paced to the window and stared out at the garden, seeing nothing there of the rambler roses or the beauty of this golden evening, or the long shadows creeping across the lawn.

Suddenly he turned and spoke huskily.

"I wish to God we hadn't this deep gulf of misunderstanding between us after long years of married life. Do you think I'm a blood-thirsty man? I have as much horror of war as you have. It's because the idea of it happening fills me with horror that I am doing what I am doing, and while I suffer anguish because of the frustrations and delays and spate of verbiage between those who ought to be getting on with the defence of the West. You say rearmament means war. I say it is the only safeguard of peace, or at least the only chance we have of survival. Don't you think I haven't the same love for our boy as you have, and for all young men like him? I write to him once a week. I think of him every day. If anything were to happen to him . . ."

His voice broke for a moment, and he turned away in deep emotion.

"My dear," said Lady Kendrick, "I know! Both of us would give up everything in the world for Mervyn's sake. Dear heart, I know that you're not one of the old fire-eaters who glorify war. But we differ hopelessly in our ideas how to prevent it. I'm for spiritual weapons and you're for steel and iron."

"If we rely on spiritual weapons alone," said the General, "we shall all be spirits above the ruin and death of Western Europe." He gave a kind of laughing groan. "What's the good of talking? All I can say, Beatrice, is that I wish to heaven you hadn't called that meeting. It's most embarrassing to me; it holds me up to public ridicule. It will cause a scandal in this village."

"Oh, they like a little scandal!" said Lady Kendrick. "It will give them something to talk about." She held out her hand again. "Let's walk round the rose garden."

The General shook his head.

"I must get on with my job," he said.

He walked out of the room and went into his study again.

CHAPTER XVIII

THE Peace Meeting in the village hall was well attended although rain was falling heavily before it began. As Lady Kendrick had anticipated, there were mostly women in the audience. They were the village women from the Council houses and cottages round about who had put their children to bed and walked through the rain and puddles on this dirty evening in late summer. Only a few men—gardeners and farm labourers—had come with their wives. A few local gentry, who knew Lady Kendrick and were curious to know what she had to say and how she would say it, had driven over in their cars or walked over from the old Stuart houses round the Green. Among them, in a front seat, sitting straight-backed and tight-lipped, was Miss Elizabeth Langtry. Next to her was Mrs. Montgomery-Jones, that sharp-tongued lady who was so observant of life and morals in Longmead. Half-way down the hall was Betty Donovan of Foxgloves. She sat next to Patricia Hastings, who had changed out of her riding kit and wore a green raincoat over a shabby frock. Her reddish hair without a hat flowed like bronze under the lights in the village hall. Dr. Paget was with his young wife, Viola, and their German maid, Hildegard. Several of the 'regulars' from Foxgloves, including the two elderly sisters, had driven down with Betty Donovan. At one end of the front row of seats was Rudi Scholl, the artist, who had resisted Lady Kendrick's wish that he should be on the platform. Far back in the hall, standing by one of the wooden pillars, was James Stewart, holding a battered and rain-soaked hat and wearing a mud-splashed raincoat over his corduroy trousers.

It was at twelve minutes past eight o'clock that the Vicar emerged from a little room behind the hall and mounted the platform, followed by Lady Kendrick, who took a chair at his right hand. The Rev. Gerald Langtry, who was received by a little clapping from some of the women, looked nervous as he took his seat behind a small table and fiddled about with some papers on it. According to an observation by Mrs. Montgomery-Jones after the meeting, he had 'blenched' when he caught the eyes of his sister, Elizabeth, in the front row.

Lady Kendrick was pale. She had not put on any artificial colour and her eyes looked very big and dark in a white face. She wore a simple black dress with a string of tiny pearls round her neck, and in the opinion of James Stewart, poet, as afterwards he told Hildegard, she had a tragic beauty like one of Euripides' Trojan women.

When Lady Kendrick appeared on the platform Dr. Paget said "Bravo!" in an audible voice, which she heard because she looked down to him and smiled. He may not have agreed with her views altogether—her extreme pacifism—but he admired courage, and with his kind heart guessed that this lady was facing a nervous ordeal of high tension.

It was obvious from the very beginning when the Vicar, as chairman, introduced Lady Kendrick with his own opening speech, that the subject of this meeting was of deep personal interest to most of those in the audience and especially to the wives and mothers. That was in some ways strange and unexpected, even by Dr. Paget, who knew the village as well as anyone. He remembered General Kendrick—not present in the hall—had spoken to him during a cricket match on the Green about the utter lack of anxiety and apprehension among the people in spite of the appalling menace which kept him awake at night.

There seemed to be no shadow on their minds, but here in this hall these women sat tense and silent and obviously emotional, as afterwards was revealed when some of them stood up to ask questions or give their own views. The ugly headlines in the newspapers, bits of talk and discussion reaching them over the wireless when they were doing their washing or their cooking, must have sunk into their minds, touching them with a fear which they had kept hidden perhaps even from their own consciousness. Now, at this meeting after Lady Kendrick's speech, it came out, showing their bewilderment, their deep yearning for peace, their hatred and horror of war.

The Vicar's introduction was well done. He alluded briefly

to his own experience as a military chaplain during the last war in North Africa and Italy. He had, of course, seen great heroism. He had marvelled at the high spirit and noble disdain of death by young men who had had no long innings of life. All that was unforgettable and in a way splendid. But as a padre, he had also seen and been very close and intimate with the tragedy and agony of war, the mutilation and blinding of boys who had not long left school; so young they were, and the death in the desert—in burning tanks, in crashed aeroplanes, under storms of shellfire and machine-gun bullets—of those boys who had come from English villages like this of Longmead. That last war, only five years gone, had not left the civilian population untouched. Here now in this village were men and women who had first come to Longmead as refugees from the blitz in London and other cities. They knew what it was to be bombed out of their little homes. They knew all about V1s and V2s. They had walked about the ruins beneath which their friends and relatives had been buried. There could be no false glorification of war in the modern mind. Weapons had become more and more destructive until with the atom bomb all human life in crowded cities was under the menace of annihilation. The next war, if it happened, would be beyond all present imagination in widespread death and destruction. In this meeting tonight, called by Lady Kendrick, they were going to discuss any possible way to prevent that next war, if there was a way by God's grace. Lady Kendrick would say something about the causes of war due to wrong thinking and evil thinking. The world had gone astray mentally and morally. That was the real cause of war. It was not 'inevitable' because thoughts could be changed and the heart of man could be changed, and politics could be changed. Ideals were stronger and sometimes more swift than jet bombs or guided missiles. Let us, as Christians—if we are Christians—look forward and work for the time when in the words of the prophet—"They shall beat their swords into plowshares and their spears into pruning hooks, when nation shall not lift sword against nation, neither shall they learn war any more."

He called upon Lady Kendrick to address the meeting.

There was a sound of clapping here and there, but for the most part the audience remained quiet and silent. Out of the silence came one clear word.

"Fiddlesticks!"

It was spoken by Miss Elizabeth Langtry.

Lady Kendrick rose from her chair and for a moment or two stood without speaking as though stricken dumb, either by intense nervousness or by emotion beyond words. The audience watched her curiously, struck no doubt by her other-worldly look with those big dark eyes in a dead white face.

Then she began to speak in a rather low voice with its 'cello-like tone, low but resonant and audible even at the back of the hall. She spoke very simply, almost too simply perhaps for a subject which was not at all simple, but somehow it held her audience because it was unaffected and deeply sincere. She began by saying that she had felt bound to call this meeting because of the world situation of which they all knew. They might think that a small village like Longmead with less than a thousand inhabitants could do nothing about the world situation and stood quite outside the issues of peace or war. But that was not so. If another war happened—it was happening in Korea—their sons would be in it and all of them would be in it. No village perhaps would escape next time, certainly no big town in England. The bombing in the last war would be nothing to the dreadful ordeal of the next, for new and more terrible weapons had been invented. So those who would have to sacrifice their sons, and those who would have to die, surely had a right to express their views, whatever they might be, on this menace which was coming close to them. She had called this meeting to get those views, to enable the women of Longmead to say openly what perhaps was hidden in their hearts or pushed away to the back of their minds.

They might think, she said, that their views were valueless and that they were quite helpless, like dumb animals driven to the slaughter-house against their will, but powerless to prevent their fate. They might think that the Government alone decides these things and the life or death of the people like Roman Caesars, who put thumbs down to the gladiators in the arena. But that was not so. No government, not even an autocratic or totalitarian government, could drive a nation to war if the mass of their people refused to march. Many would be shot, no doubt—they would be the martyrs—but their Government would have to yield or be overthrown.

So the people, even in a village like Longmead, were not utterly powerless. If they had enough passionate conviction on this or any other subject, they might light a flame which would spread to other souls in other villages and into the great cities, until this fire of people's passion would be burning and irresistible. That happened to some extent in a political election, but how much more intense should be this fire of passion, this fire of faith, on the question of peace or war!

She began to speak of the Korean war. In her opinion it was a tragic and ghastly error, which might lead to the Third World War. The United Nations by a great majority in the Assembly had condemned the act of aggression committed by the North Koreans in their attack against the South Koreans, and they were right in their condemnation. But had they been wise in resisting it by armed force?

At this question by Lady Kendrick there was an answer which rang out sharply and rather shrilly from a seat in the front row. It was the voice of Elizabeth Langtry.

"Yes! Certainly!"

"I am not of that opinion," said Lady Kendrick. "What is happening now in Korea? The American bombers are destroying the towns and hamlets of the South Koreans and spreading fire and destruction as they advance. Thousands of homeless refugees are fleeing from their fields and homesteads. It is all being done in the sacred name of justice and liberation, but the end of it is death and ruin and untold misery for those who are 'liberated'. Heaven forbid that we should ever be liberated in the same way! But that is not the worst. Who can say now what will happen when the American troops advance through North Korea to the Manchurian frontier? Over there is China, with four hundred million Chinese who do not like 'the foreign devils', as they call us and have the new watch-word of 'Asia for the Asiatics'. I pray to God——"

She hesitated and did not finish the sentence but passed to another part of her theme.

"War settles nothing. It leads only to new problems and new wars, with different enemies and different friends. That is its monstrous and ghastly absurdity. What has been the result of the last war into which we entered for the defence of Poland? We guaranteed Poland, as some of you may remember. Poland is now our enemy, or we think of it as such because it is behind the Iron Curtain and its Government obeys the dictates of Russia. We fought the Germans to the death, destroying their cities, demanding unconditional surrender, and then issuing orders of 'No fraternization' when the Allied armies occupied their country while the people lived in cellars and basements beneath the ruins. We rejoiced—I rejoiced with all of us—when the Russian armies smashed their way to Berlin, breaking through the German lines and advancing irresistibly week by week. The Russians were then our friends, we thought. But almost immediately after the war they became our enemies. They stand with enormous strength half-way through Europe and we are so afraid of them—there is fear on both sides—that we are now asking the Germans to enlist their man-power to defend or help to defend Western Europe against the Russians. That is a grisly result of the Second World War, which after five years seems to be leading to the Third World War. The Devil from whom all this evil springs might laugh at such a hellish joke—while the angels weep at the wickedness of men, or still more at man's stupidity."

"A little while ago," said Lady Kendrick presently, after another part of her speech, "I signed a document called the Peace Pledge."

"Shame!" cried Elizabeth Langtry in a rasping voice.

Lady Kendrick paused and looked towards the Vicar's sister and smiled at her.

"Someone—a friend of mine—cried shame," she said. "But I am not ashamed. I am told that it is really a disguise of Russian propaganda and that many of those who signed it are Communists or fellow-travellers. I am not a Communist, but I am willing to sign a peace pledge with anybody who professes peace, of whatever political or religious creed, with whatever sincerity or insincerity. If it is Russian propaganda, it may be a proof that the Russian people who knew the horrors of war have to be fed with peace propaganda. But if it is mere Communist trickery, let us have our own Crusade for Peace, not insincere but as a cry from our souls—a cry resounding not only in this country but throughout the Commonwealth and wherever the English language is spoken or understood. People say that we need no conversion to Peace in this country. That is true. But we need conversion to a higher and more spiritual consciousness of what we mean when we call ourselves Christians. That cannot include the use of the atom bomb which is now supposed to be our only safeguard against Russian attack. In my own heart and the hearts of all women it cannot include another war, even without the Atom bomb but with weapons of destruction terrible enough. We do not need conversion to Peace, but we need urgently an awakening—an awareness—to what is happening on the way to war. We are acquiescing in acts and policies which must lead to war unless we check them. We are accepting without protest, with a kind of dumb fatalism, the so-called inevitability of the next war. That to me is the most terrible thing—this quiet acceptance of the idea. We answer Russian abuse of us—very dreadful it is—by abuse of the Russians. We are now planning a great intensity of rearmament, which in itself is an acceptance by the British people that war is not far away. We are tied to the political mood and anger of the United States who have declared war on Communism wherever it may be found, regardless of the impossibility of killing Communism by gunfire. Not even the Americans have enough guns or men to fight the whole Communist world which now includes China. So we drift on towards world war which one day will be exploded by some incident or accident on either side. We live next to a powder magazine which may blow up the world and we watch the fuse creeping nearer and we stay dumb."

Lady Kendrick had spoken without any outward sign of emotion except by the tragic look in her eyes and the *timbre* of her voice. Now, after a pause, she came closer to the edge of the platform and looked down upon the rows of women—mostly women—and spoke to them with her hands clasped and a breaking voice.

"Dear women, and especially those of you who have children and perhaps sons old enough to be sent to war, I want you to do something on behalf of Peace, something if it is only a refusal from the depths of your souls to accept the idea of an inevitable war. We are only a small group here—inhabitants of an English village tucked away in Sussex—but your spirit may reach out to other villages and theirs in turn to great cities and theirs to other countries, until at last this spirit—these spiritual vibrations from the minds and hearts of women—may break through the Iron Curtain itself and reach out to the Russian people and let them know that all we ask from them is brotherhood and friendship. We must try to enrol all women everywhere—black women, yellow women, brown women—of all races and creeds. We have not much time perhaps, before our children are bombed and killed. We must be in a hurry. Hurry! Hurry, my dears! A little candle may light a great fire. Let us light that candle in the village hall tonight, and by its tiny flame set alight the soul of womanhood in England, inspire the courage of women, the love of women, the sacrifice of women, and their cry to God for Peace."

There was silence when she sat down and for a moment buried her face in her hands, her thin delicate hands. Then there was quiet applause and a murmur of talk. The Rev. Gerald Langtry rose from his chair and said: "Lady Kendrick will be glad to answer any questions or to hear any views. I'm sure we have all been deeply impressed by her beautiful ideals."

"Rubbish!" said his sister, in a clear, firm voice.

"Disgusting!" said Mrs. Montgomery-Jones.

One of the village women rose. It was Mrs. Longstaffe who lived in one of the 'pre-fabs' and had a family of four, the eldest of whom had just been called up. She had a Cockney accent, showing that she was no Sussex-born woman, and her face was flushed with shyness as she began to speak.

"I'm sure her ladyship has touched us all very deeply. This war talk has been going on a long time now. I'm the mother of four and my boy Tom has just been taken for the Army. I dream of him at nights, poor lamb. But what can we do about it? I'd like to ask her ladyship whether she thinks there's any use talking Peace to the Russians who are making trouble everywhere and don't seem to have any faith in God or any pity for human beings if what one reads in the papers isn't all lies."

There was a murmur of "Hear, hear!" from part of the audience and more than a murmur from the Vicar's sister.

Lady Kendrick answered the woman by name.

"I'm glad you ask that question, Mrs. Longstaffe, and I can only say that in my belief we ought to go on talking Peace to the Russians. At this very moment they are conducting a Peace Campaign. People say it is insincere, but surely we might put it to the test instead of sneering at it and ridiculing it. Our own Government ought to take the lead in calling a Peace Conference of all the powers. Even if it failed with the Men in the Kremlin, it would prove to the Russian people that we are not warmongers preparing to attack them."

Another village woman rose from her seat and spoke rather angrily.

"What are the Churches doing? Why don't they preach the gospel of Christ instead of supporting any war which happens to come along? That's what I want to know."

Lady Kendrick answered again.

"I agree with you, my dear. I think the Christian Churches have failed in their spiritual leadership by not combining to denounce war as mass-murder and the greatest betrayal of Christ's gospel. I don't know whether our Vicar would like to speak a few words on that point."

The Rev. Gerald Langtry rose reluctantly, looking embarrassed and uneasy.

"As chairman of this meeting," he said, "I had hoped to avoid any expression of my own views. I cannot go as far as Lady Kendrick in denouncing every war as criminal murder, though I am whole-heartedly in favour of a Peace campaign and abhor the tragedy and horror of war. But I suppose a nation has the right to defend the life of the people against unprovoked attack——"

Lady Kendrick interrupted him with a smiling question.

"Isn't that hedging, Vicar? Isn't it letting us down?"

"Answer the question," shouted a man's voice from the back seats. "Haven't the Churches betrayed their Master?"

The Vicar was silent for a moment. Then he spoke in a straight-forward way, honestly.

"I can hardly deny that. The history of the religious wars is lamentable. In the First World War—and the Second—national churches prayed for the victory of their own side and assumed that God favoured their own cause. Now, however, I believe that Christendom is anxious to unite, and is indeed uniting to challenge the powers of Evil which threaten to destroy civilization."

There was a harsh laugh from the back seats and a man's voice shouted a question.

"Isn't that another religious war? Communism against Capitalism?"

A sturdy-looking man who was known to everybody in Longmead as the village blacksmith rose to his feet and grasping the back of a chair gave a gruff, good-natured laugh before speaking in a loud voice.

"I'm not one who wants war, but I don't see as how we can prevent it. Not by soft words. Not by signing peace pledges. Not by a meeting like this, mainly made up of women folk—and God bless 'em. But what I think is that man is a fighting animal. He'll fight for his wife and kids the same as orang-outangs. He'll fight for his bit of earth. He'll fight for his own side—right or wrong—if it's attacked by some damn' fellows who want his land or his trade. Now those Roosians seem to want to lord it over the rest of the world. They've got to be stopped, haven't they? If any of 'em come to Longmead I shall have a go at 'em with my blacksmith's hammer, dang me if I don't!"

There was a gust of laughter from the audience as he sat down, but Lady Kendrick took up his challenge.

"Now, John Wimshurst! We can't let you get away with that, you know! It sounds very brave and fine but it's just the point of view we want to avoid. What do you think would happen if you killed a Russian in Longmead with your big hammer? The village would be burned to the ground. The women and children would be massacred. Would that seem very good to you? Wouldn't it be better to prevent the Russians coming to Longmead or to England by making a friendly Peace with them before they come?"

"You can't do it, lady!" shouted John Wimshurst.

"Then if we can't do it," said Lady Kendrick, "the things we love will be destroyed. This England of ours will be laid in dust and ashes, by atom bombs and rocket bombs."

"Better that, my lady, than show the white feather," shouted John, the blacksmith, sturdily.

"Now, John Wimshurst," cried a young woman, "you go back to your bellows and make the sparks fly. You've as much sense in your head as Mrs. Widdershaw's donkey, and perhaps not so much!"

She turned towards the platform and spoke to Lady Kendrick.

"Don't you listen to John Wimshurst, my lady. Every woman in this room is grateful to you for arranging this meeting. It's we women who will have to suffer most if another war comes; suffering in our minds and hearts I mean, as well as in our bodies. Didn't we half starve during the last war, queuing up for food which wasn't there—not for ourselves, but for the men and the kids, or the kids without the men? Didn't we weep our eyes out when there was a knock at the front door with a telegram to say our fathers or brothers or sweethearts had been killed. Died on the field of honour they called it. The field of honour! Not much comfort in that for a girl who lost her best boy or a married woman left alone in the world with two kids and one coming. If you can show us any way to work for Peace we'll follow your lead, even if we have to go barefoot from Longmead to Land's End."

The loud applause from many women which rewarded this speech revealed the emotion which had been hidden in the hearts of these women and now found expression at this meeting. Several other women rose and made little speeches timidly, with flushed faces and shining eyes. They wanted Peace beyond all things—the word Peace came like a prayer to their lips.

Suddenly Miss Elizabeth Langtry rose and her rather high, strident voice rang out through the hall.

"I have no patience with all this," she said. "I have listened to Lady Kendrick's speech with astonishment and disgust and I am ashamed that my own brother, the Vicar of this parish, should be presiding over this orgy of nonsense and disloyalty. Lady Kendrick dared—yes dared—to suggest that the people of this country, the women of England, should overthrow their own Government rather than support its policy of rearmament."

"No, no," said a quiet voice, which was that of Dr. Paget.

Miss Langtry turned to glare at him.

"I say yes. It was a plain incitement to revolt and the whole tenor of her speech, her most disgraceful speech, was to tempt these women—our poor simple village women—to throw themselves into the arms of Communist Russia and allow this country to be occupied by those Mongols and murderers."

"No, no," cried several women angrily. "Sit down."

"Chuck the old cat out!" said one of the younger women.

There was no need to use physical force against Miss Elizabeth Langtry. She poked about under her chair for a pair of gloves, then rose and walked out of the meeting with her head held high and tight lips, and a short umbrella grasped like a field-marshal's baton. She was followed by Mrs. Montgomery-Jones who had warmly applauded her remarks with many noddings of the head and loud clapping of her gloved hands.

The Vicar watched the departure of his sister with much relief. It had been exceedingly embarrassing to him to see her there in the centre of the first row of seats. During Lady Kendrick's speech he had seen Elizabeth's face flush with anger and her eyes flash fire with suppressed rage. 'She's certain to make a row at question time,' he had thought. She certainly had not spared him in front of his parishioners. Now and then his sense of humour had come to his rescue. 'I asked for it,' he thought, 'and now I've got it. Elizabeth has the spirit of Queen Bess combined with that of Bloody Mary.'

As chairman looking at the audience, he was able to study the faces of the people here—the women listening with intense interest and emotion to Lady Kendrick's address, with now and then a whispered word to one another, or with the nudge of an elbow. That old blacksmith sat with a grin on his tanned and weathered face, contemptuous of all this peace talk. At the back of the hall James Stewart, the poet, stood motionless against one of the wooden pillars, curiously like John the Baptist in a dirty raincoat, because of his beard and moustache and tousled hair. One interesting face, thought the Vicar, was that of the young Austrian artist, Rudi Scholl, obviously foreign in the midst of these English types—thin featured with sharp cheek bones and deep set eyes, with a lock of dark brown hair falling over his narrow forehead. He sat listening to Lady Kendrick with a queer smile, as though secretly amused by her speech, amused and cynical. Perhaps he knew the weakness of this plea for a spiritual defence against war, the pitiful and pathetic weakness of it. As the Vicar listened to Lady Kendrick he was gradually and painfully overwhelmed by scepticism and doubt.

As a Christian, a priest of the Anglican church, he agreed with her—how could he disagree?—that war was a frightful contradiction of Christian faith and teaching and that the fundamental cause of war was evil thinking and bestiality—the lust of power by devilish minds, hatred and intolerence and racial rivalries. All that could not be defeated by guns or bombing aeroplanes, but only by raising the minds of men to a higher standard of morality. He was the last man to deny spiritual ideals but such ideals were only held now by a tiny minority of civilized minds surrounded by a sea of barbarism and brutality. What was the use of this simple plea to womanhood by Lady Kendrick? Could it possibly check for a single instant the enormous forces of evil seething in the modern world? Could it change the minds of those men in the Kremlin plotting to spread their creed and rule in every part of the globe? Was it not childish and unrealistic? Perhaps he had been a fool to take the chair tonight. Down there was Elizabeth with all her claws out. This meeting might put him into an awful mess with many of his parishioners. He had yielded weakly to Lady Kendrick's persuasion partly out of good nature, partly because she had made him uneasy in his conscience as a preacher of the Christian doctrine. . . . Elizabeth would make life intolerable for him at home. Mrs. Montgomery-Jones down there—a wicked old cat—would spread scandal about him through the village.

These thoughts passed through the Vicar's mind as he sat listening to Lady Kendrick's address. Several times they made him lose the thread of her discourse. Now he would have to pull himself together. He would have to look bright and alert. He would have to express faith in the spiritual plea she had made.

He rose from his chair and leaned forward with a smile, with his hand on the table in front of him.

Any more questions?

There were no more questions. The village women were whispering among themselves. Dr. Paget was grabbing for his hat which he had placed under his chair. That pretty young wife of his was waggling two fingers at Patricia Hastings.

"Well, ladies and gentlemen, it only remains for me as chairman to propose a vote of thanks to Lady Kendrick for her most beautiful and thought-provoking address. I am sure we shall all go away thinking more deeply of the grave problem which faces us in the world today, casting a shadow over our minds and hearts. It has all been very moving and I for one feel uplifted by the spiritual ideals . . ."

After the meeting a number of village women crowded round Lady Kendrick to have a few words with her when she came down from the platform. One old woman with a face like a Normandy pippin and very bright blue eyes, took both her hands and kissed them.

"God bless you, dearie," she said. "It was nice listening to you and you said it lovely. But it's no good for us females. We can't do nought about it. It's men who makes the wars and men are just hopeless. No sense in their heads and no religion in their hearts. In my judgment, dearie, the Devil has been let loose in this wicked world and we're all going to be destroyed by the atom bomb which is one of his toys. But it's no use worrying, dearie, if it's God's will."

Outside the hall the rain was pelting down and the puddles had turned into small ponds.

CHAPTER XIX

THIS Peace meeting at Longmead was the cause of much discussion in the village, reaching out to neighbouring villages here and there because of a fairly full report in the Sussex papers.

The Vicar of Longmead came in for a great deal of criticism, not only at his own breakfast-table, tea-table and dinner-table where he could not avoid a running fight with Elizabeth Langtry, but from some of his most influential parishioners, such as Colonel Martinshaw-Sneed, who had always subscribed to the church funds very handsomely, and Mrs. Gladwyn-Wycherley, aunt of the Earl of Hardingley, who were among the members of his congregation whom he could hardly afford to offend. But they were very deeply offended. The Colonel—an upstanding old gentleman whose memories went back to the Boer War—walked down from the Manor House one afternoon to call at the Vicarage and register disapproval.

"My dear fellow," he said, when he was shown into the Vicar's study, "well do I know your difficulties in trying to keep on the right side of your congregation and trying to please everybody. But you allowed yourself to be trapped by that extraordinary woman, Lady Kendrick, into taking the chair for her at that preposterous meeting. Deplorable! She advocated complete pacifism—non-resistance—and surrender to Communism. I was staggered when I read the report."

"It was quite harmless, Colonel," said the Vicar, with a laugh. "Just a public affirmation of Christian principles. I don't regret having taken the chair."

Colonel Martinshaw-Sneed, getting on for eighty, had a spasm of coughing almost as though this answer had choked him. Having recovered, he thumped himself on the chest and spoke angrily.

"Damn it, Vicar, don't talk nonsense like that. Christian principles? I hope I'm a God-fearing man, but I can't stand for the unadulterated rubbish talked by pacifists, Communists and fellow-travellers. Christian principles tell me that we have to fight the powers of Evil."

"Not by the weapons of Evil," said the Vicar.

"By any weapons," answered the old soldier. "The atom bomb, if necessary. How do you think we defeated the Boers? Not by sprinkling rose-water on 'em. My God, sir, I ought to know! I was a young gunner in the relief of Ladysmith."

The Vicar refrained from saying that most intelligent people now regard the Boer War as a somewhat discreditable episode in the story of the British Empire and that having defeated the Boers at great cost to ourselves, we had given them back their independence, thereby making friends of those who had been our enemies. In logic and common sense, to say nothing of Christian principles, it would have been better if we had not fought them.

"I don't want to argue with you, Colonel," answered the Vicar, mildly. "I am very grateful for all you have done in the parish."

Colonel Martinshaw-Sneed wheezed noisily and spoke again after taking a deep breath.

"I warn you, Vicar, that I may do less in future. I may have to alter my Will. I've a damn' good mind to do so. I intended to leave a bit to build the new vestry, but if you're in with that woman, Lady Kendrick, I shall have to reconsider it. Does she want us to be over-run by those infernal Russians? What we need now is not less but more guns—not disarmament but rearmament. God, of course, is on our side—as always. But God won't be mocked. Isn't that good scripture? He would be mocked if we let the Devil ride rough-shod over us or if we failed to defend ourselves. Don't you agree, sir? How the devil can you disagree? Weren't you a padre in North Africa? Didn't I help to appoint you to this living because you had a good record with the Eighth Army as General Kendrick told me. General Kendrick! Bless my soul, what does he think of that demented wife of his?"

He had another spasm of coughing and afterwards thumped his chest heavily.

"My dear Colonel," said the Vicar, "it's my duty as an Anglican priest to preach the gospel of peace. I won't say peace at any price—I'm not a complete pacifist. That perhaps is because I'm a poor Christian and don't aspire to a martyr's crown. That needs more courage than I have, alas!"

The Colonel rose, steadying himself on his stick.

"You're a young man," he said, "and I'm an old one. I won't bandy words with you, sir. If I let go of my temper I may have a stroke or something. Good day, sir. And if you want a new vestry don't expect me to pay for it. In future I shall attend the church in Mirfield."

A painful interview. An unfortunate incident. The Vicar of Longmead had counted on getting the old man to put up the money for the new vestry.

His talk with Mrs. Gladwyn-Wycherley was even more unpleasant. She was driven up to the vicarage in her very old Vauxhall of 1924 and was shown into his study by the woman who came for a few hours each day. He was writing his Sunday sermon and in a most unchristian way said, "Drat the old woman!" under his breath when her name was announced.

She was a very thin and sharp-featured old lady who always reminded him of the witch in the pictures to *Grimm's Fairy Tales*, which he had had as a boy, though he had to admit that she was a generous old soul in many ways and belonged to the old Quality as it used to be called. In her veins, probably suffering from hardening of the arteries, was the blood of the Plantagenets, though now she lived in the old Dower House with only one maid and a chauffeur-gardener.

"Vicar," she said immediately on entering, "you're a disgrace to the parish!"

'What have I been doing to disgrace myself?" he asked with a good-natured laugh.

"What's that?" she asked. "Wait till I've put my ear-aid on. What's that you said? You admit making a fool of yourself?"

"I'm always making a fool of myself," he told her. "I don't get wiser as I grow older. Do you?"

For a moment there was a glint of humour in her eyes.

"To be honest I can't say that I do. There's no fool like an old fool. I admit that. But there are degrees in foolishness. I haven't quite lost my wits yet, and I'm certainly not going to be taken in by Peace propaganda organized by Russian Communists to dupe sentimental imbeciles."

The Vicar groaned slightly.

"I imagine you are alluding to that Peace Meeting."

"I am!" said Mrs. Gladwyn-Wycherley, "and it will take you some time to live it down, if you ever do. That woman Beatrice Kendrick ought to be scragged."

"My sister Elizabeth agrees with you," said the Vicar.

"Very sensible of her. I'm glad insanity doesn't run in the family. What made you take the chair for that ridiculous and disloyal piece of elongated ectoplasm? She advocates non-resistance to Russian Communism. She asks us to hold out our hands in brotherly love to those murderers and torturers. She must have gone mad. I'm deeply sorry for dear old Bill Kendrick—a fine soldier and a nice fellow. But that's beside the point."

The Vicar gave a heavy sigh, glancing at the manuscript on his desk—that unfinished sermon.

"What is the point, dear lady?" he asked, in a tired voice.

The old lady tapped the end of her stick on the floor.

"It's a pretty sharp point, Vicar. You're under suspicion of being a Communist. We don't stand for that kind of thing in Longmead. I don't stand for it. I warn you that my purse will shut up with a snap as far as this parish is concerned if you don't take steps to prove your loyalty."

The Vicar smiled at this fierce old woman who had been very generous with her subscriptions to the church funds.

"I have no sympathy whatever with Russian Communism," he assured her. "I detest its cruelties. I loathe its intolerance. But as Christians—if we are Christians—we are bound to pray and work for Peace. Didn't our Lord say blessed are the peacemakers?"

"Not Peace by appeasement with devils and demons," said the old lady. "Not Peace by surrender to those maniacs in the Kremlin. Not Peace by undermining the old loyalties to King and country. That woman, Beatrice Kendrick, is a female

Quisling. She ought to be put into Holloway. Unless you break with her, Vicar, you break with me, and you'll get broken yourself, my man. I'll see to that. The Bishop happens to be my second cousin once removed. He's a Gladwyn-Wycherley on his mother's side. That's to say he has guts and upholds the old traditions."

The Rev. Gerald Langtry lost his temper for a moment. His nerves were badly ruffled by this interruption of his Sunday sermon, and by this argument with hostile critics.

"Blast it!" he exclaimed. "Don't you think I have a few guts myself? I'm Vicar of this parish and I decline to be insulted by a pack of malignant old women. Kindly leave me to get on with my work."

"Don't you go damning and blasting me, young man!" said Mrs. Gladwyn-Wycherley. "For two pins I'd use my stick on you."

"I'm sorry," said the Vicar, filled with remorse for this sudden rage.

"You'll be more sorry later on," answered the old lady. "I shall write to the Bishop today. I shall ask him to shift you into some slum parish where your choice of language will be more appreciated. Billingsgate, perhaps."

She rose with great dignity, a tall and formidable old woman with a back as straight as a poker. She was remarkably like that picture of the witch in *Grimm's Fairy Tales* which he had had as a boy.

"I'll forgive the blasting and damning," she said, "but not that reference to malignant old women. That signs your death warrant as far as Longmead is concerned."

"I apologize," said the Vicar. "I deeply regret——"

He opened the study door for her and then the front door. Without another word she got into her car and gave a direction to her gardener-chauffeur, who touched his cap to the Vicar.

"Mrs. Montgomery-Jones, please, Charles."

"Yes, ma'am."

The Vicar returned to his study and his sermon. He gave a short harsh laugh to himself.

"That's torn it!" he said, in the language of the Eighth Army.

It was difficult to get back to his sermon.

The Peace Meeting had repercussions, favourable and unfavourable, in the Black Knight on the other side of the Green. Some of the men who came in for a pint of beer after their day's work discussed it among themselves.

"My missus went to the meeting," said William Rusty, one of the farm hands on the Earl of Hardingley's estate. "I'm all in favour of Peace myself. I've been through two world wars and I don't want to see another. Most of my pals were killed on the Somme. And what came out of it? The War to end War they called it. War is all blood and bunkum for the men who fight and die."

"That's God's truth," said Harry Farren, gardener to Colonel Martinshaw-Sneed. "But as far as I can see there's no getting out of it. One war leads to another. The Russians wopped the Germans, now they've come too far and we want the Germans to join us in pushing 'em back. The Americans knocked hell out of the Japs and now the Chinks are coming into the picture—four hundred million of them. What's going to be the end of that?"

"I'm on the reserve," said Sam Stanstead, the village postman, "but if they call me up again, I'm not hearing it. I'll be deaf in both ears. I'd rather do a stretch in Dartmoor."

Bill Hurley, the landlord of the Black Knight, leaning forward with his elbows on the bar, gave a hoarse chuckle.

"You boys make me laugh," he said. "You shoot a lot of stuff out of your mouths and it means nothing. Of course we all want Peace, but at what price? Are you going to let those Oriental barstards from Russia come marching through the sunny fields of Kent without opposition? I can see you letting 'em, with your wives and kids waiting to have their throats cut and their little houses burnt over their corpses. Not on your life! Peace? Yes, that's all right. No man in his senses wants war. But not the peace of death. Sam Stanstead, my lad, if you're called up you'll go, and you know it."

"It's the politicians that make war," said a young fellow by name of Tuckwell who worked in the garage up the street. "Why in hell can't they talk reasonable to Stalin and his lot?"

"Talk reasonable?" asked the landlord of the Black Knight, who had been in the Royal Navy, as witnessed by the blue anchor and a red serpent tattooed on his right forearm. "How can you talk reasonable with men like Molotov? Their brains don't let in the light of reason, my child. It's shut out by the Iron Curtain."

"Politicians!" said young Tuckwell. "They're playing the same game as ours—catch-as-catch-can. In my belief the Russian people are as human as ourselves. They want Peace the same as ourselves. They have their wives and kids, the same as us. It's the people on top who makes the trouble. Out for power, I expect."

A thin cadaverous young man in a tattered raincoat broke into the argument.

"Tuckwell's right in my opinion. Power and glory is the cause of war. Look at the Americans. What are they invading Korea for? Why are they declaring war on Communism? Because they're drunk with the pride of their own power. There's quite a bit to be said for Communism—theoretically."

"Not in this pub, Larkin," said the landlord of the Black Knight. "If anyone puts in a word for Communism I'll chuck him out and give him a kick in the pants. We don't want any of your Daily Bilge in here, my lad."

There was a chorus of laughter from the other men.

"That's right!" said Harry Farren, the gardener. "I've no use for them Reds nor for the Tories neither. What we want back is the old Liberal Party."

"Dead as mutton," said Bill Hurley, the landlord.

"Now I'm asking you," said young Tuckwell, "what are we doing in Korea?"

"Resisting aggression," answered the landlord. "Isn't that a good enough answer?"

"Aggression, my foot!" said young Tuckwell.

The landlord of the Black Knight glared at him.

"Keep a civil tongue in your head," he said fiercely.

Sam Stanstead put another question.

"What do any of us care about the South Koreans, or for that matter the North Koreans? That's what I'd like to know. Why should this village of Longmead be laid in dust and ashes because the Yanks are marching to Chu-Chin-Chow and Ma Jong? I don't see no sense in it."

"You wouldn't!" said Bill Hurley. "You haven't enough sense to see any sense in it. If you'd been in the Navy you'd know that what happens in Hong Kong or Singapore or Port Said or Gibraltar, is pretty important to life in Longmead. You'd all starve to death if it wasn't that the Navy keeps the sea routes open."

"Granted," said Stanstead, "but submarines is submarines, if you see what I mean."

"What the hell do you mean?" asked Hurley.

"I mean that war means sunk ships and empty bellies and shortage, and more rationing and starvation next time for the wife and kids. Say what you like, but I'm against war."

"You're against war, are you?" exclaimed Hurley with his big husky laugh. "Maybe you're against thunderstorms and typhoons and volcanic eruptions and Mother Nature herself!"

There was another gust of laughter from the other men who appreciated the humour as well as the beer of Hurley, the landlord.

"We've left out something from this argument," said a little man with sad eyes, who had been listening without taking part in the discussion. It was Mark Verity, the grave-digger, whose profession seemed to have cast a shadow over his mind and soaked him in melancholy.

"What's that?" asked one of the men.

"God," said the grave-digger.

There was a moment's silence. The men glanced at Mark Verity disapprovingly.

"This is a pub not a church," said young Tuckwell. "You haven't come to dig anybody's grave, have you?"

"God won't be mocked," said Verity. "If you leave out God you let in the Devil. That's what's the matter with the world. That's what makes wars. Wasn't that what the Vicar and Lady Kendrick was reminding you of? Aren't we Christians?"

The landlord of the Black Knight rebuked him mildly.

"Now, Verity, we all respect you as a man who digs a good grave when wanted, but keep that sort of talk out of this pub. Our friends come here for a drink and a game of darts and agreeable conversation. A church is a church and a pub is a pub and I won't allow any blasphemy in the Black Knight. Keep the name of God out of it."

"Hear, hear!" said several men.

"You can't keep God out of anything," said Verity. "Not even out of the Black Knight. Seeing as we call ourselves Christians——"

"I've told you, Verity," said the landlord sternly. "Religion is not discussed in this pub. Christianity is one thing and a game of darts is another. Likewise, beer and a cheerful sing-song. Leave religion out of it, my friend."

"Verity always tries to break our hearts," said Sam Stanstead. "He wants us to waller in misery before we gets into our coffins."

The door of the saloon bar opened and spirits which had been low rose again at the entrance of old Wimshurst, the blacksmith, who greeted the company cheerily.

"Good evening, all. What's the matter with 'ee? Expecting the atom bomb or the end of the world?"

"It's this peace talk," said the landlord. "It's got 'em down."

"And no wonder," said the old blacksmith with a wheezy laugh. "Her ladyship gave me a pain in the guts. Man is a fighting animal, as I told her. Be Christian, she said. Be English, I says to myself. Them early Christians were always fighting among themselves—weren't they?—from the time of Moses onwards. Yes, I'll have a pint, Bill Hurley, thank 'ee."

The balance of opinion in the Black Knight was against war, but doubtful about the possibility of Peace. The Vicar, they thought, was a good sort, and anyhow it was his job to talk in the way he did. Peace on earth, while there was a bloody mess in Korea. No doubt he had to be civil to Lady Kendrick. She was all right, too, in a way. She contributed regularly to the funds of the cricket club, to the football club and the Women's Institute.

CHAPTER XX

THERE was, of course, much comment and discussion on the subject of Lady Kendrick's Peace Meeting in many houses and cottages of Longmead. Mrs. Paget talked it over with the doctor that same night, when they sat up late with a pot of tea between them.

Viola felt rather excited about it, being half amused and half impressed by Lady Kendrick's speech and the discussion which had followed.

"I must say she has almost converted me into turning pacifist," she said. "What do you think, witch-doctor?"

Dr. Paget was putting on a pipe and answered after some deliberation.

"If you mean by pacifism complete non-resistance, I don't go as far as that. It would mean surrendering this country to Russian Communism and the N.K.V.D., or whatever they now call their secret police. There would be mass executions of all who disagree with Stalinism. There would be torture-chambers, concentration camps and slave labour. English children would be taught to betray their parents after being converted into pure little Communists. There would be no freedom of speech or freedom of thought. Loud-speakers would blare out the virtues of Father Stalin by day and night. Canterbury Cathedral would be turned into an exhibition of the Godless State."

"You're an old humbug!" said Viola. "You're a Mr. Facing-Both-Ways. You called out 'Bravo' when Lady Kendrick came on to the platform."

Dr. Paget smiled over his pipe.

"I admired her pluck, and anyhow she was suffering from stage fright. I thought a friendly hand might help."

"Old-time chivalry!" laughed Viola. "Much out of date now."

"Anyhow," said the doctor, "I'm on the side of the peace-makers. I agree with her a hundred per cent on that. If we can go on talking with Russia, let's go on talking. If they offer any concession let's take them up on it. Our trouble is that the Americans are so darned belligerent."

Viola gave a light laugh.

"I can't bring myself to believe that there's any reality in all this war talk. It freezes one's blood for a few minutes and then one puts it out of one's head. But wasn't Miss Elizabeth Langtry absolutely priceless? An old—well—lady dog of the bulldog breed. I'm sorry for the Vicar."

The doctor laughed and was much amused.

"Yes, he certainly asked for trouble in the vicarage."

Viola was thoughtful and silent for a few minutes. Then she spoke again.

"I expect Mervyn will be ragged at Sandhurst if his mother's speech is reported in the local papers."

"What's happened to that boy?" asked the doctor. "He hasn't turned up lately. Have you broken his heart yet?"

Viola blushed slightly, but answered lightly.

"Exams are keeping him away."

"Providential, perhaps," said the doctor chaffingly.

James Stewart had some serious talk with Hildegard about the Peace Meeting. It was when she took tea with him again—for the second time—at Foxgloves. That was two days after the meeting in the village hall. It was unfortunate that Mrs. Montgomery-Jones happened to be walking past the gate of that guest house with the Alsatian upon whom she lavished most of her love. It seemed to her darkly suspicious that this German girl—Dr. Paget's help—should be walking as bold as brass in broad daylight into this haunt of vice. It seemed to her more darkly suspicious when James Stewart who, she understood, wrote highly immoral poetry, came to meet the girl down the path and called out 'Hullo!' Patriotic Englishmen would not, she thought, call out 'Hullo!' to a German girl who was nothing more than a domestic servant.

After that greeting, Stewart led Hildegard into the big tea lounge where a few of the 'regulars' were already seated at the little tables. They looked at this young man and woman with the natural envy of old-age for youth, sometimes resulting in suspicions and gossip.

"I saw you at the Peace Meeting," said Hildegard.

James Stewart nodded.

"I found it curiously dramatic and emotional—a scene out of one of Hardy's novels. Those village women were good types. What did you think of it all?"

"I do not think I dare to tell you," answered Hildegard. "My thoughts are very dark."

James Stewart smiled faintly and made an irrelevant remark.

"Have a crumpet, won't you? Let's eat and be merry because tomorrow——"

"I feel a pity for England," said Hildegard. "The English people do not understand. In Germany we understand. There is nothing we have not suffered. There is nothing we have to hope. So we look at life with understanding and what you call stark, that is to say, without illusion."

She poured out two cups of tea from a pot brought to her by Betty Donovan, who smiled at her in a friendly way.

"I like a little illusion," said James Stewart, "but I'm willing to hear what the German people think they understand. It's probably all wrong. They've been wrong now and again."

"It is like this," said Hildegard, cutting off a small piece of buttered crumpet. "It is the end of Europe. It is the end of European civilization. There was a book written by Spengler called *The Decline of the West.*"

James Stewart nodded.

"Not an enlivening book," he said.

"It comes all true," said Hildegard. "The East arrives. The West declines. The last of Europe is a small peninsular with a great hinterland of Asia inhabited by hundreds of millions of Asiatics. They are moving. Russia is their vanguard—is it not what you call a vanguard? Behind them are the Chinese. In a little while they will fly like locusts over Europe. They will march like vermin to the Channel coast. They will swarm like rats across the narrow sea round England. There will be Mongols in the village of Longmead. They will park their armoured cars in St. Paul's and Westminster Abbey. Shall I pour you out another cup of tea?"

"Please do," said James Stewart. "Will there be time for me to drink it before the Mongols come?"

Hildegard looked at him sharply and saw the glint in his eyes.

"You laugh at me," she said in a low voice. "You mock at me."

"I haven't laughed," he told her. "But it's best to laugh. Boccaccio's merry tales were told by a company in the time of Plague. One may as well die a-laughing."

"Will you please talk seriously?" asked Hildegard. "Please do not treat me as a little schoolgirl."

For some extraordinary reason there were tears in her eyes which she tried to blink away.

James Stewart perceived this and spoke good-naturedly.

"My dear girl, I have quite a respect for your intelligence. But one has to shelter one's soul in this brutal world by a shield of mockery. Otherwise one would not have the courage to go on with one's job as a poet or a plough boy."

He fell into one of his deep silences which the German girl respected and did not interrupt.

It was after a third cup of tea that he spoke again.

"There have been some very dark periods in human history. Probably you've read more about them than I have. The Black Death. The Thirty Years' War. To those living then it must have looked like the end of all things; the annihilation of civilization; the extermination of the human race. But man survived. Perhaps it would have been better if he hadn't survived. But the spirit of the poor devil is unconquerable. He begins all over again. He starts building up again. Somehow he hangs on to the remnants of some sort of civilization. He goes on—learning, creating, producing. A few poets appear again. They reconcile him with life. They reveal beauty. They give him another dream. He interprets the Voice of God to them. They promise him immortality and some reward hereafter for all his suffering here and now. So he goes on. So he goes on."

"That is true," said Hildegard. "Man goes on but from

martyrdom to martyrdom and always beginning again to do what was done before."

James Stewart nodded.

"One must cling on to the spirit. That can't be annihilated. The beauty of the stars can't be wiped out even by tyrants. Perhaps it is possible to love even in Communist Russia. Such things are left to one—if one is lucky."

"Yes, it is lucky to be loved," said Hildegard with a deep sigh.

"One has to look for it," said James Stewart. "Sometimes it's not easy to find. There are lonely souls who never find it."

"I am so sorry for them!" cried Hildegard. "It is dreadful never to find one's love."

By the depth of her emotion her voice became raised. It reached a thin-lipped lady knitting a pullover after finishing her tea. She dropped her work on to her lap and looked over at Hildegard with raised eyebrows. She happened to be a friend of Mrs. Montgomery-Jones, to whom she reported this strange remark by the German girl which surely, she thought, was not in very good taste, to say the least of it.

In Foxgloves there had been already serious discussion of Lady Kendrick's meeting. It took place in the private sitting-room off the big lounge used by Donovan and his wife, and favoured friends of theirs like Patricia Hastings and occasionally, to Betty's annoyance, Rudi Scholl, who was not much favoured by her.

It was Betty Donovan who raised an argument by announcing in her blunt-spoken way that she had a jolly good mind to clear out of Foxgloves and hop it.

"Hop it why, and hop it where, mavoureen?" asked Donovan, pouring himself out two fingers of whisky.

"England is becoming too dangerous," said Betty. "Everybody thinks this war is going to happen. So why stay and be annihilated?"

"Ah, sure now," said Donovan, "it's mostly newspaper talk. That's why I do the football pools. Besides, where would one go as a refugee, my poor little rich girl?"

"Do you think the Russians would go as far as Ireland?"

asked Betty. "Are they as foolish as that? I expect they've read a bit of history. Anyhow, weren't the Irish neutral in the last war?"

"They were," said Donovan, "but that didn't prevent thousands of young Irishmen volunteering for service in the Army and Navy. But if this war happens, which God forbid, you'll have to stay and look after Foxgloves, for on the very first day I shall be recalled for active service."

"Then you'll come home to find me dead," said Betty. "And that for me would be the best way out."

There was a sudden silence and it was as though a ghost had walked.

"Don't let's be morbid," said Patricia Hastings. "If it hadn't been for that woman's Peace talk we shouldn't be giving a thought to war. It's all this talk that gets one down. Far better play a game of golf or get busy grooming a horse. Besides, she talked a lot of slush. Non-resistance, holding out the hand of brotherhood to those stone-headed Russians. It nearly made me sick."

"I thought her speech was very beautiful," said Rudi Scholl, who had come into the room after this discussion had started.

"You *would* think so, you little Bolshevik monkey!" said Patricia. "I expect you've been duping her by a lot of your lying propaganda."

Rudi Scholl looked at her reproachfully.

"If I didn't love you so much, dear lady," he said, "I should take offence."

"Yes," said Donovan good-naturedly. "You ought not to goad our little friend so much, Patricia. It's unkind. You haven't even the excuse of being his wife."

"Thank heaven for that!" exclaimed Patricia with a shrill laugh. "I can't think why I tolerate this little pavement artist."

Donovan gave a hearty laugh.

"You two people seem to make love by abusing each other. But coming back to this Peace talk, I must say I'm sorry for poor old General Kendrick—a very fine type of soldier and always very civil to me."

"Nothing much up here!" said Rudi Scholl, touching his forehead. "It's men like that—traditional and narrow-minded—who insist upon the necessity of war for the encouragement of heroic youth, ear-marked for the slaughter-house. What seems to me so wonderful is the spiritual vision of his lady wife."

"I'm always sceptical of spiritual vision," said Donovan. "Hitler was filled with spiritual vision. So was Oliver Cromwell who massacred the Irish in the name of the Lord."

"Lady Kendrick ought to be walloped," said Patricia Hastings, "and I believe you had a good deal to do with the nonsense she talked, my Rudi."

Rudi Scholl raised his hands with a gesture of hopelessness.

"My dear people," he said, "do you not admit—do you refuse to understand that every word spoken by Lady Kendrick, who has been good enough to give me her friendship, was to save the youth of the world from annihilation? My good friend Donovan here knows as well as anyone that there is no defence in the West against the overwhelming strength of Russia who have only to put on their boots for a parade march to the Channel coast. Who is going to stop them? Not the Germans shivering in the midst of their ruins. Not the French, who are forty per cent Communist. Not the Italians, who are too civilized to fight. You bank upon the Americans, but they will arrive only in time to hear the death rattle of European civilization. What, then, is the most sensible way of avoiding that calamity? To offer friendship and goodwill to the Russians. To make an amicable arrangement with them, to allay their fear of being encircled and attacked; to break down the Iron Curtain not by guns or atom bombs but by the overwhelming emotion of peace-loving peoples, going forward with outstretched hands and a burning fire of love and comradeship in their hearts. I speak with sincerity and emotion, having been so much a victim of war's insanity."

There was silence after this outburst for a second or two. It was broken by a squeal of laughter from Patricia Hastings.

"Our little Rudi," she cried, "almost believes in his own eloquence which he knows to be sheer hypocrisy and filthy nonsense."

"For once," said Rudi, "I am sincere. For once I speak without cynicism. It is because—I confess—I am terrified of another war. We sit here in comfort, in warmth, in our good companionship. We talk of war as though it were an intellectual argument without reality, or something far distant which may never happen. But I have a sensitive imagination. I have terror in the night. I have not your English phlegm nor your English disbelief in the things you do not wish to happen. But as a mid-European—you jeer at me for that—I have the historic consciousness of war's terror and tragedy, of enemy occupation, of shootings and hangings and massacres, and purges. At night in the silence of this English village, this sweet and peaceful village, I hear the tramp of armies, I hear the wild shouts of blood-intoxicated men, the screams of women and children. In the night sky so quiet now above us I hear the drone of bombing aeroplanes, Russian planes, thousands of them with parachute troops, with atom bombs. I hear the rush of rockets on their way to London and other English cities. I am haunted by this dreadful vision. I lie quaking in my bed. I want to scream out. I want to shout out: You fools, you English people without imagination, so calm and unperturbed, so unafraid! Will you not understand that these things are near to you while you do nothing but poke up Russia with gibes and insults? Can I not make you know that this plan of rearmament which seems to allay your anxieties—your little mild anxieties—is worthless and futile because Russia will not wait and in any case her armed strength will still be overwhelming. It is useless for you to prepare for war, for if war happens you will, in any case, be destroyed. You must prepare for peace instead of war, and for that you will have to make many concessions which the Americans call appeasement. I speak with sincerity. I give myself away—my fears, my terror, my cowardice, if you will call it so."

Again there was a silence. Patricia Hastings looked across to Rudi with a kind of smiling pity, as though at a little boy frightened in the dark. Betty stared at him with grave searching eyes, and once while he spoke gave a little shudder as though his fear had touched her own soul.

Donovan broke the silence by a laugh.

"Rudi," he said, not roughly, "you ought to see a doctor, my boy. You ought to call in old Paget. These night terrors of yours are due to an overheated imagination and disordered nerves."

"I have given myself away," said Rudi. "I was perhaps a fool. Forgive me."

He rose from his chair. His face was white and his eyes sombre. He pushed back the lock of hair which had fallen over his forehead and without another word left the room.

They waited until his footsteps had gone down the corridor outside.

"He's got the jim-jams," said Donovan.

Patricia Hastings gave a sceptical laugh.

"I believe it was all play-acting. It's like actors and actresses who shed real tears and feel tremendously emotional because of the words they speak, and then leave the stage and laugh at some silly joke in the wings. Rudi is incapable of sincerity."

"I believe he was sincere," said Betty. "He frightened me. He may be right. We may all be dead in a little while."

Donovan shrugged his shoulders and laughed again.

"One can only die once. And it's best to meet death with courage. Let's put all this stuff out of our minds. Betty, my beautiful one, don't look so distressed! Have a cherry brandy. Meanwhile I want to ask Patricia an impertinent question."

"Must you?" asked Patricia. "Well, I needn't answer it."

Donovan went to a cupboard and brought out a bottle of cherry brandy. There was a smile about his lips, as he poured out a dose for Betty, and then filled a little glass for Patricia.

"I'm not much of a psychologist," he said, "being a plain and simple sailor man, and I confess I'm baffled about your exact relationship with our little pavement artist. Do you detest him or are you in love with him? Do I know you well enough to ask for precise information on that point?"

Patricia laughed and a little colour crept into her face.

"A most impertinent question," she said, "but in view of all the free drinks you give me I feel bound to answer it. I detest him, but I'm in love with him."

"Most illuminating!" said Donovan. "An interesting psychological case."

"Rudi," said Patricia, "is a little liar, sometimes deceiving himself by his own lies, as he did tonight. He is a little thief —if the regulars leave packets of cigarettes lying about."

"Very pardonable," said Donovan good-naturedly. "Any other criminal instincts?"

"He has leanings towards Communism," said Patricia.

"A form of madness perhaps," said Donovan. "It seems to infect a lot of our semi-intellectuals. I'm in favour of summary execution. But why do you love this detestable fellow, my glamorous girl?"

"He appeals to my mothering instinct," said Patricia. "And he makes me laugh, and he has underneath it all a kind of sweetness, a kind of tenderness and pity for the tragedy of life. Also he is in a way romantic. He appeals to my simple girlish innocence."

She ended with a burst of laughter.

"Thanks for the explanation," said Donovan. "It seems to me very convincing. Certainly the human mind, I understand, is capable of hating and loving at the same time. I believe there's a technical word for it, but that escapes me. Have another cherry brandy, dear lady. I'm sorry for you, because Rudi will never afford to make an honest woman of you. Art is so very precarious."

Betty, his wife, rose with a vexed kind of laugh.

"I'm surrounded by lunatics!" she said. "The whole world is mad. Well, I'm off to bed. Good night."

CHAPTER XXI

MRS. PAGET was very pleased to see Mervyn again and just a little scared. Scared of herself just a little, and scared for his sake even a little more. Scared of herself? How silly that was at her age and as a happily married woman. Could anyone be so idiotic? But she had found herself wet-eyed one day like a silly schoolgirl because it had been so long without seeing Mervyn and because he had not written a line to her. Every morning she had expected a letter from him. Several times she had made a dash for the front door before breakfast at the sound of letters being put through the letter-box. Nothing from Sandhurst. She wondered if he were ill or if he had no more affection for her because she had pushed him off a little last time. It was when she found herself crying that she became a little scared of herself. 'Good heavens!' she thought. 'What's all this about? Why am I being so ridiculous? I thought I was perfectly sure of myself—an old woman like me! —well anyhow, old enough to have got over romantic passion and all that nonsense and perfectly loyal to my dear doctor who trusts me without a tremor of anxiety. "Be your age, kid!" as they say on the movies. Don't be a little ass, or a little slut, at your time of life, my dear!'

So she spoke to herself, within herself fighting against some temptation, some touch of fever in her blood, some yearning for forbidden fruit. She was ashamed of herself for even having such secret thoughts. She ridiculed herself for even dallying with the absurd dream of playing Juliet to Mervyn's Romeo—a middle-aged or almost middle-aged Juliet to a boy seven years younger than herself. It was some psychological disturbance, interfering with her common sense. Her old witch-doctor would understand if she confessed it to him, but of course she couldn't do that. There were things she had to hide even from him—just a few.

When one afternoon she heard Mervyn's well-known knock

at the door—a kind of tattoo on the knocker—her heart gave a little leap, but she restrained herself from going to the door and repeated that American catch-phrase to herself. 'Be your age, kid!'

Hildegard opened the door and showed Mervyn into the sitting-room.

"Mr. Mervyn, madam."

"Oh, hullo, Mervyn!" exclaimed Mrs. Paget in a perfectly normal voice. "I thought you were dead or something."

"Nothing like that," he answered with a laugh. "Final exams and an awful swot."

He waited until the door was shut and then came forward, hesitating, but with obvious eagerness. She knew that he wanted to kiss her or hoped for a kiss from her. Inside herself she said 'Better not!' and then seeing the yearning in his eyes leaned forward and kissed him.

"Thanks frightfully," he said, in a humble way.

"I thought you'd forgotten me," she told him. "Why haven't you written? It's two months since I've heard from you."

"I know," he answered, "it seems like two centuries. But I did write—reams, as a matter of fact."

"I never had them," she protested.

"No, I tore them up."

He laughed in an embarrassed way, as though wanting to hide some guilty secret.

"Why did you do that?" she asked. "I was longing to hear from you."

"I couldn't say what I wanted to," he said. "I wrote them late at night. In the cold light of day when I read them over they seemed rather—well, slushy. So I tore them into very small pieces and chucked them into the W.P.B."

"What a waste of fine prose!" exclaimed Viola. "Didn't you make carbon copies of them? They might come in handy for somebody else."

She spoke teasingly and felt more pleased with herself now. In the presence of this boy who had come into her dreams—she had dreamed about him quite a lot—she felt fairly sure of herself again. She could re-establish her mental attitude towards him—that of an elder sister.

"I knew you would pull my leg!" he said at this gibe. "I'm getting used to that operation."

"Not from me," answered Viola. "Not for two months, Mervyn."

He told her there had been a lot of leg-pulling at Sandhurst.

"It was the report of my mother's speech in the local rags which excited them. They read it aloud with roars of laughter. I'm now known as the Pacifist Warrior or the Conscientious Objector to Major-Generals."

"Yes," said Viola, "I thought you'd get into a spot of trouble about that."

"The extraordinary thing is," said Mervyn, "that some of the fellows rather agree with her—at any rate, as far as wanting to continue talks on a high level with Molotov and company. They're not at all anxious for World War Three. Not even one of our staff colonels who gives us hell from time to time. He admitted the other day that he thinks the Americans are a bit too belligerent. 'We mustn't have this war', he told me on the quiet. 'It would be the end of all things, and anyhow we're not ready for it'."

"That's interesting," said Viola.

Mervyn laughed.

"Oh lord, let's forget all that! I didn't come here to talk world politics or World War Three. How splendid to see you again! How lovely you're looking, Viola, if you don't mind my saying so."

He was looking at her with adoration in his smiling eyes.

"I don't mind your saying so," answered Mrs. Paget. "I like to hear you say so, though well do I know the limitations to my own loveliness. But we must avoid personal remarks. I hear the heavy footsteps of Hildegard who is bringing in tea."

"Must she?" asked Mervyn.

Further conversation of a personal kind was prevented when Hildegard brought in the tea things and according to habit, unless otherwise warned off, joined them at the tea-table greatly to the annoyance of Mervyn Kendrick, though being a polite young man he refrained from revealing it.

Mrs. Paget deliberately kept Hildegard lingering over the

tea-table. She had an uneasy feeling that Mervyn was in an emotional mood, dangerous for him and dangerous for her. He looked extraordinarily handsome because of his perfect physical fitness and because even in two months since last she had seen him, he seemed to have grown older—in his mind, in his look. But he could not disguise or hide the adoration in his eyes. She shirked being alone with him lest she should lose control of her own emotions, her own common sense.

"Do have another piece of cake, Hildegard," she said more than once.

"Oh, no, thank you," said Hildegard. "I have made a very good tea and I wish not to get too fat. Besides, I must go and wash up."

"Oh, leave that for a little while. Tell us about Germany."

Hildegard could never resist the temptation of talking about the woes of Germany. She stayed another twenty minutes while Mervyn crumbled a piece of bread, fidgeted with nervous hands, crossed and re-crossed his legs and once gave a heavy sigh. At last Hildegard left the room carrying out the tea-tray. Mervyn rose to open the door for her, and when he had shut it behind her, turned and took a deep breath and laughed.

"I thought she would never go, that young woman! Why did you keep her chattering like that?"

"Weren't you interested?" asked Mrs. Paget, smiling at him.

"Not much!" he answered. "She has wasted my precious time with you. Very soon I shall have to get back to Badgers. My mother is waiting for me."

"Oh, don't keep her waiting, poor dear!" exclaimed Mrs. Paget. "She doesn't see much of you now and you know how she worships you."

"Yes, I know, but I've come to see you. I wanted to ask you something."

"Is there anything I can do for you, sir?" she asked, smiling at him. She hoped to goodness he wasn't going to ask anything foolish.

He blushed very deeply and seemed to find it very difficult to ask that question.

"Viola," he said, in a low voice, "am I making an ass of myself if I think that you love me a bit?"

What could she say to that? How could she answer without hurting him too much?

"Quite a little bit," she told him laughingly.

"I mean really love," he said. "Body and soul and all that. That's how I love you. I want you to know."

Mrs. Paget felt herself get a little pale. This was going to be difficult. She would hate to hurt this boy. He looked so wistful, so timid, so—desperate.

"It's nice to be loved," she said, "especially by you, Mervyn. But don't love me too much. It might lead to trouble, you know. It might mess things up."

"How?" he asked. "Why?"

"It might spoil our friendship."

He was silent for a few moments. He sat there in front of her with his hands between his knees and a smile on his lips but a frown on his forehead.

"I want more than friendship," he told her. "It's no use pretending."

"I can't give you more, my dear," said Mrs. Paget. "I'm a married woman. I don't want to play the slut. Besides, Mervyn, you're too young to be worried about me or anyone. Wait a bit for some nice girl. There's heaps of time."

"I'm old enough to die," he answered, in a matter of fact way. "If I'm old enough to die, I'm old enough to love while the going's good."

"What do you mean?" asked Mrs. Paget, aghast at those words. "To die?"

"In Korea or somewhere," he said. "Lots of fellows younger than myself are being killed out there. And if there's a Third World War lots of us will have to die. So if we love each other now it's no use wasting time. Haven't we a right to get all the joy of life we can? It's a pity to miss it for ever."

"Mervyn!" cried Mrs. Paget. "I hate to hear you talk like that. It gives me the cold shivers."

"One has to face it," he said. "I've been thinking quite a lot about this kind of thing. I wrote it all in those letters which

I tore up. Viola, do you think you could leave everything for my sake—I mean cut out Mrs. Montgomery-Jones and village scandal and all that? We could go away together. I would chuck Sandhurst. We would live in a fairy-tale. We would go riding through the forest of Arden, if you know what I mean. Of course, it all depends whether you love me as I love you—beyond anything else in the world—beyond convention and tradition and ordinary morality. Our love would make all that seem trivial and unimportant."

For one moment Mrs. Paget, seven years older than this boy, forgot the difference of age between them. How wonderful it would be, she thought, to go riding with him beyond this dreary village of Longmead, this village of old people, into the fairy-tale of youth which he had imagined. They would love each other as boy and girl. She would hold his hand and walk with him through enchanted woods. They would lie together under the greenwood tree far beyond the observing eyes of Mrs. Montgomery-Jones and the knitting ladies of Longmead. It would be the supreme height of joy, the ecstasy of body and soul, the love-song of youth for which she had waited, which never she had known. So she was tempted for that one tick of time until she saw the madness of it and awakened to reality.

"Mervyn," she said, "you've got it all wrong. I can't love you like that. I'm loyal to my husband."

"He's old enough to be your father," said Mervyn in a low voice. "It's a sham marriage. He has no right to you."

"What makes you think that?" she asked. "Have I ever said so?"

"Only by laughing at him," said Mervyn. "Only by wanting to get away from all the old fogeys, including your old witch-doctor, as you call him."

"I am very fond of my old witch-doctor," said Mrs. Paget.

Mervyn raised his eyebrows and then gave an uneasy laugh.

"You think it necessary to be loyal? The ordinary convention!"

"Don't you?" asked Mrs. Paget. "I'm shocked at you. I thought you belonged to the old tradition. An officer and a gentleman and all that. Sandhurst!"

Secretly she was shocked at herself. She had had that moment of temptation. How could she blame this boy?

"I believe in the loyalties," he told her. "But supreme love is more spiritual than any ill-made marriage. One ought to be loyal to the higher loyalty, which is love itself."

"My dear," said Mrs. Paget, in a voice of distress. "I have an awful feeling that all this is my fault. If so, I ought to be flogged. I thought I had been careful with you. I thought I had enjoyed only a lovely friendship with you. Have I ever made love to you or let you believe that I loved you in a silly amorous way? If so I could kill myself."

"No," he said. "But when I looked into your eyes——" His voice broke and he cried out her name. "Viola! I want you. I can't go on without you."

Mrs. Paget went over to him and put her arms about him and laid her cheek against his.

"My poor Mervyn," she said. "I'm so sorry. I'm desperately sorry."

He gave a kind of sob.

"Forgive me," he said. "I've been a cad. I thought—I had a damn' silly idea. . . . Oh, Viola, I love you most frightfully."

"Go on loving me," she said. "But let us be sensible about it. Let's get back to our beautiful friendship. You can kiss me if you like. There's no harm in that, my dear. I'll try to comfort you. I'll try to make things easy for you. I mean you must help me a bit by respecting me as a married woman and all that. I don't want to be a little slut, you know. I want you to be my young knight, *sans peur et sans reproche*. That sounds slushy, as you call it, but one must be slushy sometimes. Mervyn, dear, don't cry!"

She felt the wetness of his tears on her face.

It was at this moment of tense emotion that the door opened and Dr. Paget came in. He looked at his wife and Mervyn for a second with raised eyebrows and a smile on his thin lips.

"Hullo, you young people," he said good-humouredly.

"Mervyn doesn't feel quite well," said Mrs. Paget, abandoning her embrace of the boy. "He's upset about something. It's my fault."

Mervyn's face was very white, but he looked Dr. Paget in the eyes.

"No," he said sharply. "That's untrue. I've been making love to your wife, Doctor. I've been making a cad of myself. I asked her to chuck you and come away with me. You may as well know."

"Thanks for telling me," said Dr. Paget quietly. "That's honest and I like honesty. I say, Viola, do you think Hildegard could get me a cup of tea. I feel in need of it."

"I'm afraid she's gone out," answered Mrs. Paget. "I'll make some tea for you."

"I'll be going," said Mervyn.

"No, don't go," said Dr. Paget. "Have a cigarette with me, my dear fellow."

"No thanks," said Mervyn coldly.

"Well, another time," said the doctor. He held out his hand and after a moment's hesitation, Mervyn took it rather limply, and blushed as he did so.

"Come and see Viola as often as you like," said the doctor. "She loves having you. Don't you, my dear?"

"Mervyn knows that," said Mrs. Paget.

For a moment Mervyn looked stupefied. He stared down at the carpet with a frown on his forehead.

"I told you I've been making love to her," he said, looking at the doctor again.

"That's all right," said Dr. Paget. "I've no objection. It doesn't do her any harm. I dare say she likes it."

"Well," said Mervyn. He hesitated. His face flushed, then he gave an uneasy laugh.

"I'm sorry for making such a damn' fool of myself," he said, looking at the carpet again.

"It does one good to make a damn' fool of oneself now and again," said Dr. Paget. "That's the way one learns. I'm constantly doing it myself. Well, if you must be going——"

"Good afternoon," said Mervyn.

"I'll see you out," said Mrs. Paget.

"Oh, no, please don't trouble."

She went to the door with him and in the hall raised both his hands and put them to her lips.

"Sorry, my dear," she said. "Be brave!"

"I'm done in," he told her. "It's the end of all dreams, I suppose."

"You have plenty of time for other dreams, my dear," she told him.

He went down the steps and she watched him turn in the courtyard and raise his hat. She kissed her hand to him, but he did not return that salute and went out of the gate with a white face and a beaten look.

When she came back, Dr. Paget smiled at her.

"I'm sorry for that boy," he said. "But he'll get over it. Twenty, isn't he? Not grown up yet. At twenty I fell desperately in love with my landlady's daughter in Pimlico."

"It's the first I've heard of it," said Mrs. Paget. Then she gave a little cry. "John, he wants me so badly! And I was tempted just for a little while. I love him very dearly."

"Of course," said Dr. Paget, smiling at her again. "To you he seems to personify the beauty of young manhood—a young Adonis."

"He wants me to go away with him," said Mrs. Paget.

"But you won't go," answered her husband. "You've a lot of sense in your head. You have a very thoughtful little mind, my dear, and you're no longer a child who believes in fairy-tales. What a foolish fairy-tale it would be if you went off with young Kendrick, a boy without money, without a career. How would you look his mother in the face? I'm not going to talk about morality in which I happen to believe. I'm just thinking of the awakening to reality which would come to you before you had been an hour away from Longmead. And you'd be conscience-stricken, thinking of me with no one to make me a cup of tea when Hildegard is out and knowing in your heart that you had messed up a boy's life. My dear little wife, I know how your mind works, and it doesn't work that way. I mean the way of a loose lady like the Kyprian woman who was Aphrodite."

Mrs. Paget went to him and put her head on his shoulder.

"John," she said. "You silly witch-doctor, keep hold of me

tight. I nearly slipped away from you. For a second I nearly slipped away from you."

"I can't spare you for a second," he said.

"I'm not safe," she said. "I feel very unsafe. I'm a frail woman inside my heart. I have all the instincts of a slut."

"Bosh!" said Dr. Paget, good-naturedly. "You have a highly developed sense of humour. That guards one against all sorts of foolishness. You can see the absurdity of running away with a schoolboy."

"Sandhurst!" said Mrs. Paget. "Old enough to die in Korea or the next world war. He told me that, and it's true."

Dr. Paget looked startled for a moment.

"Poor lad," he said with deep compassion. "So that shadow is over his mind, eh? He wants to grab at the joy of life while the going's good. I can understand that."

"How do you know?" said Mrs. Paget, looking astonished. "Those were his very words. 'While the going's good'."

"That's how we felt in World War I," said Dr. Paget. "That accounted for most of the war marriages and the unmarried girls with babies. We knew life might be darned short—a week or two more, a year or two more, and we had had no experience of life. We hadn't tasted love. We were eager and greedy to get all out of life before it was taken from us."

He suddenly gave a groan and raised his hands above his head.

"How frightful that it should all be happening again! How damnable that another generation of boys should be under the shadow of death before they've learnt to live! I agree with that boy's mother at least in her horror of this sacrificial call to youth."

"John," said Mrs. Paget, "keep hold of me lest I slip away. I'm young, too, you know."

He put his arm round her and drew her close.

"Wild bird!" he said. "With a fluttering heart in this cage with an old buffer. Don't be frightened, my dear. It's all right."

She wept on his shoulder as Hildegard had done to his annoyance, but he was very tender with his wife, Viola—so young, so exquisite, he thought.

CHAPTER XXII

As summer waned and the short dark days of autumn followed, General Kendrick became anxious again about the world situation. The campaign in Korea had been an amazing affair. After their first retreat with small forces of untrained boys, the Americans had steadily gathered strength in men and material, and under the generalship of MacArthur, with his headquarters in Tokio from which he made frequent air trips to the battle line, were driving the North Koreans steadily back. MacArthur himself was jubilant and optimistic. 'Home by Christmas' was his latest message to the troops. All that was good, but General Kendrick was not alone in being doubtful as to the wisdom of going beyond the 38th parallel. He had been summoned to a conference as a military expert when this point had been raised. He had noticed a certain amount of anxiety among this group of distinguished men lest an advance to the Manchurian border might not be dangerous. What about China? It appeared that certain doubts of His Majesty's Government had been expressed informally to Washington with the hope that General MacArthur would not act in any way without the consent of the United Nations, and it was satisfactory to learn that he had agreed to this in principle.

"That's all very well," said one of the men across the conference table, "but the United Nations is dominated by American influence as regards Korea—their men are doing most of the fighting—and the slightest breath of criticism against MacArthur is resented by the entire American nation. So he does what he damn' well likes, and the United Nations agrees in advance."

"What do you think, General?" asked another member of this group, addressing Sir William Kendrick. "I mean about the crossing of the 38th parallel?"

The General had answered cautiously.

"It's difficult to see how MacArthur can round off the job

if he stays on the 38th parallel. It would leave the North Koreans in a position to pull themselves together and reform for future attacks. From a military point of view, that is self-evident. But there's the political question. What do we know about the intentions of China? That alarms me, gentlemen. It all depends upon the American Intelligence Service, and I'm afraid that is not functioning very well. Their reports seem to be very sketchy and inadequate. At least nothing reaches us which to my mind is at all reliable."

No decision was taken at the conference table, but on the doorstep General Kendrick had a few words with Stephen Hartley with whom he had taken breakfast one morning.

"I share your anxiety, General," he said. "That fellow MacArthur may come up against a hornet's nest. I regard him as a menace to world peace. A magnificent soldier, of course, but soldiers ought not to control policy. I tremble to think what may happen if we get involved with the Chinese—four hundred million of them—by the Lord Harry and all very race conscious and nationalistic after their defeat of Chiang-Kai-Shek and his corrupt gang."

"It's taking a risk," said General Kendrick.

Stephen Hartley nodded and gave an uneasy laugh.

"We're all walking on the edge of a precipice. This Korean campaign is absorbing all the available fighting strength of the Americans, to say nothing of our own contribution. Meanwhile, Russia watches and waits. Where's our own defence in Europe?"

"Nowhere yet," answered Sir William Kendrick. "Nothing beyond plans and propositions. We're interminably slow in getting anything done. Isn't that up to you—the Government of this defenceless country?"

He looked at this politician with a challenging smile.

Hartley shrugged his shoulders.

"We haven't our hearts in it," he admitted. "I for one loathe the idea of rearmament and all that it involves in replacing war-time controls, new taxation, another period of austerity. How can we put all that on to the people who are fed up with it? Surely to God we want to avoid World War III! It's those Americans who are asking for it. They're madly belligerent. As an old pacifist, I deplore this constant nagging against Russia, this daily exchange of challenge and abuse."

"I agree to some extent," said General Kendrick. "But to remain unarmed and defenceless is to ask for annihilation—if and when Russia decides to attack."

He looked towards the towers of Westminster.

"You fellows over there in the Talking Shop don't seem to realize the danger. They're still busy with little party politics. They keep on talking about trivialities—the cutting down of the meat ration, the nationalization of steel, an extra allocation of sugar for Christmas puddings! Those whom the gods wish to destroy they first make mad."

Stephen Hartley grinned at him.

"It's our democratic system," he said. "It works out all right in the long run."

"We mayn't have a long run this time," said the General gloomily.

"Oh well . . ."

Stephen Hartley raised his hand and went up Downing Street at a sharp pace.

The General agreed with the fellow to some extent about the American belligerency. It was a mistake, to say the least of it, to take it for granted that Russia intended to make war in the near future. The Russian game perhaps was to get everybody else to fight her war. Those long-headed fellows in the Kremlin, cold-blooded as fish, busy over their maps of the world, night not think it worth their while to attack the West. They were Orientals. The East might be their main objective. Beatrice believed in their Peace propaganda. She was getting into very queer company, going up to town with that young painter fellow, Rudi something, meeting people who called themselves pacifists, but were undoubtedly Communists and fellow-travellers.

He gave a deep sigh as he walked into Whitehall. There was an intellectual estrangement between himself and Beatrice after long years of love and comradeship. He was a lonely man. He couldn't get down to Longmead even for the week-ends now, except occasionally, and when he went down, Beatrice could think and talk of nothing but her Peace propaganda. Even Mervyn held aloof and was very silent and uncommunicative. There was something worrying the lad. Perhaps he had fallen in love with some girl. Very natural that, at his age, but unsettling. He would soon be passing out of Sandhurst. He would be posted to some regiment. He might be sent out to Tripoli or Malaya or Germany. The Korean show would be over unless . . . .

At that thought the General suddenly stopped in Whitehall as though shot. Unless . . It would be too frightful if MacArthur had been wrong in taking the gamble of going as far as the frontier of Manchuria. Supposing the Chinese attacked him? That would be a new war and a very hideous war. We might get involved in it. We were tied to the American chariot. In that case young Mervyn might find himself in Korea, young Mervyn and many boys of his own age. That was a terrible thought. Beatrice would take it badly. All this Peace stuff of hers was inspired, unconsciously no doubt, by her passionate love of Mervyn. That was at the core of it. If anything happened to Mervyn it would break her heart. Not only her heart, poor dear. It would be a heavy blow to him also, an unthinkable blow. Beatrice and he had doted on that boy. He was the centre of all their hopes.

The General gave a heavy sigh and walked on again with a glance at Big Ben. A quarter to one. There was that American fellow coming to lunch with him at the United Services: William Leggett, who was over in Europe again as a kind of ambassador extraordinary, reporting back to Washington on conditions in Western Europe—one of others no doubt in direct touch with the White House.

The General quickened his pace until he reached his club in Pall Mall. The Commissionaire who had served under him saluted impressively and then spoke a word or two about the weather.

"Getting chilly, sir! They say we're going to have a hard winter."

"I hope not," answered the General.

The hall porter greeted him respectfully.

"A dark morning, General."

"Has my guest arrived?"

"Not yet, sir."

In the hall, dimly lit, one or two men stood about. One of them grabbed the General's arm.

"Hullo, my lad! What's the latest? What are you fellows doing in the W.O.? Still sleeping soundly while the smell of burning gets up one's nostrils?"

It was a retired Field Marshal, except that a Field Marshal is never supposed to retire. Anyhow, he was incredibly old but still with a straight back and a twinkle in his eyes.

"What do you think of things, sir?" asked the General, counter-attacking by another question.

"Beyond thinking about!" answered the Field Marshal. "But for heaven's sake don't call me sir. It makes me feel as old as death."

He gave a shrill old man's laugh.

"I am as old as death. I go on living beyond the normal span. All my friends are dead. To me this club is inhabited by ghosts. Come and have a sherry, young fellow."

"No thanks," said the General. "I'm waiting for a guest."

"It's a funny thing," said the Field Marshal, "that whenever I ask a fellow to have a drink he's always waiting for a guest or just off to another appointment."

"Bad luck," said the General.

This was probably true, he thought. The poor old Field Marshal was a most infernal bore, fighting forgotten campaigns over again, Omdurman, the Boer War. He pretended that he remembered the Crimean War, but that was incredible.

"Your guest, sir," said one of the footmen.

"Glad to see you again, General," said an American voice. "It's good of you to invite me here. I appreciate it as a favour."

It was Mr. William Leggett with his long lean New England face and keen eyes behind horn-rimmed glasses.

"You'll have a sherry, won't you?" asked General Kendrick.

"I certainly would like some of your old brown sherry," answered Mr. Leggett. "But I must first get rid of this hat and coat. I know the way to the cloakroom."

Over his sherry, he smiled at the General and then glanced round the smoking-room at the portraits of famous soldiers.

"This club," he said, "reeks of history. I think of all the wars fought by Great Britain in the time of her unrivalled power, and of the famous Generals who commanded your Red Coats. A very wonderful record of a fighting spirit, sir."

"Now," said General Kendrick, "the power has shifted to your side of the world. Our little forces are put under American command. Times have changed."

He could not stifle a sigh and it was heard by the quick ears of his American guest.

"Yes, sir! And the responsibility of power is giving us a headache. We're taking on a good deal. It may be a rather crushing burden. I'm not sure that our people in the mass are quite aware of the sacrifice which is going to be demanded of them. Of course, at the moment, their attention is rivetted on the campaign in Korea where our losses are not light. They don't see the world problem in its full magnitude. President Truman's fireside chats are designed to get all this in its right proportion—the defence of civilization of which Korea is only a side-show."

"Shall we go to lunch?" asked the General.

Over the luncheon table in the corner of the dining-room Mr. Leggett revealed certain anxieties.

"Europe," he said, "is lagging behind in Western defence. That makes it difficult for President Truman and our Secretary of State to consolidate public opinion in favour of continuing and increasing aid to Europe on the matter of rearmament. The President has great powers, but he has to carry Congress with him. He has to carry American opinion with him. And the old Isolationism is by no means dead. No, sir! It has very powerful advocates, especially in the Middle West which is a long way from London, Paris, Rome and the Scandinavian countries. The President has many political enemies and a vicious isolationist press. Unhappily we do not close our ranks on the subject of foreign policy and keep it out of party politics as you do. His Majesty's Opposition stand solidly behind the Government when it comes to a question of national defence. In the United

States there is no such tradition. On the contrary, some of our politicians will make use of the slow-moving pace of European contribution to rearmament as a weapon to stab the President and thwart his plans for passing many billions of dollars for that purpose—dollars which, after all, have to come out of American pockets by increased taxation already very steep."

"That is very understandable," said the General.

There was no need for him to talk much at this luncheon table. His American guest preferred a monologue, pausing only to make sure that he was holding the interest of his host or to ask a question which the General answered briefly.

"You will agree with me, General, that the greatest menace to world civilization is not in Korea but right here in the heart of Europe. That is fully realized by Mr. Truman and his advisers—men like Mr. Acheson and General Marshall, not to mention General Eisenhower. But I should not be a good reporter of the European situation if I disguised the painful fact that Europe herself—Western Europe—is lamentably slow in meeting the Russian menace. I have just come from Paris. The French Government is obstructing every effort on our part to raise and equip a European army by the inclusion of German manpower."

"I can understand their anxieties," said the General.

Mr. Leggett glanced at him sharply and gave a short laugh.

"Yes, sir! But risks have to be taken in the face of a greater menace. Western Europe can attain no fighting strength in manpower unless the West Germans raise an army on equal terms—that is their very reasonable condition—with the other free nations."

"I agree," said General Kendrick. "But the Germans, I understand, are reluctant to be rearmed."

Mr. Leggett shrugged his shoulders.

"There are thousands of young men in Germany who would enlist tomorrow for the sake of regular employment. They went into the last war as boys of eighteen—even younger. They know nothing but soldiering. And they detest the Russians. I've been talking with old man Adenauer——" He broke off abruptly and lowered his voice. "Say, General, it's not for an

American to criticize England and I think you know that I am not one of the hostile critics, but I confess that I'm alarmed by the lack of awareness in the English mind and in the English Government in face of the peril which confronts us all. You are still, if I may say so, pursuing a policy of appeasement towards Russia. A great many of your people, according to reports I have, still have the wish-dream that it is possible to make friends with Soviet Russia. Your Government, your Secretary of State for Foreign Affairs, favours Four Power talks and is critical of our occupation of Formosa and our refusal to admit a Chinese Communist to a seat on the United Nations. All that is very disconcerting to the American people. We have made up our mind on good evidence that this war is coming and won't be long delayed. We are sick and tired of Russian insults and trouble-making everywhere. We're prepared to fight Communism wherever it rears its head. But we fail to get the full support from our friends in Europe. We are doubtful even of British enthusiasm for the same cause. That may have very lamentable results in Anglo-American relations."

The General saw that he was under a searching, anxious look from those keen eyes behind horn-rimmed glasses. This American was trying to draw him out. Anything he said might be reported back to Washington. He answered guardedly.

"We wish to preserve peace if there is any chance of doing so. That's not a policy of appeasement. I am one of those preparing plans for a great programme of rearmament. I confess we've been slow in getting off the mark. As for fighting Communism everywhere—isn't that extending our military commitments rather far? Do you include China? There are four hundred million Chinese!"

"Yes, sir," said the American, "and we are prepared to knock hell out of them if they play any monkey tricks."

General Kendrick was silent for a few moments. Then he asked a quiet question.

"You are not anxious about General MacArthur's advance to the Manchurian frontier?"

"Anxious?"

Mr. William Leggett put down his knife and fork. He gave

a harsh laugh as though this question amused him and at the same time startled him. What bee was buzzing in the bonnet of this English General? Had they gone timid? Had they lost their guts, these English?

"The Korean campaign is over," he said. "The boys will be home by Christmas. General MacArthur has proved himself to be the greatest living soldier."

When the American had left him after lunch, the General went into the smoking-room of his club and settled down for twenty minutes before returning to the War Office. He thought over the conversation he had just had. It was not reassuring. That American fellow, one of President Truman's envoys, represented no doubt the American mind and mood—dangerously belligerent, very challenging, mighty sure of their own strength, convinced that the Third World War was at hand. They hadn't been so knocked about as we had in the last war. Next time we should be Target Number One for every form of guided missile. There would be red flames in the sky again round St. Paul's and in every part of London. London would be uninhabitable. There would have to be a mass exodus from all the great cities. The Americans were ready to fight Communism wherever it reared its head. Perturbing that! Supposing there were a military alliance between Russia and China. Hadn't it already happened? He was uneasy about that approach to the Manchurian frontier by General MacArthur. Reports were coming in that the Chinese were massing great armies on the other side of the frontier. Would the American boys be home for Christmas? Mervyn would have passed out of Sandhurst in a few months. It seemed only yesterday that he was a schoolboy coming home for the holidays. Now he was a fine upstanding young fellow ready for the command of men. The Kendricks had all been soldiers for several generations. Beatrice jeered at that. She had gone completely pacifist for Mervyn's sake—as though pacifism and non-resistance would save her boy's life. A false reasoning that. Utterly wrong! If there were a war young Mervyn would have to do his duty like everybody else. He would have to take the same risks. . . .

For a few moments the General dozed off.

Then he opened his eyes, pulled himself together and went to get his hat and coat. Most of the men had left the club.

The old Field Marshal came up to him.

"Come and have a glass of port, young fellow. I'd be glad to have a chat with you."

"Sorry!" said General Kendrick. "I must get back to the War Office."

"It's always the same," said the old man. "You youngsters are always pretending to get busy when I want to have a talk with you. But nothing gets done. This country is doomed and it damned well ought to be doomed. We've lost our grip on things. We don't produce the right men. Where are Roberts and Kitchener and old Plumer? They had guts. They defended the Empire which we've now given away with both hands. In my judgment, my boy——"

"Sorry, sir," said General Kendrick.

He went back to the War Office.

CHAPTER XXIII

Lady Kendrick was seeing a good deal of Rudi Scholl and now and then of Rudi Scholl's friends in London. They belonged, he said, to the poverty-stricken intelligentsia.

"They're all workers for Peace," he told her. "They believe in the same ideals as yourself, dear lady. They are artists who believe in the beauty of life; refugees who have escaped from concentration camps; men and women who are Christians at heart, although they may be agnostics and sceptics and intellectual rebels."

He took her to a Peace Meeting in the Caxton Hall and she was a little embarrassed when she was asked to take a seat on the platform. The Chairman, who was a silver-haired, florid-faced Bishop of the Anglican Church, beamed upon the audience and then rose to introduce the chief speaker, whom he described as Fleet Street's Apostle of Peace. This was the editor of a paper called *The Peace Messenger* which Lady Kendrick received regularly by post, although she paid no subscription for it. He was a cadaverous-looking young man with a lock of black hair falling over his forehead and a great gift of emotional eloquence. On the platform with Lady Kendrick, according to a programme slipped into her hand, were two or three well-known actors and actresses—she certainly had heard their names—a Labour Member of Parliament and several titled ladies like herself, one of whom sitting near her was an old friend of hers. It was Lady Virginia Merivale whom she had known in India years ago.

"My dear Beatrice!" exclaimed this lady, before the meeting began. "How wonderful to see you here. Come to my flat afterwards. We simply must have a talk."

"Won't you change places with me?" asked a polite young man sitting between them.

"Oh, thank you so much!"

Lady Virginia slipped into the chair next to Lady Kendrick and squeezed her hand.

"It's years and years!" she said. "How's dear old Bill? I used to flirt with him outrageously. So handsome! So shy!"

"He's still handsome and still shy," said Lady Kendrick with a smile. "But he thinks I've gone mad."

"How delightful!" exclaimed Lady Virginia Merivale. "My husband used to think the same thing. That was when I took up theosophy and after that Yogi."

"What are you now?" asked Lady Kendrick, smiling at her again.

She remembered this raddled-looking woman when she was a young girl, pretty, vital and audacious. There had been a few little scandals about her in India and a divorce which had been a big scandal.

"What else could I be?" she answered. "A Communist, of course! It's the only satisfying creed in this modern world. Not that there's anything new in it. It's as old as Christianity. The early Christians were Communists. They shared all things in common, according to the teaching of their Master."

Lady Kendrick felt rather alarmed. For a moment or two she had the feeling that she ought not to be here on this platform. The early Christians might have been Communists, but Mr. Stalin and Mr. Molotov were not early Christians, to say the least of it. She was here on this platform not as a Communist but as a lover of Peace.

"Are all these people Communists?" she asked.

Lady Virginia Merivale smiled and shook her head, rattling her emerald ear-rings.

"Good heavens, no! I wish I could say they were. They're the poor bewildered little people who see themselves being dragged into a war which they haven't the courage to denounce. Some of them, I admit, are Quakers and therefore conscientious objectors, of course. Others are the intellectuals who try to think things out for themselves and get it all wrong. A few East End clergymen, no doubt, those underfed-looking young men who wear their collars the wrong way round. So ridiculous, don't you think? . . . But here comes dear Mr. Mellinger. He speaks like an angel."

The Editor of *The Peace Messenger* was certainly eloquent

and very self-assured. He criticized the conduct of the Korean war and the abominable cruelty of flinging into that cold hell boys of eighteen, mostly untrained and, at the beginning, ill-equipped and ill-clad. "This war is being fought," he said, "in the fine-sounding name of resisting aggression—a new slogan for war-makers. It is to liberate the South Koreans, but do they want to be liberated? Have they asked to be liberated? Do they like this form of liberation? Their towns have been bombed and blasted and their industrial works destroyed. Hundreds of thousands of them are refugees, starving, homeless, terrified. They have been forced to leave their homesteads and their paddy fields to make a clear field of fire for their liberators.

"Russia had been named as the aggressor, but is there any evidence that this has been instigated by Russia? Where is that evidence? The arms used by the North Koreans are mostly those captured by the Chinese Communists from the armies of Chiang Kai-Shek. It might be that Russia has sent them supplies, just as we had sent supplies to other countries, and as we are now doing while rearming against Russia. But that is not considered to be an act of aggression. In any case this war in Korea, like other wars, would settle nothing and benefit nobody. It would leave only a trail of death and new causes for new wars." He spoke as a pacifist who believed that war was the greatest degradation of humanity and a crime against the civilized mind.

"You ought to be put into Brixton prison!" shouted a voice from the gallery. "You and your fellow-travellers . . ."

There was some commotion in the gallery. The man who protested was thrown out by the stewards—somewhat inconsistently, perhaps, in a meeting proclaiming the creed of non-violence.

When the commotion had subsided, the Editor of *The Peace Messenger* resumed his speech. He warned his audience that Great Britain, once so strong in leadership, was tied to the chariot wheels of American diplomacy and world strategy.

"Our greatest danger," he said, "comes not from Russia but from the United States where public opinion is inflamed, where its Press whips them into the madness of war fever, where those so-called victories in Korea under General MacArthur—that military dictator—that Roman pro-Consul—have made them believe that they are invincible and all-powerful."

"You're glad to get their dollars, aren't you?" shouted a voice from the gallery. "Don't we owe them a vast debt? Haven't we been living on Marshall Aid——"

"Throw him out!" shouted several voices. "Chuck him out!"

There was another scrimmage. The Editor of *The Peace Messenger* smiled and stroked his lean jaw as overwhelming numbers of sympathizers bore down upon this heretic and pushed him out.

"We must assume again our own political and spiritual leadership," said the speaker. "We must free ourselves from the bonds of the Almighty Dollar. We must unharness ourselves from the grinding power of the American war machine. What we need is a new diplomacy, a new gospel, a new faith, or at least a renewal of faith in human brotherhood and peace on earth to men of good will."

He spoke of the horrors of a Third World War which would utterly destroy Western civilization and leave nothing but ruin and death. If the atom bomb were used—and it would be used—we might all be blotted out, or survive only as small groups of wretched people hiding in deep shelters unable to walk about in radio-active areas, reduced to semi-starvation, made sterile and diseased by those new and atrocious weapons. "This is not a fancy picture," he said. "It is one described by eminent men of science. Indeed, I have spared you many of the details of horror which they set down."

The audience, mostly of youngish people, listened to him silently. Lady Kendrick from the platform could see many of the faces down there. They had a tense expression. Not a sound came from them, not a rustle of paper, not a cough or a clearing of throats.

'Those poor young people!' thought Lady Kendrick. 'Those good-looking boys who are probably students somewhere! My heart bleeds for them. They look the same age as my Mervyn.'

"That Third World War must not happen," said the Editor of *The Peace Messenger*, advancing to the edge of the platform.

For the first time there was a sudden burst of applause. It came in a scattered way from the front and back seats and the gallery above.

"It will not happen if we refuse to let it happen. We must all be conscientious objectors to this war, not merely a few brave souls here and there, lagged by the police, sent to prison as solitary martyrs, but the whole nation, the whole of our young manhood and womanhood. They must send out a shout of refusal to allow this thing, this horror. They must insist—they have the right to insist and the power to insist—that this country shall remain neutral and non-resistant if that Third World War is declared. Further than this they must, by a spiritual leadership in this country, secure the allegiance to Peace of other European countries—France, Italy, Scandinavia, telling the United States clearly and firmly that no act of war on their side, no provocation against Russia, no sudden flare up of mob passion in New York or Chicago, will be binding upon us or will induce us to share their panic or bear the brunt of battle not of our own choosing. We must be the defenders of civilization, not by a war which will destroy it, but by a Peace of the spirit which will avoid it. There is no need for the Third World War. There is no danger of it if here in this country we resist the evil and foolish policies which are preparing for it, as the grave-diggers of civilization."

It seemed that Mr. Mellinger had a grudge against the United States and adopted the Russian thesis that they were the warmongers.

There was another shout from the gallery in a woman's voice, shrill and clear.

"You're all cowards and traitors! Better death than slavery!"

The Bishop in the chair looked perturbed and raised a plump hand.

"There's an organized opposition here," said the Editor of *The Peace Messenger*. "The warmongers have their agents."

There was a murmur in the audience. People were talking to one another quietly. A note was passed to Lady Kendrick.

"Will you say a few words?"

The Bishop leaned sideways and smiled at her benignly.

That was unexpected. Lady Kendrick's face flushed and then turned pale. This was more frightening than a village meeting in Longmead and she had been very frightened then.

"How delightful of you!" said Lady Virginia Merivale in a whisper, as Lady Kendrick rose.

She came forward a little on to the platform. The Chairman was introducing her to the audience, but she did not hear what he was saying.

"We are now going to hear a few words from a very distinguished lady who is doing noble work on behalf of Peace. Lady Kendrick is the wife of a distinguished soldier, Major-General Sir William Kendrick, who like many other soldiers, as we must gladly admit, has seen enough of war to be a good lover of Peace. Lady Kendrick."

Lady Kendrick stood there with her hands clasped. Then she found herself speaking, but was so nervous that afterwards she could not remember a word she had said. At least she was not intellectually aware of formulating an argument or arranging her sentences. The words seemed to come by themselves out of the very deeps of her subconsciousness. They were a kind of prayer that the Third World War might be prevented by some miracle of grace or by some tidal wave of the human spirit, surging over frontiers and reaching the soul of all humanity. She thought mostly of the younger generation—the young men, the young girls, the children. People as old as herself might face whatever came—even the atom bomb—with resignation because they had known life and need not fear death, but the younger generation had a right to life. Why should they be sacrificed in the slaughter fields of war, under the bombardment of cities, in the fury and flame of war, because of hideous errors in the diplomacy of statesmen and politicians and the evil policy of cruel-minded men. Some people said that the alternative to war would be enslavement by Russia, with secret police, mass executions, concentration camps and torture-chambers.

For a moment Lady Kendrick was startled by a ripple of laughter, a kind of unbelieving laughter, ridiculing the idea of such things being done by the Soviet State. One of those who tittered was Lady Virginia Merivale sitting next to her.

"So utterly ridiculous!" she exclaimed. "Newspaper falsehoods!"

Lady Kendrick wondered why this laughter came. Had she said anything funny or made some silly mistake? She must go on talking for a few minutes longer. It was expected of her. She must say something more to all these people.

"I think there is a better alternative than that," she said. "I believe it is still possible, at least I pray that it is still possible to reach out to the Russian people themselves so that they will refuse to make war upon their fellow-men, or to be the unwilling instruments of destruction. They know to the very full the agonies of war. These Russian mothers love their sons and their babes. There is, I am told, in the Russian mind, in the minds of their peasants and workers, an idealism which may be suppressed but has not been killed in their hearts. It is to that we must appeal, breaking through the Iron Curtain by messages of good will and loving comradeship——"

The Chairman who was the Bishop, seemed to be getting nervous. He did not seem to like the reference to Russia and its Iron Curtain, and its police state and torture-chambers. It was not the policy of his friends to admit the existence of such things.

"Thank you, Lady Kendrick," he said, leaning towards her with a smile. "Thank you so much."

Lady Kendrick did not quite realize that he wanted her to stop speaking. She came a little more forward to the edge of the platform.

"I can see that we have a young audience here," she said. "I can see the faces of young men, boys of eighteen and nineteen, perhaps. I have a son of that age. Perhaps that is why I feel so deeply about this menace of war which is very close upon us. I am just one of the mothers of England. My dear young people, all of us older people here only want to save you from annihilation. We want you to survive. The fine flower of youth must not be cut down by flying scythes of steel nor burnt in the furnace fires because of the folly and wickedness of men lustful for power and ruthless in their ambitions. Do not accept the inevitability of war. Fight against the powers of darkness by the sword of the spirit, by the flame of love—even by the courage of Christian martyrs. Must we be driven as dumb beasts towards the abyss? I do not think we are so helpless. Let us urge our leaders to try to establish friendly contact even with those who are suspicious of us and who insult us."

"Thank you, Lady Kendrick," said the Bishop in a firm voice. "That is enough, thank you. Most kind of you, I'm sure!"

Lady Kendrick understood that he wanted her to sit down and, as she did so, feeling relieved that this ordeal was over, there came from the body of the hall a wave of applause. The young people in the audience were clapping. Something in the simplicity of her speech, in its sincerity, had touched them. It might be great nonsense—her ideas might be unworkable—but this woman, this tall lady with dark eyes luminous in a white face, spoke to them from her heart and the warmth of her love for the younger crowd came through and reached them.

Rudi Scholl had slipped out of the lecture-room and was waiting for Lady Kendrick in the central hall as the audience began to stream out. They were mostly young people with a minority of old fogeys and harassed-looking women of middle age. He knew all the types from his study of English life. The youngsters were probably students from the London School of Economics or King's College in the Strand. As they passed him he heard some of their comments.

"Gosh!" said a boy in a sports jacket and flannel trousers. "I suffered exceedingly. Why did you bring me here, Jenny? Never again! It was all Russian propaganda."

"That tall woman was the best," said a girl in a light green raincoat of some shining material. "The others just talked the usual clichés. She spoke from the heart."

"It's a pity she didn't speak from the head," said the boy

with this girl. "Does she honestly believe that pious sentiments are going to stop the Russian hordes?"

Two young men passed Rudi as he stood there listening and watching.

"The only way of Peace is for England to go Communist."

"I agree," said the other. "But they won't. They're too stupid."

Another boy and girl passed. The girl's hand was slipped through the arm of her companion, a hatless young man with longish hair and a pimply face.

"It makes one frightened," said the girl. "Do you think war is really coming?"

"I'm making plans for next year," answered the young man. "I hope to get through my exam before I'm lagged as a conscientious objector."

Lady Kendrick came into the central hall with Lady Virginia Merivale. Rudi slid towards her and took her hand.

"A very beautiful speech!" he exclaimed. "Most inspiring!"

Lady Kendrick smiled at him.

"I really don't know what I said! I spoke like one in a trance."

"Probably you were in a trance, my dear," said Lady Virginia. "Quite likely some spirit was speaking through you. But I must say it was a very naughty spirit for saying such untrue things about our dear Russia—accepting all the libellous stories published by our gutter Press."

"One can't ignore them," answered Lady Kendrick. "Terrible things are done, Virginia."

"I don't believe a word of them," answered that lady. "I have the greatest affection for dear Mr. Stalin. Such a charming man! So benign, so devoted to the Russian people, poor darlings!"

Further conversation on this point was prevented by Rudi's friend Peter Oldenburg, who came up and spoke to him with one hand on his shoulder.

"May I have the honour of being presented to Lady Kendrick? Her speech was very wonderful—very moving, if I may say so."

Rudi introduced him.

"This is my friend, Peter Oldenburg. We were in a concentration camp together during the Nazi régime in Austria. We are still good comrades."

"How very touching," said Lady Kendrick, holding out her hand to Peter Oldenburg. "I'm very glad you are safe in England. Virginia, my dear, this is Mr. Oldenburg, one of the victims of Nazi persecution and a friend of my dear Rudi who looks after me so well—almost as if he were my own son."

"Delightful!" cried Lady Virginia Merivale. "This is a most interesting afternoon. Exciting! I suggest that you all come to my flat for further conversation. I am devoted to conversation. One learns such a lot. One meets such charming people. Oh, there is Mr. Slattery, the Editor of *The British Proletariat*. Do come and take a cup of tea in my flat, dear Mr. Slattery."

"Thanks so much," said that gentleman, who was a tall dark young man in a black suit with a red tie.

"Hullo, Slattery!" said Rudi's friend, Oldenburg.

"Hullo!"

They exchanged a smile with each other.

It needed more than one taxi to convey Lady Virginia's friends and acquaintances to her flat in Princes Gate, Kensington—a spacious and elegant flat on the first floor.

Rudi Scholl was impressed by its magnificence. Once he had been a prisoner in a verminous hut behind barbed wire. In pre-war Vienna he had lived in attics and basements as a poverty-stricken art student. Now here he was in the luxurious apartment of an aristocratic lady. His quick eyes roved round the pictures on the walls—a portrait of his hostess as a younger woman by Lazlo; good, he thought, in its chocolate-box style; a portrait of an English general, possibly the husband of Lady Virginia; a portrait of a young airman of the First World War by Orpen—certainly by Orpen, very strong and sensitive—masterly, he thought.

He glanced round at his fellow-guests—a very odd assortment. His friend, Peter Oldenburg, was standing with a cup and saucer talking to the bland-looking old Bishop in gaiters, with a silver cross on his stomach. A sudden thought made

Rudi smile. He wondered what the Bishop would think of Peter's Italian wife in one of her drunken moods, as that day when she had burst into wild abuse of the Soviet system in front of two innocents whom Peter was trying to convert to the pure gospel of Leninism.

There was Slattery of the *British Proletariat* subsidized by Russian money as everybody knew—everybody except the innocent outsiders—and doing rather well on it, with chambers in Lincoln's Inn, an office in Blackfriars, an expensive-looking car and an expensive-looking dame whom he called his wife.

A very agreeable thing to be subsidized by Soviet Russia, thought Rudi Scholl, conscious of his own impecunious state. Lady Kendrick passed him a little bit now and again—"for expenses, my dear," she said, in her charming way—he was really very fond of her, but it didn't go very far, not much farther than cigarettes and drinks and a new pair of shoes and other little necessities of daily life, such as Gillette blades, shaving soap and his sweet ration. Mrs. Donovan—Betty—was getting fed up with him again because he hadn't paid his quarter's bill.

His eyes continued to study the company in Lady Virginia's rooms. There were two or three very elegant young women with the fresh innocence of English girlhood. They had never been in a concentration camp. They had never suffered hunger like the women in Dachau and Ausswich. They had been shielded from the brutality and degradation of life. Now they listened to Lady Virginia with starry eyes and belief in what she was telling them about a conducted tour she had made in Russia with that smiling and benevolent Bishop and other fellow-travellers.

"It was all wonderful, my dears! No horrors. A happy people. Summer holidays in the Crimea—a lovely climate you know—for the workers in factories. Fine hospitals. Well-equipped schools. We had a most intelligent and charming guide who told us everything and answered all our questions . . ."

Rudi heard Lady Virginia say these things and a cynical smile stayed on his lips. Lady Virginia had not seen what happened in the Lubyanka prison, the breaking down of men's bodies and minds by ingenious methods of lights and drugs, and threats of torture. She had not seen the marching away of young and middle-aged men conscripted from villages for work in the mines and the timber forests, from which they would never return. They would die of starvation, pneumonia, typhus and the other miseries of slave labour by enfeebled bodies. Lady Virginia, that chatty, smiling lady, had never sat at midnight in an overcrowded room when there had come a knock on the door and a shout of 'Open!' There would be a woman's shriek when four men of the N.K.V.D. thrust their way in, turned their torches on to the face of a half-awakened man and said 'Get up. You're wanted.' She had never seen a political purge, nor heard the rifle shots of an execution squad. As a tourist in Russia she had been very much impressed by what she had been shown by a very intelligent young woman.

Rudi Scholl knew all that. He had friends who had escaped beyond the Iron Curtain, from Latvia and Estonia and Lithuania. Once he had been a Communist. One could believe in Communism if one were starving and verminous. Theoretically there had been something which appealed to the underdog like himself. Perhaps it was the idea that he might be an overdog one day, taking revenge on those who had had all the luck of life. The dictatorship of the proletariat! It sounded fine at the beginning before the proletariat realized their serfdom, and a new tyranny so organized that a whisper to one's neighbour, the jerk of a head, a cynical smile, was enough to put one behind barbed wire.

Rudi had been a Communist in the German concentration camp and afterwards. He had accepted the arguments of his friend Peter that the police state was necessary in the early stages of the Soviet system, and that its ruthlessness would no longer be necessary when everyone was a faithful and loyal believer. Then, it was argued, there would be prosperity and happiness in a class-less state. The end justified the means. For days, months and years in the concentration camp he had listened to all this and talked all this with fanatical enthusiasm. Now lately, he had become a cynic and a sceptic, due perhaps to his English environment and friends. They were so decent, these English people he met—stupid, unintellectual, exasperating at times, narrow-minded and traditional—but very decent. The English way of life in a village like Longmead was perhaps the ideal of life anywhere, at least in comfortable conditions, for everyone, freedom of speech, absence of terror. He had drifted away from his Communist friends, still mouthing those phrases based on the creed of Karl Marx and Lenin, still believing them, still working underground like Peter Oldenburg.

He was rather sorry in a way that Lady Kendrick was being caught up in this set, partly by his own influence. He felt a twinge of guilt about that. It was like betraying an innocent child. She was a very charming lady and was kind to him. It was hardly fair to introduce Peter Oldenburg without telling her that this man was a paid agent of the Soviet and according to her code an immoral and unprincipled scoundrel, though very likeable in some ways. There was no guile in women like Lady Kendrick and that other one, who was the hostess of this tea party—Lady Virginia. They were devoted emotionally and spiritually to the cause of Peace. They still believed, poor ladies, that it was possible to establish friendship and co-operation with the Soviet State. Perhaps even that smiling Bishop was not intellectually dishonest, consciously and deliberately. They were just the dupes of men like Oldenburg who laughed at them secretly. Now it was an easy game for the Communists in England because the pacifists and the peacemakers, millions perhaps of ordinary English folk like those women in the village hall of Longmead, were beginning to be frightened by the menace of war and suddenly awakened to this fright by the fighting in Korea. They were going to Peace meetings. They would be susceptible to a Peace propaganda put out by Russia to weaken the Western powers and sabotage their plans for disarmament.

These thoughts pursued each other in the mind of Rudi Scholl, ex-Communist and very impecunious artist, as he stood in the drawing-room of Lady Virginia Merivale with that faint mocking smile on his lips.

One of the pretty young women brought him a cup of tea and a piece of iced cake.

"A most interesting meeting, wasn't it?" she said, smiling at him. "Lady Kendrick was marvellous!"

"Yes, she is a very sweet lady," said Rudi. "Devoted to Peace."

The girl, a young woman of twenty something, with frank smiling eyes, lowered her voice when she spoke again.

"None of us want another war, but I'm not a pacifist like most of the people here. If Russia attacks we shall have to defend ourselves. I would rather die than be under the Russians with their secret police and all that."

"I'm afraid we shall have to die anyway, if Russia attacks," said Rudi, smiling at her.

"Gloomy thought!" exclaimed the young woman. "Oh well, I hope for the best. Are you an out-and-out pacifist? If so, don't give me away to Lady Virginia."

She laughed and slipped away from him to hand round some cakes to other guests.

Oldenburg and Slattery came up to Rudi Scholl and beckoned him to a corner of the room by the tall purple-curtained windows looking out to Kensington Gardens beyond Princes Gate, with the winter trees faintly etched through a white mist.

"Look here, young fellow," said Oldenburg in a low-toned voice. "Do you still go to Lady Kendrick's house now and then, or is that one of your imaginative lies inspired by your incurable vanity?"

Rudi laughed and shrugged his shoulders.

"You needn't believe it, but as a matter of fact I take tea with her at least twice a week."

Peter Oldenburg gave Slattery a quick smiling glance.

"He might be useful to us, this young fellow," he said.

"Yes, indeed," said Slattery. "But I don't think it's quite safe to talk about it here." He gave a nervous glance over his shoulder.

"Talk about what?" asked Rudi, suspiciously.

His friend Oldenburg assured himself that nobody was listening to this private conversation. The other guests were all talking and laughing.

"Slattery and I want to have a talk with you," he said. "It might be worth your while."

"In what way?" asked Rudi, now very deeply suspicious.

"Financially, my dear laddie. Would £500 be worth your while? Perhaps a bit more according to results."

Rudi stared at him and grinned.

"Have you gone mad?" he asked. "£500?"

"Or a bit more," said Oldenburg.

"I don't think we ought to talk here," said Slattery, looking more nervous. "I suggest we meet tonight at the Green Dragon."

"Better come round to my flat," said Oldenburg. "Perfectly private. That Italian slut has bunked off. I'm quite alone."

He put his hand on Rudi's shoulder.

"What about it, you little gutter rat?"

"I'm not sure," answered Rudi. "I suspect you've got some dirty work on."

"Just as you like," said Oldenburg irritably. "Go to the devil if you like. But don't forget you owe me £10."

Rudi stared at him again.

"Did you say something about £500? Or was that a *façon de parler*?"

"Or a bit more I said," answered Oldenburg. "Of course if it isn't worth your while."

"What time?" asked Rudi.

"Nine o'clock. Is that all right for you, Slattery?"

Slattery nodded.

"I must be going."

He moved off to take his leave of Lady Virginia Merivale.

"So delightful of you to come!" she told him.

Rudi went over to Lady Kendrick.

"Can I be of any little service to you, dear lady?" he asked.

She took his hand and patted it.

"It's due to you that I have met so many nice people here today," she said. "I am really very grateful."

CHAPTER XXIV

APART from the Vicar perhaps, it was Dr. Paget who knew most what was happening in the minds of people in Longmead and the neighbouring villages. Until the Korean campaign and the Government's sudden announcement that rearmament was necessary and urgent, they had mostly been wholly unperturbed by the international situation. It was only intellectuals like James Stewart and a few others who had worried about it. General Kendrick, hardly to be classed as an intellectual, but very knowledgable in his own line, had had sleepless nights because of the defenceless state of the country, and Viola had shocked her husband once or twice by saying that they would all be 'atomized' one day. But the village women whom the doctor treated for ailments and accidents had never once talked to him about the menace of war. Nor had their men, being much more interested in the Test Match or the football results. But now, after the Peace Meeting in the village and a flood of newspaper reports with grim headlines and broadcast speeches by the Prime Minister and others, they were getting apprehensive and alarmed. He met this anxiety on his rounds.

"Doctor, do you think we're going to have another war? The papers seem to take it for granted. It's too awful!"

One young mother in one of the council houses, who had burnt herself at the ironing-board, spoke very bitterly.

"I'd rather be dead than face another war. I went through the London bombing when I was working in a laundry. I crawled out of the ruins of a little house in Camberwell, with my father and mother buried under the rubble. Night after night we used to sleep in an Anderson shelter hearing the bombers come over and the crash of the bombs and the noise of houses falling in the same street. My young brother was killed in Normandy, just a kid. Now I've three kids of my own. Is it going to happen all over again?"

What could he answer to that? How could he comfort them unless he lied?

"I pray that it won't happen," he said. "It's certainly not inevitable—yet."

He noticed among the men a kind of hostility or suspicion towards the Americans.

It was young Grainger—his father kept the garage in Longmead—who put this view bluntly.

"It's the Americans who want us to line up for the next war. They want to knock hell out of Russia and they want to make England a base for their bombing aircraft. They're already doing it. That means that if they get their war, we shall be in it up to the neck and Target Number One for rocket bombs and every old thing. Why should we be tied up to American policy or wiped off the earth because they've gone mad with war fever in New York and Chicago?"

Dr. Paget bandaged up a sprained ankle and wondered what the right answer to this might be.

"The American leaders have pretty cool brains," he said. "Men like Acheson and Marshall aren't going to be stampeded into war."

"But they *have* been stampeded into war," argued young Grainger. "They're trying it out in Korea. Once having tasted blood, they're ready to try it out anywhere in Asia or Europe. I know 'em. I know how they talk. All swank and bounce, ready to lick the world."

"No, no!" said the doctor. "I don't believe that's true. American fathers and mothers don't want to sacrifice their sons any more than ours do. Their war in Korea—we're in it, too—was to resist aggression. They've acted under the United Nations' authority."

"Poppycock!" said young Grainger contemptuously. "Why the hell should we be trapped into a world war because a lot of dagoes—Latin-Americans and such like—put thumbs down for other fellows to fight and die? Have they sent any contingents? Not on your life! They support the American policy and proclaim their beautiful faith in the principles of justice and some damn' fool document like the Atlantic Charter, which

I and my friends have not been asked to sign and don't know what's inside it, except perhaps a sentence of death for the likes of us."

"One must stick to principles," said Dr. Paget. "One must uphold justice. There must be law and order."

"I don't agree," said young Grainger, sulkily. "There have already been two world wars fought on a point of principle as far as I can make out. Both fought for law and order, no doubt. Something to do with Poland last time, wasn't it? Where's Poland now? What law and order did the last war produce? Nothing but chaos and new hatreds. I'm against principles. Some fanatics would sacrifice the whole generation of youth for the sake of a blinking principle, and then forget it."

Dr. Paget laughed good-humouredly.

"You're a pragmatist," he said.

"That's as may be," answered young Grainger. "Not knowing I can't say. But I fought in the last war—anyhow, I drove a lorry behind the fighting men and I'm fed-up with that kind of thing. I want to marry a nice girl and have a couple of kids and live happy."

"A very reasonable ambition," said the doctor. "Good luck to you, my dear fellow. That's how life ought to be."

"Yes, but is it going to be? That's what I'm asking you, Doctor. Supposing the Americans insist on having war with Russia?"

Dr. Paget was against this suspicion of the Americans. He had come across it before. It seemed to him dangerous and unfair. We should be sunk if we quarrelled with the United States. It seemed to him that the only chance of survival for civilization was to stand in firmly and loyally with those people.

"We owe an immense debt to the Americans," he said. "We should have starved and had a mass of unemployment if it hadn't been for Marshall aid. Now they're coming to the defence of Western Europe. They're going to spend billions in helping to rearm and get some strength where now we only have weakness."

"That's the way to war," said young Grainger, with deep pessimism. "The guns will go off. The Americans will be all right, three thousand miles away, but meanwhile we shall be wiped off the map. I see it coming. If I could get out to New Zealand——"

He was not the only one looking for some way of escape, searching their minds for geographical knowledge of some nice safe spot in the world where there would be security and peace. Not easy to find in a dangerous world! Not easy for a little family in Longmead village to up-stick and go out to the pioneer life in one of the Dominions.

It was another woman in one of the council houses who spoke to him about this one day. That was Biddy Loveday the mother of delectable twins, whom he had brought into the world four years ago. Her husband was a pleasant-spoken fellow who earned a fair living as a jobbing gardener.

"Doctor," said Biddy, when he had eased her mind about the children's health—not measles this time—"is there any chance of getting out to Australia or South Africa? Ted is a handy man. He could do most kinds of work. Don't they want people like us?"

"What's the idea, Biddy?" asked the doctor.

"It's this talk of war. It gives me the shivers."

"Forget it," said Dr. Paget. "Don't worry about it. Be merry while you may, my dear."

He felt the utter insincerity of his own words. It was impossible not to worry. Not that he worried about himself. It was for people like Biddy that he worried, foolishly perhaps. There was nothing he could do about it.

"I can't be merry," said Biddy, "when every newspaper is stuffed with articles that prophesy doom. The nine o'clock news gives one the hump!"

"Switch it off," said Dr. Paget. "Listen to Wilfred Pickles in 'Have a Go'. That cheers one up. The spirit of our people comes through it somehow—brave, sturdy, laughing, fearless people."

"That's putting one's head in the sand like an ostrich," said Biddy Loveday, who was an intelligent young woman. Viola had made the same accusation against the doctor one day.

"Do you think it might be worth while going up to Australia House?" asked Biddy. "I mean, we might put our names down as would-be emigrants. If this war's coming, I don't feel like waiting for it. I'd rather live in the wild grubbing up a bit of land. The twins . . ."

Dr. Paget drove through Longmead that evening after dark. Lights gleamed behind the curtains in cottage windows. There was a bright moon veiled now and then by scudding clouds which touched the roofs and chimney-pots of these old dwelling-places, some as old as Elizabethan England. It was a sweet place, he thought, this village of Longmead. It seemed utterly peaceful and secure below the little low hills. But under every roof there was this sense of insecurity creeping close, threatening their lives, threatening to destroy civilization itself. That was incredible. It had never happened in history before. Perhaps it was all a mad, bad dream.

'It can't be true!' thought Dr. Paget. 'It mustn't be true. I pray to God . . .'

He drove into his own courtyard, put away his car, and went into his hall.

"Hullo, Viola!" he called cheerily.

She was reading a book called *1984*.

"My goodness," she cried, "I'm glad you've come back. This book has given me the jim-jams."

"Why read it?" asked the doctor. "These modern novelists are terrible fellows. They wallow in pessimism. I feel like a drop of gin, old dear."

"So do I," said Viola. "Let's take to drink."

"Fine idea!" said Dr. Paget, "but give me a kiss first. I need womanly comfort, I want to be mothered."

She gave him a kiss, a butterfly kiss, just touching his cheek.

CHAPTER XXV

BETTY DONOVAN spoke to her husband one day about Rudi Scholl.

"Our little pavement artist seems to have come into a bit of money lately. Where do you think it comes from?"

Donovan laughed, and looked up from his papers in their private sitting-room.

"He's certainly throwing it about a bit—standing drinks all round. There was a wad of notes in his wallet last night. I expect he's won it on the football pools. If so, he's kept it devilish dark."

"It doesn't seem to make him happy," remarked Betty. "He has a shifty worried look. He avoids looking one straight in the eyes, like a man guilty of some crime. Do you think he has been stealing?"

Donovan grinned at her.

"You've always been prejudiced against our little Austrian. It's my belief—if you want the honest truth—that he's been sponging on her ladyship at Badgers. I think she's fallen for the lad. 'Orrible scandal in Longmead village! Titled lady runs off with romantic young artist. Mrs. Montgomery-Jones is delighted. She always feared the worst."

Betty rewarded this piece of fantasy with a smile.

"Rubbish!" she exclaimed. "Lady Kendrick is old enough to be his mother. Besides, she's not that sort. She's like a saint in a stained-glass window."

Donovan shook his head.

"You never can tell. Even saints are tempted. Rudi has charm, you must admit that; he has a plausible tongue. And he's certainly up at Badgers two or three times a week. Putting two and two together and making it come to five according to Irish arithmetic . . ."

Patricia Hastings had also noticed that Rudi exhibited a certain affluence and she questioned him on the subject one evening at Foxgloves.

"Yes, I will have a glass of port, kind sir! But may I ask whence the shekels come to pay for it? Have you robbed a blind man lately, or broken open the church money-box?"

Rudi laughed, but looked annoyed at this jibe.

"I don't think you're behaving quite like an English gentlewoman," he told her. "It's not the way to accept a friendly offer."

Patricia Hastings much enjoyed this rebuke and gave a squeal of laughter.

"Rudi," she said presently, "you have the look of Eugene Aram."

"I don't know that fellow," he answered. "Is he good-looking? Would he commission me to paint his portrait?"

"He had a guilty look," said Patricia. "He committed murder. He was afraid of being found out."

"Was he found out?" asked Rudi, swallowing the last drop of his port.

"He was!" said Patricia. "He was led off by the cops, properly handcuffed."

"Poor devil," said Rudi with an uneasy laugh. "I'm always sorry for the criminal."

"You would be, my little mid-European," said Patricia.

"Let's have another glass of port," said Rudi, "or some of Donovan's fine old brandy."

"Great idea!" said Patricia. "And I like to see you pay for it. How much money have you got in that wallet? It's bulging!"

Rudi coloured up hotly.

"That's my private affair," he answered sulkily. "Do behave yourself like a lady, my beautiful one."

Patricia Hastings behaved less like a lady after a glass of Donovan's fine old brandy. That is to say, she only laughed when Rudi became sentimental.

"Patricia," he said, dropping his voice because other people had come into the lounge, "will you stop jeering at me if I talk seriously—if I reveal my heart-secret to you?"

"I don't believe I could bear it," she answered. "And I doubt whether it's quite proper for you to tell me. Is the secret of your heart really quite nice for a young girl of my innocence and upbringing?"

"You jeer at me again," he said, as though deeply hurt.

"I can't stifle my sense of humour," she told him. "If I tried I should suffocate."

He was silent for a few moments. Perhaps he had been drinking a little too much, for his hand trembled slightly as he took another sip of brandy. But it may have been that he was stirred by real emotion, if there were anything real in his emotions.

"I admire your sense of humour," he said. "We have laughed together very often, have we not? We have laughed at this strange adventure of life. We have laughed when otherwise we might have wept, being lonely souls in a cruel world. But our laughter does not mean that we are heartless or incapable of sentiment and passion."

Patricia raised her eyebrows with a quizzical look.

"What is this leading up to, my dear Rudi? Are you going to tell me that you have murdered someone, like Eugene Aram? If so, I shall have to tell the police."

"It is leading up to something very beautiful," said Rudi. "It is leading up to the fact that I love you very terribly."

Patricia laughed but gave him a warning.

"That ancient dame in the corner is straining her ears to catch what you're saying. Terribly, did you say, my poppet?"

"I owe you a very great debt, Patricia," said Rudi, with an air of solemnity.

"Oh no, only a few drinks now and then," she answered carelessly.

"Not that kind of debt. I owe you a lot for your friendship, for your laughing spirit, for your kindness to a beggarly refugee."

"Don't mention it," said Patricia, refusing to take him seriously. But she had an idea, an extraordinary idea, that for once he was talking sincerely and that he was actually revealing himself below the surface of his cynicism and pretence.

"Dear lady," he said, in a low voice, "dearest Patricia Hastings, I know you think I'm a little rotter—isn't that what you say?—and I don't defend myself, knowing my own weakness and rottenness, but perhaps all that may be wiped out, burnt out, because of my love for you which is like a flame, a pure white flame, consuming me—perhaps even illuminating me."

"All that is very touching," said Patricia, "but I warn you that the old cat in the corner has sharp ears. She knows you're making love to me."

"Damn the old cat," said Rudi.

"By all means!" agreed Patricia.

"Dearest heart," said Rudi, "we have fought intellectual duels with each other. We have fenced with each other and drawn sparks. You have jeered at me and I have pretended to be angry with you. We have caused some very amusing scandal in the guest house though we have been as innocent as a boy and girl—brother and sister—walking hand-in-hand to church."

"Not quite as innocent as all that!" protested the truthful Patricia. "We have occasionally been over-sophisticated in our views on life. But what then, Rudi, what then my little amorous Austrian? You're making love to me, aren't you? Or am I mistaken?"

"I am making love to you," he said. "I am making love to a laughing lady who will never be serious. Patricia, be serious for just one minute. Believe me for just this time, when I bare my soul to you. You think I'm a charlatan—and that's true. I am a *poseur*—I put on a mask—but there is a real man behind the pose and behind the mask. There is a Rudi Scholl deeply melancholy, frightened by the cruelty of life, desperately in need of comfort and comradeship, yearning for the love of one soul on earth who will understand him and pity him and cherish him. It is this Rudi Scholl who speaks to you now and tells you that he loves you with a very great and humble love."

Patricia saw that he had tears in his eyes. She wondered for a moment if they were tears caused by excess of alcohol, but somehow he convinced her that he really was speaking with sincerity, that for once she was in contact with the real Rudi—a frightened Rudi, afraid of his own loneliness, yearning to be comforted and cherished, the poor little naked soul of the real Rudi Scholl.

"My dear child," she said, not unkindly. "You want to make me burst into tears, but that old cat in the corner is watching and listening."

"Damn the old cat in the corner," said Rudi.

"Certainly," agreed Patricia.

Rudi leaned forward and spoke in a low but vibrant voice.

"I want you to come away with me. I want to get away from Longmead. I'm in what you call a jam—a scrape. Let us go away to some other place. We will marry and live happily as man and wife. You may jeer at me always and I shall not be angry. You shall be my laughing lady and I shall be your beggarly refugee."

"Is that still the real Rudi talking?" asked Patricia. "Or have you put on your pose again, and your mask?"

"It's the real Rudi," he told her. "It's the man I am who speaks to you, pleadingly—desperately."

Patricia gave a little laugh and touched his hand for a moment, regardless of the old cat in the corner whose eyes blinked at this shameless action.

"Miss Patricia Hastings," she said, "has received the kind proposal of Mr. Rudolf Scholl and thanks him for the same. She will be glad to have time to consider so important a matter and to consult with her Mamma."

"Let's go tonight," said Rudi eagerly. "Let's go now."

Patricia raised her eyebrows at this alarming suggestion.

"Do be reasonable, my dear," she said, "I shall have to give a month's notice to the riding school. I can't let them down. And if we're going to be married—do I understand you want to make a respectable woman of me?—I shall insist on the banns being put up in Longmead Church. None of your hole-and-corner stuff for Miss Patricia Hastings. No, sir!"

"A month!" exclaimed Rudi, with a look of despair.

This scene of emotion was interrupted by Donovan who came to take a chair at Patricia's table.

"Let's have a game of twenty questions," he suggested. "It sharpens the intelligence."

"One has to have a bit to start with," said Patricia.

"Excuse me," said Rudi.

He left the table and went out of the room.

"Been quarrelling?" asked Donovan.

"Not exactly," answered Patricia.

"A queer little romantic," said Donovan. "He seems to have something on his mind. I believe Lady Kendrick has a pash for him."

Patricia gave a squeal of laughter at this very absurd idea. It was equally absurd that Rudi had a pash for herself. It was more than mere *blague*. She might have to take it seriously.

CHAPTER XXVI

At Badgers Rudi was accepted by the servants, almost as one of the family. He was there almost every day for a while helping Lady Kendrick to answer the large number of letters which came to her from pacifists and peace-lovers who had read reports of her speeches or had seen her name in journals devoted to Peace. He helped her with little articles she was asked to write for those publications. She was grateful to him for these services.

"I really don't know what I should do without you, dear Mr. Scholl," she told him more than once. "I don't know how I can repay you."

He was not entirely without repayment. Very shyly now and then she slipped a few notes into his hand, with a kind of apology.

"I'm sure you will need this for your expenses."

"You are too generous," he assured her.

He knew how to type and that was a help to her in answering the letters after she had bought a second-hand typewriter in the neighbouring market town. She dictated the answers slowly enough for him to take them down in long-hand, or sometimes to type them straight away on the machine. This was in the drawing-room and that worried him a little.

"Wouldn't it be better for me to type them in Sir William's study?" he suggested one afternoon. "Out of the way of your visitors."

"Oh, I think not," said Lady Kendrick. "My husband regards his study as his sanctum. He doesn't like even the servants to touch his papers."

So it was in the big drawing-room that he did his typing on a little table between the windows and the fireplace while Lady Kendrick sat on the sofa opening the latest batch of letters or reading them carefully before dictating the answers. Some of them were very touching, she thought. Many of them were from young people who wanted to be active in the cause of Peace.

"Listen to this one," she said one afternoon.

She read out a screed from an unknown correspondent:

"*Dear Lady Kendrick,*

I am an art student in London, twenty-two years of age and as poor as a church mouse because my father is an underpaid curate in an East End parish. I heard your speech in the Caxton Hall a few weeks ago and since then I have been thinking about it quite a lot. I would give up everything in the world—even my Art, which I love so much—if I could do something, however small, to prevent another war. But I am very much bewildered about it all. Some of this Peace propaganda is certainly put out by Communists in this country who want us to disarm and remain weak while Soviet Russia increases her strength. Bertrand Russell thinks that, and I believe he is the wisest man we have. But I don't see how another War can be avoided if the world is divided into two systems rearming intensively against each other, building up piles of atom bombs and inventing new and more terrible weapons. You seem to think that spiritual weapons are stronger than guns and bombs. I wish I could believe that! Has it been so in the past? Did all the prayers of all the people stop the wars which began in 1914 *and* 1939*? You seem to be a complete pacifist and to believe in non-resistance, but wouldn't that let in the Russians with their frightful cruelties and debauchery of young minds? Isn't it a terrible dilemma? How are we going to defend the beauty of life if rearmament leads to war and if non-resistance leads to the killing of the soul and the death of all that is meant by the civilized mind? Forgive me writing like this but your face and the tone of your voice and the things you said in the Caxton Hall made me feel that you were talking from your heart and not as a partisan or a fanatic of the Communist creed.*

"One of our intelligent young people," said Lady Kendrick, "and one of many others who write to me. They are thinking things out, poor darlings. They have awakened to the dreadful reality of a menaced world, overshadowing the joy of life. I find it very difficult to answer letters like that. I can't fob them off with a few insincere platitudes. I have to be honest with them. I have to be honest with myself."

"It's a difficult letter to answer," agreed Rudi in a non-committal way.

Lady Kendrick thought out her answer and Rudi typed it:

"*I am so glad to get your letter. It is splendid that young people should be thinking seriously about these perils and problems that face civilization today. It is going to be your world, the world of the generation now growing into young manhood and womanhood. We elders can only hope and pray and give perhaps a little guidance. I share your own perplexities. You have put the dilemma squarely enough. There is no easy answer to it. Perhaps the best answer I can give—and I know it will seem to you like wishful thinking or the pious aspirations of a foolish woman—is just this: Fanatical Communism is a religion, or at least a faith, held by the minds of men and women in many countries. It is in its way a spiritual force but, as we may think, the force of the Evil Spirit. This cannot be countered or defeated by material weapons. There must be a spiritual challenge to it—the challenge of a spirit of goodness instead of evil, pity instead of cruelty, comradeship instead of secret police, the spirit of Christ instead of the spirit of Satan. Therefore every individual mind like yours, my dear, must add to the spiritual power of our own creed and faith. However insignificant, the individual may add to those spiritual vibrations and support those spiritual thoughts and words which will weaken and perhaps defeat the propaganda of the opposing creed. We must proclaim our faith in the liberty of the mind and the true values of life—beauty, love, compassion, truth and our belief that peace is preferable to war, and friendship to hatred and world co-operation more reasonable and more productive of human happiness than a conflict ending in death and ruin and perhaps extinction for both sides. If millions of people—especially millions of young people—think this way, send out this message to the world, not once but every day by every means of thought transmission I believe—I dare to believe—that it will reach and touch the minds of those now blinded by ignorance and embittered by false teaching.*"

Very slowly and with frequent pauses, Lady Kendrick worked out this answer, which Rudi typed on his machine.

"What do you think of that?" she asked, with her normal humility.

"Very good!" said Rudi. "Very helpful to a bewildered young mind." He smiled at her over his machine and something in his smile made her doubtful for a moment.

"I think you are mocking me a little!" she said.

He looked startled and the smile left his lips.

"My dear Lady Kendrick, I assure you that I think it's a wonderful letter. Most inspiring. Very beautiful in its sentiments."

"I want you to be quite sincere with me," said Lady Kendrick. "I have a very poor opinion of my own ability. I do value your help and advice."

"I am delighted to be of the slightest service to you," answered Rudi, in his charming way.

"Well, that's enough for today," said Lady Kendrick. "Perhaps you would like to have a wash. You know the way."

Yes, he knew the way. He was becoming familiar with the rather dark passages, the little steps up and down, the various doors, in this old Stuart house. He made tea for himself and Lady Kendrick one day in the big kitchen when the servants were out. It was on that day that he discovered that a door opposite a little cloakroom which he guessed led into the General's study. That seemed to interest him. He opened it stealthily and looked into the forbidden chamber. He ventured a few paces across the floor with watchful observant eyes. A noble room. The library of an English gentleman. The walls clothed in well-bound books. All the world's knowledge there, but doubtful whether all of it had entered the head of an English General. English Generals were not notorious for intellectuality. Perhaps some of them had been maligned.

With a quick stealthy step—it would be awkward to be found in this room—Rudi advanced towards the desk. It was very tidy. Some papers were there in a neat pile. Not a sheet out of place. There was a writing-pad with blotting-paper, red sealing wax and a brass seal. There was a big inkpot, probably of the French Empire period, very handsome.

Rudi's quick eyes saw every detail of this room, but he could not linger there. He stood still listening intently. There was a noise of footsteps in the hall. He went quickly and silently out of the room and into the little cloakroom opposite. He stayed there for a few moments and then went into the hall and came face to face with young Mervyn, who greeted him without enthusiasm.

"Hullo. You here again?"

"Yes," said Rudi. "I'm helping your mother. It's a great pleasure. She gets so many letters now."

"Oh, I see."

He went upstairs to his own room looking rather miserable.

Lady Kendrick had noticed for some little time that Mervyn seemed worried and unhappy about something. She missed the long talks they used to have together when he was home on leave. Lately he had been very silent and moody and went out for long walks, whatever the weather might be, coming home white-faced and sometimes wet through.

She had questioned him several times—were things going wrong at Sandhurst?—but he would not admit that anything was the matter with him.

"It's quite all right, Mother. I'm perfectly all right. Please don't fuss."

She had to 'fuss' as he called it. She had always fussed over him from his babyhood onwards. She had nursed him through the usual illnesses of childhood—measles, chickenpox, whooping cough—worrying over-anxiously, no doubt, if he had a temperature or lost his appetite. She had been utterly wrapped up in him when he was a small boy, watching the development of his mind and character with pride and delight because of his unusual intelligence—perhaps every mother thought that of an only boy—and his sweet disposition. She had taught him to read, had told him fairy stories, had played interminable games of Beggar-my-neighbour and Snap when he was old enough to like cards. Then one day she had wept bitterly and felt that her heart was broken, and that she was utterly desolate. It was the first day he went to boarding-school. Her husband had insisted on that though she had fought hard for letting him go to a day school.

"You'll make a namby-pamby of him," he said. "You're spoiling him utterly, Beatrice, or at least you try to."

"Love never spoils anybody," she told him. "Children need love—as much as they can get in a cruel world."

But her husband would not yield. Mervyn had gone off to a preparatory school in Sussex and afterwards to Harrow. In a way she had lost him. He was more at school than at home. She lived for the holidays, when she could wrap him round with her love again. But rapidly, with frightening speed, he grew out of the little boy stage. He became a tall lad, self-reliant, hating to be fussed over—as he called her devoted love. . . . Now he was a young man about to be commissioned as an officer, ready for the next war, that terrible and haunting menace. Was he going to be sacrificed to Moloch like a whole generation of youth in her own young womanhood—on the Somme battlefields or in the Ypres Salient? That mustn't happen. She would rather die a thousand deaths herself if she could save her handsome Mervyn.

That night when Rudi had met him in the hall he went to bed early with some excuse of feeling a bit 'chippy'. He had been very quiet and untalkative at supper. She was worried about him. Before going to bed herself she stood listening outside his door and her heart seemed to miss a beat when she heard a kind of moan come from his room.

She tapped at the door and called out.

"May I come in, my dear?"

There was a moment's silence and then he answered.

"No, it's all right. Don't come in."

She turned the handle of the door. It was not locked and she went in. He was sitting on the edge of his bed with his hands up to his face, and when he dropped them at the sound of her coming in, she saw that he had been crying.

"Mervyn!" she cried. "What's the matter, my dear? Tell me."

"I'm all right," he said. "I asked you not to come in."

"You're not all right," she answered, "and I *must* come in. I'm your mother, Mervyn. Tell me what's worrying you. Oh, my dear!"

She went over to him and kneeling on the floor by his bed put her arms round him and kissed his wet face.

"There's nothing to tell," he said. "I suppose I can make an ass of myself if I want to, can't I?"

He spoke harshly and tried to thrust her away, but she held on to him and answered soothingly.

"Of course, my darling! We all have a right to make asses of ourselves. I do so constantly. I can feel long ears sprouting out from time to time like old Bottom the weaver."

He smiled at that and brushed his sleeve across his eyes and spoke without that harshness in his voice.

"I haven't been aware of them, Mother, except perhaps this pacifist stunt of yours. Do go to bed."

"I can't go to bed until you've confided in me," she said. "Surely there's nothing you can't tell me? You used to tell me everything once when you'd been naughty and all that. Do you remember?"

He gave a short laugh.

"I was a kid then. Now I'm going to get my commission in a week or two—one of the brutal soldiery, one of those strong silent men who made England what it is—God help us all!"

She rejoiced that he was talking with his usual humour, but there were still the traces of those tears on his face. She must know what had caused them.

"Have you done anything wrong, my dear?" she asked. "Whatever you've done I shall forgive you and try to put it right. Have you got into trouble about money?"

"Good lord, no!" he answered impatiently. "Do you think I've been faking my mess bills or pinching notes out of the Colonel's wallet?"

"Have you fallen in love with some pretty little slut?" she asked. "If so, I'll invite her to tea."

This seemed to amuse him slightly. The idea struck him as being funny.

"She's not one of those!" he answered.

It was an incautious answer. He had given himself away. Perhaps he wanted to give himself away to this adoring mother to whom he had taken all his troubles as a boy.

"Who is she then, darling?" asked Lady Kendrick. "She's a jolly lucky girl if you've fallen in love with her. Tell her that I'll be a very kind mother-in-law—in due time. Say five years from now, or three, if you both feel desperate about it."

"Mother," said Mervyn after some hesitation. "You may as well know. I told you I've made an ass of myself. I'm very deeply in love with a married woman. It's Mrs. Paget. I love her most frightfully."

It was certainly a shock to Lady Kendrick. What could she answer to that? What could she say to this boy whom she had found weeping in his room?

Mervyn had risen from the bed and walked towards his wardrobe, which he opened and then shut nervously before speaking again.

"It's quite hopeless, of course. She's loyal to her old doctor. She won't come away with me."

Come away with him? That was a staggering thought. He was hardly twenty-one. He had no money except his allowance; he had not yet passed out of Sandhurst.

Lady Kendrick spoke tenderly and without criticism or rebuke.

"She's very charming. I find her quite beautiful. I was so glad when you went riding with her—you two young people. I envied you."

"It began like that," he said. "In fact before then. It was the night she dined with us at Foxgloves. I'm glad you think her beautiful, Mother. I think she's the most beautiful thing on earth."

"Well, I wouldn't go quite as far as that," said Lady Kendrick cautiously. She would have to be very cautious in what she said. She could only help Mervyn if she were completely sympathetic and understanding. He would jib instantly if she spoke one word of criticism or moralizing. Perhaps later she might have to do that. Not now.

"Viola is a very sweet girl," she said. "I can imagine anybody falling in love with her. She's so vital, so frank, so fresh."

This tribute to Mrs. Paget was very pleasing to Mervyn. His eyes lit up.

"I'm so glad you think that, Mother. It's terribly nice of you to say it instead of cursing me for falling in love with a married woman."

Lady Kendrick smiled at him and put her fingers through his hair as he sat down on his bed again.

"My dear boy," she said. "I wouldn't curse you if you fell in love with Mrs. Montgomery-Jones—but of course I should be sorry."

The idea of falling in love with Mrs. Montgomery-Jones was so preposterous that Mervyn had to laugh.

"Mother, you do say the most ridiculous things!" Then he became grave again and gave a little groan. "What am I going to do about it? How am I going to carry on?"

Lady Kendrick took one of his hands and put it to her lips.

"One has to carry on," she said. "My father taught me that. When my eldest brother was killed on the Somme—the apple of his eye—he said to mother: 'we must carry on, my dear. We mustn't show the white flag'."

"That was different," said Mervyn. "A soldier expects to be killed, according to the odds. But the love of a man for a woman, isn't like that. He can't carry on in a normal way if he's absolutely desperate for her, body and soul."

"It's very difficult I know," said Lady Kendrick. "At any rate all the poets seem to think so, especially the Elizabethans who were very passionate, no doubt."

"Oh, curse the Elizabethans!" said Mervyn, as though their passion were nothing to his.

"It's a pity Viola is a married woman," said Lady Kendrick, after a fairly long silence, and as though this idea had only just occurred to her, though it was the fundamental cause of Mervyn's misery.

"She's not really married," said Mervyn. "That damned old doctor is old enough to be her father. She would be perfectly justified in leaving him."

"Does *she* think so, poor girl?" asked Lady Kendrick.

Mervyn hesitated and then answered truthfully, though it was a painful truth.

"No, she doesn't. She talks of loyalty. She pretends she loves the old quack. That's what puts me into an awful mess. It makes everything—hopeless."

"She's a little bit older than you, isn't she?" asked his mother, who as a matter of fact knew the exact age of Mrs. Paget.

"Not worth bothering about," answered Mervyn. "Seven years. Besides, she's young in her mind and young in her heart. That's what really matters."

"Yes, I agree," said his mother, who in her own mind disagreed totally. Seven years make a vast difference between a man and a woman, a boy like Mervyn only just touching manhood, and a woman charming but sophisticated, like pretty Mrs. Paget. When Mervyn became twenty-eight she would be thirty-five. Mervyn now was hardly more than a schoolboy. The thing was too utterly absurd except for his heart-break, his first heart-break.

"I must say you're tremendously understanding, Mother," he said gratefully. "Most mothers would make a row and say beastly things about a girl like Viola. I mean because she's married and all that. I'll have to stick it out, I suppose. I'll have to walk about with a bleeding heart and a stiff upper lip. Isn't that the tradition? Isn't that the code of my rotten old ancestors?"

He spoke with bitterness again, the bitterness of a boy who has unjustly been punished by Fate the schoolmaster, or has been hurt in an accident by no fault of his own.

"Not rotten ancestors, Mervyn!" she said. "Men of courage who served their country. High-minded men on the whole. I must say I admire their tradition. It's really the only way any of us can face a tragedy in life. One's heart bleeds, but one doesn't let everybody know. What's that Shakespeare said about wearing one's heart on one's sleeve?"

"You're the only person I've told," he said in self-defence.

"Thanks for telling me," she answered. She went over to him and held his arms and kissed his forehead. "Mervyn dear," she said, "try to be brave. You feel horribly hurt. For the moment the colour has gone out of life for you. But life is still here—the colour and beauty of it. In a little while the pain won't be so hard to bear. Even a broken heart gets mended."

"Not mine," he said. "Never!"

She smiled at him.

"Never is such a long time. But meanwhile, my dear, I will try to help. A mother's love must seem worthless compared with the other kind, but such as it is it's yours, wishful for your happiness, loyal in your unhappiness, whatever the cause of it, or the blame of it."

In her mind she blamed Mrs. Paget. That young woman, she thought, must have led this boy up the garden path knowing perfectly well that it was baby-snatching. She was probably an immoral little hussy, though she looked so charming and had nice manners. One day she would give her a talking to, but not yet. She felt comforted. Mervyn would get over it, just as he had got over the measles and whooping-cough. He would meet another girl one day, not already married. She would surround him with pretty girls. It was a pity that Viola Paget lived in the village—that would make it more difficult.

Mervyn seemed grateful.

"Thanks, Mother," he said in a low voice.

"Good night, my dear. Try to sleep."

She kissed him again and left his room.

Her baby boy now was a young man in love with a married woman. It made her feel very old and sad. She wept a little in her own room.

During that week-end she spoke to her husband who had come home with his usual mass of papers which kept him up late in his study. Mervyn had gone out before tea-time—she wondered if he had gone round to see Mrs. Paget again—and was not back by seven o'clock, which was when she tapped at the General's door and went in without waiting for an answer. He was sitting at his desk making notes on one of the folio sheets on which was the War Office stamp.

"I want to talk to you," she said. "Can you spare half an hour?"

He gave a heavy sigh and then swung round in his chair.

"Of course! And glad to be interrupted."

"It's about Mervyn. He's in trouble."

She saw the quick look of anxiety in his eyes.

"In trouble, poor lad? What sort of trouble?"

"He's fallen in love with a married woman," she said. "Mrs. Paget."

The anxiety left his eyes and he smiled.

"Good heavens, I thought it was something serious!"

"It is serious," she told him. "He tells me that he's bleeding at the heart."

General Kendrick burst out laughing.

"The exaggeration of youth! The pangs of calf love! I had them myself at his age. I fell passionately in love with a girl called Ada. She was a mother's help looking after my two little sisters."

"You never told me about Ada!" said Lady Kendrick.

"She was a plump little thing," said the General reminiscently. "I met her again some years ago. She was the mother of four—they must be older than Mervyn—and she looked remarkably like Queen Victoria in her middle age."

"William," said Lady Kendrick, ignoring this ancient romance, "I'm really worried about Mervyn. He wants to run off with that Paget girl. He talks of throwing up Sandhurst."

The General was startled by that.

"Good heavens!" he exclaimed. "I never heard of such a thing."

Lady Kendrick saw that he was startled out of his levity. It was no laughing matter—a boy's agony.

"I wouldn't mind him leaving Sandhurst," she said. "I would rather he were almost anything than a professional soldier."

The General's face flushed slightly.

"Don't forget I'm a professional soldier," he reminded her. "And don't forget that in time of war the life of the nation is in the hands of professional soldiers."

"Not always with admirable results," said Lady Kendrick dryly. She regretted that cynicism after having spoken the words. She didn't want to exasperate her simple-minded husband. "Sorry, William. We won't argue about that. The point is that Mervyn is desperately in love with young Mrs. Paget. What are we going to do about it, my dear?"

The General rose from his chair and paced to the fireplace with a heavy frown of thought, but a faint smile on his lips.

"I'm sorry for poor old Mervyn. These things are very painful at the time. But the affair really depends upon Mrs. Paget. We can't do anything about it, but if I have any knowledge of character I don't mind betting that that young woman will handle the situation with delicacy and tact. She looks one straight in the eyes. She's an honest wench and very charming."

"Charming certainly," agreed Lady Kendrick. "Perhaps a little too charming. I mean, she may have been flirting with our poor Mervyn. She may have led him on. Her husband is very much older than his young wife. She may have been tempted by Mervyn's lovely young manhood. Such things happen, don't they? I don't want to be malicious or suspicious, but I want to know the truth about this."

General Kendrick shrugged his shoulders.

"You and I had better keep out of it," he said. "It's a private affair between Mervyn and Mrs. Paget. We have no right to interfere unless we're asked for our advice, and then it won't be taken, anyhow. I put my money on Mrs. Paget. I give her credit for commonsense. Her head is well set on her shoulders and she won't let Mervyn make too much of a fool of himself or too much of a fool of her. She's quite a bit older, isn't she?"

"Seven years!" said Lady Kendrick, raising her hands with a gesture which seemed to say that seven years was a lifetime's difference between a man and a woman. But she felt comforted. All through life in moments of illness and family anxieties, she had leaned on the rock-like commonsense of her husband, his refusal to get ruffled, his calm and sometimes exasperating confidence that the worst wouldn't happen when she had always feared the worst.

"I hope you're right," she said now. "I almost think you are, Bill my dear."

He smiled over to her.

"Don't spoil it by that 'almost'."

She left him to his work again.

He had refused to get ruffled, nearly always, but for some reason he became extremely ruffled that evening. Half an hour after leaving him she heard him give a call from his study.

"Beatrice! . . . For heaven's sake . . ."

There was something urgent in this call, as though he had been taken ill, or as though the house were on fire.

She went quickly to his room.

"My dear! What's the matter?"

He was down on his knees looking under his desk. Then he stood up and stared at her with a look of dismay in his eyes—or was it fear?

"Beatrice," he said quietly, "I've lost some important papers. I left them on my desk when I last came down. Now they've gone."

"They can't have gone," said Lady Kendrick.

"They've gone," he said, raising his voice. "I tell you they've gone. They're very secret. Has anybody been mucking about in this room? Spring cleaning or any nonsense like that?"

Lady Kendrick smiled and shook her head.

"Spring cleaning in this chilly autumn?"

"Beatrice," he said in a low voice, "I must find those papers at all costs. Has any servant——"

"They have strict orders not to touch a paper in this room," said Lady Kendrick. "Mrs. Craddock knows that perfectly well. So does Mary."

"Do they come in here to dust?" he asked.

"Mary hoovered the carpet on Wednesday."

"I wish to heaven she wouldn't hoover the carpet," said the General. "Where's Embry? Send for him. I must see him at once, Beatrice."

"I expect he's doing the boiler," said Lady Kendrick. "I'll call for him."

She paused at the door.

"Will the heavens fall if you can't find those papers?"

He raised his hands with a gesture of angry despair and then gave a queer laugh.

"I don't know about the heavens, but other things will fall if they've got into the wrong hands. No, it's impossible! I'm losing my nerve, I suppose. They must be in this room somewhere. I may have put them into some other place absent-mindedly, although I can't think I did."

He searched under the cushions and behind the curtains and even in the coal-scuttle before there was a tap at the study door and Embry, his old batman, came in.

"Anything I can do, sir?"

The General nodded.

"Come in and shut the door, my dear fellow. I've lost some important papers. Very secret papers. Do you think that girl Mary could have put them in the dustbin or used them for lighting fires?"

Embry shook his head.

"She's not such a fool as that, sir. Besides, she's been told not to touch any papers whatever. I've told her myself more than once. Most likely you've put 'em down somewhere and then forgot."

"Well, for the love of Mike have a look round," said the General. "If I did that I ought to be shot—and I'm certain I didn't."

His man looked in all the places which had been searched by the General. Every drawer was opened, every cupboard, every shelf.

"Not a trace," said Embry. "What you might call an 'opeless quest."

The General stood watching him with a deep furrow on his forehead and anxious eyes.

"No," he said at last, "it's no use looking. They've gone."

"Afraid so, sir. Didn't leave them at the War Office, I suppose?"

"I wish to heaven I had!" answered the General. He stood staring down at the floor and then asked a question. "Do you think anybody could have come in here without your knowing it? A stranger? A thief?"

"Most unlikely," said Embry. "He would have to come in at the front door. I keep an eye open for gypsies and that like.

A fellow came to examine the gas-meter a week ago but he showed his card."

"I suspect that girl," said the General. "These women who tidy up things are enough to drive one mad. I expect she used the papers for lining the kitchen shelves or some nonsense like that. But I'd rather she had done that than not know where they're gone. If they got into the wrong hands——"

"I'll have a word with her tomorrow," said Embry. "But she wouldn't do such a thing. Too much sense in 'er 'ead."

"Most extraordinary!" said the General. "Most infuriating. Well, thanks——"

"Very good, sir." He turned at the door and spoke a few sinister and surprising words. "I wouldn't worry over it, sir. When the end of the world comes there won't be anything more to worry about. Pardon me."

He left the room silently and solemnly.

CHAPTER XXVII

Dr. Paget was having one of his lonely evenings—Viola had gone up to town with Patricia Hastings to see a play called *Ring Round the Moon*—when Hildegard tapped at his door and came in looking curiously shy and embarrassed, following a ring at the front-door-bell and some low-toned conversation in the hall.

"Who is it?" asked the doctor, looking up from a book he was reading—that terrible work called *1984* which had got Viola down one evening.

"Jamie would like to see you," said Hildegard.

She gave a little splutter of laughter and then blushed very hotly.

'Now, what's the matter with that lass?' thought the doctor, 'and who the dickens is Jamie?'

She enlightened him on the subject by giving the full name.

"Mr. James Stewart. He likes me to call him Jamie."

"Oh, he does, does he? Very amiable of him, I'm sure. Well, show him in."

The Poet of Longmead came into the room looking gloomy. He was in his old raincoat with a woollen scarf round his neck.

"Hullo, Stewart," said the doctor genially, "anything the matter with you?"

"Almost everything," answered Stewart with a faint smile. "But this isn't a visit for medical advice. I just want to waste your time for ten minutes or so on a private matter of some slight importance."

"Good!" said Dr. Paget. "Take off that coat and scarf. Sit down and have a whiskey. Tell me something amusing. I've been reading the most infernal book which has given me the horrors. Glad to see you, my dear fellow."

"Well, I have something amusing to tell you, as a matter of fact," said Stewart. He gave a deep-throated laugh, as though there were something very comical in his mind.

"That sounds promising," said the doctor. "Tell me."

"I think I'll have a touch of whiskey first," said Stewart. "It doesn't do to tell a funny story until one's moral atmosphere is warmed up a bit."

"There's something in that," agreed Dr. Paget, getting up to pour out two tots of whiskey. "How is the divine afflatus? Have you been inspired lately?"

His eyes twinkled as he glanced at the poet who had taken off his raincoat and scarf and flung them on to the doctor's sofa before sitting in a deep chair with his long legs outstretched.

Stewart caught his smiling glance and grinned back.

"Well do I know your contempt for my work," he said good-humouredly. "But then it's not written for the likes of you—Philistines and Pharisees. Not that I have any conceit about my own verses. From time to time they fill me with loathing and despair. Poetry—verse-making—is utterly futile when all arrangements are being made for the suicide of the human race."

"Now look here!" said Dr. Paget. "Don't you get on to the international situation or the war in Korea. I've just been listening to the seven o'clock news on the Light Programme. Did you hear it by any chance?"

James Stewart nodded.

"The Chinese have attacked in force. General MacArthur says it's a new war. The Americans are in full retreat after being told that they'd be home by Christmas. It fills one with terror. Four hundred million Chinese in friendly alliance with two hundred million Russians—a beautiful prospect for civilization! The Third World War is near at hand, Doctor. That's why we should grab a little happiness while the going's good. That's why I'm going to tell you something amusing."

"Tell me now," said Dr. Paget. "Anything about Mrs. Montgomery-Jones? A juicy bit of village scandal, or some new joke you've discovered in the works of Aristophanes?"

"Doctor," said James Stewart after some hesitation, "this will make you laugh with considerable hilarity. I've fallen in love with your German *Mädchen*. I'm going to marry her with your permission. I'm afraid you're going to lose your domestic help. Please give my excuses to Mrs. Paget."

The doctor laughed heartily.

"My dear fellow, forgive my ribald laughter, but you asked for it. I'm more than delighted. I can give Hildegard excellent references—a good cook, a very good needlewoman, tidy in the house, and very knowledgable in the works of Hegel, Kant and Bertrand Russell."

"She's marvellous," agreed Stewart, secretly enjoying the doctor's amusement. "She understands things I've written to which I confess I'd lost the cue. She reveals their underlying meaning. She gives me that reverence and adulation which are so necessary to the creative soul. And as you say, she is a good cook."

"Can you afford to marry the girl?" asked Dr. Paget in his candid way.

Stewart shook his head.

"No, that's part of the joke. Before our love gets stale, before the fire of passion burns low, we shall both starve to death. It will be a happy death, clasped in each other's arms, and I hope it will precede the arrival of the first atom bomb."

Dr. Paget looked him in the eyes with a searching smile.

"Stewart," he said, "let's drop all rhodomontade for a second. Take off your mask and let me have a look at your real soul. I believe that underneath your intellectual camouflage you're a straight and simple-minded man with the ordinary instincts of humanity. The point is, do you love the girl? Are you going to be kind to her? I feel a certain amount of responsibility for her happiness and welfare."

Stewart's face flushed slightly at this searching challenge, but he laughed and answered humorously.

"My dear Doctor, don't strip me naked. Don't winkle out my poor little soul and hold it up to the light. Let me assure you that I shan't beat Hildegard or drag her round the room by the hair."

"Good!" said Dr. Paget. "Let's have her in. I expect she is listening through the keyhole, anyhow."

But Hildegard had gone up to her own room like a perfect

lady. When she came down in answer to the doctor's call she was very shy and smiling. Dr. Paget went up to her and patted her hand which he clasped in his.

"My dear child, I'm very glad."

"And I am very, very happy," she answered. "I owe it all to you, dear Doctor."

"Well now," said Dr. Paget, "we must celebrate the occasion. I have an excellent bottle of old port given to me by a grateful patient whom by accident I failed to kill. Hildegard, *gnädiges Mädchen*, get three wine glasses and don't indulge in amorous dalliance with a poet while I fetch the wine."

When he returned with a bottle which looked very old and cobwebbed, he found Hildegard in the arms of James Stewart. She was crying on his shoulder.

"You'd better put on your raincoat again, Stewart," he said gravely. "That young woman once cried on my shoulder and I found it very damp."

"This time I cry for joy!" exclaimed Hildegard, releasing the poet and mopping her eyes.

Dr. Paget poured out three glasses of port with a steady hand. He raised one of them and his smiling eyes beamed at the two lovers.

"My dears, I congratulate you both, and if ever you are in danger of starvation, send for me and I will bring a tin of bully and some digestive biscuits. Hildegard, my Wagnerian beauty, I fear you are going to marry a very poor man. Poetry and Art are the only commodities which have not gone up with the cost of living."

"I am not afraid of poverty," said Hildegard. "I should be more afraid of being rich. That would be very frightening."

"I don't think you'll ever be frightened by that," said James Stewart. "It's not one of the perils which confront us in this terrifying world."

After one glass of port which was very warming to the heart, Hildegard sat on the floor with her head against the knees of James Stewart, who was deep in an armchair pulled up to the doctor's hearth where a log fire was burning.

"It's a queer thing," said Stewart presently, "but I don't

care a damn because the Chinese have invaded Korea. It will probably lead to a flaming hell on earth and I'm sorry for the Amercian boys out there, but one's personal happiness—the happiness of one's miserable little ego—wipes out all other emotions including pity and blue funk. Here for a moment in this fire-lit room I have a sense of warmth and happiness and spiritual comfort. This is very good port, Doctor."

He was stroking Hildegard's brown hair with his thin bony hand.

"That," said Dr. Paget, "is the instinct of one's own survival value. I remember being in the trenches in World War I when there was heavy shelling on the right or left. We felt very cheerful about it so long as we were being left alone. 'My word, those fellows on the left are copping it all right,' we said. Or, 'those fellows on the right are getting it pretty hot, poor bastards'."

James Stewart grinned and bent down to kiss Hildegard's hair without any affectation or shyness.

"Yes, I suppose if we were hyper-sensitive we shouldn't be able to carry on. One has to shut out the tragedy of other people's lives. Boccaccio told his merry tales when masses of people around were dying of the plague."

Hildegard had something to say on this subject.

"It is perhaps the reason why poets are so often unhappy. They're too sensitive to the unhappiness of others. Is that not true, my Jamie?"

"If you call me Jamie before other people," said Stewart, "I shall divorce you after a week of marriage. But what you say, my love, is very true. We poets are miserable swine."

"It is necessary to be unhappy in order to know the deeps and the heights of tragedy, is it not?" asked Hildegard. "Shakespeare, Goethe, Schiller, knew those deeps. It was necessary for them to taste the bitter cup of agony."

Dr. Paget ventured to quote some lines of verse.

> "Who ne'er his bread in sorrow ate
> Who ne'er upon his bed has sat
> Weeping in the midnight hours
> He knows ye not ye heavenly powers."

Hildegard shifted her position on the floor to look at this doctor with raised eyebrows.

"You know that? It is by our great Goethe."

James Stewart gave a satirical laugh.

"Our doctor is an old humbug! He pretends to be a simple and ignorant man. He hides his erudition."

"No, no!" exclaimed the doctor. "I'm only an ignorant quack—a very ill-educated fellow."

"We Germans," said Hildegard dreamily—the doctor had given her another glass of port—"have suffered more agony perhaps than most other peoples. We have lost everything. We have eaten the bread of humiliation. We walk amidst the ruins of our former cities, defeated, hopeless and starving. Out of that misery may come one day a new genius, a new vision, a renaissance of Art and Beauty. That may happen if we are not enslaved by the Russians or massacred in a new war which would finish everything."

She yawned a little. The port wine had made her very somnolent in a beautiful dreamy way.

"Not a very cheerful thought, my Gretchen," said James Stewart. "Let us laugh and be merry for tomorrow we die."

The doctor laughed at both of them.

"I must say you two young people take your pleasure sadly. Be a bit brighter about it, my dears. Make love gaily. Don't mind me. Have another glass of port, Stewart?"

"Thanks, Doctor. But love doesn't express itself in gaiety. It conduces to a beautiful sadness. Romeo and Juliet were not gay. None of the great lovers were gay. Hildegard and I decline to be gay but we're very happy, aren't we, *mein Schatz*?"

"I would like these moments to last for ever," said Hildegard, snuggling closer to her future husband.

"You see, Doctor," said Stewart, thoughtfully, "supreme happiness which only comes through love—a new experience of mine—is saddened by the thought that it cannot last. There is death as the divider. The kiss must end. Somebody must cook the dinner if there is anything to eat. One is dragged from the sublime to the ridiculous by the material necessities of life. That will happen to Hildegard. She will have to wash my shirts because I can't afford a laundress. Poor little German refugee!"

The German refugee did not answer this remark. She was fast asleep with her head against James Stewart.

He winked at the doctor and spoke in a lower voice.

"Doctor, I expect this is the first time such a thing has happened to you. Shameless love and a sleeping beauty in your own sitting-room."

"I like it," said Dr. Paget. "I'm on the side of all lovers."

"You're a poet," said Stewart. "You have the heart of a poet."

"God forbid!" exclaimed Dr. Paget. "I want to make people happy. Poets make them darned miserable—you modern poets who are wallowers in gloom."

"I'll write a merry satire," said Stewart. "I'll make the world laugh at its own folly. I'll make them laugh like hell."

"Have another glass of port," said the doctor.

"Thanks," said James Stewart. "But we mustn't wake this sleeping nymph."

They talked in low voices. Once Stewart made the doctor laugh and Hildegard stirred in her sleep. Sometime later, Dr. Paget noticed that Stewart's head was drooping. The warmth of the fire, the warmth of the port, love and happiness, took him away from the terrifying world into the dream land of his own. His hand slipped over Hildegard's shoulder. His eyes closed. He was alseep.

Dr. Paget looked at them both with a benevolent smile. He had been a matchmaker. He had brought these two young people deliberately in contact with each other.

Presently he heard the sound of a latchkey in the front-door lock. It was Viola back again from her trip to town. He went out into the hall to greet her.

"Don't talk too loud," he said. "Two Babes in the Wood are here. Very touching!"

"What on earth do you mean?" asked Viola, laughing at him.

"Look!" said the doctor, taking her by the hand and pushing his door wider open.

Viola looked in. The poet and the German girl were sleeping like two tired children.

"Good heavens!" exclaimed Viola, greatly astonished.

"Isn't life wonderful?" said the doctor.

Viola didn't quite see it in that light.

"I shall have to give that girl notice," she said. "Cheek, I call it!"

"She's giving *us* notice," said Dr. Paget. "She's going to get married to James Stewart.

Viola's sense of humour asserted itself.

"Well, they can't make a nuptial chamber of your sitting-room, John. And what would Mrs. Montgomery-Jones say if she heard of it? I must say they look rather sweet."

The sound of her voice disturbed the two lovers. James Stewart stirred, stretched his long legs and sat up in a bewildered way.

"Oh lord," he said, "I must have dozed off."

Hildegard sprang up, confused and embarrassed.

"Excuse me!" she said. "It was perhaps the wine. A thousand pardons."

"The wine of love!" said the doctor. "Don't apologize. It was a very touching little episode in a doctor's consulting-room."

"Congratulations to you two dears," said Viola. She went over to Hildegard and kissed her cheek. It was, of course, necessary for Hildegard to burst into tears.

CHAPTER XXVIII

THE Vicar of Longmead knew as much about his parishioners as Dr. Paget did of his patients. In fact very often these two men coincided at the same little houses and cottages, the doctor going there for sickness and the clergyman for spiritual comfort, but the Vicar, having no great conceit of his own power in that respect as well as a sense of humour, accused the doctor more than once of trespassing on his domain.

"The fact is, Doctor, you have no faith in your own drugs and you rely entirely on your bedside manner and the usual tricks of a psychiatrist. You forget that I'm supposed to be the soul doctor. I've a good mind to prosecute you for poaching."

That conversation took place outside the cottage of old Wimshurst, the blacksmith, who had developed pneumonia after an attack of influenza.

Dr. Paget laughed and hit the Vicar a light blow on the shoulder.

"I cheer up my patients," he said. "But you parsons depress them dreadfully. I know when you've preceded me. The poor devil hasn't a smile left in him after you've reminded him of his immortal soul and his failure to overcome original sin."

The Vicar laughed at this thrust, not taking offence.

"They don't get much of that from me. What they want and what I try to give them is a sense of honest to God comradeship in sickness or in health. I don't put on any side. I don't pretend to any spiritual superiority. I know that many of them have far more heroism, far more true saintliness, than I shall ever attain—the mothers of kids always at it from morn till night, these labouring chaps doing their job in all weathers, honest to the bone and quick to do any pal a good turn if he's down on his luck."

Dr. Paget nodded.

"The more I know them the more I admire them. The salt of the earth, Vicar! The old stuff hasn't gone out of 'em. I mean the spirit of their forefathers. The old heroic spirit is still here in these cottages and council houses. They know now that there's danger of another war. It comes to the women over their washtubs with the wireless turned on at full blast. The men are talking about it in the Black Knight. It doesn't amuse them, that idea of a new war. They know that if it comes it will mean death and destruction. They remember the last, and some of 'em, the First World War. They've no illusions. But what is so damn' wonderful is that there's no panic, no showing of the white feather, no mob hysteria in village or town. I take my hat off to our own people."

He took off his hat though a cold wet wind was blowing.

"Doctor," said the Vicar, "how are we going to stop that next war? It just mustn't happen. I'm utterly bewildered and conscience-stricken. I'm a clergyman of the Church of England. How can I reconcile the Christian faith with intensive production of atom bombs, or other diabolical weapons. On the other hand, how can I adopt the full pacifist position of non-resistance which would hand over this country and other nations to Communism and its debauchery and serfdom of the human mind? I'm torn in half, spiritually and morally, by this dilemma."

Dr. Paget laughed and shrugged his shoulders.

"Aren't we all in the same boat?" he asked. "Doesn't the same dilemma bedivil most minds in this country? I don't envy our politicians who have to make the decisions, poor devils. Some of them are instinctive pacifists. Some of 'em went to prison as conscientious objectors. Now they have to back a rearmament programme, half-heartedly and with frightful doubts. Mr. Facing-Both-Ways, the right honourable member for——" His eyes twinkled and he did not finish that sentence. "I must be going," he said. "You'll find old Wimshurst a bit better, thanks to my tender care. Don't drag him down by talking about death and damnation."

"Doctor," said the Vicar, "you're an older man than I and a damn' sight wiser. Is there any way out of this mess? Do you think we ought to rearm at full blast? Or do you think we ought to go on striving for an arrangement with Russia? I want your advice. What am I to say in the pulpit? How am I going to get straight with myself? At the moment I feel like a hypocrite and a liar."

Dr. Paget gave a quiet laugh but there was a look of sympathy in his eyes—a look of pity for this bewildered man.

"My dear fellow," he said, "I can't be your father confessor or your spiritual guide. I'm only an old quack. I rather think we must try to reconcile the irreconcilable—Christian charity and big and better bombs; rearmament, quick and urgent while keeping the door open for negotiation with Russia, and now with China—refusing to be stampeded into war by American rage and impatience which is very natural—completely justified no doubt—but very dangerous in our time of weakness." He held out his hand and gripped the Vicar's. "I, too, am Mr. Facing-Two-Ways," he said. "But I must be off."

He raised his hand in salute and walked to his car which was a few yards down the lane.

That afternoon the Vicar walked over to Badgers in the hope of taking a cup of tea with Lady Kendrick, who had first disturbed his mind by her challenge to his sincerity as a Christian and clergyman by her pacifist views. Perhaps that was an exaggeration now he came to think of it. He would have been tortured anyhow by the irreconcilability between the teaching of Christ and the threat of atomic warfare. All that Lady Kendrick had done was to bring it more forcibly to consciousness by her advocacy of non-resistance.

She was at home working with the Austrian refugee who acted as her secretary. When he was shown into the drawing-room the floor was littered with letters and envelopes and the typewriter was clicking away under the quick sensitive fingers of Rudi Scholl.

"Sorry, Vicar," said Lady Kendrick, smiling and holding out her hand. "We use this room as our workshop. You know Mr. Scholl, of course. He is my devoted assistant in the cause of Peace."

"Splendid," said the Vicar. "But I'm beginning to think that the cause of Peace is a lost cause. I'm in very low spirits about it. The Chinese attack in Korea fills me with alarm."

He had given his hand to Rudi Scholl who held it limply and then went down on his knees to clear up the litter of papers. The Vicar noticed that as he did so he seemed nervous and ill-at-ease, and that afterwards, when tea was served, he was very silent and avoided the Vicar's eyes when directly addressed in order to bring him into the conversation.

'That young fellow looks rather ill,' he thought, 'or worried about something. Perhaps he's had a row with Patricia Hastings.'

Further talk about Peace was interrupted by the arrival of two other callers—the elderly sisters who were 'regulars' at Foxgloves. Their conversation was on trivial matters such as the weather and the ridiculous cuts in electricity at the most awkward hours.

"I hesitate to mention it in the presence of the dear Vicar," said one of them, "but I was plunged into darkness in the midst of a bath. What could I do?"

Lady Kendrick laughed in her deep-toned voice.

"Most embarrassing, I must say! What *did* you do?"

"I lay there for half an hour in the utter darkness, asking why God allowed the Labour Government to drag down this unhappy country to the level of the Dark Ages."

"Did you get any answer?" asked the Vicar blandly, with a smile in the direction of Lady Kendrick.

It was the other sister who replied.

"The answer is obvious. We are being punished as a people for betraying dear Mr. Churchill in the last Election. Wasn't it Mr. Gladstone who said that a nation gets the government it deserves?"

"Or was it Lord Salisbury?" asked Lady Kendrick. "Let me pour you out another cup of tea, my dear."

"How sweet of you. And such nice tea!"

The General put in an appearance and was polite to the company but absent-minded and thoughtful. Presently he glanced at the Vicar and said: "Come into my study, Vicar. I'm sure the ladies will excuse us."

"I'm not sure that they will!" said Lady Kendrick teasingly.

But she allowed the Vicar to depart and on the way to the

study the General gripped his arm and spoke in a lowered voice.

"I thought I would rescue you. You must find these tea-parties intolerable. Those two old dames are a bit trying, don't you think?"

The Vicar laughed.

"As a parson I have to do a certain amount of penance—tea-parties included."

"I can't bear tittle-tattle," said the General.

He led the way into his study where a log fire was burning in the big old-fashioned chimney-place.

"Have a cigar?" he asked after shutting the door.

"I'd prefer a cigarette," said the Vicar.

The General pushed over a silver box and then stood with his back to the fire. On his desk was a pile of papers and a reading lamp.

A good-looking spaniel settled down to sleep again after a pat from his master. The Vicar took a glance at this tall heavily-built man standing there under the portrait of one of his ancestors in uniform—the old scarlet tunic of the Georgian era.

'The same type,' thought the Vicar, 'the same quality—courage, devotion to duty, loyalty to the soldier's tradition. Young Mervyn is made in a more delicate mould. He gets that from his mother.'

It was odd perhaps that he should have thought of Mervyn at that moment, because the General's next words mentioned that young man.

"I'm a bit worried about Mervyn."

"Not too well?" asked the Vicar.

The General gave a quiet laugh and then sighed.

"The boy has fallen in love with a married woman. This is between ourselves, Vicar, I thought I'd ask your advice. I expect you come up against cases like that."

The Vicar had heard rumours that Mervyn Kendrick was having a love affair with Mrs. Paget. Or rather, they put it the other way round, these scandal-loving ladies of Longmead. 'Mrs. Paget who ought to know better was playing fast and loose with young Kendrick. Baby snatching! Too disgusting.'

He had heard something like that from Mrs. Montgomery-Jones upon whom he had to call now and then.

He raised his hands slightly.

"Nothing much to worry about, General, in Mervyn's case. He's very young and impressionable. He has his career to make. Sandhurst won't stand for that kind of thing."

"He talks of chucking Sandhurst," said the General gloomily. "But of course that's ridiculous, especially at the present time. One doesn't desert in face of the enemy, so to speak."

'One doesn't desert in face of the enemy. That's the old tradition,' thought the Vicar. 'I like to hear him say that. It's so wonderfully typical of the man and his caste. Mid-Victorian. The younger crowd are rather apt to chuck tradition. They think it comical.'

"I suppose I can speak in strict confidence?" he asked, with a smile, not to make things too serious.

"Of course," answered the General.

"I mean one's not supposed to mention ladies' names."

"Do you know her?" asked General Kendrick.

"Mrs. Paget, isn't it?"

"How do you know?" asked the General.

The Vicar laughed quietly.

"My dear General, Longmead, like every other English village, is Argus-eyed and it's a whispering gallery for any little tit-bit of scandal, imaginary or over-dramatized. The first time Mervyn went riding with Viola Paget it was noted by observant ladies behind lattice windows. The second, third and fourth time made them fear the worst and pity the poor doctor!"

"Frightful!" said the General with a laughing groan. "I dare say they've made up a bit of scandal about me."

The Vicar had heard several bits of scandal about General Kendrick. He had been seen talking to a pretty gypsy girl on the heath. He had stood chatting to Patricia Hastings when she was waiting outside old Wimshurst's smithy for a horse to be shod. He had been seen in London at the Café Royal and the Ivy restaurant with Gladys Trent, who had played the part of a bad woman in a play by Somerset Maugham. Besides, why did he stay up in town so much? There were perfectly good fast trains from Waterloo, up to a late hour. The War Office was, of course, a very convenient alibi.

"I wouldn't be surprised," said the Vicar, keeping those things dark. "But why I mention the name of Viola Paget is that she is a very charming girl and as straight as—well—a silver birch when it's straight."

The General's eyes brightened and he looked greatly relieved.

"I'm so glad you've said that!" he exclaimed. "That's my own idea. That's what I tell Beatrice. She's a young woman with her head well screwed on her shoulders. She won't do anything foolish with Mervyn. Of course he's lost his head, poor lad. It's his first love-affair and she's an attractive young woman. I'm devilish sorry for the boy. That kind of thing hurts. It's not all honey, this love business. When I was a young subaltern——"

He checked himself and laughed.

"Well, that's another story. The point is, do you think I ought to talk to him? I hate the idea of playing the heavy father. As a matter of fact I'm devilish shy of butting in on a delicate affair like this. You know what young fellows are, especially with a father!"

The Vicar nodded.

"Always a bit of a strain between father and son at a certain age. I used to resent my own guv'nor jawing about my private affairs and prying into the secret chambers of my heart—however full of trash and nonsense. Mothers can do it better."

"I agree," said the General. "Beatrice has played up well, I think. No reproaches. Sympathy and understanding. Isn't that the best line?"

"Certainly the wisest," agreed the Vicar.

The General was silent for a few moments. Then he spoke again.

"Of course I love every hair on the boy's head. He means almost everything in life to me now—I mean apart from duty and all that. I don't see much of him but—well—he's always here—if you know what I mean." He put his hand on his heart with a shy kind of laugh, remarkably like the shy laugh of his son Mervyn. "One doesn't want to sentimentalize," he went on, "but an only son has a rather special place in one's personal life. Beatrice, of course, dotes on him—always has done."

"Very natural," said the Vicar. "I'm all on the side of mother-love. I didn't get enough of it, myself."

"It can be overdone," said the General thoughtfully. "It may weaken a fellow. And I shudder to think what would happen to Beatrice if anything happened to Mervyn in this dangerous world. I hope I shan't live to see that. But of course a soldier has to take the usual risks. I wouldn't like Mervyn to dodge a soldier's life and its inevitable chances. I mean family honour and all that. Patriotism and so forth."

The Vicar saw how his eyes had softened at this talk about Mervyn. Underneath that military mask, so firm, so clean-cut, so strong in its lines, there was this love for a boy, this tenderness, this—fear of what the future might hold for him.

"Well, General," said the Vicar, reassuringly. "I don't think your boy will come to any harm with young Mrs. Paget. She's not one of those young hussies who lie in wait for innocent youth!"

"Thanks, Vicar," said the General.

"Of course, if you would like me to have a talk with him——"

"I'm afraid he would jib at it," said the General.

The Vicar rose to go, but could not resist a question about the international situation. Here was a man with inside knowledge. Probably few men had more.

"Do you think we shall get out of this mess without a war?"

The General shrugged his shoulders slightly.

"Things are becoming more dangerous every day. God forbid that we get involved in a full-scale war with China. I'm afraid of American impatience. The American people are seeing red at the moment, of course, and it's not to be wondered at, but they have some cool heads at the top. We mustn't disperse our available strength by military commitments in the Far East. Europe is the vital line of defence." He groaned slightly. "Everybody is so slow! Rearmament is such a long term affair, especially when there's a lag in will-power, a reluctance to face facts. Will the Russians wait for us?"

"Is it quite ruled out that Russia may want Peace?" asked the Vicar.

The General looked at him sharply and then smiled.

"I forgot! You're a pacifist, aren't you? Like my wishful-thinking lady."

The Vicar hedged.

"Not a hundred per cent. Perhaps I'm not brave enough to go the whole hog. Not enough spiritual faith."

The General made a startling admission.

"I should be a pacifist tomorrow—today—if I thought it would work. I would meet the Russians at any conference table if I thought they would be open to argument and good will. Do you think I want the guns to go off? Do you think I have anything but loathing for war—and a war which next time will leave very little standing above the ruins? Do you think I want my boy and millions of other boys to be blown to bits? But I can't see any way out but the way of strength to resist attack."

"Is that a way out?" asked the Vicar. "Shan't we be blown to bits, anyhow? Will victory mean anything if we are all destroyed?"

"I don't believe in the white feather," said the General. "If we have to go down let's go down with our flags flying."

"Wouldn't it be better not to go down?" asked the Vicar. "Is there no possible way of avoiding all that by wise diplomacy, wise statesmanship, a desperate attempt to understand the other fellow's point of view and to prove our own good will?"

"Not when you're dealing with the fanatics of a frightful creed," answered the General. He laughed and then held out his hand. "It's your job to pray, Vicar. It's mine to speed up the material for defence. Perhaps both jobs are worth while. I'm glad to have this talk with you."

The Vicar felt himself dismissed in the most courteous and friendly way.

CHAPTER XXIX

THE theft of General Kendrick's papers had been as easy as taking a slice of bread and butter from Lady Kendrick's tea-table.

That lady had left Rudi alone in the drawing-room typing the letters she had dictated to him, while she went out to a meeting of the Women's Institute, of which she was the local President. All he had to do was to go out into the hall, listen intently for any servant who might be about, slip into the little cloakroom, listen again, and then open the unlocked door of the General's study, walk to his desk and take the pile of documents with the War Office heading.

That is exactly what he did, but not without hesitation, a sense of fear, and some agony of mind. There is no doubt that he was both frightened and conscience-stricken. In a subsequent argument between Betty Donovan and Patricia Hastings, it was maintained by Betty that Rudi was entirely devoid of conscience and that he was just a little sneak thief, afraid of a policeman's hand on his shoulder, but Patricia, who knew him best, declared that he had many delicate sensibilities, that he was really worshipful of beauty, that he wanted to be honest, except in trifling things—a packet of cigarettes lying about—and that all his instincts were humane, generous and rather childish in their innocence.

When Betty Donovan laughed in an incredulous way, Patricia burst into tears and cried out in a heartrending voice.

"Hasn't he proved what I say by what he has done?"

That conversation, however, is an anticipation of events. It was several weeks before then that he was seen by William Hurley, the landlord of the Black Knight, getting into the bus going from Longmead to Mirfield. Hurley took the seat next to him and entered into friendly conversation. He noticed particularly that the refugee, as they called him, was nursing a brown paper parcel about which he seemed anxious and uneasy.

"Shall I put that parcel on the rack for you?" asked Hurley, good-naturedly. Rudi Scholl muttered something about being absent-minded and wanting to keep his eye on it.

"It's an old suit that I'm taking to the cleaner," he said.

"Going up to London?" asked Hurley presently, not liking to sit next to a silent man. The young fellow, he said, was quiet-like and pale as though he had a pain in the stomach.

He said he was going up to London, but would be glad to get back to Longmead.

He caught the eleven-twenty fast train to Waterloo. There was no doubt about that because Mrs. Paget met him on the platform and travelled in the same carriage with him. She, too, thought he looked worried and unwell, but he chatted with her pleasantly enough when she was not reading the morning paper or glancing at some illustrated magazines. He returned to the idea of painting her portrait and she was afraid that she rather snubbed him about that, so that he became moody and silent. She noticed that he held on to the brown paper parcel as though afraid of losing it.

Nobody saw Rudi Scholl disappear into the underground or get out at South Kensington after changing at Charing Cross and walk down the Fulham Road as far as the greengrocer's shop above which his friend, Peter Oldenburg, had his rooms.

Oldenburg answered the door bell. He was unshaven and in pyjamas under a dirty old dressing-gown of tattered blue silk.

"Oh, it's you!" he exclaimed in German. He stared at Rudi and then saw the brown paper parcel. "Not an atom bomb, I suppose?" he asked, and then laughed at his own joke and said: "Come in, my friend. You look in need of a drop of gin and scared about something."

"I *am* scared," said Rudi, "scared stiff. I wish I hadn't done it."

"Done what?" asked Oldenburg harshly. He stared at the brown paper parcel which Rudi had put on his table. Then he spoke in a low voice.

"Are those the papers?"

"Yes," said Rudi.

"*Gott in Himmel!*"

His fingers trembled as he tried to untie the string. Then he grabbed a pair of scissors lying on the table and cut the string below the knots. He unwrapped the brown paper and pulled out the pile of documents on each of which was the War Office stamp and the words underlined twice—*Very Secret.*

Suddenly he began to laugh in an asthmatical way.

"Very secret! It's too good to be true. Look at the dear little War Office stamp! This is marvellous. *Wunderbar!* Worth their weight in gold on the other side of the Iron Curtain. Very secret. Yes, indeed! Highly confidential as they say in the government offices. Of course I don't know what information they reveal. But official papers are not marked *Very Secret* unless they are—well—let us say Very Secret."

He coughed and laughed explosively. Then suddenly he patted Rudi Scholl's cheek.

"Rudi, my little comrade, you have done well. This is what the English journalists call a 'scoop'. You will be paid for it, my little one. You will not need to starve. You may get drunk every night. You may dance among the fleshpots. How much did I say? £200?"

"You said £500, and a bit more," said Rudi sullenly. "I wouldn't do it again for a £1000. It's a betrayal of my friends—my only friends."

"You will make other friends," said Oldenburg. "One day when they hear of this they will heap favours on you. Important friends, my little one. The future rulers of the world, my sweet innocent boy. I shall like to see you Kommissar of Art and Culture with your headquarters in Chelsea Town Hall." He laughed again until he had a frightful fit of coughing. "Let's get down to these papers," he said presently. "Let's see if they're really important. They may be worthless after all. Pour yourself out a dose of whiskey, my little miserable one. Don't stint yourself. Hand me over that cough mixture on the mantelpiece. This cough will kill me. Oh dear, oh dear!"

After two hours study interrupted by exclamations and oaths in several languages, Oldenburg agreed that the papers taken from Major-General Sir William Kendrick's study were important.

"Full of most interesting information on certain plans for the Defence of the West. Very technical. Very detailed. Very, very, secret."

Rudi Scholl went back to Longmead by the nine-forty-five to Mirfield. It was a coincidence, but not a very remarkable one, that the Vicar was on the same train. Every Wednesday he went to town to visit his father and mother, getting very old now, at their flat in Lexham Gardens and this happened to be a Wednesday. He spotted Rudi Scholl and with his usual good-nature suggested that they should have a cup of coffee or something in the restaurant car. They found two seats and sat opposite each other. But the young Austrian, generally so talkative, sat rather silent and glum, so that presently the Vicar turned to his *Evening Standard.* Rudi had ordered a bottle of beer and when the man put the bill on the table for both of them, Rudi said, "I'll pay," and pulled out his wallet.

"No, no!" said the Vicar, "it was my invitation."

He knew that this fellow was generally 'stoney-broke'. He had heard that from Betty Donovan and others.

"That's all right," said Rudi.

To the astonishment of the Vicar, he pulled out a one-pound note and seemed to have quite a packet of others in his wallet. 'He must have sold a picture,' thought the Vicar. 'He must have had a stroke of luck, poor fellow.'

"How are things going at Foxgloves?" asked the Vicar. "I expect the Donovans are having a difficult time, aren't they?"

Rudi nodded.

"Donovan says he's always staring ruin in the face. It's all right as long as it doesn't hit one in the face. I lived with ruin, so I know."

'One of the refugees,' thought the Vicar. 'He was one of Hitler's victims. In the background of his mind is a concentration camp, verminous, crowded with half-starved men, under brutal guards who knocked them about, typhus, pneumonia, every kind of horror in a pest-house. Poor devil!'

They took the bus from Mirfield to Longmead, but had no

further conversation as the Vicar gave up his seat to a woman with a small child.

It was after that visit to town on that particular Wednesday that Patricia Hastings and others noticed that Rudi Scholl seemed to have come into money. And it was about four weeks later when Rudi Scholl asked Patricia Hastings again to go away with him from Longmead.

For the first time since she had known him he spoke with a kind of desperate sincerity, dropping all cynicism and verbal highfaluting, scaring her a little by a kind of urgent passion.

It was rather late in the evening after dinner at Foxgloves. The old couples had departed for bed; Donovan and his wife were working in the little room they used as an office. Patricia sat in a deep armchair which she had pulled up close to a log fire. She was reading a magazine, with a lighted cigarette on a little table by her side. Outside there had been a fall of snow covering the fields with an ermine mantle. Rudi came in from his studio with flakes of snow on the shoulder of his raincoat, which he took off and threw over a chair.

Patricia looked up and grinned at him.

"Hullo, Eugene Aram! Have you buried the body yet?"

He came over to her and spoke urgently in a low voice.

"Patricia, I want your answer to the things I said last time."

She raised her eyebrows and pretended not to understand.

"What did you say? I've forgotten. Was it important?"

"I told you I loved you. Isn't that important?"

Patricia stubbed out her cigarette in the ash-tray on the little table and laughed.

"My dear Rudi. You've been telling me that ever since you came to this low dive. In return—because you amused me—I stood you many little drinks and innumerable cigarettes. Haven't I played fair?"

Rudi stood looking down at her with sombre eyes.

"You jeer at me always! You mock at me! It's because I liked to make you laugh and hid my real self from you."

"Have you a real self?" she asked. "Is there anything honest and true inside your layers of camouflage and insincerity?"

He was silent for a moment, standing there with his back

to the log fire, with a pale face and his lock of dark hair falling over his forehead. The grandfather clock in the corner of the lounge beat with an audible tick-tick in the quietude of the big room.

"You are cruel to me," he said. "You do not believe a word I say. When I say I love you, you laugh. You think I say only damn' foolery. How can I make you believe?"

Patricia answered with smiling eyes.

"My little Austrian poppet, I'm very fond of you in a way. I should miss you if you went away from me, just as I might miss a little puppy dog."

His face flushed heavily.

"You insult me," he said. "You scorn me. I am a damn' fool to love you but I cannot help myself. I have loved other women. I knew many girls but with you it is different. You are intelligent. You have a civilized mind. You are more than a pretty girl with whom one plays about. You stir a very deep passion in me. We belong to each other. It was destiny which made us meet."

Patricia laughed again.

"You little play actor!" she exclaimed. "How you like dramatizing yourself!"

Suddenly he went down on his knees and put his head on her lap and gave a kind of sob. She was startled and rather touched. She put her fingers through his hair and said, "Hush, you silly boy!"

"I am unhappy," he said. "I have no joy in life. I want to be loved. I am a refugee alone in the world. Please love me. I implore you to love me."

He raised his head and spoke in a tearful way. She saw that his eyes were wet. They were real tears.

"For goodness' sake get up," she whispered. "There's someone coming."

She pushed him away and he stood up. Someone came into the lounge. It was Donovan who came to put out the lights. He had already switched off one when he saw the two people in the room.

"For the love of Mike!" he exclaimed. "I thought everybody had gone hours ago. Are you two people indulging in illicit love? Go and do it somewhere else, children. I have to economize in electricity. The Minister of Fuel and Power——"

He looked at them with his shrewd smiling eyes.

"Clear out, Rudi," he said, "or I'll give you a kick in the pants."

Rudi turned on him savagely in a sudden rage.

"That is all I get in this cold hell!" he said. "A kick in the pants. You have no pity. Your women have no pity. You despise all foreigners. You treat them like dirt. Wait until the Russians come. They will be here before long. Then it will be my turn to laugh when your women are abused and your men have to dig their own graves before being shot."

"The lad has gone mad!" said Donovan, astonished by this hysterical outburst.

Rudi Scholl grabbed his raincoat and flung himself out of the door and then through another door into the courtyard.

"What's up with him?" asked Donovan.

Patricia smiled but looked a little distressed.

"A nerve storm," she said. "I feel a little sorry for him. If you hadn't come in I should have flung my arms about him and said: 'I am yours, my motherless orphan. Take me or leave me.' "

Donovan seemed to think this very funny.

"You ought to be spanked," he said. "You've flirted with that little spalpeen for six months or more, led him up the garden path and then refused to give him what he wanted. Heartless I call it. He's quite right. Englishwomen are essentially cruel. Not like the kind-hearted Irish."

"It's too late to argue that," said Patricia. "I must go back to my dog kennel. Is it still snowing?"

"The snowflakes are spreading a white magic over the landscape," said Donovan. "Have a drop of gin, old dear."

"Good night," said Patricia, getting into a raincoat which lay over one of the chairs. She pulled out her torch from a pocket and flashed it into Donovan's eyes. "You immoral Irishman!" she said. "You've always tried to make love to me. Betty ought to be grateful to me."

"Good night," said Donovan. "May God forgive your heartlessness."

CHAPTER XXX

General Kendrick was fairly certain that Mary Newton had burnt his papers. He had cross-examined her and she had admitted that she had taken away a bundle of newspapers from his study and used them for lighting fires. Most probably she had, he thought, taken up the other papers as well and used them for the same purpose. He remembered what had happened to Carlyle's manuscript of the French Revolution. No great harm had been done. There were two copies in the War Office. The only danger had been that they might have fallen into the hands of enemy agents, deliberately stolen with sinister intent. Next time he would be more careful, and put them into a locked drawer. He would never be able to get back for a week-end at Badgers unless he brought some of his work. He brought it back on another week-end and after sitting up late one evening put the papers in the bottom right-hand drawer of his desk. That girl, Mary Newton, fool as she was, wouldn't go to his drawers for waste paper to light the fires. He meant to lock the drawer, but had mislaid the key. Anyhow, it was quite all right. There were no Russian spies about in Longmead, as he thought to himself, with a smile at the absurdity of the idea.

The following evening being Sunday, he went to dine with Dr. Paget and his wife. Beatrice had cried off not feeling very well—a bit of a chill. He was glad to have the opportunity of seeing Viola Paget again and confirming his opinion that she was a sensible young woman who would not take advantage of Mervyn's infatuation. "As straight as a silver birch, when it's straight," the Vicar had said. He remembered that odd simile. . . .

It was ten o'clock that evening when Lady Kendrick, who had been sitting by the fire in her own bedroom writing some personal letters, pushed away her blotting-pad and note-paper, gave a little sigh and put on a blue silk dressing-gown. She certainly had a cold. There was a hot feeling at the back of her nose. It might be as well, she thought, to take a couple of aspirins. Unfortunately, she had left the little bottle in her writing-desk in the drawing-room. She was wearing a pair of bedroom slippers lined with fur. They made no clatter down the stairs. She went down as quietly as a ghost. Suddenly when she was in the hall she heard a noise in her husband's study. It was a very slight noise, like a drawer being opened stealthily, and then a faint rustle of paper. She stood for a moment outside the study door. She had not yet switched on the hall light, being able to see by a faint shimmer of moonlight which came through a tall window in the hall. But there was another light in the study. The door was open and she could see the tiny light of a torch moving about the room. She felt the touch of fear. Could it be a burglar?

"Who's there?" she called out sharply.

The tiny light flashed off. There was no sound in the room. Her hand reached out for a switch just inside the study door. In a second the room was flooded with light.

Rudi Scholl was there. He had turned swiftly away from the desk and was standing rigid with a file of papers clutched in one hand. His face was as white as a sheet of foolscap.

Lady Kendrick cried out.

"Mr. Scholl—Rudi—what are you doing here?"

For a moment he seemed unable to answer. Then he spoke in a nervous frightened way.

"I left something here. I came in to get it. Excuse me."

"How did you get into the house?" she asked.

"Through the back door," he answered. "It was open. Your servants do not lock up as well as they should. Pardon me. I am so sorry. It's really unforgivable."

She came closer to him.

"What are those papers under your arm?" she asked.

"Just papers," he told her. "I have been writing—some sort of a novel—very foolishly I left it in this room when the General asked to see me about something. I'm so sorry to have disturbed you, Lady Kendrick. I will be going now if you will forgive me."

She stared into his eyes which avoided that searching look, in which there was a kind of horror.

"Those are my husband's papers," she said. "You are stealing them. It was you who stole the others."

He dropped the file of papers on to the floor.

"Yes," he said. "I am the thief. I have betrayed the one woman in the world who believed in me and was kind to me. I am a Judas." Suddenly he went down on his knees and wept and cried out through his weeping. "I beg you to forgive me! I ask you to forgive me. I wish I had killed myself rather than do this thing. Dear Lady Kendrick, my very dear lady——"

He tried to clasp one of her hands but she drew back from him.

"I believed in you!" she said in a low voice. "Why have you stolen those papers? I don't understand."

"I sold them for money," he said. "I was very greatly tempted. Forgive me."

"Who wants those papers?" she asked. "Who pays for them?"

"Those who deceive you," he said. "Those who pretend to be pacifists but take their orders from Moscow. I am a pacifist. I did not deceive you about that. I swear to you I did not deceive you about my love for Peace. My dear lady, forgive me! I will pay it all back. I will serve you with my whole heart and strength. I worship you as a saint."

He caught hold of one of her hands and raised it forcibly to his lips and made it wet with his tears.

"Don't touch me!" she said, dragging away her hand. "You have lied to me. I trusted you. I loved you almost as a son. But you are a reptile, a snake in the grass. What shall I do with you? How shall I dare to tell my husband? How can I go on working for Peace not knowing who is lying as you have lied?"

"Forgive me!" pleaded Rudi again. "I hate myself worse than you can hate me. I have made my own hell."

"Get up," said Lady Kendrick sternly. "I ought to ring for the police."

"No!" he cried in a kind of terror. "Not that!"

"Go," she told him in a harsh voice. "Leave this house. I shall have to tell my husband. He will deal with you."

"Not the police!" cried Rudi. "I will make amends. I will tell everything."

"Leave me," said Lady Kendrick. "I will never see you again."

He wept again and tried to speak. Then suddenly he gave a startled panic-stricken look and dashed out of the room. There were heavy footsteps in the hall. It was General Kendrick who had come back from his dinner with the Pagets. He came into the room and was startled to see his wife there standing like a ghost with a dead white face and tragic eyes. He stared at her and then saw the file of papers on the floor.

"Beatrice!" he exclaimed, "what has happened? Those papers!"

"Somebody has tried to steal them," she said. "We've had a thief in the house. It's Rudi Scholl whom I thought I could trust."

"Good heavens!" said General Kendrick.

It was the General who telephoned to the police, that is to say, to the one village policeman who upheld the Majesty of the Law in Longmead; kept his eye on stray dogs, boys with catapults, motorists with out-of-date licences and young louts who had destructive tendencies. He had an extensive beat reaching out to the heath and outlying cottages.

"I'll let him know when he comes in," said his wife.

It was two hours before he came round and it was too late to do anything about Rudi Scholl.

At about half-past eleven that night, Donovan, who was sitting up late playing gin-rummy with Betty and Patricia Hastings, suddenly looked up from his cards in a startled way and said, "What's that?"

"What's what?" asked Betty. "You're not seeing ghosts again, are you?"

"It sounded like a shot."

"A poacher in the woods," said Patricia. "Good luck to him."

"Too close for that," said Donovan. "It sounded as if it came from one of the barns."

He left the card-table, went out into the hall, took down the hurricane-lamp which hung on a peg and went across the courtyard to Rudi's studio. Snow had fallen freshly and his footsteps were muffled. There was a light burning in the studio but there was no answer when he gave a bang at the door and shouted out:

"You all right, young fellow?"

No answer—that was queer. The door was locked and resisted Donovan's attempt to get in.

"Rudi!" he shouted. "Are you awake, man?"

No answer.

Donovan was a heavy man and when he put his weight against the door it forced the lock and he crashed in.

"For the love of Mike!" he said in a frightened voice.

Rudi lay crumpled up on the floor. One hand clutched a small pistol. From under his head which was face down on the floor there was a trickle of blood.

Donovan stooped down, holding his hurricane lamp.

"Holy Mother of God!" he said, crossing himself in the presence of death.

He looked round the studio. It was in disorder with clothes strewn on the floor. There was a half finished portrait of Lady Kendrick on the easel. Other canvases were stacked against the wall. The camp-bed had not been made and its blankets trailed to the floor.

Donovan went back to the two women. Before going into the room he stamped the snow off his shoes. It was Patricia who saw the whiteness of his face. She half rose from her chair.

"What's the matter?" she asked. "Somebody hurt?"

Donovan looked at her and there was pity in his look. Patricia had been fond of Rudi Scholl in a funny way.

"It's Rudi," he said. "He's shot himself."

Patricia gave a little cry.

"Dead, do you mean?"

Donovan nodded.

"Steady, my dear," he said.

She had moved away from her chair and taken two steps as though going to the studio. Then she swayed and would have fallen if Donovan had not caught hold of her.

"Rudi!" she cried. "My poor little Rudi!"

"Get a drop of whiskey," said Donovan, speaking to Betty who had not uttered a sound but looked white-faced.

"No!" cried Patricia. "What's the good of that? Is Rudi *dead*? I can't believe it. Why should he be dead? I was unkind to him. He loved me, you know. I laughed at him."

She put her hands to her face and wept convulsively. Betty put her arms round the weeping girl.

"I'm sorry," she said. "I'm sorry."

It was then that the village policeman, Bob Marples, came to the outside door and rang the big bell. Donovan went to open it.

"It's a bit late," he said apologetically, "but I want to speak to the young Austrian fellow. Something about some stolen papers."

"He's dead," said Donovan.

"Dead? You don't say——"

Nothing like that had happened in the village of Longmead in the experience of a village policeman.

They sent for Dr. Paget. It was a few minutes before midnight when they heard his car drive into the courtyard.

Presently he knelt beside the body of Rudi Scholl and turned it over.

"Poor boy!" he said. "What did he do that for?" he asked.

At the inquest in Mirfield, evidence was given by those who knew Rudi Scholl and had seen him shortly before he killed himself. Among them were Donovan and his wife, Patricia Hastings, Dr. Paget whose evidence was purely medical as to the cause of death, and Lady Kendrick.

Then the stealing of the General's secret papers was revealed when Lady Kendrick was being questioned by the Coroner and it created a sensation in court.

"Did he receive any money for them, as far as you know?" asked the Coroner.

"Yes, he admitted that he had been paid for them," she answered.

"By whom, do you think?" asked the Coroner.

Lady Kendrick hesitated and then answered in a low voice:

"By his Communist friends."

The Coroner adjusted his pince-nez and paused before his next question.

"Have you been—are you in fact—associated in any way with the Communist party or those who are called, for some reason unknown to me, 'fellow-travellers'—that is to say, sympathizers and secret supporters of the Communist creed and activities in this country?"

There was a murmur in the public gallery. The Vicar's sister, Elizabeth, was there and said in an audible voice, "Yes, indeed!"

"Silence!" cried the usher.

Lady Kendrick answered quietly.

"It is possible that there are Communist sympathizers using our Peace Movement—the work of all peace-lovers and pacifists—as an opportunity for their own purpose. They are not friends of mine. They are unknown to me. I do not believe in Communism."

"This young man," said the Coroner, after another pause, "—this Austrian refugee—he was an intimate friend of yours, Lady Kendrick?"

"He helped me with my work for Peace."

"He was a frequent visitor to your house?"

"He acted as my secretary."

"Had you any suspicion that he was a Communist in close touch with other Communists in this country?"

Lady Kendrick hesitated again for a few seconds.

"Once or twice I had a vague idea—hardly a suspicion—that as a younger man he had leaned towards Communism. But I believed that he could not be a Communist now."

"What made you so certain of that, Lady Kendrick?"

"He hated cruelty. He had pity for human suffering. He had a horror of war."

"And yet he stole your husband's secret papers and sold them, you believe—we have no direct evidence about that—to Communist friends?"

"He yielded to temptation," said Lady Kendrick, "a desperate need of money."

"It was a great betrayal of your trust, was it not?"

"It has been a terrible blow to me. He was always so charming and obliging. I believed him to be a noble-minded young man."

There was a subdued laugh in the public gallery, sternly hushed by the usher.

"According to the medical evidence," said the Coroner, "this young man shot himself. What induced him, do you think, to take his own life?"

Lady Kendrick was silent for a moment or two until the Coroner repeated his question.

"I think he suffered an agony of remorse when I discovered his treachery. It was like Judas who betrayed his Master and went out and hanged himself."

This answer caused another sensation in court, but this time there was no laughter.

The Coroner seemed anxious to discover the real motive behind Rudi Scholl's suicide. He was sharp in his examination of Patricia Hastings.

"You were almost the last person to talk to the deceased?"

"Yes."

"You were sitting together in the lounge of the guest house known as Foxgloves?"

"Yes."

"You were alone with him?"

"For most of the time until Commander Donovan came into the room."

"What time was that?"

"About half-past eleven."

"Half-past eleven at night. How long had your conversation lasted with the deceased?"

"For perhaps an hour."

"He was quite cheerful?"

"No, he was not cheerful. He was upset."

"Was there a quarrel between you?"

Patricia hesitated.

"Not a quarrel exactly."

"What do you mean by exactly? Was there anything like a quarrel?"

"He was upset because I laughed at him."

"You laughed at him? What caused your laughter."

"He was talking rather—foolishly."

"He was making love to you?"

"Need you ask these questions?" said Patricia angrily. "They seem to me offensive."

"I must ask you to answer my questions, Miss Hastings. Was this young man making love to you at that late hour?"

"He said he loved me," answered Patricia.

Suddenly she burst into tears, but recovered herself quickly.

"Did he make some proposal to you?" asked the Coroner in his bland inquisitive manner.

"He just said that he loved me. Isn't that enough?"

"And you thought that was comical? Why did it strike you as being funny?"

"I suppose I have a right to my own sense of humour?"

"A very odd sense of humour," said the Coroner. "Next witness, please."

The inquest ended in the only possible verdict. It ended in court but not in the village of Longmead where for many days it was discussed at tea-tables, wash-tubs, and the public bar of the Black Knight. Among some of these village commentators was the belief that her ladyship had been 'diddled' by the Austrian refugee who, of course, was a Russian spy getting into her good graces, poor innocent soul, in order to steal her husband's papers.

"A dirty dog!" said old Wimshurst, who had recovered from his attack of pneumonia. "And there are lots of dirty dogs of the same breed. We let 'em in to undermine this country which stinks of Communism."

"But why did he shoot himself?" asked William Hurley, the landlord of the Black Knight.

"Afraid of the police, of course. Knew the game was up."

That was not a satisfying explanation to some of those who had known him well—not to Patricia Hastings, nor to Lady Kendrick, nor even to Donovan, who had found him dead.

"He wasn't a complete villain," said Donovan. "A complicated character, I should say. Weak, of course, and hysterical, an easy prey to temptation—aren't we all?—and then full of contrition and remorse when he was found out. Poor little swine! I can't help feeling sorry for him. God rest his soul!"

"You'd give extenuating circumstances to Satan," said Betty. "I always knew he was phoney to the marrow of his bones. There was nothing real in him. He was a fake all through."

It was then that Patricia Hastings defended him, or at least proclaimed her faith in Rudi Scholl's sincerity.

"He wanted to be loved. He felt desperately lonely. Underneath his mask there was something real."

"He stole the General's papers," said Betty. "He betrayed the woman who had mothered him and trusted in him—poor Lady Kendrick. Why all this soppy sentiment about the little wretch?"

"It's a psychological problem," said Donovan. "Why did he shoot himself?"

"Afraid of an English prison," said Betty.

"More in it than that," said Donovan. "I believe he shot himself because he had disgraced himself in the eyes of those who had befriended him. A sudden disgust with himself, a hatred of his own treachery. A Catholic priest would understand all that."

Patricia Hastings wept a little She had the awful thought that Rudi Scholl had shot himself because she had jeered at his love. That perhaps was the only sincerity in his soul.

"He was just a little play-actor," said Betty.

"Anyhow, he shot himself," said Patricia, glaring at Betty angrily. "That wasn't play-acting. It was the real Rudi who shot himself after secret agony and despair and self-accusation."

"Let's forget him," said Betty in her hard matter-of-fact way.

"I shall remember him," said Patricia. "He loved me. He was my last lover."

"Ah, now you're talking nonsense!" said Donovan. "Have

a glass of port, my dear. You're still a very attractive young woman. I'm in love with you myself."

That was the inquest on Rudi Scholl, not in the Coroner's court but in the guest house of Foxgloves where perhaps his ghost walked.

CHAPTER XXXI

At the breakfast-table one morning, Mrs. Paget received a square-shaped envelope. She knew the handwriting on it. It was from Mervyn. She had not seen him since that evening when he had scared her by being too emotional. She took out a card and studied it with a smile on her lips. It was an invitation to a Sandhurst Dance. In the corner in his neat handwriting were the words "Do come!"

She pushed it across the table to the doctor, who was reading the headlines of his morning paper while busy with a minute piece of bacon—there was the usual shortage—and some buttered toast slightly burnt on one side by Hildegard who always burned the toast since her engagement to a poet, though psychologically that was difficult to explain.

"What do you think?" she asked. "Shall I go?"

The doctor examined the card.

"Certainly," he answered. "Why not? It ought to be pleasant."

She said no more until breakfast was over and Hildegard had carried out the tray.

"John," she said, as the doctor was folding up his *Times* before going into his consulting-room. "You're quite sure I ought to go to that dance? Isn't it rather asking for trouble? I mean, is it quite fair on that boy, opening things up again?"

"That's all right," he said. "Nice for both of you."

Mrs. Paget looked at him in a queer way, with a secret smile.

"It might be too nice—for both of us. I'm not an old woman, you know. I have dangerous moments. Youth and the joy of life—they're very tempting sometimes."

Dr. Paget did not show signs of alarm. He showed signs of being amused.

"Even at my advanced age," he told her, "I'm not immune from such temptations. But I resist them. That's all that can be expected of us between the ages of nineteen and ninety."

"Supposing I don't resist?" she asked teasingly.

"I should deplore it," he answered, "but in this case, wild heart, I think it most unlikely. I'm not worrying. Where's that pipe of mine? I could have sworn I put it on the mantelpiece."

"Hildegard took it out on the tray," said his wife. "So you're not worrying, eh? Gosh, I've a good mind to give you something to worry about, you old optimist!"

He came over and pulled her ear—a very pretty ear—and kissed her on the cheek.

"I must go to my panel patients," he said. "We'll resume this sprightly conversation at lunch-time."

The Sandhurst dance meant that Mervyn Kendrick and other young gentlemen of his own age had received their commissions. In due course he would be gazetted to some unit of the British Army. Mrs. Paget wrote accepting the invitation and enclosed a little note with the formal card.

Dearest Mervyn,

It's sweet of you to ask me. Of course I shall come. It's a long time since I've been to a real dance, so that I'm quite excited about it. I shall put on my best bib and tucker, so as not to disgrace you before your brother officers.

All my love to you,

Viola.

On the evening of the dance she put on a frock of rose-coloured silk. She had spent a couple of hours in the hair-dressers in Mirfield. The frock fell away from her shoulders —pretty shoulders, as she was bound to admit when she looked at herself in the long mirror.

"Gosh!" she said aloud. "I look so young—and I'm so old really. I'm so abominably old."

Hildegard came up to put some finishing touches.

"*Wunderschön!*" she cried. "You look like a fairy princess."

"Nonsense," said Mrs. Paget. "I'm as old as one of the Ugly Sisters. I don't think I'll go after all. It's ridiculous!"

"You look enchanting," cried Hildegard. "I wish my Jamie could see you. He would write a poem about you. But it would be dangerous for me. I could not risk it. I am myself so very unbeautiful."

Mervyn came to fetch her in a car. He waited for her in the drawing-room and when she came downstairs, he looked abashed at the sight of her.

"Hullo, Mervyn!" she said in a jolly kind of voice. "Do I look all right?"

"You look stunning," he told her, avoiding her eyes as though her beauty were too dazzling.

"Oh well, as long as I don't disgrace you! It's frightfully kind of you to ask me."

"It's frightfully kind of you to come," he answered with one quick look of adoration.

'I ought not to be going,' thought Mrs. Paget. 'It isn't fair on him. My old witch-doctor ought to have warned me off. Mervyn's still emotional about me, poor boy. I shall have to watch my step. I shall have to play the elder sister for all I'm worth. I mustn't give him any chance of being—sentimental. How lovely he looks! How shy and noble—and how young—how young!'

He was in his officer's mess dress—a blue tunic with white gorgettes, and blue trousers with a red stripe. She sat next to him when he took the wheel of his car. He put a rug over her lap and said: "I hope you won't feel cold. It's a bit foggy, worse luck."

It was quite foggy, and he had to drive slowly, sometimes at almost a crawl, peering through the wind-screen to see the edge of the road. The headlights were blurred by the thickness of the fog. Once he had to put on his brakes suddenly to avoid running into a car ahead.

"Sorry!" he said.

"It's exciting," she told him. "I'm enjoying it."

"I don't want to put you into a ditch," he said.

"No. It might be a little damp," she admitted.

She heard his quiet laugh over the wheel.

He fumbled his way through the fog without accident. They saw a blur of light which was Aldershot. Then Sandhurst, and a dazzle of light inside the dance-hall and a welcoming warmth out of the chilly night, and a military band playing dance music.

Viola put her cloak away and in another minute found Mervyn waiting for her at the door of the ballroom. He was saying something to another young officer—commissioned that day—and then turned to Viola with a smile.

"They're playing a waltz. Shall we take a turn?"

"I'd love to."

He danced well, as she knew. He was tall and strong but moved lightly and had a sense of rhythm.

"Are you glad to be an officer, Mervyn?" she asked presently.

She felt the slight shrug of his shoulders.

"I don't feel much different. But I suppose I'm lagged."

"Lagged?"

"An Army career. Oh lord!"

"What's wrong with that, my dear?"

He laughed a little bitterly, she thought.

"The usual conversation in the mess. The same fellows saying the same things—year after year. Subject to interruption of course."

"What kind of interruption?" asked Viola.

He hesitated for a moment, and then laughed again.

"The next war they keep on talking about."

Mrs. Paget was holding his left hand. His right was against her body with a light touch. She tightened her hold on his left hand.

"Oh, don't mention that grisly idea!" she said distressfully. "Don't spoil the evening for me."

"Sorry!" he said. "I'd hate to do that."

Presently he smiled down at her.

"It was jolly decent of you to come!" he told her.

She laughed into his eyes.

"It was jolly decent of you to ask me! An old frump like me."

"An old frump? Good lord, you're the most beautiful girl in the room. Everybody thinks so."

"How do you know?" asked Mrs. Paget. "I have only been here ten minutes and you haven't talked to anybody except me."

"I see it in their eyes," he said. "My brother officers goggle at you as they pass."

"What nonsense! How absurd you are, Mervyn!"

But she liked this absurdity. She was very glad, anyhow, that she passed in a crowd. She felt rather good-looking tonight. She had an idea that her rose-coloured frock suited her. The hairdresser had been a bit of an artist. But perhaps her frock fell away from her shoulders a little too much. One or two of the other girls—young creatures not long out of school—smiled at her as they passed and looked at those white shoulders she had powdered after her bath.

'I look younger than I am,' she thought. 'I'm a fraud really. In a few years I shall be middle-aged.'

She was sorry Mervyn had said that about the interruption of war. It was a horrible reminder of the outside world—a cruel and dreadful world. The morning papers had had beastly headlines. When the waltz ended and she walked across the polished floor with Mervyn, she looked at this crowd of young officers with their girls. They all looked so young. Some of them had tiny moustaches like the downy hair of newborn babes. They were just boys like Mervyn—so young, so young! But they were pledged in honour to service in any war that might come along. The Next War. They would be the young lieutenants to be mown down at the head of their men—gun-fodder—the first victims of sacrifice in some ghastly conflict due to powers over which they had no control. All these good-looking boys who had been dancing—her dear Mervyn. . . .

She gave a little shiver.

"Cold?" asked Mervyn, anxiously.

"No, not at all. This room is beautifully warm."

"Let's wander towards the buffet," suggested Mervyn. "After that cold drive——"

He found a seat for her and brought her some hot coffee. All round them was a buzz of laughter and chatter.

"This is like a dream," she said. "I feel like Cinderella at the Ball."

"It's not a bad dream," he said. "With you here it's——"

He didn't finish that sentence, except by the look of adoration he gave her just for a second. Then he added something else with a half laugh.

"I'll hate to wake up in the cold grey dawn. You will have gone. I shall be here, hearing a blasted bugle blow and knowing I'm lagged."

"Cheer up, dear!" said Mrs. Paget. "I shall be Cinderella again doing a bit of washing-up. My old witch-doctor will be wanting me to brush his overcoat before he goes on his rounds."

She saw a shadow creep into his eyes. She could see that he winced at this reminder of her husband. She had given him that reminder deliberately. She couldn't let this boy forget a very important fact. She couldn't let herself forget.

They were playing a fox-trot.

"Shall we?" he asked.

"Of course!"

He was very silent during that fox-trot. She could see that he had a little frown on his forehead.

"A penny for your thoughts," she said presently. "Very serious thoughts, aren't they?"

"Highly tragic!" he told her, laughing away part of the tragedy but leaving some in his eyes.

"No tragic thoughts tonight, Mervyn!" she said. "Let's keep the dream happy."

"Good idea! How are you feeling about it?"

"All this is enchanting."

Between two other dances the young man to whom he had spoken in the hall came up with the obvious intention of being introduced to Mrs. Paget.

"Hullo, Mervyn!" he said. "Going strong?"

It was impossible not to introduce him without a lapse in civility.

"Hartley Graham," said Mervyn. "Mrs. Paget."

Hartley Graham had one of those tiny moustaches with down-like hair on his upper lip. He had china-blue eyes and the complexion of a new-born babe.

"I hope Mervyn is behaving like an officer and a gentleman," he said. "Has he brought you anything to eat or drink?"

"A cup of lovely strong coffee," said Viola. "We eat later."

"Mervyn, old boy," said Hartley Graham, "will you give a dance to my sister over there? That kid in the blue frock. Brothers are not quite satisfying all the time. See what I mean?"

Mervyn looked at Viola as though to get an answer from her, which she gave with a little nod.

"Certainly," he said. "Of course."

"That's very sporting of him," said Hartley Graham, with a laugh. "Of course he doesn't want to leave you, Miss Paget."

"Mrs. Paget," said Viola.

He raised his eyebrows.

"Incredible! Still I suppose it can't be helped."

They both laughed at this absurd remark. He began to talk about Mervyn.

"One of the best. A born soldier. *Sans peur et sans reproche* and all that nonsense."

"Nonsense?"

"Well, one can be a bit too noble, you know. Mervyn is other-worldly. I suspect him of being a poet. He's one of those spiritual fellows—the soul of honour and all that. I confess I'm one of the earthy. Horses, dogs, shootin', fishin', huntin' and all that sort of thing. Low-brow stuff and all that."

"Very pleasant," said Mrs. Paget. "Mervyn and I are fond of riding."

"Any relation of the lad, may I ask?" said Hartley Graham.

Mrs. Paget hesitated and then smiled.

"Something in the nature of an elder sister."

"A charming relationship," said this young officer, "but quite incredible in your case, if I may say so."

"Why?"

He gave a sideways glance, amused and admiring.

"Not that difference in age, my dear lady."

"You'll go far in your Army career," said Viola. "You say the right things at the right moment."

"No, honour bright," he said. "Shall we do this dance? I'm a bit clumsy on my feet, but I have a kind heart."

Mervyn was dancing with his sister and looking rather miserable about it. Viola smiled at him as they passed, but he looked daggers at Hartley Graham.

In due course he returned to Viola.

"Curse that fellow!" he said grumpily. "Just like his cheek. Shall we go and feed?"

"A beguiling idea," said Viola.

They could not, of course, get a separate table. They squeezed in with a group of other young people. Mervyn had to introduce several of them. Mrs. Paget noticed that he dropped the Mrs. and called her Viola Paget. It seemed to make things easier with this little crowd. Before the evening was over, several girls were calling her Viola as though they had known her all their lives, even two of the young officers who insisted on dancing with her.

She had to accept—how could she refuse?—though every time she danced with one of his brother officers Mervyn looked unhappy. She was sorry about that. It was his night to be happy and she wanted to make it good for him, so that he might look back to it in after years—the night he was commissioned—as one of his best memories. In after years he would have fallen in love with someone else and married perhaps, with children. She would be the middle-aged wife of an old man.

Towards the end of the evening, he came up to her looking desperate, though with a smiling kind of desperation.

"I haven't seen you for years. Everybody grabs you away from me. And I don't believe you mind. After all, why should you?"

"I've been watching you," said Viola. "You've been dancing with very pretty girls. That one in the pink frock is ravishing."

"Quite brainless," he answered sulkily. "Besides——"

"Besides what, my dear?"

"I want you," he said. "This room is a desert without you."

Later in the evening he gave a kind of groan.

"Good heavens, this is the last dance!"

"It's yours, Mervyn," she said. "Don't let's waste a second of it."

She gave herself into his arms and they went round the room silently until presently he said something to her, something rather startling.

"It may be our last dance ever. I don't want it to end."

"Mervyn!" she exclaimed, looking up at him. "What do you mean by that? It sounds tragic."

"Who knows?" he answered. "Things happen. In the Army one never knows. I may be sent off somewhere. Posted to some plague-spot."

"Foreign service, do you mean?"

He nodded.

"Quite likely. I shall miss you like hell."

"I shall miss you, too, dear Mervyn. But it might be good for you to get away a bit, to see new places, to meet new people——"

"You mean to forget you? To be beyond reach of you?"

"In a way," she said. "You love me too much, Mervyn. It's dangerous for me as well as for you. I don't want you to be—foolish. I don't want you to make a mess of life almost before it's begun—your young manhood."

"Wherever I go and whatever happens," he said, "I shall never forget you. Will you remember that?"

"Of course. And wherever you go and whatever happens I shall remember our friendship—our loving comradeship."

"But not our love," he said. "You would never let it get as far as that. Perhaps you were right. I expected the impossible. I made an ass of myself. Forgive me. Do you forgive me?"

"There's nothing to forgive," she told him. "It was my fault, if there's any fault. But there's never been anything wrong, Mervyn. I love your love. When I'm an old woman—pretty soon now . . ."

She tried to lighten her tone to get away from emotionalism, to play fair with this boy.

He smiled down at her again.

"You never get tired of that joke," he said. "That and the Elder Sister stuff."

"It's more than a joke," she answered, smiling at him. "It's the painful truth. Seven years difference. Seven years makes an elder sister. I'm sorry to remind you. I'm sorry in a way to remind myself. But we must be honest, mustn't we? You and I? Anyhow, we must try to be sensible—you and I."

"How appalling that sounds," he said impatiently. "To be sensible, how cold that is! Isn't it better to be mad sometimes?"

She hoped he wouldn't be too mad on the way back in the car in the small hours of the morning, this boy-lover of hers. He hadn't a chance. Four other people crowded into his car. They lived in a village four miles farther on than Longmead. In the car they flirted outrageously, laughed in gusts, sang in chorus, while Mervyn sat silent at his wheel peering through the fog. He didn't want to kill them all, though he felt like it because they had spoilt the journey back when he might have been alone with Viola.

He was posted to the Gloucesters. Viola wondered whether he had worked that by pulling secret wires. The Gloucesters, forming part of the 29th Brigade, had gone out to Korea in 1950. Mervyn was sent out with reinforcements in mid-May of the following year after two courses of training which kept him away from home until he said good-bye to her. He came round to see her before going and she put her arms about him and kissed him on the lips and did not weep until he had gone.

"Take care of yourself, my dear!" she said as women had said to their men in the First World War and in the Second, as though by taking care they might avoid bursting shells and spasms of machine-gun fire and the gleam of naked bayonets.

"Thanks for everything," he said.

He took hold of her hands and raised them to his lips and kissed them and gave a kind of sob for a moment.

"I'm afraid I behaved like a cad," he said. "It was because I loved you so much. Of course I went a bit mad—because I loved you so much. I'm frightfully sorry."

"Don't be sorry, dear Mervyn!" she cried.

"No, I'm not really," he admitted. "I just couldn't help it."

He was brave enough to be half humorous, to laugh though there were tears in his heart like a boy going away to boarding-school, she thought, or like a young man going to a dangerous job with perhaps the risk of death in his mind.

"Give my kind regards to your witch-doctor," he said.

"He would like to see you," said Viola. "He would like to

say good-bye. He likes you so much."

Mervyn smiled.

"I hated him once, you know. But that doesn't matter now . . ."

"Good-bye!"

He kissed her for the last time.

It was hardest for his mother.

Lady Kendrick broke down when she heard that Mervyn was ordered to Korea with the Gloucesters—this boy whom she had brought into the world. It was to save him that she had become a pacifist and non-resister though that motive for her passionate advocacy of Peace was hidden from herself in her subconsciousness and was linked up with pity for all boys whom she wished to save from the horrors of war. It was the General who told her that Mervyn was being sent out with reinforcements for the Far East.

She turned very white and asked a question in one word.

"Korea?"

"Yes," said the General. "I'm afraid so. It means that."

He went over to her and put an arm round her.

"Be brave about it, my dear. He'll come back. The worst is over. We must be both brave."

She went away from him and gave a cry of anguish.

"Hush!" said the General. "Hush, my dear. After all he has become a soldier and he's the son of a soldier. It's his duty. I wish to God I were going in his place."

He glanced at his wife and felt anxious about her. She had turned away from him and was suffering an agony of soul, as well he knew.

"He wants to go," said the General. "We can't hold him back. He could have been gazetted to another unit. He arranged it with Metcalfe without saying a word to me. I was hoping he would join the Queen's."

Lady Kendrick turned her white face to him.

"If he's killed it will be your fault," she said. "You and your military tradition. I tried to fight against it but you were too strong for me. I tried to save him but you made a soldier of him because you had been a soldier and your father and your father's father. From his babyhood you put a service badge on him. Your son, of course, must join the Army. He was pre-destined. He had no choice for himself. I had no say in the matter though he was my son."

She spoke in her low-toned voice with tragic bitterness.

"Beatrice," said the General quietly, "I know what a blow this is to you. I'm terribly sorry for your sake. But, my dear, nowadays a soldier's life is no more dangerous than that of any civilian. Remember that. If another war comes we shall all be in the front line, we shall all be under fire—the old people as well as the young—you and I."

That did not comfort her at all.

"It is your kind of mind," she said, "which is arranging for that Next War. You will make it come. Aren't you planning for it now. Those papers which were stolen by poor Rudi—weren't they the blue-prints of the next world war? I'm glad he stole them. I wish there had been no copies of them."

"Beatrice," said the General, "you are talking wildly."

"I'm talking the truth," she said. "Wasn't I right about Korea? What have you done there with your guns and your bombing aeroplanes? What have the Americans done except make a graveyard and a desert of scorched earth in which the Koreans—those who still remain alive—hide and starve and freeze in the ruins? Your beautiful liberation! Now we're at war with China. What a wonderful victory for General MacArthur. What a wise and statesmanlike diplomacy! You are all mad. You are sentencing the world to death—all that we call civilization is condemned to death—in the lovely name of resisting aggression. Those whom the gods wish to destroy they first make mad. Do you remember learning that at school? No, you have forgotten!"

"Beatrice!" cried the General.

She began to weep convulsively. For a moment he thought she had really gone mad.

She cried out in a voice of anguish.

"Mervyn, my son!"

He strode over to her and held her in his arms.

"Beatrice, my love! My dear wife! Calm yourself. You were always so strong, so brave. Mervyn is my son, too. Both of us must think only of him. We mustn't let him see that we have any fear. We must hide that from him. We must only be proud of him and pray for him. You believe in prayer. You are a saint, Beatrice, aren't you? The saints were brave, weren't they? They had faith and resignation. There are worse things than death, Beatrice, even for Mervyn. You know that, don't you? You believe in a spiritual life. You're so much better than I am at that kind of thing. You're one of the world's Christians. A Christian mother. Beatrice, what can I say? I want to comfort you. I want to give you courage. I want you to comfort me. I want you to give me courage, too. If anything happens to Mervyn——"

His voice broke, and there were tears in the eyes of Major-General Sir William Kendrick, D.S.O., the father of an only son.

Something in his words startled her. Something in his voice touched her. She put her hands up and clasped his head and drew it down while she wept in his arms. It was her time of agony and Mervyn never knew the wildness of it nor the fierceness of her grief.

When he came home before embarkation for the Far East he was astonished at the calm way she took it. He had expected a bit of a scene, but she seemed fairly cheerful and strangely quiet and, of course, very loving as always she had been to him.

They had some long talks together. Once he got something off his chest, so to speak.

"I'm glad I'm going. I got into a bit of a mess—quite hopeless."

She was on the quayside at Southampton when he went up the gangway of the troopship. She lost him in the crowd of men and officers but stood there, fluttering her handkerchief.

She didn't weep again, this mother of Mervyn, until she turned away when the ship had warped away from the quayside and was moving down the Solent.

THE END